Between the Lines to Villainy

For my friends and family,
who somehow put up with me
every single day.

And for everyone who didn't ask:
"Are you still working on that book?"
"And those who did…"

Foreword

This novel explores conflict and war as forces that have historically driven progress and invention. It presents characters who embrace the belief that struggles and contention are necessary. Later, those views will be challenged by opposing perspectives. The intention is to tell a story while simultaneously encouraging readers to deeply consider conflict or war's role in shaping advancement, and to question, challenge, and reflect.

This idea first came to me junior year of high school, though I can't trace its exact origins. Over the past three years, it has evolved to be more concrete and specific. To create a world with too much 'peace' (as a bad thing) was quite challenging, but after much research and studying infamous historical figures who had the belief, I've finished what's written below.

I intend to simply examine war's place in history and in human thought. Can peace alone foster advancement, or does conflict force change? I invite you to step into this world with that question in mind—and decide for yourself.

Chapter 1

~Ringing swarmed my head, replaying memories in flashes~

ARIS SHELIA

"Roar!" Micha shouted, gleefully knocking over another cardboard wall. He swung his stuffed blue dinosaur over the *catastrophic* wreckage and grinned, eyes gleaming, barely visible through his fraying black-and-white ashen hair.

Sunlight spilled through the curtains, casting long shadows on our make-believe ruins. I collapsed to the rough carpet, draping my arm over my head. "Oh, no! My house!"

With the stegosaurus held high, he ran over to me, dodging toys, art supplies, and a clock across the floor, 'like a ninja.' He jumped over the clock, which beeped as he landed at my feet. I sighed and sat back up. The light in his eyes died instantly as if he knew what I was about to say.

"Sorry, Micha, I've got to get—"

"Aris! Time for school!" My mother's voice rang from downstairs. The faint scent of peanut butter and jelly wafted through the air, coming from the open bedroom door.

Micha's smile instantly deflated to a pout. He stomped. "No! She's busy playing with me!"

I moved to my knees and wrapped my arms around him. "I know. We ran out of time. I'm sorry, bud."

"No, I don't want you to!" He grabbed my arm tightly, voice shrill. In his other hand, he lifted the dino. "Chomper doesn't want you to either."

"Hey." I peeled his hand back. "Maybe we can play after school?"

"You promise?"

I *hope* so. I rose to my feet, meeting his wide, pleading eyes, and kissed his forehead. I *really do.*

"We'll have to see," I said.

I descended the stairs and snatched my bag by the door, shouting goodbye over my shoulder. The door slammed closed as I headed out, its pound creating a dull ringing behind my eyes. An ache deepened in my chest.

****

Sunlight reflected off pristine buildings, which were lined with rooftop gardens, straight into my eyes. I shielded my face with a hand, sticking to the sidewalk. Outdated solar panels embedded in the roadways gleamed as emission-free cars drifted over them, running on either electricity or water. The air they blew onto me as they passed smelled artificial.

In a shop window, a serene voice faded in, recapping 'updates' about the USA on the TV. Next to it flickered a holographic sign promising 'A Brighter Tomorrow.'

I snorted under my breath. *They should focus on improving today first, starting with that sign.*

I entered Lumea Square, skirting the edge to avoid the center. Seeing the same bronze statue every day, with Shelby Feyth—one of the two people holding the spiked crown inscribed with 'Victory Over Villainy 2042'—felt redundant and repetitive. A lot less like inspiration and more like hey, look! Nothing's changed.

The hairs on the back of my neck prickled. Even around them, the same holograms dragged on, replaying their triumph over villains in a loop, cheering. I turned my earbuds' volume up.

Citizens I weaved around exchanged cheerful, ignorant waves as they strolled on their merry way. Several police roamed the square in khakis, casually leaning against walls or parked cars, laughing and chatting over coffee. None glanced my way as I passed the hedges and ducked out, entering a large shadow.

Overhead floated a daunting variety of metal and stone buildings, including a distant Skyship and a library with its sweeping point, connected by wooden-like bridges. Dull patches of paint spotted the exteriors of the buildings, especially worn around the elevator set for those without Air powers. The jittery elevator still functioned, but no one cared to improve it. It's as if they thought: 'Why bother when it works well enough?'

There must be a better way.

A couple of heroes flew or scurried past me. One of them soared and unleashed a stream of fire. The heat washed over my face and seared the tip of my nose. I flinched back, eyes watering. *Idiot.* I touched my nose, then leaned out, trying to see what he aimed at—only for another hero to narrowly miss body-checking me.

She barreled past, shoving a massive rock aside as if I weren't there at all. It reminded me of those pointless posters where people drag square stones up hills. Only, that hill was full of people.

Thank goodness interactions like this weren't typical. Most heroes, like those from the six designated colleges on my continent, guarded the prisons instead of stupid display work. Colleges that had each established their name and importance for specializing in and mastering different styles and techniques of magic.

Squeals carried over to me from kids as young as four and as old as ten, who played unsupervised in a nearby park. There, fenced fountains sparkled, their bases ringed with dark solar panels. Its water danced in patterns that delighted some of the children.

Micha would definitely tug at my sleeve, nagging me to let him join them. I chuckled, the absence of his little hand in mine unsettling. *I'll have to take him here when I get back home.*

Besides the kids, a small group of elderly citizens tended a community vegetable patch, exchanging stories and snacks with each other.

I exhaled, forcing myself to move on and pick my way

over a rickety wooden bridge. Not far ahead, my green-brown school peeked from its corner, on the ground like any high school. Teens flowed inside and out of the worn concrete walls, 'reinforced' to protect us from any natural disasters.

Or so we're told.

Windows spread throughout it, sure, but would they hold up during a tornado or flood? Or was it 'good enough' for now, like everything else?

I slipped inside and made my way through the wide halls to my classroom. The students gave me no heed, talking amongst themselves, caught up in their individual problems and lives.

One boy at the edge of his group even got his hat knocked off, which skipped in front of me, settling right before it hit my shoe. I stooped down and picked the baseball cap up, handing it back to him. He snatched it without a word, already turning away and continuing his conversation.

Okay, then. I bit my lip and forced a shrug, proceeding down the narrow hallway. If that was the first time it happened, maybe it would've bothered me. But people acting like that were normal.

I didn't really mind it anymore.

A commotion of voices snatched my attention as I neared the principal's office. The doors were propped open, allowing Mr. Halden's voice to spill into the halls. "This is not a debate, Brendan. You had warnings."

"I'm not debating!" a voice replied evenly. I turned to see a boy standing at the doors with his arms crossed. "I'm saying it's not fair. Half the students here think what we memorize is useless. The school isn't doing enough to encourage our success. So why can't you change the curriculum to adapt to our generation?"

"Fairness is irrelevant," Mr. Halden replied coldly. "This school was built to prepare students for a world where the best heroes maintain order. If you can't respect that, you have no place here. And watch your tongue."

A wave of murmurs rippled through the students walking in the halls. I tightened my grip on the straps of my backpack.

"So that's it?" His voice cracked. "You're going to kick me out because I don't agree with the way this school teaches?"

"No more," Mr. Halden said, stepping into the hallway with a stack of papers in hand. "Questioning our curriculum is forgivable. Disrupting class and undermining authority is not, especially when you speak so freely... I say this with a heavy heart, but you are no longer a student here. Your expulsion is effective immediately. Please keep the peace as you exit."

Disrupting class? All he did was ask questions. I lifted my head, brushing off my hood.

The hallway fell silent. Brendan stood frozen for a moment. With a shake of his head, he turned and stormed down the hall, the crowd parting to let him through.

I held out my hand, catching his eye as he passed. The heavy slam of the front doors echoed down the corridor, ringing behind my eyes. A cold knot formed in my stomach. "That isn't right," I said, catching a few people by surprise. Then I closed my mouth and tugged my hood back on.

He didn't even have any warning. So if I say anything outloud, who's to say they won't retaliate? How long would it be before my thoughts slipped out and I got expelled, too? I stared after him. Or... what if it happens to Micha?

The gossip around me flooded in like a tidal wave. "Can you believe that?"

"He was asking for it. You don't argue and expect to stay. Complaining has consequences; it's not unreasonable."

"Brendan's got to be one of the reasons hero colleges are downsizing."

Another voice laughed. "No, according to Ezrat's President, our recruitment is still pretty high."

My chest squeezed as the hallway emptied.

I entered my class, taking a seat at the back-row edge—a place where a demon could easily drag me away. The thought made me smile. I brushed the dull grey textbook waiting on my desk. Tablets were more common than books these days, but this teacher particularly loved them. The cover was worn and frayed, titled in hard-to-read print: History of Human Achievements.

Inside, the 'modern' advancements it listed felt like relics from decades ago, especially when they're the same 'breakthroughs' taught since I was a kid. Even the digital projector sputtered to life with a groan, as though it, too, was tired of repeating the same lessons year after year.

The desks pressed close together in perfect rows, uniform and narrow, leaving just enough space to funnel us in. It was a small room with a few windows on the far wall.

Sunlight struggled in through them, thin stripes that never reached my chosen corner.

By the time the tardy bell rang, nearly all the students were present and seated, facing the board. The desk next to me sat empty, as usual.

The teacher stood from his metal desk in the front corner, which guarded a series of wooden shelves behind it, piled high with various glass containers, liquids, and substances. "I reckon you lot are excited 'bout the year wrap-up when it's barely begun," he started when the class settled down, his cockney accent thick. "Those of you with magical fam will soon clock if you've got it too. And even though it's a right slim chance, it's still on the table, yeah?"

Yeah, a one-in-a-million. Unless both of your parents and grandparents had them... then it's like one in ten. We've heard the basics of this before. I twirled the pencil in my hand. My cheek rested on the other, propped up on my desk. *My family has powers, but I'm not going to get my hopes up for nothing. After all, my older sister turned up empty and left to study in another country with my dad.*

Though I guess the generic information of magic or hero schools can be useful, even if I don't receive them.

"However," my teacher continued, lifting a finger. "I wanna give you a heads up before we talk more about this at the end of the year. For them that ain't as clued, 'round seventeen or eighteen is when one's powers'll pop up, along with the weak spots to battle 'em. If it does, you'll go to hero college. Those without will continue onto normal advanced studies."

In the front row, a boy eagerly raised his hand, extending it higher and higher. He didn't wait to be called on. "We'll become as strong as Altruistic, right? That's awesome!" My teacher gave a thumbs up like he wanted to continue, but the boy carried on, "I remember she mentioned something about all villains being old or in confinement. Is that true?"

"Most disturbers are like that, yeah. Course, we'd be fools to think a few don't slip through now and then, no matter all the protocols we've got to stop 'em. Yet they never make a big enough dent to gain attention, but that's why we still train." A few students glanced at each other, brows raised. "And for the heroes, nah, there's always a need for more selfless blokes to lend a hand or guard 'em prisons, especially when powers can help during or preventing natural disasters or crises."

Right. I narrowed my eyes, biting the edge of the pencil.

Truth was, we haven't had a bad disaster, like a cyclone season or tornado in years. Villain attacks are almost nonexistent. Our world isn't crying out for heroes like it used to, especially when most real threats get handled before reaching the public.

So what is the point of training to be one? Why are we memorizing old tactics instead of learning to live in the world we actually have? I hesitantly raised my hand, only for more hands to shoot up with clamor.

The teacher shook his head. "Oi, mates, I know, I know. You've got a hundred questions. Some of this stuff ain't covered till next year, but you'll 'ave time for more questions at the end of school or with your future teachers. Or if you keep yer ears open, maybe even today! But for now, we gotta crack on with our lesson."

I lowered it and looked out the window. My fingers curled around the edge of the seat, the lesson fading into background noise like any other day.

****

Weeks blurred into months until it was spring. At some point, the days stopped feeling real. I'd wake up, play with my little brother until school, force myself to push through endless mind-numbingly bland classes, and head straight back home where my mother would be waiting for me.

The moment I walked in the door, shrugging off my bag, she'd call to me from the kitchen with her airy voice, "Aris, you're back! How was school?" And she would have food prepared, with a place cleared for me to study on the table, ready to help with whatever I needed, no matter how busy she was.

Not that I did, but I hugged her anyway. "Thanks, Mom. School was not bad. How was work?"

"Same old, same old." She rubbed her eyes with the palm of her hand. "The spaceship I was telling you about is preparing to launch soon, so they've been keeping us busy ensuring the designs are perfect and that our prototypes test well."

"I'm sure you're doing great."

Laughter exploded from upstairs. We both looked up and then at each other. I smiled and slid into my chair, dropping my bag next to my leg.

"I'm guessing Micha's upstairs?"

Mom chuckled. She kissed my forehead before walking to the stairs. "Micha! Aris is home. Why don't you come down to eat?"

A squeal followed, paired with the footsteps of someone very small scrambling downstairs. Typically, the little rascal would already be jumping at the door or running around waiting for me. *He must've gotten distracted by Chomper.*

When he rounded the corner, Micha gleefully shouted my name and leaped to my side with his full body weight. I barely managed to catch him on the chair without knocking anything over, bringing him into a tight hug.

"Hey, bud, how was school and daycare?"

"I only had school today, because we had—we had a field trip to, uh, a big place with-with lots of fish." He squirmed in my arms, eyes bright. "There was a big blue one making weird faces. And I think Mr. Andrews said it was an aquarium and showed us cool sharks and stingrays and these tiny fish that ate at your hands! It tickled. I do not want to do that again!"

After I managed to sit him next to me, we ate around his excited chatter, and like usual, I ended up convincing him to put on his shoes to bring him to the playground, joking I couldn't wait.

Mostly I did it so my mom had a second to breathe.

"Whoa, there's lots more kids than yesterday," he gasped, his hand swinging in mine.

"Yeah, there is. Look at all the dogs in the field," I said and pointed. Some additional heroes lingered off to the side, one rolling her eyes and shifting her body into the form of a golden retriever. She darted out, catching a kid's frisbee in mid-air. "Make sure not to pet one unless the owner says you can, and you ask."

Micha nodded, passing a sign that listed approved abilities 'for your safety' and pulling me towards the slides. I eventually let go after asking him to stay within my sight, which he immediately groaned about, then stopped himself.

"Why? The other kids don't have supervision."

"Mom prefers us sticking together. You are allowed to play alone, but she wants me to walk you here and back."

"Oh, okay."

At that, he shrugged and darted off. It took less than ten seconds before my little brother joined ten other kids playing 'lava monster' on the playground, screaming and darting away from whoever was it and confined to the woodchips. One onlooker hero flicked his hand, and a hologram of volcanic lava spread across the ground.

How do you do that so easily, Micha? Why is it so simple for you to walk up to someone and just play?

If I did that, I'd be laughed at. I told myself I preferred to be alone and stick to myself. That it was okay. Yet for some reason, the pressure in my chest lately grew heavier and heavier as I watched Micha from a distance. Sometimes, I had to straight up walk the perimeter in an attempt to shake the expanding emptiness burrowing inside. To not let my eyes blur from thinking.

It *had been so long since* I... I recalled a kid named Malik. He's said "hi" to me in the halls since we were five, but nothing came out of it. To be fair, I would never respond, pretending I didn't hear him, though that didn't exactly seem to deter the man.

But it's okay. I had Micha. And mom.

On the TV across the road, the news lady hyped up the upcoming Victory Over Villainy festival like it was the event of the year (without much to compete against, it was.) People would grin from ear to ear, of course, and the streets would be filled with cheers, colorful parades, speeches, and tributes to past heroes. You'd be looked at weirdly if you weren't enthusiastic.

"That day, a hundred and fifty years ago, the heroes had saved us," they said in a recap. "They'd built this world to keep us safe."

And it worked. Or at least, it was supposed to.

What they avoided saying was that each year brought more and more security and rules—sorry, *precautions*.

I eyed the group of heroes from earlier, where the shapeshifter dropped the frisbee at one of her teammates' feet.

Rules of what defines a hero and a villain. Of what was acceptable or led you to jail, in order to protect citizens, then heroes. And maybe it wasn't that bad. Yet lately, the more we became shielded, the less we were allowed to move. Like being in bubble wrap until you couldn't breathe and suffocated.

My teachers liked to say: "Why change if what's working works?" I agreed back then.

What was I supposed to do?

Yet, after gradually watching how creativity and new ideas were repeatedly squished down and discouraged, like it was with Brendan. After seeing certain phrases being restricted and punished, or the same old school lessons and fighting styles repeated year after year, I don't think it's working at all.

It's as if we're stepping on eggshells, and if you step wrong, it will send a butterfly effect that collapses the entire city. Because what comes with rules and order is an idiotic fear.

****

Mr. Poistio counted down the class, ignoring the heroes flying past our window, seemingly in a game of tag. He picked up a marker, uncapped the lid, and began drawing on his whiteboard. In silence, I fiddled with my pencil until he finished. A collective gasp rippled through the classroom.

"You're going to teach us more about magic?" a boy beside Malik exclaimed.

Smiling, the teacher capped and set down his marker. "Yeah! School's 'ardly got long left, ya know." Gesturing to the eleven words on the board—listing the four elements to shadow, light, and more—he scanned the room. "Who can tell me what these words mean, then?"

Malik raised his hand, and the teacher called on him. "Those are the different categories of powers."

Magic. Rules of magic...

I looked up as Mr. Poistio nodded. "Lovely done. Would

you like to explain?"

Scratching the back of his neck, Malik chuckled as he leaned back. "I don't know anything beyond that."

"S'pose that's fair. We're 'ere to learn, ain't we?" The teacher's gaze met mine. "Aris? What'd ya know?"

Straightening, I reread the words, lingering on the last two, Power Manipulation and Electricity. My thoughts churned. *Rules to keep the peace and to keep things the way they were... Of course they didn't question it. I had to be the only one still thinking about what he'd said earlier that year.*

"Uhm, sir, can I ask you a question instead?" I replied softly, shrinking as if the chair itself could swallow me whole.

He blinked, then inclined his head. "Go ahead."

It felt as if the entire class focused on me. My heart pounded against my ribcage, trying to break free.

Just stay quiet. It's not worth all the attention, a part of me argued.

I have to know, another insisted.

"A while ago, you confirmed that most villains are locked away. If that's the case, there's no real threat or pressure to achieve anymore. So how and why will our world continue to progress if there's no reason to? After all, why change when what works, works?"

The students immediately glanced away, as if anything else in the room was more interesting than the conversation.

Shifting from a smile, his lips pressed into a line. The

creases at the edge of his eyes deepened. "My, that is a puzzler," Mr. Poistio said slowly. "Progress ain't all about good and evil, yeah? We'll carry on fine and even better as a community without it." He straightened. "Though, it's worth sayin' that some of our best ideas, like improving flyin' and some of the early uses of el'ctrickery came from desperate times. Desperation birthed some of our brightest ideas. But now we polish what we've built. Make things more... comfortable." He stared at his hands.

"I don't think so," I replied, low enough that he could ignore it, and he did. I bowed my head and retrieved the pencil, pressing myself against the wall. *He didn't fully answer the question. It makes no sense to 'polish what we built' instead of improving it. Like using cleaner and more efficient energy sources than solar-panel roadways.*

Another girl perked up to my relief, shifting the attention to her. "So how are they categorized, sir?"

"Great question, Arlene. Magic falls into eleven general groups. The Elements, Emotion, Mental, that sort. Most folk have one main type and a few little ones."

"You can have more than one?"

"Kinda." He scratched the side of his face. "The smaller ones can be unique from the main one. But your primary's what shapes you. Take Lighter, whose main is light, and his secondaries are plant identification, cloud walking, and omnilingualism. Be mindful that some power groups are kept a closer eye on than others 'cos they might cause a right bother."

That made the room go still. My pencil halted.

"What d'you mean?" the same kid prompted.

"Let's just say, some levels of magic's not encouraged. Bit too disruptive or unethical, yeah?"

We know. Gosh, everyone's kept in line, even if you have magic. I propped my head on my hand, elbow on the desk. *No powers allowed without permission. We get it. Yada yada yada.*

The teacher flashed a smile. "Anyhow. Back to the board."

The discussion continued, and I ended up drifting off until the bell chimed, its high-pitched ring ricocheting in my head as I struggled to exit until the room emptied. Students cut in front of me as if I were a wall. In the halls it was no better; they gathered in their groups, creating an impenetrable maze. Before I could make it out the door to freedom, a hand grasped my shoulder, then immediately loosened when I tensed.

"Whoa, sorry, I was trying to get your attention. I almost missed you," a familiar voice said. "Where are you off to in such a hurry? It's like you're allergic to human interaction."

Shrugging his light-toned hand off in a spin, I came face-to-chin with Malik. He wore his typical plain tailored uniform, which suited his dirty blond hair and dark blue eyes.

Why is he talking to me again? What does he want?

Since when were you this paranoid about him?

It has to be nothing good. Kids here are always trying to mess with me. It'll be my luck if today's when he starts.

I exhaled slowly. "Home," I curtly said, sidestepping. "I'm headed home. If you'll excuse me—"

"Hang on." He stuck out his arm, blocking my path,

then lowered it slightly as if reconsidering. "I've said hi to you since, what? Elementary? Yet you still act like I don't exist." His mouth twitched like he regretted saying that. "All I do is try to talk to you. Did I do something wrong? Can I fix it?"

His tone sounded so earnest. Is that why I couldn't shake the sense that it was fake?

I backed up, my eyes narrowed. "No, I'm not in the mood right now. I need to go."

"Oh." He blinked, eyebrows furrowed. "Are-are you sure? I didn't realize—" he cut himself off, something genuine yet confused and conflicted crossed in his eyes. "Ah, that's not an excuse. I can shut up. Or can I at least—?"

I whirled to the doors, shoving them open with my shoulder. I found myself letting out a long breath when he didn't follow.

What an idiot. He doesn't actually care about you.

Even if that's true... I don't want to be rude.

After a few more steps, it became impossible to ignore the pit expanding in my stomach. Yeah, right, he wants to be friends. The last time I trusted someone besides family, I ended up alone and embarrassed. It was a complete mess, I will—no, this would be no different.

I'm not someone people want to get to know or befriend.

Removing my hood, I trailed along the sidewalk, heading to the place I sat each day. Countless slow-drifting clouds hovered in the sky, casting soft shadows across two fields that were already splashed with budding trees, their leaves gently rustling. Smooth metal fences lined the edges, extending far enough to contain a sprawling oak full of knots.

I wiped the pollen from my nose, dropped my backpack at its roots, and leaned against its familiar bark. A long sigh escaped my mouth as my eyes closed. Cool wind curled against my face. *Halfway done with another day; only a month or so until summer.*

"You look lonely for such a wonderful soul, dear."

My eyes snapped open. At my left stood an older woman. Great-grandma-old, with dark skin, short braided caramel brown hair, and amber eyes. On her wrist dangled a silver with red bracelet, and in one hand, she pinched bronze sunglasses that she slid into a pocket.

The hell? Why is she talking to me? "Do I know you?" I folded my arms, stifling a yawn. "Are you lost?"

Tilting her head, the woman smacked her lips. "No, dear. Where are your friends? Or are you here alone?"

My body stiffened. I shifted my weight off the tree. "Awfully inquisitive for a stranger speaking to a teenager on school grounds, aren't you? Shouldn't I be the one asking questions?"

"Oh no, no. I apologize if I'm giving off the wrong idea. Here." She lifted her arm, wind picking up and surrounding her as she slowly sat on *nothing.* A faint cinnamon-honey scent tickled my nose. "You see, I'm not just a typical stranger, honey."

"Magic? Your main is Air?" I blinked, forcing my face to

stay neutral, and shook my head. "You still haven't answered who you are."

She exhaled. "Let's just say I've watched the world long enough." Adjusting her blouse, the old woman shot me a side smile. "As for magic, yes, perhaps these days, though when I was young, we had thousands more. Alas, it tends to dwindle after the oppressor ceases."

I squinted before squaring my shoulders. My hands clenched into fists. "Are you messing with me?"

"No, dear. I've seen what happens as the world tips too far into the 'light.' Magic-wielders, our government, think they're heroes, and maybe they are in their own eyes. But they've stripped away the urgency that inspires true innovation, falling back to safety and harming families 'for stability.'" She tilted her head. "What do you think?"

That's similar to what I asked Mr. Poistio earlier... Is she stalking me? I scanned her over. Her words pricked in my mind. "I don't know. I think... something about it feels wrong. Is it something you're wondering about?"

Humming softly to herself, the older woman turned in her air chair. "Mm, good. You're paying attention. You'll learn more eventually."

"You still haven't said who you are or what brings you here. Do I need to take you back to a retirement home?"

"Oh, child, you'll see. For I preserve what's being erased. I'll meet you here in a week's time. If you decide to take a chance and listen to my words, we will then meet again beside Taftside Peak, toward the setting sun. There, I'll tell you what you want to know about it."

I didn't move. "You're asking me to blindly follow a stranger. With powers. Who showed up at my school to talk to me. Why don't I call the police?"

"Oh, I'm merely offering you a choice. You don't have to do anything you don't want to. But you deserve to know what they refuse to say, especially when your family crossed a line and you'll be directly affected."

Crossed a line? I realized I was leaning rigidly toward her. Awkwardly straightening, I bit my tongue, eyes locked with the grandma. *Pft. There's no way my family crossed a line. She must be lying.*

Why is she?

This old lady is willing to answer my questions that everyone else shuts down. It might be good to know.

How do I know if I can trust her?

"Why do you think I'll come meet with you?" I reached my hand out. "I still don't know who you are. Can't you speak more clearly? Tell me what makes you credible to answer the questions I don't know?"

I wasn't going to even touch her mention of my family crossing a line.

She paused, her eyes flicking down as if considering something, and continued hesitantly, "Taavi. My name is Taavi Higgins. I am what is known as one of the last *villains* of today. I am what's left of the truth no one teaches anymore. And if you're brave enough to hear it... I'll be waiting, Aris."

Chapter 2

ARIS SHELIA

"Why do you have to go to school agaaaaain?" my little brother whined, tightening his clutch on my leg. I tied my shoes at the doorway, struggling around him.

"Because it isn't summer yet." I wiggled him off and slung my backpack over my shoulder. "Don't worry, I'll be back before you know it. And maybe, if you're good, I can take you out for some ice cream." I messed with his hair, then bent down and hugged him before opening the door.

Sniffling, he rubbed his nose. "Can't I go with you?"

The floorboards creaked. I glanced over my shoulder as Mom strode to Micha. She picked him up under his arms. Her green eyes stood out brightly yet prettily against her long, stark white hair. "Don't fret. You'll get to go to kindergarten next year! That'll be fun!"

"I do!" He gasped delightedly, laughing and pulling down his shirt. "Why not now? I wanna go to school with Aris 'cause she gets to go to a cool hero school next year."

A tiny orb of water, more like a floating blob you'd see in a tacky 90's Halloween movie, weaved from our kitchen. It shimmered, rising above my mother's head and playfully splashing above Micha's face. He squealed with a mix of complaints, laughter, and joy, using my mom's shirt to wipe it off.

"Moooom! Why'd you do that?" he part-whined, part-giggled the last word, struggling against her grip.

Smiling, I waved and exited as two police cruisers parked in front of our driveway. Two armed men and a woman with handcuffs stepped out, their expressions carefully blank. All closed their doors in unison and authoritatively stride over to me, hands on their uniform's belts.

"Officers." I widened my stance just outside the doorway, fully aware that the door hadn't been fully closed.

"Is this your mother?" one of the men asked, sticking out his hand, revealing a picture identical to my mom.

Tilting my head, I took the photo. Everything was the same, from her very tan skin to her diamond-shaped head. I lowered my hands. *It was her. What do they want?*

"What's this about?" my mother interrupted from behind me. She placed both her hands on my shoulders.

Two of the officers immediately pushed past me. They dropped behind her as the first drew his hands to the gun. "Ma'am, you are under arrest for multiple felony charges. All rights are at liberty as by law, you may only speak when a lawyer or attorney is present."

"Sorry, what?!" my mother exclaimed, placing her hands behind her back.

My little brother peeked beyond the door. "No! She isn't a bad guy!" he cried and ran out, grabbing and yanking the woman's arm. "You can't take her! She's MY MOM."

"That's for the judge to decide, sweetie," the woman replied gently, removing his hands. She guided him to me. "How old are you two?"

"I'm seventeen. My little brother is six." I stepped in front of him, my breath hot in my throat. "What's this about?"

"I am not allowed to say," the woman said curtly. "I'm simply following government orders."

"Then you can't arrest her without proper reasoning!" I snapped, wrapping an arm around my little brother and fully stepping in between my mother and the officers. My other hand curled into a fist. "What are you accusing her of? This isn't—"

The two police officers, one with my mother, split to go around me. I instinctively nudged Micha behind my legs, then held out my arms to block them, to fight them even if it meant she could escape. Yet, my mother shook her head as she passed. "Don't fight, sweetie, it will only make it worse."

"Mom," I started, voice cracking as I looked over my shoulder. My blood boiled. I'm not letting them take you.

She shook her head again and walked with the police officer, who escorted her to one of the cruisers. I stepped to go after her, but my mother threw her head over her shoulder like she knew I would.

"Aris, don't worry. I understand, and we'll get this figured out. Please don't act rashly. All I need you to do is be strong and look after your little brother for me. Please."

'Don't act rashly.' The muscles in my shoulders and legs strained. *Then what am I supposed to do?* I swallowed, wanting to throw up and punch someone simultaneously.

Yet her plea knocked on the back of my mind, reminding me of a quote she often told us: '*Don't let the world decide what kind of good you are. We're not perfect, but hold onto yourself.*'

I reached back, half-hugging Micha's little body, trying to force myself to relax. My chest rose and fell rapidly.

"That will be quite difficult, I'm afraid," the lady next to me said, clasping her hands together. "I'm sure you'll see each other after school and daycare, but you'll be placed into separate foster homes until this gets sorted out."

What? Two badges on her chest glinted. One was a shield captain badge for Lumea, the other a circle for CPS. *Separate foster homes? Why can't we stay together?* A hole grew in my stomach. I twisted, tightening my hold on my little brother to stop myself from tearing off her nose or knocking her out. *How do I get them to answer me?*

"Aris, what does the lady mean?" Micha asked, wiping a tear. "Is Mom going away? What's going on?"

"Shh," I whispered. "I'll handle this." I closed my eyes. '*Be strong and look after your little brother for me.*'

Agh, I want to. I know I can take care of him and help you. So why do they act as if I have no say in this matter? Like

I'm some helpless kid? Why do I have to accept it and allow them to take you?

Our government, heroes, police. They were supposed to keep the peace. Keep us safe. Its rules were there to protect us. Perhaps that's what they think, but with every new restriction, it wraps around like a vine, placing you in a chokehold. The Presidents of Heroes and Lumea City's Council seemed to watch over every street and monitor every tiny spark of magic closely. Magic was supposed to be a gift, but if you committed a few mistakes or selfish acts, you'd be sent away and labeled a villain.

Taking away my mother and separating me from my little brother is not a way to 'maintain' peace.

My eyes flew open. "No, absolutely not. You let her go and answer me. Why take her? Why separate foster homes? We did nothing!"

"This is beyond your understanding, sweetheart. You can see her later." The woman looked at me with her lips puckered out. "You wouldn't want to disturb the peace, would you?"

Disturb the peace? Isn't that what you're doing? I almost moved my arm, but inhaled deeply instead, glancing at my little brother. Tears streaked down his cheeks, his arm pulling at me as he tried to go after our mother, calling out in broken gasps. *Anything I do will make it worse for him.* I forced myself to remain still, meeting the woman's smile and biting back all my remarks.

"Go get your backpacks," she said with a wave. "I'll make sure you arrive safely at school and pick you up after."

Can I let them take us to school after this? Do I even have a choice?

After a second of her eyes on me, she added, "You have no other friends or family in the state, correct?"

"You will answer for this." I lowered my head. "And yeah. My older sister and father are living in another country for the next five years."

"For the international research assignment?"

"Yes."

Nodding, she gestured with her hand. "Alright, that's what we thought. We'll find you somewhere." Micha's sobs racked my head as the officer nudged us back inside. There was nothing I could do. But I'll fix this. I have to. If not for me, for Micha, who strained against my arms.

I will make them listen to me. They won't get away with this. They won't break apart my family.

****

I arrived at school in a daze. Each step felt wrong as I passed groups of friends full of laughter. The chatter became a static noise in the background, like I was underwater. *"They will be placed into separate foster homes..."* I clenched my teeth, stiffly making my way to my class. I sat at my desk and took out my laptop, searching for local foster laws and any other information that I could perhaps use.

By the time my teacher began class, announcing something along the lines of presentations, I confirmed that nothing I said would hold weight against the city taking my mom and splitting us apart. Especially since I was a minor directly involved with the situation.

I closed the tabs as the teacher called us, one-by-one, down the row, assigning presentations. He wanted the class to learn more about the varying levels and limitations of each main power and then to share our findings with each other. Being last on the list, he assigned Shadow to me, then signaled us to start.

The work had been extensive. I knew most of the groups had three to five levels, ranging from beginning to advanced, but Shadow had *seven*. To be honest, I didn't get through much after that, trying to take my mind off the fact that my brother would be taken from me. That they took my mom to who knew where. And despite anything I said, nothing would change that. I clenched my teeth and reopened the tabs, scrolling through to double-check what I'd read.

Halfway through, someone approached quietly behind me and touched the back of my chair. "Aris," Malik said, causing me to jump. "Do you want to work together?"

"No, thanks." I pointedly turned my back to him, my knuckles turning white against the keyboard.

You're powerless. No one listens to a kid.

Isn't this world supposed to be peaceful?

Pulling out the chair next to me anyway, Malik sat and opened his laptop. "The teacher said we had to work in groups of up to four. All the other groups are maxed out, and he told me to work with you."

Groaning, I opened the share tap and pushed the

laptop to him. "Okay, get at it and don't bother me."

Another kid approached from the side, with stand-up white hair, dark skin, blueish-gray eyes, and loose-fitting athletic attire. "Sorry to crash your party. Mind if I hang with you?"

"Sure!" Malik answered quickly, lifting my laptop to the newcomer so he could enter his email. I lowered my head, snatching my laptop back after he finished. "Drystan, right?"

You did nothing. You were useless, Aris.

And I'll make sure that won't happen again. See you at lunch, Taavi.

"Yep. And you're Malik and Aris?" he asked in a New York accent. Malik nodded. "Great to meet ya! So, I was thinkin', since we gotta do like sixteen slides—y'all cool if Arlene joins in? She's MIA today, so she ain't got nobody."

Shooting me a glance, Malik grinned. "Of course!"

****

Midday, I found myself beneath the shade of the familiar old oak tree, attempting to silence the barrage of thoughts in my mind to think more clearly. They were forming into a tornado. The cold, prickly grass and bark felt harsh against my hot skin. *They don't deserve this.* The morning endlessly looped in my mind like a stuck record player about to snap. *Hopefully, this will help silence it.*

Taavi hovered cross-legged in front of me, scarves lightly draped over her neck. Her amber eyes caught the late afternoon light in a way that made her look otherworldly. I couldn't shake the feeling she knew a lot more than she let on.

I'll let her talk. If there's a chance I can get them back with her help, I'll take it. I cast a wary glance her way. *Though it's still weird that she acts as if she knows me. It was like she was waiting for me to cross her path.*

Her gaze never wavered, her expression nearly amused as if she knew I'd been on edge. She fidgeted with the red and silver bracelet clasped on her wrist.

"What do you want?" I asked dryly, refraining from letting my voice sound eager or desperate.

The old woman slid a clipboard from her bag with a satisfied smile and held it in front of her face. "I'm glad you came around." No doubt she spotted the frown fighting on my face. "I sense a change mixed itself in. The inner turmoil of your soul speaks volumes." She lowered her clipboard a smidge below her eyes, enough to meet my gaze. "What is it you seek, child?"

My hands curled into fists, fingernails engraving into my palms. "That's personal. Look, you said stuff about good and evil earlier. Is it even possible to fix an empty world you call 'peaceful' when it's more of a cage we're all trapped inside?"

"Ah, Aris," she said, tilting her head. "An unjust world does not mean it is not good nor peaceful. People are simply trying to do the right thing with the little they understand." She clicked her tongue thoughtfully. "Balance itself is not achieved through mere harmony. It requires the intertwining dance of opposites."

"Uh... okay?" I scrunched my face.

She continued with zero reaction to my tone, "Have you ever tried standing on one foot for too long? You tip over. That's what happens when the world has too much of 'good' or 'evil.' Unless, of course, someone evens the scales."

Flipping the board over, she revealed a drawing of two people locked in combat. I stared at her before looking at it closer. One person was Shelby Feyth, the woman one of the statues at Lumea Square was modeled after. "Progress comes through struggle. History has proved this, time and again." The knot in my stomach relented.

"Shelby Feyth's peace brought us stability, but even she understood it wasn't perfect. Sean Weaver sold the world a dream, and the people embraced it. The heroes may have won that day, but what if they've stolen the world's ability to dream beyond comfort and fear as well? What's left for someone like you in a world where progress has been locked away?"

"Okay, that's one way to put it." I frowned. "Why are you telling me this? I can't do anything about it. Let alone change the way our country is structured."

Taavi set it aside on the spikey grass. She adjusted her short, curly hair. "You're right. You can't do anything yet, but soon, the time will come when all villains will be confined or hidden, snuffed out. And if the heroes succeed, the world will become nothing but empty peace for future generations."

Micha. I shifted foot to foot and lifted my head back. "I can't do anything yet, but soon I can? What, when I'm twenty-one? Or if I somehow have powers?"

"How about earlier than that? Let's say three days' time. Meet me at Taftside Peak toward the setting sun. It won't fix anything yet, but you can stop another thing from happening. Perhaps you'll understand more then."

I want to know, but... "Taftside—why should I trust you enough to meet you there?" I crossed my arms. "You showed up out of nowhere, spouting riddles about peace and balance and whatnot, then expect me to follow you? Give me a reason why I don't walk away to report you right now."

"You sought me out today. You know I'm right. Deep down, you've always felt it, dear. This world isn't what it seems. It's full of problems to fix. Ones they are not willing to face."

I shook my head. My voice wavered, mixed with a breathless laugh, but I tried to keep it firm. "That doesn't mean I trust some stranger on a floating chair." My mom's face flashed in my mind. I straightened. *This is something I can actually choose.* "Okay. I'll think about checking it out."

"That's fair," she replied calmly, levitating backward. "You'll see things differently when the cracks in your perfect world begin to widen. Until then, I'll be waiting." With a wave of her hand, her feet touched the ground, and she walked away.

As her figure grew distant, I knelt and picked up the clipboard she'd left. I swallowed, tracing a thumb along the paper. *She's willing to talk about what I asked in class. I don't get a sense of danger from her. In fact, my neck doesn't feel so tense. I* touched Shelby's face. *My family, all of us, are trapped in this twisted world of rules and 'peace.'* A world so saturated with blandness and unfairness I didn't want for any of us. Maybe a world rid of villains wasn't as spectacular as it was made out to be. I'll have to see.

"Who was that?" a voice wondered from a few yards

away.

I cursed, almost dropping the clipboard, and pressed it against my chest with a sigh.

Malik sat down across from me. "Do you know her? Are you okay?"

"It doesn't matter," I muttered, backing up and sliding against the tree. "And it's none of your business. Why were you watching me?"

His bright blue eyes widened a fraction, more startled than offended. Propping one knee up, he draped his arm over it. "I wasn't. I saw you on the way back from class and came over to invite you to sit with my friends and me."

"Nah, I'm good." I covered my face with the board, the tension in my shoulders easing a fraction.

Opening his mouth then closing it, Malik brushed away his hair fluttering over his eyes. "Okay," he said, pressing his lips together. "If you prefer, we can come over here instead. That way you don't have to move."

Sighing, I lowered my hands and staggered to my feet, brushing off grass from my tight sweats. "Why are you so insistent I be with you? Why can't you just leave me alone?" I winced at the sharpness of my own voice, especially when the light behind his eyes died slightly.

"Why do you always want to be alone? I just—" Malik shook his head. "You seem to be a really cool person." He frowned faintly. "I only want to be your friend."

Taken aback, I looked at him. A mix of feelings within

seemed to battle with one another. *What? No, that's a joke. Someone had to have put him up to this.*

Yeah... Well, my words seemed to have genuinely hurt him.

It doesn't matter if it happens to you. Why should it matter if you do it back?

That's not how you do things. Though it doesn't mean I trust him anymore.

The muscles in my hand ached from clenching so hard. After a long silence, I eventually lifted my hood. "Hasn't it ever occurred to you that I don't want one?" The fabric snagged my ear piercing and I flinched.

"I... don't think I can believe that," Malik admitted. "Why are you so defensive all the time?" Rising, he kept his careful distance but trailed after me as I sped to the entrance of the school. "Aris, please. I promise I won't—"

"Just leave me alone—" *Before I say something I can't take back.* I slipped into the crowd as the bell rang. *Gosh.*

Dude, what are you doing? I gripped my backpack straps tightly.

No. He has to want something. That is why he's so persistent. Then he'll throw you away like friends always do. I ducked into my next classroom.

Why would he do that? He's given no reason for you to think that.

There's always a reason. I've always been better alone.

****

By the time I got home with the police officer, sweat clung to my forehead and my breathing was heavy. As we neared my house, the air shifted. *Right.* Two of the police officers from before and a man in a suit waited for me in the driveway. My front door was wide open, and Micha was nowhere to be found. Apparently, my house had been searched. I tightly clutched the straps of my backpack, getting out and stopping only a few feet away from them.

"You have an hour to pack any essentials," the burly man with a handlebar mustache gruffly told me, typing on his phone. He pointed to his CPS badge briefly. "Another social worker will be here soon to see if you need any help."

"I'm going to be placed into foster care? What about my brother?" I asked, setting down my backpack. "My mom asked for me to watch him."

His eyes skimmed over me as he briefly glanced up. "You'll be fine. Your brother was already placed in another household. And I don't know." He sensed my next question. "Someone else will go over all that with you."

Anger swelled in my throat, enticing me to shout—right when my mother's voice came back to mind. I swallowed it, pushed past my door, snatched a spare backpack, and climbed upstairs. I shoved my clothes inside, only taking a second to breathe before moving on to other essentials. When it was full, I went to my door and paused, looking back to see the blue stuffed dinosaur my little brother loved, with faded purple markings. *No matter how long it takes, no matter what I have to do, I'll bring Micha and my mom back. I'll find him.* I picked it up and squished it inside.

As I climbed back downstairs, I kept my head lowered. "Where am I going?"

"You'll probably jump around a few homes until a decision is made, or you turn twenty-one and are placed at a shelter. They'll tell ya." The man placed a hand on my back and escorted me outside.

A fancy black SUV pulled up, skidding to a stop. Rolling down the window, a woman smiled brightly behind the wheel. "Hi, Aris! Ready to go?" With one last glance at my house, shrubs and ivy hugging the walls, I opened the front door and climbed in. The man went in the backseat with no complaint.

"There's a nice old lady who was eager to take care of you," the woman said, pulling out onto the road once I was ready. "She got recently certified, too. It was lucky timing due to our remaining foster homes being quite full. Most only have room for one child each."

Many people don't want to accept teenagers. I know you're avoiding that information to protect me. I'm not stupid.

I stared out the window. My teeth clenched. They had taken my family, the illusion that my choices mattered, and perhaps even my future. Soon, I lost myself to imaginary figures, free to do what they pleased, parkouring over trees and rooftops. They had no limits. They had freedom. Unlike me.

****

The kidnapper van rolled up to a small house, hanging on at the edge of the city, near the mountain with a fenced-in yard. Pulling into the driveway, the social worker parked and got out with the man. I opened my door reluctantly, ensuring the stuffed spinosaurs, Chomper, remained inside the bag, and double-checked that I had left nothing inside the vehicle.

We rounded the sidewalk, leading up the stairs to a white door. The lady knocked briefly, tablet in hand.

"One second," an indistinct voice called, followed by creaking floorboards and footsteps. Minutes later, it opened, and a sharp scent of cinnamon honey hit my nose. Inside stood a familiar old lady with bright amber eyes.

My breath hitched. *Taavi?*

"Oh, is this Aris? It's so nice to meet you." Taavi smiled as she stepped back with a gesture. The red and silver bracelet on her wrist slid as she moved her arm. "Please come inside."

The man stayed at the door while the woman stepped in with me, handing Taavi the tablet. After filling it out, Taavi showed the woman and me my room. The woman left after examining the house, closing the front door in her wake.

"How did you know I needed a home?" I asked Taavi right after the car drove away, setting plates on the table while she cooked. "Aren't you supposed to be in hiding?"

"Soon, dear. At Taftside Peak," she answered, her tone soft and melancholy. A pot of stew simmered on the stove, swirling as she stirred.

I lowered my head and exhaled, placing two water cups down as Taavi began to hum. "How do you expect me to follow you when you won't answer any of my questions? If I'm staying here, you owe me answers without all this nonsense."

Only silence responded as she added spices to the pot.

"What if I report you to the authorities?" I pressed.

"You said you were a villain. So what's stopping me?"

Pausing, Taavi looked up, locking eyes with mine. "Oh, Aris. Of course I'm no hero. And we both know that's an empty threat. You see what I can do. After all, I chose you for a reason."

I straightened. "So you have been watching me. That's a little creepy." I shook my head as my stomach growled. "What is it that you want? Do you know where my little brother is or what happened with my mother? What did you mean by 'my family crossed a line?' Can you get me in touch? How did you become my foster parent?"

"I will show you at Taftside Peak. You agreed." Returning to the stove, Taavi dipped a spoon in and tasted it. Her eyes lit up. "Now, if you're done with all the questions, let's have dinner. It's been an eventful day for you."

"I'll have dinner *after* I unpack. And if I'm staying after eating, you have to tell me."

****

The sunset splashed the horizon, washing the sky with cool colors. The clouds looked like strokes of paint as the fading light kissed their edges. As the land darkened, a particular point from the base of the mountain glowed. I made my way over sage and crabgrass. The stillness of the landscape was jarring compared to the storm churning inside me, simmering beneath my skin.

Under a limb of a tree in the distance, Taavi sat, her dark legs crossed and arms resting over them. The crunching of the grass caused her to look up. A faint glint sparked in her eyes.

What if this is a mistake? What if Taavi is some crazed old woman who'll land me in jail? I recalled Micha. His tear-streaked face as the officers dragged our mother away, his tiny hand gripping mine. I couldn't protect her or him then.

Taavi's the only one willing to give me a choice. As frustrating as her methods might be...

I stopped at the mountain's base, staring up at the path ahead. *This is insane.* I could turn back now, forget I ever met her. But she might have answers to get them back.

Standing, Taavi picked up her lantern. She gestured for me to follow her. I kept close as we made our way over the rocky landscape and partially up the mountainside. A distant trickle of water reached my ears. Flowers bloomed on branches, briefly visible from her bouncing light. A tinge of pollen and murky underbrush hung in the air.

Up ahead, a divot appeared, widening into an opening of a cave. Taavi took a sharp turn inside, her silhouette slipping into the cracks. I slid after, rocks scraping my palms, sending them skittering or piling up like sand.

Inside, a vast chamber opened with numerous outlet tunnels. Only a few edges near us were illuminated by the light swaying in Taavi's hand. She broke off to the farthest left, descending a set of crumbling granite stairs. At the bottom, Taavi faced me, winked, and swept her hand outward. An explosion of light surrounded the rooms, torches bursting into flames, aiding another unknown source.

"Come here." I approached, examining the yawning cavern that seemed to be over the size of a tennis court. A full-sized mirror lay to my left, a carpet wrapped in the middle of the floor, and a wooden desk pressed against the far rough stone wall. The walls had about twenty white half-oval outlines the size of a door across them. "Look in the mirror."

"Why?"

"I will show you."

Oh my gosh. I let out a tight breath. Slowly, I held out my hand until I brushed it. It was caked in dust, leaving grime on my fingers. Wiping more off, I tilted my head. My slightly diamond-shaped face looked very tan for being inside all winter. My black and white ashen hair was ruffled, falling to my midback, and a couple of strands strayed over my dark green eyes. Both of which I took after my dad. Tucking back a loose strand, I tightened my earrings.

"What do you see?" Taavi asked softly.

"Myself." I glanced at her. "It's a mirror."

"Look closer. Who else?"

I skimmed the mirror and sighed. "If you're referring to my family, I don't see them. I only see myself."

"Perhaps you need some help." Taavi strode to the side, her fingers ghosting over the mirror. In response, a wisp began to collect at my feet in the mirror. It solidified an identical model to my little brother.

I stared, taking a second to collect my thoughts. "That's my little brother." *I've heard of magic items, but I've never actually seen them used.*

"Yes." Both of our images vanished, replaced with the city. Nothing about it was unusual. "Now, what do you see?"

"My city."

"Well, yes. This was seventy years ago. Has any of it changed?"

"I can't see what had." I squinted. *Seventy years ago? No way.*

A cloud blew over and covered the mirror, then released the same cityscape. This time, two buildings changed colors, and numerous trees spotted throughout the area. Otherwise, there was nothing besides spotless streets. An AI delivery drone hovered lazily above the square, its design identical to the ones in the first image. The streetlights flickered as though their time was running out.

"And this is your city a hundred years from now. Besides rebuilding the structures the same way, not much changed," Taavi murmured and stepped back. "This is what happens when peace reigns too long."

"Surely it'd shift much more than that. Though it doesn't seem too bad," I said as the images morphed back to my reflection.

"In a world that knows only peace, there is no urgency for more." She waved her finger. She went to one of the half-oval outlines and pressed a rock next to it. Inside, a bright green, cloudy portal appeared. She waltzed inside.

It was like briefly walking through fluffy cotton candy. The scenery spilled open underneath. Taavi and I floated in the sky, peering over my school. The building's color faded slightly, and the trees have grown much more. The bell rang, causing swarms of teenagers to crowd out. After it thinned, I saw a familiar face exit. His mix of black and white hair was the same after all these years, but my little brother was much taller. With him were two other boys and a girl, all laughing and grinning.

They parted ways later, with my brother jumping into a car. I could barely make out his face beyond the tinted window as the light died in his eyes. He slouched against the doorframe, resting his head against the glass as the car drove away. *What's wrong? Doesn't he have anything to look forward to?*

The scenery shifted to a factory, full of working people. All had bland expressions, tirelessly doing their jobs. One was my mother, frail as a fish bone. I stiffened, leaning closer. Her skin sunken in, but she still happily worked around her amethyst chains.

Switching again to overlook the city, following the car my brother hopped into, the streets filled with children laughing and everyone at ease, going through life.

Except Micha, everyone looks so content, even my mother. I inhaled sharply. *What is the problem? Why is she showing me this? Why is he not okay?* Scratching the back of my neck, I met Taavi's knowing gaze, as if she sensed my question.

"That it isn't obvious to them either." She sat in her invisible chair.

I knelt at her side. "They're safe and look happy. Except my little brother."

"He might be safe," Taavi said, nodding to the car my brother's in, "but not free to choose anything beyond the path laid for him. To live and experience life in all its colors. Safety without freedom is a cage. Without threat or challenge, there's no drive to create, no thrill to overcome. No reason to do more." Taavi hummed. "The Presidents, Coast specifically, believes stability and safety came before anything else. After all, to them the wars of the past had claimed enough lives."

I opened my mouth, then closed it. "You're saying too much of our peace is bad?"

She tilted her head. "If there is no need for vigilance, no challenge, no desire for something greater, then people settle for what they have. They're like a world without shadow, which knows no thrill of light. What is good without evil?"

"Too much darkness would destroy everything. Isn't peace, dull as it may be, better than destruction?"

A faint smile curved her lips. "An untended garden will die, and its roots will rot, despite no disaster around it wrought. When fire is set to a forest, later the seeds may grow from black and flourish."

She gestured again, the scenery changing to a battlefield, full of cannons and guns, killing countless people. Siblings hugged each other. Half of them coughed and looked pale, still bracing in front of or behind their dead parents. More images bloomed around us: great discoveries and bursts of invention, all in times of war. It stopped inside a building, where countless men and women in white lab coats typed at computers or played with chemicals.

"Take a look at the history of innovation. How was penicillin made?" She didn't wait for an answer. "During wartime, in a chaotic, desperate attempt to save lives, penicillin was created by accident while a man researched a common type of bacteria called Staphylococcus. Do you know how many other inventions or advances came from conflict?"

"I know atomic bombs were then largely banned, but that's about it."

"Many." She drifted closer to me. "To name a few: communication, aviation, computers, medicine, synthetic materials, mass production, nuclear energy and efficiency, rocketry, certain psychology, transportation, planning and reconstruction, farming machinery, food preservation, global organizations, and women entering the workforce."

I blinked.

After a few seconds, Taavi prompted, "You see? Change doesn't happen without a hand to shape it. The question is who?"

"You're suggesting I... what, become a villain? Villains hurt people, I refuse to—"

"Who decides what a villain is? If someone breaks a rule to protect their family, are they evil? If someone uses their power to challenge injustice, are they selfish? Despite what society thinks, villains aren't defined by their actions. We're defined by those in power."

That sounds right. I rubbed my chin, deciding to repeat what teachers had told me my whole life to see what she'd say: "Rules are supposed to exist to keep people safe from villains, and maintain peace so more don't come. They keep things orderly."

"Did the Presidents' rules bring you peace when they shattered your family?"

My chest tightened. "I—"

She cut me off. "And yet, they call themselves heroes. Always for the 'greater good.' But whose good? Theirs? They say villains are selfish and destructive because we refuse to play by their rules. But some rules need to be broken for the world to move forward."

"To a certain extent. If everyone breaks the rules, like I said, wouldn't that just cause hell?"

"Not everyone needs to, child. Only one." Taavi's smile deepened. "You want a better life for those you love, don't you? A life with purpose and choice. Something you can control. Do you think the Council will give that to you? Or will they decide what's best for Micha like they did for your mother?"

"What if becoming a villain makes everything worse?"

"Worse than what? A world where your brother grows up afraid to step out of line? Where people like you are caged by rules? Heroes preserve what is. Villains tear it down to create a gateway to what could be. The future only belongs to those bold enough to claim it."

My pulse quickened so much that I could feel it in my thumb. *A better world for my family, for Micha.*

"You want a better life for those you love, don't you? A life with purpose, choice, and control. Who better to shape that future than you?"

One I can control. One no one gets hurt.

Could I do this? I've never heard of a hero versus villain fight happening since, well, Shelby. I'm sure they happen, but...

Do you have any other choice? The other part of me

reasoned. *There's no going back. They won't listen. You have to make them.*

Disrupting our lives, I can create a place where people don't sleepwalk through peace and live with purpose. I recalled Micha's face. I couldn't let him live in such a hollow world. *If I don't do this, someone else will. And I won't take that chance.* I blinked, my mouth pressed into a thin line, and my fingers trembled.

"I'll help you only if we do it my way. You will plan with me," I stated firmly, meeting her gaze. "No one touches my mother or Micha."

"Good, then you know what has to be done." She clapped. Around me, the world disintegrated, and I was back beside the mirror.

****

END OF THE SCHOOL YEAR

"Hey, y'all! That's enough for today; tomorrow is your last chance. If ya pass and prove your worth, by chance, you can get into the Ezrat Institution." Shanessa sheathed her sword, undoing her ponytail and letting the blue bonnet shift from its pinned place above her ear. "If ya got powers, that is. You're free to go."

I sheathed the katana, setting it on its stand. Malik stuck to my side. "That was a tough workout. Good job," he managed between pants, his voice clear. He wiped his brow, sweat glistening on his hand.

"Thanks." I briefly smiled at him before scooping up my backpack, passing through yet another doorway.

"You know, I really thought you would've warmed up to me by now." Malik retrieved his bag and fell in step beside me. "But I'll take that response as an improvement."

I pulled my backpack tighter, lowering my head.

"Say, did you hear that they're changing part of the air training next year? I'll be part of the first heroes to incorporate a newish technique involving sound vibrations."

I weaved around barricades of people and barely peeked up enough to see his face. "Nah, I'm not interested."

"Not interested?" He gaped at me, incredulous. "At least you gotta admit it's kind of cool."

He wants to use you. This friendship of his is like plastic pretending to be fish in the sea.

"Why do you care what I think?" The question came out sharper than intended. We descended the stairs, our steps more of a clatter than thuds against the tile.

Malik didn't flinch. "Okay, rough day or year, I get it. Give me six months with this new training. I'll master that and be moving tornadoes with my pinky before the next Victory over Villainy festival."

"Uh-huh. Or blow yourself into a wall. You're not even a first year."

"Pft. Either way, it'll be fun." Scratching the side of his head, Malik took a few tentative steps. "If you're not too busy, do you mind if we spar later? I could use a partner. And I can show you what I've learned."

Yeah, right. My breath hitched as I clenched and

unclenched my fists. *Seems genuine. They do to the point I almost want to, but I can't. I just— I can't.*

Why not?

You know why. I breathed. *No one actually cares about you, except your family. And I've been trying to reach them for the past year with no luck. The stupid CPS workers and police ignoring me— Agh, but that's a completely different fiasco. No, if anything, he'd use you like people always do. Make you a laughing stock, and dump you with less than you had before. It's better to prevent it from happening than to take the risk.*

My family... Who even knows what's happening to my mother now?

I don't have time for this. "Sorry, I have to go," I muttered, picking up my pace.

"Wait!" Malik easily kept up, keeping enough space between us. "What's up? Did I do something?"

His voice made me pause, feet from my locker, adjacent to my class. "Malik. Why do you even bother with me? I know you want something, so spit it out."

"What do you mean?"

"Just why?" I forced out the words, unlocking the door and taking out a book. "You have friends, family, and a future. You don't need me dragging you down, and I don't want to be your next charity case. So can we skip the false pretenses?"

Malik frowned, slightly tilting his head and ruffling the collar of his uniform. A wisp of his blond hair fell in front of his eyes. "Is-is that what you think? Seriously? That I'm just...

doing this for appearances so more people like me or something?"

"Isn't it?"

His crystal blue eyes searched me, as if he were dealing with a complex puzzle he didn't have all the instructions to. "No? I get you like your space. I respect that. But I'm not doing this for 'social points' nor do I plan to leave you in the dust. It's, well, I don't know how to put it right." He rubbed the back of his neck. "We heroes need to stick together to protect and serve. I feel like I notice some things. I don't love pretending I don't see it, even if I don't understand it."

Closing my locker, we locked eyes for a solid minute. I could've sworn the shadow at his feet twitched. "I don't need friends or for someone to 'look out for me.'"

"Alright, then don't think of me as that." Malik nodded, shrugged, then stepped back. "I don't think any less of you, and I'm not great at disappearing on people. So I'll still be around as a friend, acquaintance, or classmate. Whichever." He shifted his weight, eyes flicking away.

God, stop being so insistent! Why does he sound like that? I dragged my fingers over my face. *I don't believe a single word this man utters.* But his eyes didn't seem like someone lying. I stood there, Malik a foot away, waiting. *This world took your family without a damn. The government and society don't see the problems it's creating. He'll become one of them. And if I tell him, trust him, or let him in, he'll try to control me like they do. Take away the one chance I might have to do something about it.*

No one is on your side. You're the only one who can get

your family back. Give Micha the life he deserves. A life that's not suffocating creativity.

"I'm busy. See ya." I pushed past him into my last class. He didn't follow.

Taking my usual place in the far corner, I waited for the teacher to begin. I tried to focus on anything else but Malik. The smooth chairs, the chatter, the mixed scent of honey and body spray, and a disgustingly excited atmosphere. Thankfully, the aroma reminded me of someone else.

Her words rang through my head. *"Remember, you can make this world a better place. You know what has to be done."*

Am I the only one able to? I studied my hands. If not me, who will? I can change my future. I can get my family back. If Taavi is right... If the world needs conflict to grow and I'm the only one who sees the cracks in this peace, maybe I'm the only one who can break them open.

The bell rang. In response, the students grew still, facing the board. Walking out from his wooden desk, Mr. Poistio passed out a piece of paper. On it were the eleven categories of known magic, with large boxes under each one.

"This is a simple worksheet. One you should all 'ave no trouble fillin' out." He uncapped a marker. "But until school's finished, I want you to use it for yourselves instead. Who already knows some of their abilities?" About five people raised their hands. Blinking, the teacher shook his head. "Blimey, that's incredible!" Gesturing to Arlene, he faced the board. "What is it, then?"

"I can light up anything I touch for up to five minutes." She straightened, then added quietly to the person next to her,

"Say, do you suppose that if heroes wear reflective suits in battle, we can create a walking disco ball?"

"A minor power, not half bad." Mr. Poistio wrote her name under light and called on another kid.

"I can help animals manage their emotions."

Raising an eyebrow, the teacher wrote his name under nature and called the rest. "Now, these are all little powers, and as you can see, don't mean they are heroes only. In the next year, those receiving ought to figure out all of 'em. One to three minor powers are the norm, an' it's rare for a few to snag four to five. Usually, a strong—major or main they call it—power will also arise with it." Taking a sip of water, Mr. Poistio continued, "For the majority of them who don't know if they've got powers, flip the paper over."

I complied.

"This side's what powers you'd expect or like to 'ave. If it shows at all, it'll be within 'alf a year. For the majority it won't, you will be sorted into a different school than those with when the new year rolls in." He locked eyes with me. "Make the most of it, yeah?"

Chapter 3

PRESIDENT COAST

The others should be here soon, he thought stiffly, a smooth glass bottle in his hand. He took a swig, the cold beer sharpening his mind. Droplets landed on his scruff. *Damn it.* He gently wiped it away with a napkin tucked inside his pocket.

That morning, he did his hair and trimmed his black beard so it would not look unkempt like a wilderness survivor. A few droplets of beer would ruin his hard work.

We all know appearances matter more than people realize, especially when stability depends on perception.

Papers in an open Manila folder rested on the long brown table in front of him. It contained reports of recent magic activity of meddling students (who decided decorating their city's prized statue in plants, drawings, and bright new colors was an excellent idea), propositions for new laws or inventions, and schematics to "improve" safety.

Red "Rejected" stamps glared up at him like warnings

across all the pages. At least they've substantially dwindled in the past years, much to Ezrat's President's relief. He'd learned to see that as progress.

President Coast flipped through them slowly, his fingers tracing the bold lines of one blueprint in particular. The design promised clean power using a new design of nuclear energy, proposed by a student named Brendan. The same kid who was promptly expelled for not following orders. He set it aside, his lips pressed into a thin line.

He tucked the papers underneath the others. "It's not worth the risk of ruining a peace we've fought to maintain. Manageable problems are all we need. Let the people enjoy their festivals and monuments, chalk their peace up to Shelby's use of the crown, but we must ensure their safety at all costs."

The upcoming festival, "Victory Over Villainy," was a full-blown annual event, a cornerstone of their society with plays, music, and games. Two more years will mark one hundred fifty years since that day. His grandfather had been amongst the first to take charge and establish new rules, herding in villains to create this new era.

He traced the outline of a faded photograph on his desk, peeking out from under all the papers. To the left of his grandfather and Sean Weaver, smiled Shelby Feyth, holding a bronze crown adorned with five embedded crystals. Their expressions were one of exhausted triumph, chests puffed out, and bags clinging under their eyes. "*For the good of the people, to keep us safe.*" These people did everything they could so that citizens and heroes would have peaceful lives. And President Coast had every intention to keep it that way.

To keep potential *villain* behavior at bay, they had

shown many videos to citizens and heroes of what the world used to look like, back when villains ran amok. He helped film them, even if they were supposed to be 'history,' they were, of course, greatly exaggerated. The cause was worth it. Without what they taught, the devastation and death, like in the videos, would be insurmountable.

Every small, minor disturbance quickly ran up the chain to him and the civilian leaders. Nothing would go unnoticed. Everything had to be accounted for.

His eyes flicked to a report at the bottom of the stack, detailing the successful containment of a rogue artifact. A student at Tesril had attempted to smuggle a blue-silver pocket-watch out in a handbag, claiming they wanted to "study its potential applications." President Coast snorted, seeing it was the same student who had been flagged over one hundred times for questioning their teacher and ranked toward the bottom of the six-hundred students.

"Negative tendencies," he murmured. The artifact now lay secured deep beneath reinforced barriers, alongside dozens of others inside Tesril. The student was reprimanded and placed under closer observation.

Coast tapped the report with his pen and signed off on it without hesitation. He added a secondary authorization beneath his signature, extending surveillance protocols for students flagged under repeated behavioral reviews. If they were asking the wrong questions now, it was better to watch them closely before those questions turned outward.

A soft knock echoed through the room, and his guard opened the door to admit the other Hero School Presidents one by one. First Mala, then Hyzrit, followed by Tesril and

Higgins. As expected. Tesril and Higgins are a lot more lax with their students. It's very risky. Safety doesn't come with freedom. They must be more careful.

"Welcome." He stood with open arms, walking to shake each hand by hand. After they were all in their chairs, an electric air settling over them, he sat back down. "After the usual, we have much to discuss." He eyed Tesril.

They worked through the pleasantries and paperwork rather quickly, combing through laws and minor disruptions. Halfway through, they took a break. When everyone returned, President Coast clicked his tongue as Tesril's President was the last to arrive and sit. "Tesril, your approach is rather increasingly risky," he began. He glanced directly at their school president, who bristled but said nothing, his gaze hard. "You all know safety comes from discipline. Why are you so lax?"

Higgins frowned, leaning forward. "Discipline has its limits, President of Ezrat. We can't mold our students into our society's version of an ideal hero. They're meant to think—"

"And I understand your reasoning," President Coast cut him off. He gestured to the pile of rejected proposals on the table. "Innovation is important, but history—like the Great Depression born of unregulated growth and finance—has taught us the price of unmonitored *progress*: devastation, destabilization, and suffering. It took decades and war to recover." He stood. "Our responsibility isn't only to preserve peace, it's to protect the lives built on it so no one has to live through the horrors of the past again. Our people trust us to ensure its stability, and we owe them that. You've seen our rules succeed for the past century."

Higgins opened his mouth to protest, but President Coast raised a hand, silencing him. The other two school Presidents nodded.

"The festival must be flawless. Moving the jewels or not, it's vital for the people to see the statues, eat the food, hear the speeches, exchange the gifts, and feel the weight of what was won."

Mala's President adjusted her hat. "They need to believe the balance is holding."

"Exactly. If they start questioning that... if they start thinking we've let our guard down..." He shook his head. "Villains have tried to rise, and we quickly put them back in place; only a few have intentionally reached the public eye. They stand no chance against our heroes and technology anymore. With that in mind, we keep a close eye on the prisons and any red-flagged students or citizens."

He did not miss the way Higgins stiffened at that.

The meeting soon adjourned, and the others filed out, their conversations trailing into murmurs as the door closed behind them. Coast remained seated, his hands clasped tightly on the table. The curtains swayed slightly, a faint breeze finding its way through the cracks. *I don't need to consider Tesril and Higgins words closely. It's absurd, frankly.* He reached for the photograph again, his fingers tracing Shelby Feyth's silver crown. "For the good of the people."

Chapter 4

~What led me to be here~

ARIS SHELIA

The dummy swayed, taunting me to strike it down. I aimed for its side, but my limbs burned, and my movements were too sluggish. It moved diligently, causing me to stumble to the side.

"Stop thinking like a hero," Taavi snapped in her calm way. "I thought you wanted to save your mom. You ain't going to do that, holding back, second-guessing, or playing it safe."

I gritted my teeth. Around me, I demanded the shadows to draw near, pulling them like a rope. They responded, swirling around me like a living entity. Like a bowstring, I released them to the target. It shredded under the force of the blow, splitting apart with guts of white fluff spilling to the floor. I dropped my arms, panting.

"Better." She nodded approvingly. "Yet I sense you're still fighting yourself. Let it go. You're going to have to manage yourself if you want to get anything done."

The muscles in my neck tightened. *Of course, I want to do this for them. To prove I have control in the matter.* I tried slowly rolling my shoulders to loosen them.

What if doing what Taavi asks meant losing the last stable thing I have? What would happen if she wants me to go further than I'm willing to? What if she's using me to get what she wants—

My mother's shout to me cut into my head, pleading for me to watch my little brother as they dragged her away. The way Micha cried, begging me to tell him 'what was going on, why was mom being taken?' right before they dragged him to another home without seeing me again.

They separated us so easily. If they could do that without remorse or guilt. If they could ignore me—

"I'm not afraid," I stated firmly. "I will keep my word, and no one dies."

"Good." Taavi's expression became unreadable. "The world doesn't care about you or your intent. It only cares about strength and your actions. Progress is born in fire, so if you want to help this world and the people you love, you must work for it. You want to save your little brother and mother, don't you?"

Is that even a question? I closed my eyes as a small voice rose inside me. *I'm doing this for a reason. That's why I asked you to train me.*

Perhaps she's giving me the tools to carve my own checkmate.

I opened my eyes and nodded.

"Tear down the system that tore your family apart. The only way to protect him is to destroy their rules and peace." She waved. "You're done for today." I followed her out to the cave, stepping around the dummy's guts.

The now-less dusty mirror and old wooden desk rested in their usual places inside Taftside Peak. Dim outlines of semi-circles lined the jagged stone walls, as if not a day had gone by since the first time I stepped inside the cave.

Taavi clasped her hands in front of her, her wrinkles by her eyes deepening. She reached out and handed me a rag from the desk. Her braided hair frayed everywhere as if she had been the one training.

Sooner I learn, the sooner I can get them back.

I wiped it against my face. "Thank you again for letting me stay with you. I appreciate you helping me."

She hummed in response.

Once I know they're safe, I'll thank Taavi and help her with the rest of her plan to encourage change. I rubbed my forehead. *What happened to my mom?*

After living with Taavi for a few weeks, I managed to figure out an address to a holding 'house.' The police assured me that's where Mom resided after I confronted them with it. I also asked about Micha, and they dismissively said him too. The same day I got to the rickety old house, surrounded by empty farmer fields, I found it rather abandoned, with not a soul for miles. Then I stormed back; the men at the front desk shrugged, telling me to wait in the corner for someone to bring me back. No one ever did. In fact, I was only talked to when they asked me to leave to lock up. I argued, politely at first and more harshly the longer they ignored me.

Over the next few months, I attempted various other times to locate my family. To get into contact with someone instead of the police—like my social worker—who's at least talked to me or heard about their whereabouts. Whether it was following anyone or leveraging my omnilingualism, no one would answer or help me. Taavi said she tried when I asked during dinner one day, and would keep looking, but other than that, the police were frustratingly curt. The front desk for the City Council wasn't much better. It's like a teenager had no sway or importance to them.

I sharply bit my bottom lip, suppressing a harsh sigh. *If they're not willing to talk, fine. I'll keep training until I am able to sneak and bypass their security, then search every building myself.*

Until I become someone they can't ignore.

"Have you been practicing your powers outside of training?" Nodding, I backed into the shadows. It wrapped around me in an embrace. She clasped her hands. "Good. Any more surface?"

I shook my head.

Over summer break, three had emerged: enhanced physical abilities and omnilingualism as my minor powers, and the major I practiced earlier, Shadow.

The physical enhancements, specifically, were estimated to be about 150% of an average person's, including the five senses, vertical jumping, and speed. Compared to a person with it as their major power, though, it's barely sufficient to keep me on their trail.

I'll figure out a way. I'll make do with what I have.

Pinching the bridge of her nose with her head lowered, Taavi went up the stairs. I trailed after her, tossing the rag to the floor behind me. After we surfaced, she sighed and shook her head, "Despite their insufficient surveillance, they still have the advantage. You're not ready."

"What? What more can I do?" I asked fervently and dodged a deep hole. "Am I doing something wrong?"

Stepping over a fallen log, Taavi gazed into the distance. "Don't worry, it'll be dealt with when the time comes. Only then can you take back what's yours. Now it's almost time for bed."

"Wait!" She continued forward, leaving me to jog after her. *How is she so freakishly fast for an old lady?* "You can't not elaborate. How do you expect me to learn? To be good *enough*? Don't you want to make this city better like I do?"

She waved her hand, the silver and red bracelet shifting on her arm. "Dear, be patient. There are objects of magic out there that will aid you. We'll go over them in due time. But you must be wary, as for now, all you can do is prepare and hone those skills. Our plan to make them heed us may begin by the end of your second school year."

I stopped in my tracks, letting the distance between us grow greater. *How do you expect me to do this? What if I can't get them back? Or help society grow? Make it become more interesting for us and future generations?* My breath came short.

It sounded like you'd give me the control and chance to do that. You made it sound so inevitable, like growth was a fire that had to consume something. But did it? Couldn't society advance without chaos, without villains? All it needed was obstacles to progress. Something I could do without malice.

Or was Taavi right? Am I too weak to see what it takes? Agh, why can't anything be easy?

****

The grass swished and crunched underneath my tennis shoes. It changed as I went onto the sidewalk, music blasting in my ears. Songs were the only thing lately that kept my voices out of my head. That kept the memory—no. I shook my head, pushing my legs to walk faster.

Floating gray towers hovered over Ezrat, with upper-level students flying or walking on the bridges in between. I passed under my college's ever-present arches, which were cemented to the earth, to its front yard, noting the lush, meticulously planted green moss or ivy woven into the structures. Smooth stone pathways starred out, lined with luminescent flowers, and wound around the main square, passing ancient trees that bore markings of spells long faded.

Clutching the straps of my backpack, I slipped past the first glass doors into the building. Weariness, like a weight, stained my heart, pooling in my gut. The thought of facing people twisted my stomach as if medicine had been plastered over my tongue.

Shoving past the occasional crowd, I rounded a corner and sluggishly climbed the marble steps. Its rough black railing scratched my skin and snagged my hoodie when I reached the top, ripping it and leaving a small tear at my side. I cursed, pinching the edge.

Second year, yet nothing's changed. This place hates me.

Down the hall, walls brimmed with flower vines, rocks, and the rare stream of water. I brushed a strand of my ash hair behind my ear and entered my first class. I collapsed in my spot, the back corner adjacent to a window, and slipped my backpack off and under my desk. A new teacher stood from his blackwood desk, talking to two students.

It was a larger class. About seventeen people. It made sense, since history and laws of magic and science were a requirement all heroes had to enroll in. That, and various ethical courses (Mental, Power Manipulation, and Emotion heroes had to take the most out of everyone here).

An older kid strode in, about six feet tall, taking a seat next to me. Warmth radiated from him in waves. I couldn't see his face very well from the corner of my eye, only his messy black hair, but I could make out that he had a fine build beneath his tight white shirt and denim jacket.

"Welcome to yet another year! Or if you're a first-year, I hope you'll enjoy it." The teacher, Mr. Atherly, picked up a pile of papers and began handing them out. Small arcs of electricity ran across his skin, leaving faint lines like kiss marks. "Today, we'll briefly review what you'll learn over the year."

Nearing, he made eye contact with me. A wise glint crossed his eyes, like he knew what I asked last year. As if that question was big enough to spread to each hero teacher in the world, classifying me as someone they should be careful around. But he blinked, and it was gone, replaced with an electric kind smile.

When he finished distributing the papers, he scratched his beard. Little sparks of static shot from his fingers. "I suppose I'll start with this. Magic's not solely raw power. You might come across items like the Spiral Staff, an item that can bind any individual with any magic to complete stillness, or enchanted daggers for generic defense. Out of the six schools in the world, each crafts its own unique set of tools. Our neighbor, Mala, for instance, is famed for its focus on magic artifacts, while Tesril specializes in combat." His gaze swept over the class. "Our institution, Ezrat, focuses on blending power with practicality for better control."

Mr. Atherly tapped the board with his chalk. "Remember, while powers and magic can be a gift, it's a privilege the government monitors closely. Each spellcaster and artifact falls under the eyes of the Hero Council. So, if you ever feel a spark to practice something unconventional, make sure it's recorded and allowed. They aren't known for leniency when it comes to unauthorized use, and we've all seen how they handle rule-breakers..."

The orientation video skimmed through my mind of powers being stripped for weeks to the user's own powers and weaknesses being used against them.

"We're lucky to live in a safe, peaceful society. Best not to forget why, wouldn't you say?"

I shifted my attention over to the window, the droning continued, and like a miracle, the bell eventually rang. I slung my backpack wearily over my shoulder, standing only for the man with fire powers to abruptly cut me off, heading out. It was brief, but he turned enough that I caught his face. He was definitely a last-year student.

Fits his ignorance and indifference.

The corners of my eyes tugged as I headed downstairs, brushing past the mossy corner, and across a hall to the courtyard outside. I pushed open the hot metal doors. The sun immediately blazed down on my head and back. Sweat beaded upon my forehead as the smell of freshly cut grass hit my nose.

I cut through the lawn, ignoring the sidewalks that outlined the courtyard and separated the walls from the grass, scanning for my agility class. In the center lingered a cluster of students, with one in particular standing off to the side. Malik. He passed another kid from my high school, Reed, who messed around with his friends, all of them shouting to make our ears bleed. The hairs on my arms prickled at the sight of the latter.

Around the group and courtyard, trees swayed. Benches dotted the grass as well, some snuggling to the trunks.

In front of the students was Shanessa, a teacher from my high school, and an upperclassman at Ezrat. A soft, glowing aura hugged her body, even the blue bonnet she wore pinned above her ear.

I dragged myself over, reaching my class as the tardy bell rang. With a sharp nod, she carefully scanned each of us. "Welcome, folks. Grab a partner and line up. Y'all gonna be together for the whole year, so choose who ya trust or work well with."

Winking, Malik made his way over, high-fiving or fist-bumping a few kids as he passed. All of the other students immediately paired off with their friends, leaving us and a third person who joined the teacher. She motioned for us to stand closer together, turned, and began walking. *Whatever. I'll take him over Reed any day. Malik's annoying... but he isn't that bad.*

I followed in the back of the line as the teacher led us back into the school, through some halls, and out the back doors. We were like little ducklings being led to the slaughter.

The grey sidewalks continued straight from the school into the grassy fields. In the distance arose two heavily metal-armored wooden doors. *This class may be better than I thought.* Bees buzzed over my head. Ahead, Malik talked to a man, about our age, who was half a foot shorter than him. He had stark white hair and a loose-fit sports uniform. Nothing about him signaled his power, though something felt familiar about him. Like I met him a few years ago or something.

The armored doors opened right before Shanessa was in reach and smoothly swung shut after the class, Malik and I, at the back, were clear inside.

I should've taken this class last year, though I guess we couldn't help it. I didn't know about my enhanced physical abilities yet. It's fine, I'll work hard to get a handle on them so I can get going with my—our plan. One that involved me clearing roofs...

Aside from the enormous doors, three large, smooth rock walls stood together with no ceiling. Half the place was a parkour course, reaching about four acres. Swinging rods, beams, ropes, dangling chains, shifting platforms, oddly shaped walls, and shaking ledges were only part of it. The other half was a mix of a football field, swimming pool, and interchange-able courts.

Facing us, the teacher jabbed her thumb toward the

course. "This section will be most of our unit. For today, y'all can go explore. After that, we'll play a game. Just be careful, alright? Off now."

Malik nudged me as our class dispersed among the course. To my left rose a staircase that unraveled into impossible spacing, the final steps vanishing into a set of doors that swung wide and snapped shut as if alive. The middle had moving platforms with swinging beams, leaving one option.

Taking off to the right, a frayed rope extended to the top of a smooth fifteen-foot wall. Branching off to my left was a diagonal wooden bridge leading to a swinging beam surrounded by a foam pit. I climbed the rope, reaching the top to find him sitting cross-legged in the center.

"Took you long enough." Malik smiled at me. "Great view, isn't it?"

How'd he...? I paused at his side and scanned the course. Though the platform didn't tower like the others, the arena unfolded clearly with students scattered below, some already messing around at the end. *Why don't the kids with Physical as a main get their own class?*

Dragging himself to his feet, Malik leaped off and floated down the other side. *Oh, right. Never mind, then. Air manipulation.* The rope bit my hands as I slid down. Burns etched into my palms, stinging like crazy as my feet touched the floor.

There must be better ways to work on our physical powers than a generic course. I guess it has some uses, like the ability to navigate unique terrain or use our surroundings to our advantage. But I doubt they'd improve it.

Ignoring the next obstacle, I veered to the left. It led slightly backward to a long diagonal row of glass panels that led to the middle courses. Every so often, one dropped, leaving whoever set foot on it to plummet and be buried by the foam underneath. On the other side stood the same familiar, dark-skinned man with stark white hair. He stared at me—no Malik—while leaning against a metal pole. The man nodded when Malik noticed him.

I squinted. *Wait, we did our presentation together. That's Drystan.* I peeled my eyes away and waited for the first panel to drop.

"I'll do this one with you," Malik said, dropping to a running stance, and the first panel clanked down.

Right when it reset, I bolted. Malik easily kept pace with me, eventually pulling ahead and landing next to his friend. Right when I was about to reach them, the last panel dropped, taking me with it.

I managed a not-so-solid grip on the panel's outer edge, slipping when I failed to lift myself and plummeted to the foam below. It covered me quickly. The soft and squishy substance blocked out most of the light above. Particles flew into my eyes and lungs, making me cough.

Stupid! My throat swelled as I fought to get upright, uncovering myself only for more to take its place as the foam swallowed me. *Why wasn't I fast enough?* I found my footing and located a nearby ladder leading to where Malik and the other guy should be. I... I could imagine my mom's disappointment for not making it... No, she'd still be cheering me on. She would always, even if I failed her.

"Aris, sweetie," Mom said between the crack of my door. I rolled over in my bed. "Do you want to watch a movie with me? The neighbors agreed to watch Micha tonight, so it'll just be us."

I sat up, brushing my black and white hair from my face. "Uhm, sure I can, Mom. But can we do it later?"

Something in my voice must've made her do a double-take. She opened the crack wider. "Yes, we can. Is this about the astronomy club?" Sighing, I flopped back into my bed. She asked if she could come in, and I nodded, letting her sit on the edge. "They ignored you again, huh? Did you try to talk to them this time?" I shook my head 'no' and she let out a 'mother sigh', placing a hand on my leg.

"Aris! You okay?" Malik called, jolting me from the memory.

Like quicksand, the foam attempted to bury me while I was lost in thought. I removed it roughly and struggled toward the ladder, feeling as though I made zero progress with the cubes dragging my limbs down. It was as if I waded through thirsty water. My ears grew hot and my face tingled. *They must be laughing at me. I'm such an idiot!*

What would Taavi say?

"Chill out, man. She's good."

The cold plastic greeted my hands, and I pulled myself up. *I have to do better. I will do better.* I scaled the ladder within seconds. At the top, Malik tilted his head, eyebrows in that swoop an adult has when helping a little kid with a boo-boo. My throat felt numb.

"Told ya, didn't I?" Drystan said, putting his arm over

Malik's shoulder. "Is this...?"

I inclined my head, using an arm to push past them, heading back to the front. This one had vertically moving platforms and three swinging beams.

"Yeah," Malik answered. "That's Aris."

I looked over my shoulder as one platform touched the ledge. I stepped onto it with an eyebrow raised.

The PA system came to life in the time I ducked under the first beam. Shanessa's voice echoed, clear as if she was talking in my ear, "Everyone, come back to the front. We're going to play a game."

Both the moving platform I stood on and the next touched one another ten feet in. I stepped to the second, repeating this process while ducking and eventually ending back at the start. Malik and Drystan arrived minutes later.

As the rest of the students returned, Malik tapped my shoulder and introduced us. I didn't tell him I remembered Drystan as the kid who made a presentation with us two years ago. Apparently, his hair change was a mix of being struck by lightning and dyeing it, but it was a nice contrast.

He finished talking as Shanessa split everyone into two groups. Both Malik and Drystan, unfortunately, ended up on my team, along with four other people. One seemed like a first year, and the other three appeared like third or last years.

Shanessa waved in between the groups. "Listen up, y'all! We're 'bout to give us a race to figure out some temporary rankings in this class. This here's to pair ya up with folks at the same skill level." Striding to the middle, she held her hands flat out in front of her. "One team's gonna start on your right, the other on your left. When I give the word, y'all take off and race to the other side. Stick to the first floor. Once you make it, swap sides and come back. Got it?"

People cheered, challenging each other in friendly shouts. She raised her hand, gesturing for them to quiet down. "Alright, folks, to keep things fair, we gotta lay down some ground rules." Someone on the other team booed. "First off, since many of y'all are green, let's keep it to just yer physical skill agility, speed, strength, and any enhanced sense. No other powers allowed. Second, play nice! Don't go hurtin' nobody or bein' cheap. That means avoid physical contact with the other team. We'll have time for that next class.. And third, y'all better help each other out! Everyone on your team has gotta make it back to this platform to count as finished."

Whoever arrives first will gain the class's respect and a handicap for the next class. Like a weight chained to their waist or a blindfold. They will get the spotlight and become competition, a bar to be better than. Losing will only cement what people already think about me. Not to mention, my family is counting on me. And Taavi expects me not to be weak. So I'll aim to be middle or top, like second or third, but not first.

While I was lost in thought, Shanessa pointed to Malik, who raised his hand. He scanned our group, scratching his head. "Can we go in the middle?"

"Yeah, but only one time or if ya get stuck. Best stick to your side otherwise. Malik, you may pick where to start first."

"We'll go to the left."

My group left to go wait by the first gaping step. Each

platform was a blue mat, spaced farther and farther apart until the opening and closing doors.

Someone on the other team caught my eye, laughed, and mouthed, I *saw you fall. Ready to lose, Aris?*

Freaking Reed. His light brown, curly mullet shifted over his shoulder. *You're one to speak, wearing that haircut from two centuries ago.* The man towered at a similar height to Malik, built like a farmer. His skin wasn't very tan but oddly a dull white.

Lowering my head, I stayed at the edge with the rest of my group as the others took their positions. *I'll show you.*

Drystan passed me with a pat on the back. "You think you can keep up?"

I nodded sharply, biting my tongue. Shanessa counted down and sent us off. Drystan sprinted first, followed by the four other members of our group. Malik shot me a thumbs up and made the first jump, then the next. By the time I began, Drystan had made it to the opening and closing cushion doors, clearing the large gap and diving in seconds before it slammed.

The other thing about this course is I can see how far along I am and still have to go. Taavi said I wasn't ready. This can put it more in an obvious way. I hope I'm fast enough to keep up with them.

I trailed after Malik, leaping from step to step as they grew farther and farther apart. There were about five in total, each adding another five to six feet in space. The last one was about a thirty-foot gap between it and the doors. I dove to the last platform as Malik passed the doors. My hands slammed the edge of the mat, and I rolled, barely keeping myself on.

Rising to my feet, I counted how many seconds there were before the doors closed. *Ten.* They opened again, and I took a one-step leap, reaching as far up as I could for the ledge as I sailed over foam.

I slammed the wall, fingers grasping nothing but a flat surface, missing the bottom of the ledge by mere inches.

Two hands extended down with insane speed, wrapping around my wrists. They yanked me, aiding my legs until I went over. Malik's face met inches from mine, and he shoved me behind him, throwing himself back as the walls slammed close, and landed next to me on the black rubber floor.

I rolled onto my feet, muscles burning. *Seriously?* I brushed the dust and foamy bits off my jeans and hoodie. Our team wasn't waiting for us; they were already on the second course. *Thank God no one saw that.* I fixed my sleeves, pulling them back to my wrists, and tucked the stray strand of hair behind my ear.

Hanging from a singular monkey bar, the fourth person threw it up with their body and over to the next notch, swinging between two rows of dangling metal beams over the pit. The trick was to hook the loose bar into the notches, swing your body across, then pull it out and hurl it into the next set of notches until reaching the other side, where Drystan and the others waited. Dropping to the floor with the bar, she tossed it back to the last person. Malik and I ran to him as he crossed. Upon seeing us, Drystan gave a thumbs up, turned, and began the third.

We passed the second obstacle, the third with falling blocks and shaking tiles (helping each other dodge), and the fourth, sliding under sets of moving walls, fairly quickly.

One more until the end, where we turn around. I need to get in the middle. I rolled my fingers. *Ugh, why can't this be easier? All this freaking training and I'm toward the end?*

The fifth course had stairs on the left leading to the second floor. Straight ahead had metal chains dangling at various lengths, clinging to a holey ceiling. Balls flew at it from some type of hidden machine in the wall. Another teammate went first, some of the chains falling seconds after she moved to the next one, swinging to miss the balls. By the time she crossed, half of the chains remained.

"I guess we're going through the middle," Malik said, scratching his ear.

I shifted right. It was a slide straight to a lower middle, directly into a smooth silver pole. Connecting from the top of the pole back to our side hung a rope vine. One you had to swing to get to where our team member waited.

Drystan patted Malik on the back, who glanced at me.

Rolling my eyes, I slid to the pole, using the momentum to propel myself in a jump to reach it halfway. The metal was quite smooth, warm from use, yet it gave a good grip. I scaled to the top, taking hold of the rope.

Below me, Malik was already at the pole, struggling to climb it. He made it halfway before Drystan came down. His eyes found me, and Malik shook his head. I leaned off, tightening my hold. Wind swept my hair, slowing down as the rope reached its length, and I leapt, landing next to the girl. I spun to see Malik barely snatch the vine. He made his way over, smoothly landing at my side.

Sweat collected on my forehead and arms. I rolled up my sleeves and pulled back my hood. *I have to push harder.* The sixth had ropes hanging and connecting in all directions like a spiderweb, usually attached to strategically placed poles that wrapped around a wall. Drystan, as usual, made his way meticulously across.

"Yo, damn!" His voice rang, followed by seconds of silence. "Step it up, everybody! We're fallin' behind! The other team just rolled up!"

Our four other teammates sprang on the web. Malik and I gave them time before sliding on ourselves.

Two people from the other team rounded the corner of the wall, barging their way across. They darted around our four teammates, who tried to trip them and shoved past Malik and me. The girl in particular almost made me fall. I lagged behind Malik, who climbed through it like a monkey, the slack and tightening of ropes having little effect on him and his speed. Three more of the other team rounded the corner, giving him just enough space to squeeze around them as he ducked under one of their elbows.

I reached the wall about five feet from the corner. The other team continued, forcing me to wait. As the last two of their group passed, one especially drew my attention. Reed, and he grinned wildly, sending bumps across my spine. Those orange-red eyes bored into me as he stuck his hand out and pressed his fingers against my arm.

My vision blurred. I dropped to my knees, clutching the ropes and blinking. The cold rush spread from my arm and across my body as quick poison or venom. Any object shifted without leaving its spot, as if it had a life of its own. *Too far down... I can't.* The weight on the rope slackened and dropped me lower as their group got off. The rope imprinted itself in my skin, rough and stringy, but it was the only thing between me and that drop to the foam cubes... the shadows pooling into the shape of a large, gaping mouth that stretched and yawned like it would swallow me whole and never let—

"Aris?" Malik called out. "Everyone is already past the next obstacle heading back. What's taking you so long?"

"I'm fine!" I snapped, ripping my hand from the rope. My body trembled, making it harder to crawl as I forced myself forward. Reed and his friend were already long gone. Hot flashes crossed my body. *That kid... I'm going to kill that—*

"Hang on, I'm coming."

The rope swayed. I flattened out to my stomach and clenched my teeth.

"I saw you fall," Reed had said. I saw you.

Incompetent. I closed my eyes, sliding back to my knees and hands. *I'm not...* The wall stayed to my right, brushing my shoulder. I did the one thing Taavi drilled into me, loosening the tight hold I had, and breathed out. I opened my eyes again, using it to stand and round the corner right as Malik turned.

"There you are! I thought you fell," he said, trailing off while I flinched.

"Don't worry about it," I snapped again. Taking my hand from the wall, I moved to push past him while biting my inner cheek.

"Okay... I guess I can follow behind you."

Two steps were all I could manage before it hit back in a wave. *Spinning... high up failing... falling.* I leaned back harder against the wall, slowly nudging the rest of the way around him.

"Are you scared of heights?" Malik asked softly, placing a hand on my shoulder.

"No!" I brushed his hand off. "Look, it was that freaking boy, okay?"

"What boy? What did he do?"

"I-I don't know! It's messing with my head."

"Alright." Tapping his chin, he nodded to himself and gestured to the next platform. "Would you like me to be in front? Or follow behind?"

I'm not a freaking child. The fall didn't seem so bad anymore. "No. I'm fine. I got it. T-thank you."

Parting from the wall, I scrambled across the web. A lump formed in my throat with every sway from the thought of the mouth waiting below, relenting when I made it to the next platform. With a sigh of relief, I shuffled to the middle and collapsed to my knees. I breathed in deeply.

Stupid. Why would you let him touch you? You can't cross a simple course, let alone save your family.

Footsteps grew louder, with a shadow falling over me. "Should I tell Shanessa? She did say using other powers wasn't allowed. Him using Emotion like that could've been dangerous."

The pit in my stomach began to fade, paired with the breaths I took. My hands slowed to a still. Shaking my head, I got up and rolled out my limbs.

Our group was so far away that I couldn't see them anymore. We had to hurry. Pressing my hands to the floor, I forced myself to my feet. Before us were three blurry walls; two were tall, clear plastic, about an arm's length across from each other. The third was a matted wall blocking me from walking through it.

"Great," Malik whispered behind me.

I narrowed my eyes, facing him. *Oh, I see.* "Go first."

"Will you be-"

"Go."

Nodding, he slowly walked in between the walls. Placing his hands and then his feet on both sides, Malik climbed slowly. Halfway up, he stopped, readjusting his hands and feet as they slipped.

"You don't need help, do you?" I walked below him. *That should motivate him enough to make it.*

"I," Malik huffed, falling down a few inches. "No. I can do this."

I got on, scaling the smooth walls quickly. I caught up as he neared the ledge, breathing heavily, slipping seconds after placing a hand. There was about three feet between Malik and the opening. I squeezed past him and ended up squatting on the small section that separated the walls.

Pausing, I glanced back, teetering back and forth with my weight to continue or not. *He did help you... Agh, fine.* Leaning over the ledge, I held out my hand, letting out a small smile. With a grunt, Malik jumped and grabbed it. I pulled him next to me, a scent of cool mint intermixing with sweat wafting my nose.

After making sure he wouldn't fall and ignoring this new sense of lightness blossoming in my chest, I sprang off, landing on my side and rolling to my feet. Our team was one and a half obstacles ahead.

"Thank you," Malik panted, landing at my side.

By the time we made it back, the other team was already waiting. My voice caught in my throat as I saw their expressions. *I wasn't fast enough. All my training and I still made my team lose.* Our teacher congratulated them, while our teammates ignored us. Besides Drystan, who strode to Malik, shoulders back.

"Ayo, why'd it take you so long? You and Aris were killin' it. If ya kept up, we woulda totally won!"

"I messed up," he replied, holding his hands up. "We had to deal with a rule-break, but we all still did a good job."

"Liars!" someone shouted from the other team.

Shanessa whistled, walking to Malik. "What's this I'm hearin' about cheating?"

Glancing at me, Malik raised an eyebrow. "At the spiderweb, I'm pretty sure one of the guys on their team used a power on Aris."

Across from me, Reed held a neutral expression, yet his brown eyes held a playful light. Telling on him wouldn't change anything with him. *It'll only change my team members from* hating us. Well, hating Malik. I'm fine with them hating me.

"Aris?"

I dipped my head to the boy.

He laughed, punching his teammate's arm, scrunching his plaid shirt. "Yeah, so what? You should've seen it!"

"Reed," Shanessa said sternly, folding her arms. "Your team loses on technicality, and now you've got yourself a week stripped from magic for it to be used against you. Usin' your powers, unless it's physical, ain't allow'd. Especially not against another student!"

"Relax, it was a joke!" His teammates glared at him. As he passed me, he smirked, strutting out of the arena, putting his hands behind his head. "Don't take it so personally."

Pinching the bridge between her nose, Shanessa closed her eyes. "I'm sorry, Aris. I will ensure he learns his lesson and keep a closer eye next time. You guys may go now."

The class scattered freely. My chest burned, Reed's smirk engraved in my mind like a permanent scar, daring to call him out again, heavier than the cubes I'd clawed out of earlier. My arm tingled where he had pressed his fingers. I tugged my hood over my head. *Tch. Let them think I'm weak. I know I should've kept up, but they won't think that when it matters.*

Ahead walked Malik with Drystan, heads bent together in easy banter. I flexed my fingers. *If Taavi's right, being I'm not ready, then this is where I prove her wrong. I won't be last again. I won't let them see me fall.*

Chapter 5

ARIS SHELIA

I ran with a conjured shadow sword in my hand, the moist still air licking my arms. (Usually, I wore one of my hoodies, but it needed to get washed.)

Water rhythmically dripped from above, echoing off the cave walls. The pitch-black room took some time for my eyes to adjust, never immediately switching like night vision goggles, but when they did, I could see as clearly as a cloudy day. Each fall of my footsteps made zero sound or echo. Cold air numbed my ears, biting my cheeks as I searched for its outline.

The dummy popped up in the middle this time, waiting. It moved after every attack, and could also swing back, but wasn't nearly as good as another partner.

Slashing it twice, I bounded up and off a wall, striking it again on the ceiling. The dummy waved its arm, missing my torso by a foot and then vanishing and reappearing on the floor.

My foot collided with its head as I came down and rolled, ending at the door. Turning the knob, I slipped out back into the hall, straight to the main cavern, and dissipated the sword in my hand.

Taavi waited at the desk, legs crossed. Her distant eyes regained their focus, drawing straight to me as she looked up.

After my first year, she taught me the next three levels of Shadow. Seeing in the dark came naturally — normal for level-one powers — so we started with stealth by setting up harsh lights that cast long shadows across the floor. Obstacles and walls threaded the cave, with all kinds of noisy materials thrown across the floor.

During the first few passes, weeks even, Taavi spotted me easily as I ducked, slid, or encased myself within the darkness. It wasn't until the seventh that I made it all the way, slipping under a makeshift rock bridge she used like a watch tower, climbing up, and touching her back. And not until the twelfth did I make it there and back without a sound. We planned a few riskier ones too, like me taking Taavi's teacup from her, or making it throughout my entire city unseen.

The next level prioritized my connection to the shadows. I worked on pulling that tether inside, aligning it with my thoughts. I used it to press the darkness, having it cloud and assist in pulling the light, dimming it by over half.

After, I moved to forming shadows into daggers or walls. Despite needing them to stay connected to its object of origin, I could sometimes create a dagger to switch hosts when flung. Most would destabilize mid-air and collapse into nothing. That took me a good two months before those numbers switched, advancing to moving dummies, which occasionally fought back.

The last two she mentioned were the hardest of them all, in addition to Shadow Puppets. With any shadow and proper training, a wielder of shadow magic can manipulate them to become real creatures, varying from animals to mythological to hybrids. Learning Undead, another upper-level power, and Shadow Puppets, or even planning to, was banned and punishable by death unless you had special permission.

The chance to master such a power made me almost giddy, but with the risk and limited time...

I waited for Taavi to speak. She tapped her chin with her legs crossed, scanning me up and down. The tips of her lips twitched. "You aren't half bad, dear," she said and smacked her lips, halfway smiling. "In fact, you could fight against third years! I worry..." Shutting her eyes, Taavi rested her chin on her hand. "The advanced levels of your powers aren't something you can learn from me. You're going to need assistance. Even then, I doubt you'll be—"

"I will!" I interrupted, standing straighter. Energy buzzed through my body. "I'll train as hard as I need to."

Light danced in her eyes. "Yes, there's a kindling ready to burst alight within you... Long ago, I once had high hopes for someone else, but he lacked conviction." Pausing, Taavi picked a blue piece of paper, its edges frayed, from the desk and handed it to me.

"What is this?"

"Another example for you. One inventor's lifetime

achievement that could've revolutionized energy creation."

I unfurled it, scanning the layout. "Why didn't they use it?"

"The City rejected it," Taavi said bitterly. "Said it wasn't worth the risk of destabilizing the economy and electrocuting the public. Now it sits here, gathering dust."

"You keep talking about progress through conflict, but what about the lives ruined along the way?"

Taavi didn't flinch, twisting her silver and red bracelet. "Every revolution has its costs. The question is whether the price is worth the outcome. From my experience, it is." She stood and walked towards the exit. "Oh, before I forget, there's someone else you'll meet soon."

"Who?"

"He's going to help you."

"With what? I don't need-"

Taavi whipped her head around, placing her finger on her mouth. The bracelet on her arm bounced. "Listen here. We will plan and work with him. In order to create a better world, I need you to have more power and allies."

"Taavi." I folded my arms. "Who is it?"

She paused and sighed. "Cyril Shepherd. Our world has been preparing for years in case of rising villains and it wasn't the time yet to tell you."

"Do I have to work with him? What powers does he have?"

Tensing, Taavi relaxed again. "No, it's your choice. One I highly recommend as it means life or death. I'll tell you more about him later, before he comes."

I nodded.

"It's good that you're not afraid to question things." Taavi waved her hand, climbing up the stairs and out into the world.

I turned towards the desk. A brown plastic book rested in the center of it. *Advanced Shadow Techniques: Version 1.* Tracing the corner of the cover, I opened the old books to the first page.

2025- Mastering Undead (Second half- Shadow Puppets)

Undead* **Note: *Harder and larger creatures will require power fusion, typically Water power, but a third may be needed. These animals are covered in Advanced Shadow Techniques: Version 2 and 3.*

Shadow does not restore life. It acts as a temporary conduit for the husk left behind. The higher in Power level or complexity of the creature you're controlling, the less precision you will be given of its form. If needed, those with Power Manipulation have been able to enhance our control over these puppets significantly.

Level 1, lesson 1: *Prepare a dead fly. Lay it on a flat surface, close to where you may touch. (Distance control will be taught in lesson 6)*

I skimmed over, flipping a few pages.

Level 5, lesson 1: *Prepare a dead rat.*

Level 9, lesson 1: *Prepare a dead small-medium sized animal. Examples include: a dog or a cat.*

**Ensure to cover the undead ethics located at the end of each volume.*

This is going to take forever.

****

More power and allies. How do I do either of those at a hero college? My nails tapped my lips. The whiteboard marker squeaked and squealed, replicating the earsplitting screech of a chalkboard as my teacher wrote.

"I'll be recapping and diving into depth some of the things you've learned in past years." Mr. Atherly paced in front of the classroom, tapping his marker against his hand. "Over a century ago, Shelby Feyth was one of the first heroes to figure out how to sustain capture of villains, rather than simply locking them up, creating the stepping stones for our current society." He uncapped the marker and wrote the name on the whiteboard.

Next to me, the student straightened at the mention of Shelby's name, puffing out his chest and indirectly tightening his white shirt. His hair was a lot nicer today, combed into a swoop.

Erasing a sentence on my paper, I wrote the name down. "Our country wasn't very accustomed to the idea of heroes and people openly having powers. But Feyth's friend, Sean Weaver," he said, writing down the second name as well, "was a very charismatic and intelligent individual. He persuaded much of the community to agree to the idea, as long as the government placed rules to keep everyone safe. And those with powers had to—"

A siren blared. Flashing red lights circled the room. People stood up in a frenzy, pencils and papers flying on the ground. And a chair. "Students! Stay calm and form a single file line." The teacher rushed to the door, waving his hands. People shoved each other, forcing their way to him. I threw on my backpack and waited in my corner.

"What's going on?"

"Is this a drill?"

"Fire?"

"Did someone break in?!"

The sound of glass crashing came from the next room. A blasting, leaking noise followed it, like air escaping an Instant Pot. Our teacher swore, pointing to the guy who sat next to me. "Leor! You're in charge! Get everyone out of here while I deal with this! And if anyone asks, tell them this is a drill."

Raising his hand, Leor made his way in front of the mob. Signaling another student, a woman with short hair and a tattoo of a cat on her back, he told her to bring up the rear, then walked out. I ended up with the student singled out. People crowded the hallway to the stairs, pushing past each other and me away from my class.

What's happening?

Our teacher entered the classroom next to ours. I broke off from the crowd and slipped to the side of the door. The hallway emptied as the last people left in a hurry.

Kneeling, I strained to hear past the high-pitched

sirens.

"Our gas pipe exploded," a woman's voice informed. "No serious injuries. I managed to contain it for now."

"How bad is it?" My teacher asked.

"Enough to make the siren go off. I had to shield the students from its blast."

A grave silence replaced their voices.

"How did it happen?"

"I have no idea. It doesn't look sabotaged, but we can't eliminate that possibility."

"Someone's trying to disrupt the peace," my teacher muttered.

Gas explosion? Why would someone have done that? Rising to my feet, I headed back to the stairs. Movement caught my eye as I reached the stairs. To my right, in a dark classroom, crouched a figure.

"Aris," an unfamiliar voice beckoned. "This won't keep them occupied for long, come on." Footsteps echoed through the halls. *Firemen and Heroes are here, great.*

I entered the room, closing the door softly behind me. It was very dark, except for a few small blinking lights where the teacher's desk would've sat. I sensed the figure on the other side of the room. "Cyril? Did Taavi send you?"

"No. Look, it doesn't matter who I am." This person was a woman. I saw her jawline and clothes as my night vision began to set in. There were two papers in her hand. "I had to give this to you." Placing it on the desk, the woman pulled back her neck-length red hair. "Take it to your mentor." She stepped back and vanished.

People passed the door in loud conversation. I could see the room fully now. I took the papers and flipped through them. One was an image, with lines of detailed information about magic objects on the back. The other had lots of writing with dates and times. *How and what does this woman know about me? Is she a friend of Taavi's?* Folding them carefully, I slid them into my sweats, forcing the endless questions out of my mind.

Outside was an unusual mess of people and noise. Students milled about with faculty attempting to rein them in. In the parking lot, two fire trucks and multiple police cars crowded. Arriving heroes landed next to them.

I stuck close to the school wall, following it in the other direction to the pine tree.

I dropped my backpack. It sent a cloud of dirt wrapping around my feet, fading as I took out the papers. Leaning against the tree, I held them to the light. In the picture, many items, such as jewelry and staves, rested neatly in a wood-paneled room. There lay a silver crown amidst the items, circled with a red marker, on the floor, closer and bigger than the others. In the center of the crown displayed a shiny white-bluish rock. But the other four of the five jewel spots were vacant. On the back, a list of the items was laid out, along with descriptions of what they do.

"I thought I'd find you here," a familiar voice called.

Crumpling the paper, I jabbed it in my pocket. Malik

strode up to me, hands swinging at his sides, with Drystan and a woman named Arlene close behind. Her dark brown eyes were alive, set against the warm tone of her Filipino skin.

Great. Please say they didn't see the paper or that I left the school late?

"Sorry, I know you like to be alone. But I got kind of worried." Malik scratched his head. "The rumor going around was that an explosion happened in the class next to yours. I'm glad you're okay."

I nodded, relaxing my shoulders. I reclaimed my backpack and pulled my hood back over my head, not offering a response.

Arlene ended at his side, holding her hand out. "Nice to meet you again, Aris. I'm Arlene. We had class back in high school together."

Slowly, I shook her hand and forced a small smile.

"What happened with the explosion? Do you know?"

I shook my head.

Drystan patted Malik's shoulder. "Hey, my boy here talks about you all the time. You're light on your feet," he trailed off, focusing on my hair and face, and narrowed his eyes. "Wait a sec, what's your last name?"

Pulling my hood farther out, I turned my back against them. "Sorry, I should get going."

"No, wait." Malik's hand brushed my wrist. "Can we walk with you?"

I tilted my head so they stayed in my view. *Uhm, I...*

Drystan widened his eyes. He held up his hands. "I was only curious, ya know? You kinda look like someone we fostered not too long ago."

"Fostered?" I repeated, limbs growing stiff.

Two years. I tried finding him. I searched, and nothing turned up. I vividly remember his scared eyes. His small hands clinging onto me. Two years since Mom's been arrested. She asked me to look after him, not to do anything rash, but I had no idea where she went either. Not at the typical villain jail, that much was certain. And neither of their names pulled up online.

They were taken by what these people, our society, call a perfect, righteous country.

Two years. He would be eight now.

"Was his name Micha Shelia?" I asked, facing him.

"Uhhh." Drystan rubbed his brow. "Uh, yeah, think so. You look awfully lot like him."

"How is he? Where is he now?"

He shrugged, running his hand through his hair. "I don't know. They only had us keep him for a little while. We've had dozens of placements since, so I can't exactly keep names straight."

"Who? Where was he taken?"

Shifting his weight, Drystan said, "They didn't exactly say who they were. Only did their job, and that's all."

Please tell me if it was anyone, it was not another villain or... or...

"That's not all," I pressed. "Did he look okay? Did he ask about me?"

"I can't say. I don't remember," Drystan muttered, eyes falling.

Air was sucked out of me as if I had been pummeled in the stomach and chest. The scenery around me got blurry and red with black edges. Malik opened his mouth to respond when I stumbled, managing to shift it into a jog to the parking lot.

I have to get out of here.

Someone yelled after me. Tears brimmed my eyes, threatening to break free. I blinked them back, clenching my teeth.

I kept going, passed the crowd, and kept running until I reached the cave.

****

I dropped to my hands, gulped, then coughed. The cold, bumpy cave floor gave me something to anchor myself. I refused to let the tears go. Slowly, I regained control of my breath and sat up, running my fingers through my hair. The mirror caught the light, aimed at me off to the side. I glanced at it without thinking, seeing my reflection. I punched the ground. Pain greeted my fist.

White and black hair reflected in the mirror... My own hair, everything reminded me of my little brother. I tried to shove it aside. To shove any thought of Micha, my mom, or my family aside.

I hate this. How weak I am.

I couldn't even protect my own family.

"I'm sorry, Micha," I whispered, clenching my fists. "I failed you. But I will make up for it."

Our society had to change. I had to make sure my family was protected. If anyone would do it, it had to be me.

I would control the chaos and make sure no one got seriously injured or killed. I will set this right on my terms and eradicate any future villain the chance of taking that from me, too. I will be successful.

From now on, nothing will hold me back. I will change the world for the better. I will control the chaos in order to protect those I love. Even if I can't get them back yet.

Starting with the crown.

****

The setting sun flashed in and out through the bare branches as I weaved around a stump, nearly missing a gaping hole next to the sprawling tree roots. Humid air clung to my skin. Insects swarmed the ground; some managed to jump up and bite my legs.

Taavi convinced me to wear capris, and I regret it. She tried to get me to leave my hoodie, too, but I refused. The tag underneath still had my mom's and Steph's initials. I did relent and put on a balaclava.

Days later, but not much farther now.

When I handed Taavi the papers, she thanked me yet warned me harshly. *"Don't trust strangers, Aris." Taavi shook her head, her lips pointed down, and looked closer at the papers. It was* the papers the red-haired woman gave to me that same day.

"That's why I gave it to you," I lied. "Is any of it useful?"

"There are many powerful items shown here. This crown, a relic created during a time of conflict by Shelby Feyth, could give you the powers you need for change. That is, if you can collect its counterparts. And it may help your family," Taavi said, holding up the paper. "But I would be cautious about information as deceivingly accurate as this."

I nodded and tilted my head. "What if it's correct?"

She smiled. "Then you must be careful of traps. The jewels for the crown will be spread out and hidden, most heavily guarded. Shelby's Crown will be shielded by the top heroes and at least one of the presidents of the six hero schools. Its location is only known to them and, seemingly, this piece of paper."

Following that, Taavi planned with me after my training. In the cave, another one of the semicircles, when transformed into a portal, led to an offshoot. Inside was a bedroom-sized cave, with a huge dusty table in the center, filled with precise details of our city and continent. We'd start small and simple, then increase the difficulty of our attacks and heists accordingly. The paper told most of the artifacts' locations, many of which I'm certain you can get off the internet, due to them residing together in school archives.

It wouldn't be long before Cyril joined. Taavi explained that people would underestimate him, which made him a more powerful ally. His powers played off mental abilities, using memory absorption, replication, and puzzle creation. The idea didn't stick well with me.

"*Wouldn't he try to betray us and take anything for himself?*"

"No, dear." Taavi sat in her air chair, frowning. "Cyril isn't interested in betraying us. He's been a dear student of mine for a while, and is as loyal as a dog. It would be smart to put your faith in him."

"*Even so, wouldn't he be considered a danger? To citizens, at least?*"

"Yes, he can be very dangerous or useful. However, to remain on good terms with the public eye and Mala institution, the government has to be careful with how they treat him, like anyone else. And mental heroes do have rules to follow."

Always rules. They kept people like him contained, and people like me watched.

Within the past week, I haven't seen Malik much. Only during our two classes together, where we didn't speak often. I would catch him staring at me from time to time, but nothing else. *The less the better.* I told myself, over and over. *Befriending anyone will get in the way. There's no saying what he'd do if I told him. Or anyone, for that matter.*

Swatting a fly, I accidentally crunched some leaves. *Wait, I wonder if Malik was assigned to watch me? Would he do that? That might be why he's so persistent.*

So he's watched you the past decade? Why you?

No. Only recently, like the past year, I'd guess.

You have no proof of that. He may just be oblivious and friendly.

Okay, okay. Yeah, that might be it. Until I do know, I will give him nothing worth reporting. And if he isn't, the caution costs me nothing. It's like the saying, 'keep your friends close and enemies closer,' right?

I passed a bush and broke out of the foliage. A beautiful array of colors cast across the skies as the sun sank. In the dead middle of a clearing, the hill led straight to concrete walls, which extended beneath the ground and not much above, like a retaining wall.

Within the confines, piles of stone, coal, and dirt filled all but the middle, where two security guards leaned against poles in battered, dirty clothes, half asleep. Between them, on a table, sat a black metal box. At their feet rested wrappers and other various containers, from cardboard to plastic to metal, along with tools like shovels and picks. If I didn't know better, I'd think this place was only a mine of sorts.

Stationed around the guards were parked trucks, their seats empty from what I could make out. I dropped to a crouch, creeping to the edge. *The location on the paper happened to be correct.* Inside my pocket weighed a look-alike jewel, two knives, two tranquilizers, and a lock pick. My right hand had a glove on. Due to its inconspicuous and remote location, this was the easiest and least guarded target.

In and out. Where are the cameras?

I scanned the layout. One mounted behind a wall, hidden yet easily avoidable in the dark. The three others were on display, one pointing at the box. Both portrayed like cheap bank cameras from their cases to trick a regular thief. In the center was a highly digitalized lens instead.

One of the guards stretched and yawned, and the other stood fully and waved to the other, heading below the hidden camera, where a door was, and slipped inside. The remaining guard folded his hairy arms, closing his eyes as the lights on his post switched on.

The piles were in a four-by-four. The closest, surrounding the guards, were stacks of stone slabs mixed with loose rocks, the next layer away was coal, and the furthest was dirt, all contained in thirty-by-thirty-foot boxes.

I toed the edge of the wall, leaping to a dirt pile, and then to the floor. Sticking to the shadows, I jogged to the center, avoiding any scant of light.

Behind the middle box, I found the parked truck closest to the guards, about a hundred feet behind him, and made my way over. The second guard exited the building again, with a vape in his hand, casually striding back to his friend.

I ran my right hand over the smooth glass of the tranquilizers resting in my pocket. When the second guard reached his post, I sprinted, keeping low to the ground. Both guards wore shorts, loose t-shirts, and had slouched postures. *Do they not know what they're guarding?* I first went to the recently returned guard, impaling the dart into his leg. Before either of them realized what had happened, I stabbed the second guard, and they both slouched then rolled to the floor, unconscious.

Reclaiming the tranquilizers, I swapped them for the

lockpick in my bag. *Those cameras should record over today within the next twenty-four hours.* I tried to pick open the box, the pick bending in my hand. *Snap.*

Dammit. I tossed it into the bag, taking out another. Using the tip, I carefully move it into the lock. The shadows called to me, offering their help. I took hold of that calling, using them and the needle to pick the lock open. Inside lay the gem, reflecting a clear blue and violet color. Tanzanite. I switched it with the fake one in my gloved hand, bracing myself for a trigger to set-off. One second, then ten went by. Gently, I closed and relocked the box.

Leaves crunched, echoing in the distance. I tensed, glancing around. *Did I miss something? Is someone there?* The guards didn't move as the rustling grew closer, sounding more like dirt shifting. I pulled out a dagger. A cat emerged from behind a pile, trotting toward me with a sweeping gray tail held high. I dropped my hand, letting my shoulders relax. *Thank goodness.* It padded up to the tip of the bent metal point and sent it rolling to the side. *The tip of the lockpick I broke.* Picking it up, I stuffed it into my pocket and double-checked I didn't leave any other marks or show my face to the camera. I retraced my exact route and easily scaled the wall.

One down, four to go.

I'm coming for you Mom. Micha.

****

I entered Taavi's house, putting away the items in my pockets before entering the cozy living room. Taavi floated in front of her plastic-covered couch, her legs crossed and her eyes closed. I placed the vibrant Tanzanite in her open hand.

"Good job," she acknowledged, rolling the Tanzanite in her hand as the TV rambled in the background. "All is falling into place. I expect you handled things well."

"When the guards wake up later today to be relieved, they'll see the gem is still there. By the time they report dropping unconscious and review the footage, it'll be recorded over."

She lowered her legs and stood, closing her hand over the gem. "It's progress."

I yawned, stretching my arms. The TV flashed the time and went back to its show. *An hour until school starts?* "I think I'm going to skip school."

"No." Taavi brushed past me, exiting the room. "You must keep up with your class. Don't give anyone a single reason to doubt or suspect you, and that includes not messing up your routine."

Sighing, I picked up my backpack then headed to my room to change. After getting ready, I stumbled outside and made my way to school, rubbing my eyes from the harsh sunlight pouring across the city.

The gas pipe that exploded ended up being an easy fix. People still buzzed about it, and conspiracies grew about what had happened. Teachers would shut down as many as possible, yet they kept coming, from possible villain attacks to a student losing control.

I slept through my first class, though the bell woke me up. Leor sat next to me again, despite plenty of other seats being available. It was like he didn't care. He exited the room as I packed up. In my second class, I couldn't sleep due to it being

PE. Malik and Drystan noticed my sluggish movements but, thankfully, didn't ask or prod. That surprised me. Reed wasn't there, either, much to my relief. Then, the third class before lunch was fully in the dark as we practiced.

By the time lunch came around, I had regained a little of my energy and collapsed in the shade of the tree, my eyes drifting close until a twig snapped a few feet away. I rubbed my eyes. "Malik, leave me alone."

Another voice laughed. I opened my eyes to see Reed before me, staring with disdain, tapping his fingers against the cuff of his jeans that tucked inside his muddy cowboy boots.

"You're having a good day," he noted smugly, tilting his head as if curious.

"What do you want?"

He rolled his stained knuckles against his jeans again, crossing a symbol I've seen on council enforcers at parades. A smile protruded from his mouth. "Oh, just wondering how it feels to be overlooked. Like an old car left in a barn, or an undusted trophy. But, at least you've got that tree." He gave a lazy chuckle, crossing his arms in a shrug, and rocked back on his heels. "People at least know I exist."

I pushed myself off the peeling bark on the trunk. "Cool. Is that all?"

Reed's green eyes caught the light, turning red-orange. "Not exactly. See, after that *incident* at the obstacle course last month, they tightened recruitment, and you're kind of... wasting space at Ezrat, don't you think?" He tugged a brown curl from his temple. "How about chu go to another school? Perhaps Higgins would take you in? Or if you stay, you'd make a great background sidekick."

"You're one to talk." I lowered my hood. "If you spent less time fooling around, you wouldn't be 'average' with villain qualities. Heroes might even want you on their team."

Reed's grin tilted before he covered it by wiping his lips with his wrist. "Villain? Me? Funny." He tapped the side of his forehead. "I think you're bitter that people like me don't think the world is falling apart the way you do."

"Quit acting like you know me." I stiffly picked up my backpack. A quiet growl rose in the back of my throat and I faced him. "And maybe you should. You don't see how broken it is."

"You don't know what you're talking about. Our system's with the patrols and apprenticeships kept us safe for a hundred and fifty years. They pulled us from ruin. You think you're smarter than the people who built it? The ones who made sure we wouldn't end up like them?"

I bit my tongue, tasting the copper tang of blood. *Why can't you see it?* "We're not moving forward anymore. There's solar paneled fountains that would kill whoever falls in. Buildings, signs, and roads are repaired to baseline but never improved. Even our school barely adjusts its curriculum, bouncing back any ideas. It's like we're caught in a museum cage and you're too busy playing zoo keeper to see it."

"Playing?" His voice dropped. "You think it's a game? Keeping people safe... It's rather hard. But it's better than whatever it is you think the world needs. You should be grateful you're not the one who watched everything burn."

I stepped closer, my nails digging into my palms.

Shadows curled around the tree roots, whispering promise and threat, or merely to snap the bark under his heel. "For who? The people who don't care about progress? What about the children?"

He stared at me for a beat too long. Then, with an exaggerated bow, he backed away toward the path where a cluster of students began to watch, the smirk returning to his face. "Alright, good luck, Aris. Someone like you? You'll need it." He spun and walked off, his dismissive wave hanging in the air like a challenge.

Heat burned beneath my skin, like liquid spice in my veins, or like someone took a liquid fire and replaced it with my blood. I took a measured breath. Shadows stirred at my feet, curling unnaturally around the roots of the tree. They welcomed me, coaxing me to act or trip him.

No. I slung my backpack over my shoulder, forcing myself to ignore my power calling to me. It wasn't worth it. I won't hurt someone no matter how much they deserve it. The day would come when he'd see what I was capable of. I would make life *interesting*. And they'd all regret thinking I was nothing.

****

The last three classes breezed by. I left the classroom as the last bell rang, and this time, no one kept hot on my heels. I expected I would feel grateful that people finally left me alone, but instead, there's nothing. A vacant space. Weaving through people, I stepped outside the school where students boarded buses, and cars drifted by. They floated or flew around, most in deep conversation. Some descended from the high floating towers in the clouds, like an angel from heaven without the wings.

I put in music and began to walk to Taavi's house, focused on the ground, tracing each crack and crevice. A few minutes in, I lifted my head, seeing a group of kids playing at a passing playground. They varied in age, from five to thirteen, all giggling and playing. One kid held a toy truck that ran over another kid's plastic dinosaur, screaming for its death, followed by the dinosaur's miraculous resurrection.

Micha would probably be nagging at me to play with them, which I would reluctantly agree to. He always loved people and dinosaurs. A smile edged my mouth, falling as a heaviness grew in my chest. *He shouldn't have to grow up without me. Without mom.* I recalled the last time we played together. I clutched my backpack tighter as if I could somehow shield past him.

The kids here were at peace, unaware of how amazing they had it. Like Micha, they were so innocent and curious... yet so oblivious of the boring, unjust world they'd grow into and the bland jobs they'd slave away in.

I pressed forward, staring back at my feet. *I'll get you back, Micha. And Mom. You will have a life worth living, where original ideas, like yours, will be encouraged and integrated instead of snuffed out.* My steps grew heavier as I reached Taavi's house. *People will listen.*

Inside, I set down my backpack and found Taavi back in the living room. She stood upon seeing me, waving to follow her. We headed to the kitchen, where papers were scattered across the table. Gesturing to it, Taavi waited. I scanned the diagrams and layouts of an old city hall.

"Your next mission." She picked up another paper, along with a flash drive in the back, and handed them to me. "Sneak in and out with any files you can manage. Make a mess."

"Any files? Don't you want future plans or secrets they have?" I asked. The piece of paper had a list of passwords on it, along with directions to the file room.

"Not yet," Taavi said. "I'll still have use for whatever files you manage. For now, start small. Your only focus is to create panic. Then, we'll build from there."

Chapter 6

SETH VRY

Two vials in hand, he measured them carefully and slowly dumped them into another glass of liquid. Seth stirred the mixture mindlessly with a metal stick, taking a bag from the counter and sprinkled its contents in. Mixing again, the grains vanished, and he methodically added water and waited. It switched between blue, clear, and yellow about ten times before settling.

The colors were beautiful, as always. Nothing unexpected, nothing new. Seth gave a tired smile and sighed, carefully taking the metal prongs and draining the vial down the sink, where the liquid drained into special containers to be disposed of later.

Setting his supplies down exactly where he'd found them, Seth glanced at his notes with precise, methodical handwriting. Each day's log was indistinguishable from the last. A repetition of each week, ensuring past discoveries weren't lies, he supposed.

Newton's Laws, for one, had been easy to prove. Others, not so much.

Outside of this, Seth had ideas. Ideas he never wrote down, like compact spheres to redistribute force and pressure. Or theories and other experiments that could yield real progress, that his brother could see. Ones that might disrupt the harmony society so closely cherished, that could be used by anyone to disrupt peace or save it. That would give him recognition that intellect could be as great as power.

Someday, he could use his ideas. For now, it wasn't worth it.

His brother, Ezra, might be out practicing hero magic and doing more fun things. And that's okay. While Seth didn't have his own powers, these projects retained his attention enough. His society would only be ready if it ever needed to be ready. The thought surprisingly flickered a hint of irritation, of restlessness inside him.

The elevator dinged, its chime breaking the quiet hum of the lab. Seth glanced up as the doors opened. *Speak of the devil.* Ezra and his friend, Xiomara, waltzed in, revealing a third person, a woman in her late thirties, trailing behind them in a crisp lab coat. One he'd seen stereotypical 'evil' scientists wear.

"Whatchya been up to, man!" Ezra exclaimed, a grin spread wide on his face, and he clapped Seth on the back.

He closed his logbook, putting the last tools away with a shrug. "Same old, same old."

"I've heard a lot, a lot about you," the third person, a woman, said lightly, extending her hand. On it gleamed connected bronze rings. "I'm Maren."

Seth shook her hand briefly. "I apologize, but I can't say the same."

She giggled, covering her mouth. "That's fair, I didn't expect you to." Taking a not-so-sly glance at his brother, she lifted her head. "I did, however, come to offer you to join our group. Xiomara and your brother Ezra told me about your work. They said you're a genius at what you do."

Seth took his logbook and moved to the elevator. "Depends. I typically do what they tell me. It's repetitive, but other than today, I make old medicines that treat illnesses well enough."

"Well enough?" Maren echoed, on his trail like a creeping panther. "Don't you think those tasks are a little boring?" Seth raised an eyebrow as she bounced on her toes. "Don't you want a chance to do something new?"

"I mean, yeah," he began, scratching his head, "but when the world's ready for it. Right now, the treatments work. Why fix what's not broken? There's no need to stir the pot unless it's necessary."

Stepping forward, Xiomara placed a hand on Seth's shoulder. "Seth, I can understand where you're coming from. But I also know it's not all you want." She paused, seeming to weigh her options before continuing, "What if I told you that Maren is head of an underground operation? One that can experiment without restrictions and use ideas, like air-powered flying cars, to the fullest."

"I do have ideas that I..." Seth shook his head, the words stirring something inside him. No, *that's a death wish.* He continued half-heartedly, "But I can't risk my life and be thrown into prison to never be seen again. If something needs changing, we should do it the right way through government approval."

Xiomara tilted her head, dropping her hand.

Maren stuck out hers, clicking the elevator button. "You know as well as we do that all ideas are rejected for fear of throwing away peace. At least let me show you what it's like, and you can decide there."

"You have one chance," Seth agreed, glancing at his brother, who leaned casually against the elevator wall, then Xiomara. "Are you guys in on this?"

"Not exactly; we know about it," Ezra answered as the doors opened. They all stepped inside. "But despite being *awesome* heroes, Xiomara and I aren't scientists. We don't get the invite yet; too risky."

"If this group gets caught, Ezra and I will bust you out," Xiomara added, inspecting her fingernails closely.

Seth did a double-take watching Xiomara. *Woah. She only looks at her fingers like that when she has another motive.* He narrowed his eyes, focusing on where she flicked them. *I wonder if it has anything to do with rumors about the first jewel going missing. If that's the case, Xiomara would logically think there is a new villain out there. Then she'd have to figure it out, and being part of this operation must be helpful in some way. That sounds correct.*

Maren sighed. She pulled out her phone from her pocket and pressed the button to a lower floor. The doors closed, and the lift began descending past the Mala Science Center floors Seth knew. "It's to protect ourselves. Less obvious, unlike a separate building would be."

Staring at the glowing numbers on the panel, Seth's mind raced. "If this is real, why hasn't anyone heard about it?"

Smirking, Maren replaced her phone in her pocket. "Maybe they have. Maybe that's why nothing truly revolutionary gets past the government. They can't silence what they can't find."

Ezra nudged him playfully. "Relax, big bro. You'll love it, trust me."

The elevator slowed, a soft ding signaling their arrival. As the doors slid open, Seth hesitated, his heart pounding as only he and Maren stepped off into a hallway.

At the end stood an armored door with a retinal scanner. Maren uncapped the scanner and waited as it scanned her, dinging. The doors opened slowly, revealing seven more people inside a decently sized room.

Two people stood at the entrance, as if either on watch or about to enter themselves. One held an onyx sword and amethyst cuffs, nodding upon seeing Maren. The other, with a hand on the wall, tiny lightning bolts fleeing from her arms like fleas, simply shifted closer to it.

Beyond them, two scientists picked over an armor stand, adjusting small shoulder pads and soldering thin metal over it. Most of the stand was covered in a light-absorbing black fabric, beginning to take the shape of a suit. The last three spread around the room, each working on what Seth thought to be separate projects. One worked with boots, switching between them and a computer, another with the same fabric and graphene-infused fibers, and the last fiddled over thin tubes, a type of cooling system, with a hydrophobic coating.

Seth's head spun from all the items sporadically thrown around the room with no apparent order. Here, they were free to do whatever they wanted. Supposedly. And that meant being messy.

For some reason, it made him want to smile.

"We're technically a startup. They're working on a suit we got a special order for." Maren passed the two scientists working on the stand. "It's been pretty slow."

How's this suit going to be different from others? A floral scent hit Seth's nose, and he spotted rose petals next to one of the scientists and the second computer. Out of the various items, they only had two laptops together. "I'm assuming you have limited access?"

"To supplies and technology?" Maren turned and raised an eyebrow. "Yes and no. We keep a low profile on purpose."

"What if you guys get caught?"

"We won't."

"What makes you so sure?"

"We're scientists. Two of us have electrical powers."

"But if you get caught, won't we be all put in jail, names smeared as villains, and disciplined?"

"Yeah," she said, picking up and inspecting a cylinder. "Don't you like the idea of not constantly being watched?"

Seth turned toward the armor stand. A pressure inside his chest loosened. "Okay, even with all that risk. Why are you building a suit instead of something else?"

"Money. And, it's a good test to see what our capabilities are, like in assisting heroes or other missions."

Seth nodded, refraining from staring at or touching the progress they've made with the material, though his fingers twitched. *Are they using restitching fabric? We could combine that with a conductive lattice to act like a Faraday shell, so that way the metal threads keep the electricity off the wearer.*

"I believe you can help." Maren pointedly looked at his hand. "The client needs this to be perfect. After all, it may change everything for us. And you know chemical compounds and their relationship to evolving powers better than anyone. Or would you rather keep pouring endless experiments down the drain?"

"Hmm," Seth relented and bent forward, touching the suit. "Alright, I'll bite. Show me what you have."

Chapter 7

~Looks like there's no going back... is there?~

ARIS SHELIA

Lights pierced out from City Hall's windows, cameras posted above them and along the outside. Night had taken over quickly, with few lights flickering in the near-vacant street, illuminating the handful of people who wandered, lost in thought. A single police officer surveyed the street, eating a messy taco.

I waited above on a nearby rooftop, which leveled City Hall, hidden from the edge in all-black clothing, including gloves, a bronze ring, and a mask. The woolly mask, designed exactly like a hero's, covered half of my face, to the point that others couldn't discern a single feature. I took out my nose ring and earrings too, leaving them inside my bedroom earlier that day.

A small pack swung at my side as I shifted, daggers strapped beside it.

Six people exited the building, wood decorating its walls, the last one struggling with keys, then locking the stylized door. When they entered their separate vehicles and drove off, I cloaked the shadows around me and took off, leaping toward its roof.

Unlike the obstacle course, the gap was closer than the one between the closing doors. Wind snapped at me like lassos, and I hooked the edge of the concrete, finding my footing as my shoes scraped the wall and quickly cleared the lip. Smoke wafted by my nose from the chimney nearby. The shadows stirred, straining. Not much light reached up here, but enough that the shadows could survive.

A smooth metal door stood next to a vent, encased by more concrete. I approached it, extending my arm. Like a part of me, the shadows obeyed, slipping through the lock. *Click.*

Opening the door a crack, a stream of light poured out, I connected to the shadows within, pulling them up and covering the camera lens. My breath sounded louder than my footsteps.

I entered, descending the stairs two at a time. Before emerging on the top floor, I pulled out the blueprints and pointed my finger at the black outline of the floor. *I'll be able to descend the stairs to the sixth floor without much trouble. Then I'll have to make my way to the other side, past two doors, and into the file room. Which, annoyingly, is next to the security room.*

Refolding them, I replaced them beside my daggers and reached for the shadows again, sweat breaking across my forehead and down my neck. They eagerly found the next cameras as shown on the blueprints, covering them briefly as I passed, descending two more staircases, and breaking out onto the sixth floor.

The carpeted hallway split three different ways, with a majority of the doors closed and assumedly locked. Distant voices carried across the floor, barely decipherable with their hushed tones.

"Ich habe keine Ahnung, warum sie immer noch Sicherheitskräfte haben." *I have no idea why they still have security,* a man's voice said in German.

I blinked, dropping to a crouch.

"Arrêtez de vous plaindre, vous le dites à chaque fois. Au moins, nous sommes toujours payés." *Quit complaining, you say that every time. At least we're still being paid.* The other voice, a woman, responded in French.

The hell? I thought. *Why are they speaking to each other in different languages? Do they think it makes it more coded or something?*

"It still smells like rust down here," the man continued in his tongue. *"20 years down, and we get the same pipe leak every year. They should treat us better. I hope my baby doesn't have to put up with this. It was only his second birthday yesterday."*

The woman agreed, *"Honestly, they do nothing. You hear the Board denied all fourteen technology renewal requests this quarter? My boyfriend was one of them."*

A breathless laugh, full of disbelief, responded, *"Really?"*

Their banter pursued as I crept closer, acutely aware of

each time my joints popped or the floor squeaked sullenly. Their shadows played on the ground in the security room. *Fifty steps*, I noted, and slipped inside the room next to theirs. Another bead of sweat ran down my neck, which I wiped away. *One slip could end everything right here.*

Total darkness, aside from the door, enveloped me. A desktop, its screen dark, rested on a table in the center. File cabinets lined all four walls, end to end, ceiling to floor.

If you're caught, you did all of this for nothing, a part of me reminded. I grabbed the flash drive, moved to the computer, and inserted it. *You'll never help society advance. Taavi would kick you out and you'll never find Micha or Mom.*

I clenched my teeth, switching the computer on. A sticky note stuck to the screen's bottom corner with the same username and password Taavi provided me, followed by a note reading: *In case you forget again, Gerald. Remember to remove this note and keep it on you.*

With a few clicks, I'm in. I highlighted and dragged all the files that looked important-ish over to the flash drive and copied it. The computer screen loaded, saying it would be done in fifteen minutes. *Of course. Freaking slowest and dustiest computer in a government building. Why not?*

A faint hum of machinery or pipes vibrated underfoot. The file cabinets, neatly organized from A to Z despite papers scattered across them, especially those cramped beneath boxes stacked on top. The plan gave me some idea of what they held, like lists of current residences and businesses, finances, public safety reports, and citizen service requests. Across the P section, I read previous and future plans for our city. I picked up a piece of paper.

DEP. OF URBAN CONTINUITY – 10-YR PROJECTION

Public Safety: 1.2% ↑ incidents vs. prev decade | **Hero Deployments**: 38% routine – 62% administrative disputes

Technology Renewal Requests: 14 filed / 14 deferred | **Reason for Deferral**: "Existing models meet stability threshold." | **Next Upgrade Cycle**: 12 yrs (pending)

Citizen Satisfaction Poll: 89% "content" | 71% "no need for change" | 11% "unsatisfied"

Wow, they don't have much of anything. Reaching toward the shelf, I commanded the shadows to unlock all the cabinets. They flickered, eventually relenting, crawling to paperclips, taking them and bending, then stretching its thin metal over the locks to assist pins into place. *Thank goodness these locks are simple.* A cold wave rushed through my head, causing items to dance, before I opened the shelf and rifled through the many names. Leaving it ajar, I moved to the next and down the line. Under "S", I found Malik's family name, Styri.

Hesitantly, I peeked in it, pulled out a packet of papers stapled together and read the first page.

GOV / PEACE & INNOVATION BOARD

<u>FAMILY STABILITY PROFILE — CLASSIFIED / ISA</u>

Subject: *Styri family, 884-ST-12-U.* **Tier:** *Upper-middle class, six total people. Three adults and three children, same residence.*

Risk-Factor? *Three speeding and one minor traffic violation. Deferred.* **Powers?** *FIRE-D 3M, EARTH-A 1M, 3 AIR-B 2-5M, check next page.* **Heroes?** *Two.*

Felonies? None. **Compliance Index:** 92.4/100. **On watch?** No. **Notes:** *sibling reports above-norm curiosity and inclination towards the arts; no record of deviance or dissent.*

Hero-Program Eligibility: *YES / family flagged for empathy bias. High-average grades.*

More continued down the page, but I closed it and opened the drawer above it, finding my last name with a red dot on it, and skimmed over the watermarks.

FAMILY STABILITY PROFILE — CLASSIFIED / ISA

Subject: *Shelia family, 781-ML-29-U.* **Tier:** *Lower-middle class, five total people-- four adults, one child. Three live in-city. Two located in the country Alcen Nepif. Child in foster care. Recent adult lives with Taavi Higgins. Mother sent to work, unfit to raise children. See next page. Person of interest.*

My hands shook. I pulled it back out more to reveal the words further along the page.

Risk Factor? *Six speeding and seven minor traffic violations.* **Powers?** *2 SHADOW-C 2-4M, WATER-D 3M, check next page.*

Felonies? *Three, none active.* **Compliance Index:** *63.9/100.* **On watch?** *Yes.* **Notes:** *youngest experiences night terrors. Three indicate above-norm curiosity; detailed record of deviance or dissent page five.*

Hero-Program Eligibility: *YES / flagged for perceptive bias.*

I reached into the file and tugged out the wrinkled packet fully. A chair squeaked in the other room, followed by the thudding of footsteps.

"Warte mal, ich glaube, ich habe etwas gehört." His voice dropped.

Wait a minute, I think I heard something.

"Je parie que c'est les tuyaux. Bon, c'est l'heure de notre ronde de toute façon.

I bet it's the pipes. Well, it's time for our rounds anyway.

Reaching out my hands, I stood, commanding the shadows to close all the file cabinets at once. They did so without fighting, but slowly, leaving me breathless. The files finished copying. I ejected the flash drive, ducking underneath the desk as the lights in the room flicked on.

The shadows receded to me, chased away by the light. I willed them to cover me, only managing enough to stay hidden if I did not move. I hoped. My breath grew tight and stiff. *Am I losing control of them?* My heart pounded in my ears. *Did I use too much power? Is the light too strong?*

"Jemand hat wieder vergessen, den Computer auszuschalten!" the man's voice complained.

Someone forgot to turn off the computer again!

He strode over, his black leather boots shining with light. I pressed myself back against the desk, the paper and flash drive clutched tightly in my hand.

"Don't *forget* to check that *they* haven't forgotten *anything else*," the woman shouted back.

Grumbling, he stood in front of me at the computer.

The darkness around me quivered, a blob hesitantly touching the light like a child on a hot stove. After he finished, without so much as a scan around the room, he left, switching the light back off.

I released the shadows and exhaled, realizing I'd been holding my breath. Slowly, I crawled from the desk, getting to my feet.

"Your only goal is to create panic," Taavi had said.

I smiled, becoming more awake than I had been in months. Tucking the flash drive and paper into my bag, I brought out the fire starter and began opening drawers. The shadows watched, almost curiously, as if they were sentient, while I removed stacks of folders and papers, carefully piling them next to the computer. Cardboard boxes thudded underneath and I brushed my hands.

When I finished the trail of papers, laid from the carpet leading to the stack, drenched in alcohol and gas from my bag, I lit the firestarter on the first paper. It burst into flames instantly with a whoosh, the fire spreading down the page to the next. I bolted before the sprinklers hissed awake, using the shadows to throw over tables, knock chairs, rip boxes, and fling open cabinets, along with covering the cameras from earlier. My thighs burned as I climbed the stairs, clearing three to four at a time, voices raising behind me. White lights flashed.

At the top, I saw the door closed and barreled toward it at an angle. It buckled under my shoulder and broke open, letting me free onto the roof. I cleared the gap easily, rolling to the next roof, and faded away into the night.

****

Entering the house, I skipped steps downstairs to my bedroom, threw off the small bag, and shed my clothes. Pulling on my hoodie and sweats, I rummaged through the bag and pocket of the suit I wore for the paper.

Where is it? I patted my suit and frantically cleared both pockets and the bag over ten times, turning up empty. *No, no, no. I was too worried about being followed.* I skimmed the ground and darted back upstairs, exiting the house, following closely to the trail I took on the way home.

The old city hall burst into view, smoke thickly swirling and choking from the windows. Firefighters and heroes smothered the building with shared water, a few ambulances waited at the doors. Sirens echoed, lights turning on nearby apartments and buildings. Four stretchers emerged from the building, a wooden statue tumbling after them, followed by five more who found their way around. They loaded the ambulances quickly.

No. I slid to a stop in my tracks at the end of the street, the ambulances veering past me. *That building was supposed to be empty, except for the security guards. They weren't supposed to get hurt.* My grip loosened from engraving indents into my palms, and my breath shortened. *Are they dead?* Each wail of the ambulances faded, leaving the crackle of wet ash.

What have I done? Please tell me they're still alive.

****

Morning came as if nothing happened. I leaned forward in my seat, my hood far over my head. Strands of my ash hair fell over my nose piercing. Warmth radiated off of Leor, already in his seat next to mine, wearing his typical dress pants and plaid jacket.

The whole school buzzed about the fire in a mix of loud and hushed whispers. Mr. Atherly switched on his screen before the bell rang, pulling up a livestream. An overvoice began, "Ten injured, none dead. Eight of which were part of the overnight cleaning crew. Sandra is live with the security detail from that night. Sandra?"

Flipping, the screen switched to a lady in a dress with a microphone in her hand. She stood next to a woman and two men, one with black boots. "Yes, thank you." She pointed it toward the black boot man. "Tell us, what happened that night? What or rather, who started the fire?"

"Like zey said, the electrical viring malfunctioned." I recognized his accent immediately, the man rubbing his burly hands together. He avoided eye contact with the camera and the reporter.

The woman stepped forward, around the second man, who leaned forward like he wanted to cut in, and maintained a straight posture, her shoulders back and chin lifted. "Exactement. Since our cleaning lahdy wasn't here, the building was a mess, and it just so happened ze pahpers lit on fire."

The news lady pulled back her microphone. "So it wasn't sabotage?"

"Nein," the man said quickly.

I shook my head, my neck stiff. *After all of that, with people injured, it did nothing? They're covering it up? There's no way they didn't see the trail.* Twisting my prickly piercing, I kept watching.

With a fake smile, the news lady nodded. "That matches with the police and fire departments' reports. There you have it, folks. Back to you."

With a musical melody, the screen switched to two people in seats around a long table. "Now a word from our councilmen." One of them held up a paper. "Later today, our mayor will give us a briefing. For now, she wants to ensure all citizens are aware that accidents like this happen and are rare enough that you need not worry. Especially since we have heroes to help out."

The other jumped in. "I'm glad we have the system and its heroes to ensure—

Switching his screen back off, Mr. Atherly paced in front of the room, reiterating what the news had said. Several people displayed their suspicion, to which he immediately shut down. After the comments had slowed, he switched to the lesson, bringing out a worn textbook.

"This," he began, pointing to an ancient diagram of spell circles and power hierarchies, "is one of the earliest systems developed after the Victory Over Villainy. It is the foundation of our peace today. Without it, we would have nothing but war and death, as was the case during the age of villains."

I leaned back in my seat, arms crossed as he paced. His voice droned on, reciting the same speech we'd heard a dozen times before about the brilliance of past heroes and the deliberate systems they put in place.

"Now, as you've all seen, these guidelines have ensured stability, efficiency, and safety. Any questions before we move on?"

A hand shot up from the other side of the room. "Didn't citizens oppose and riot against the ideas? Why did they?"

Mr. Atherly nodded, the electricity shooting off from his hair. "Of course. There are always those resistant to change. But their opposition ultimately failed because it was clear these frameworks, like our rules, were necessary for survival."

My hand went up automatically, before I could fully think it through, and he called on me.

"Yes, Miss Shelia?"

"I get why these rules were created, but shouldn't we question if they still work? What if we've outgrown them?"

The room went still, a few heads turning my way.

"Outgrown them?" Mr. Atherly repeated, rubbing his chin.

I nodded. My fingers curled inward. "They were made to fix the problems of that time. Now things are different, yet we are still punished for a curfew slip as if it's treason. What if, instead of preserving the past, we thought ahead and replaced outdated rules with new ones? Such as improving the school system and encouraging innovative thinking? Or, if someone makes a mistake, they shouldn't be beaten, thrown into jail immediately, or expelled and fired like Brendan was. If society has changed, our laws should reflect that and allow opposing thoughts."

Narrowing his eyes, Mr. Atherly's lips thinned, his hands clasped behind his back. "Miss Shelia, you're misunderstanding my course and these systems. Their role isn't to foster recklessness. It's to ensure that the mistakes of the past, including the Collective-Punishment Edict and the Civilian Vigilante Purge, aren't repeated."

"We could be doing so much more," I pressed, talking faster, "advancing technology or making our city better. Instead, we're stuck going over the same history and training the same curriculum made a century ago. Superheroes act like placeholders."

A murmur rippled through the room. I caught a few students exchanging uneasy glances.

"You may think you're advocating for the good of our city, but what you're describing is exactly how war begins. Disrupting and revamping established systems doesn't lead to growth. It leads to instability, disarray, a complete mess, which is something this society cannot afford." Mr. Atherly turned back to the board, dismissing me with a pointed look. "Let this be a lesson for everyone. History is not something we outgrow. It is something we learn from so that we don't repeat it. That is the foundation and the reason we're all here today. Peace has a cost. And our heroes, like Altruistic and Lighter, show that."

I fell silent for the rest of the lesson, my fists clenched under the tiny wooden desk. When the bell finally rang, I gathered my things slowly, watching as everyone else filed out. Only Leor took a second glance at me before departing.

****

At the tree, I ate, welcoming the chance to breathe. Sometimes, Malik would come by with Drystan and Arlene, but that usually came later. *Would he come today?* I closed my eyes, my muscles loosening.

Well, until someone cleared their throat.

I suppressed a groan, finding Reed shifting foot to foot on the patchy grass. He crossed his arms, his red-orange gaze locked onto me.

"So," he said slowly, as if I had asked for the fifth time to repeat what he said, "You hear about the fire? Crazy, huh?"

"Yeah, I heard about it." I rubbed my eyes with the palm of my hands, then straightened back against the bumpy bark.

With a chuckle—*did he think it was funny?*—Reed glanced to the side. "Ten people injured, rumors our government's trying to cover it up... not that *you* would know anything about that, right?"

"What's that supposed to mean?" Lifting my head to meet his gaze, I took a deep, measured breath. *I know you're trying to get a rise out of me. There's no way you actually suspect anything.*

Reed shrugged. "Oh, you know. People are saying whoever did it knew how to get around the building well. Say, wasn't your mother working there two years ago?"

I leaped to my feet. The shade snapped to my side like cobras. Before I could strike, another voice cut in, "Hey, Reed." Malik strode up, casually positioning himself between us. "What are you two talking about?"

"Just talking and messing around. Nothing to it," he added and looked between us. "It's nothing serious, dude. I doubt she needs you to speak for her."

"You're right." Malik inclined his head. "I don't. But you think you're playing around and it's not."

Reed's eyes widened briefly, as if he was surprised, before his smirk returned, and he took a step back. "Fine. Fine. Guess I'll leave you alone with your girlfriend, jeez." With a last look at me, he spun and walked off.

I returned my back against the tree, sliding down and adjusting my backpack to rest against my leg. When Reed left from view, Malik turned toward me. "You okay?"

"I don't need you defending me," I pointed out sharply as he sat a few feet across from me.

"I know. I just, well, sorry. He can sometimes be a bit... You know."

"Abrasive or egotistic?" I filled in, forcing back the faintest smirk tugging at the corner of my mouth. "Picked up on that a while ago."

Taking off his backpack, Malik chuckled. "Yeah, that."

After a few moments of silence, I tucked a strand of hair behind my ear. "Is Arlene or Drystan coming?" I found myself asking, lifting my hoodie back enough so I could see around me.

"Oh, they'll be out soon. They got to lunch late." Malik scratched his forehead. He bit his lip, his crystal blue eyes intent. "What Reed said about the fire. It's horrible that people got hurt. But it's almost like the whole thing just got... buried. Did you see how quickly they dismissed it in class?"

"Governments do what they want, as long as it

maintains peace and order." I shrugged. "What's new?"

Malik frowned. "But it doesn't make you wonder? Things like that don't happen often, but when they do, it's like no one's supposed to talk about it. People act like no one was even hurt." He sighed. "If anything like that happened to my family, and people just ignored it? I don't know what I'd do. I love my little siblings."

My throat tightened, and I looked away, swallowing. *What if that was Mom or Micha? I'm doing this for them, aren't I? No one died. Not yet. And I won't let it get that far.*

"Sometimes people get hurt," I muttered, tracing patterns in the dirt with my fingers. "That's the risk."

"Yeah," Malik agreed, almost hotly, "and I don't want that. People don't *have* to get hurt, at least as long as I can do anything about it. Maybe it's just me being paranoid... After all, it all points to faulty wiring. But it makes me worry. Especially how the city handled it."

It's not unexpected for officials to lie in order to maintain peace, I thought. *Riots and mass panic are the last things they'd want. This means I'm going to have to do something bigger to catch the government's and the public's eye.* I shook my head, catching Malik watching me.

"What about your family, Aris? You ever worry about stuff like that?"

I froze, taking several moments to respond. "I do, yet I know people have been hurt before. It's not like the government's ever been great at handling things."

His brows drew together as he nodded. "It seems... I

don't know. More recently, I worry my family will get caught up in something, whether they're involved or not. My little brother and sisters... they're pretty young still, and..."

"People get hurt no matter what we do." Beams of light burst from a floating building above, out of the Light wing. "It's inevitable."

"No one should be," he pointed out. "Sometimes it's because someone's too unaware or desperate to see what their choices are doing to others."

I stiffened, pulling the hood further out again and sticking my hands in my pockets. "People always have reasons. Some don't get to pretend everything's fine. They have to take it into their own hands."

Reaching out a hand, Malik hesitated before dropping it. "Sorry, I'm not saying people don't have their reasons. I just over..." He dragged his hand over his face. "Never mind."

Silence filled the space between us. In the distance behind him, Drystan and Arlene emerged from the doors, heading straight for us. *Oh, that's time for me to leave, I guess.*

"You know," Malik began casually, scratching his head. "Speaking of siblings, I have to babysit mine this weekend, but I've got a date, too. Don't suppose you'd be up for helping out?"

My mouth slightly hung open in disbelief. I did a double-take. "Babysitting?"

"Yeah, I know." Malik shook his head. "But I figured since you mentioned your little brother... maybe you'd know how and consider it?"

We barely know each other. I drew back, shoulders shrinking together. *What would Taavi say? I have to train.* I recalled the stuffed dinosaur sitting on my bed, my mind moving at the speed of a bullet train. *And Micha... I can't even find him or protect him.* My breath caught, and I briefly closed my eyes. *So seeing children that would be his age... I don't think I can...*

"Sorry," I began as Drystan and Arlene reached us. A set of keys fell from her purse, getting covered in the grass.

"Hey, guys!" Arlene waved, ran a hand through her brown hawk cut, then sat next to Malik with Drystan. She wore a striped shirt with a black jacket. On the other hand, Drystan wore his athletic wear.

I stood, lifting my bag's strap over my shoulder. Passing them, I located the keys in the lush grass, picked them up, handed them to Arlene, and left before she could say a word. But her voice still followed me. "Thank you! I would've freaked out without them."

****

In my almost empty room, I sat on my bed and stared at the dusty desk. The book Taavi gave me sat on top of it, its pages worn from the number of times I had gone through it. Beside it lay an open note from Micha that I received yesterday in the mail, without a return address. I assumed it was sent by the foster parents through CPS or the like.

"Dear Aris, I made a new frend 2day! His name is Benny, and he likes dinosors to. But he's not as cool as you. When you coming to viset? Mrs. Jenings says your busy, but I think your just being a cecret hero. I miss you. Love, Micha."

Mrs. Jennings? That might be a good start to finding out where he is. However common that last name may be. The stuffed dinosaur, Chomper, lay to my right, beneath the covers on the pillow. I brushed my hand against it, breathing in the faint scent of cinnamon honey.

In the middle of the night, you knocked on my door with Chomper hugged tightly against your chest, as if he'd protect you. Then you slightly opened it so light would leak through.

"Aris," my little brother called with a shaky voice, tears in his eyes. "Can I come in? I-I don't want to be alone."

"Yeah." I scooted over, patting the empty mattress next to me. "What's wrong? Did you have a bad dream again?"

He nodded and struggled up onto the bed, sliding under the blankets and curled next to me. "I don't know. My-my heart is going really fast, like a racecar or a train. And I feel really scared, li-like something bad is going to happen."

I wrapped my arms around him, setting my chin on his head. "Don't worry, you're safe here. I'll protect you."

Flashes of ruins expanded before me like fireworks, clouding my sight, yanking me from the memory and vividly showing people locked in combat, smoke rising, and blood everywhere instead. Occasionally, I would be running inside it, dodging blasts, guns, and swords, a blurry object in my hands. Shadowy tendrils spiraled around me, a dead animal leaping at my side.

Other times, I was at the edge, observing various disasters. Natural or man-driven. Then I switched to observing a ship guarded by my teacher, with her blue bonnet hair clip, Shanessa, and five outline figures behind her who were indecipherable. Her lips pressed in a firm line as if she were facing someone she didn't want to.

My little brother and mother would come into the mix, and no matter how hard I tried, they always ended up just out of reach, either consumed by the destruction or vanishing completely. Micha's laugh echoed faintly, a hollow sound that made my chest ache. *Why couldn't I hold on to him? Why couldn't I save either of them?*

Like in the third person, I watch myself with the blurred object in my hands again, glowing darkly. It cut off, the scene expanding outward, showing other cities, other lives on fire or shattering from what appeared to be sound waves. My heart twisted, and my hands ached from clenching so hard.

I was back on my bed, breathing heavily. *My brain's playing tricks on me.* Picking up the dinosaur, I hugged it, closing my eyes. *Why couldn't I catch up to Micha or Mom? Why couldn't I save them?*

Mom. Are you even thinking of me? Or have you moved on? Her laughter ran through my mind, pulling me back to the time we went swimming.

Micha wandered off to play with some new friends. Mom and I stayed at the deep end together. The pool was empty and quiet, making the water look darker and colder around my ribs. I stayed afloat, held up by the water at my Mom's command. She kept eyeing the lifeguards for some reason, a mischievous glint shining in her eye.

When they were all distracted, she lifted a hand, and the water rose between us like a ribbon—curling, looping, making a stupid little crown that wobbled onto my head.

"Don't laugh," she said, already failing, her eyes crinkling. "It's a masterpiece."

I laughed anyway as it broke apart, splashing across my scalp. Streaks ran along the sides of my face. "Mom, you need to be careful. You could get in trouble."

She waved at me. "Now, now. What's life if we can't have fun? Sometimes you need a little chaos, you know."

"Without chaos, there is no progress." Taavi's voice snapped me from the memory, echoing in my mind. My eyes flew open.

How many people have to suffer before Micha and Mom are safe? How much blood will it take? I stared at the ceiling. There has to be another way other than Shelby Feyth's or Taavi's. People don't have to die. I have to create enough unease to prove it. For my family. For those I love.

Footsteps descended the stairs, and Taavi entered the doorframe. "Dinner's ready. Can you help me set the table?"

I tucked Chomper back under the sheets, running my fingers over its worn fabric. "Micha used to hold you at night," I whispered under my breath before standing. I walked to her, exited the room, and went up to the kitchen.

"Is something bothering you, dear?" Taavi asked. I shook my head behind her, going to some cabinets and taking out cups and plates. "Is it because people were injured in the fire?"

I set the plates and cups on the table, and I go to take out the utensils. "The building was supposed to be empty."

"Besides the security guards." Taavi calmly brought over a pan and a hot pad. "I know." I filled a pitcher with water and set it on the table, and she turned toward me, her amber eyes piercing. "People are going to get hurt no matter how careful we are. That's the price."

I tightened my grip on the pitcher, the cold glass biting into my palms. I poured it into my cup. "It doesn't have to be like that. There has to be another way. People don't have to die to prove a point."

"Ah, dear, no one died." Taavi sat down at the head of the table. "I see the burden weighs on you. You're not the first to feel that way, and you won't be the last. But tell me, do you think anything great has ever been built without sacrifice?"

Taking a seat next to her, I hesitated. "I guess, just, there has to be a way to change things without... without people getting hurt."

She leaned closer, and her voice lowered to a near whisper. "Aris, necessity is the mother of invention. Do you think people invent solutions when they're comfortable?" She gestured with a sweep of her hand as if encompassing the entire city beyond the walls. "No. Comfort breeds complacency. Without chaos, people stagnate. It's only when the ground shakes beneath them, when their way of life is threatened, that they find the will to adapt, to innovate, to move forward."

I stared at her. "That doesn't mean—"

"It means," Taavi interrupted smoothly, rearranging the silverware I had set down at her place, "that the world needs a spark. And if you give a man the right motivation, he will move mountains. He won't do it for comfort or peace. He'll do it because the alternative is unbearable." She turned to face me. "Do you want your brother to grow up in a world where nothing changes? Where he's invisible and bored, like we were?"

I flinched back. "I only want him back and to not lose him. Or mom. Or anyone else."

Reaching out, her hand rested lightly on my shoulder, her touch warm but light. "You won't, Aris. Not if you are calling the shots. Waking the world doesn't mean destroying it, but forcing it to move. To give people the push, the discomfort they need to build something better. To make a place where your brother and everyone like him can thrive. You aren't their villain. You're their wake-up call."

"Why did you choose me?" I asked, picking up a fork. "There are plenty of others more powerful than me, surely. Being the first to do this..."

"You think you're the first?" she laughed, throwing her head back before looking at me again. "No, others tried to do what you're doing. And every single one of them failed." She served herself food. "They were too loud, wanting recognition and credit. That's why I chose you, Aris. You know how to stay unseen until it's too late."

"Who has tried before? And how did you know about my powers?"

"That's a lesson for another time. I'll put aside some time during training for it. Secondly, what?"

"How," I said and picked at my food, pushing it with the fork, "did you know I had shadow powers before I did?"

"The crown isn't the only magical object out there, as you know. I used one, but that's not the only reason. I watched and saw that you were coming to terms with the fact that our system is flawed."

"Can I see this object? Or use it?"

"When the time is right." Taavi took a sip of water. "Don't forget what—or who—you're doing this for."

Right. For Micha. For my Mother. I won't lose them. I can't accept people having to die for it either. Under my watch, that won't happen. I will control that.

Eating my food, my mind drifted towards the papers the woman gave me at school. One detailed the known magical objects. The other outlined locations and upcoming changes. One line in particular lingered. Two of the jewels in Shelby's Crown will be moved from their hiding spots a month before the festival. That date is set for this weekend.

I'll go after them to prove I'm capable. Under my terms, I can decide for myself. I kept eating.

Chapter 8

ARIS SHELIA

A mix of citizen and hero guards, clad in gleaming armor or suits, patrolled the area in pairs. The citizen guards had guns strapped to their backs and deep Russian Amethyst cuffs hanging at their sides. Together, the pairs were unusually alert as they scanned the docks, climbing on and off the white ship. It arrived earlier that day and now waited to be unloaded, some nailed crates already taken off.

By now, a blanket of clouds covered the sky, providing much more shade than the sun would've offered alone. I crouched near the dock wearing a black suit, mask, earplugs, and gloves. It took little time to cross, the only trouble being when I had to dive behind a stack of crates as a pair of guards ventured a few steps outside their usual patrol.

A sharp mixture of salty air and oily fumes hung in the air. The oakwood creaked under my feet, darkened by the splashing waves. I descended the stairs quickly to the poorly lit lower level, pausing as sharp Russian accents carried from behind a closed door to my right. I quickly checked to make sure the hall was clear before I pressed my ear to the cool metal.

"—to Ezrat, huh? It's a fool's errand," said one man.

"You think so? You vanna to explain dat to da Presidents or Council?" the second replied with a softer voice.

A chair scraped. "I know what they tell us vut this crown isn't just for show."

The second man huffed. "We've got heroes guarding it. They've got no clue what the extent of power the gems have together, and ze Presidents just cares about making their speech sparkle."

There was a pause. "When the truth about the crown leaks, what then? You think there won't be blood? That's why we were brought in. To keep the lid on this, to make sure these pieces stay out of the wrong hands. You saw what happened in Evora—"

"Our job is to follow orders," the second snapped, cutting him off. "Move ze gems, protect ze shipment. Dat's it. Leave ze big-picture worries to people higher up ze chain." The second man sighed, the chair squeaking again. "You worry too much, my friend. Besides, we're not sticking around to see the festival anyway. Once the ship's unloaded and gems hidden, we're gone. Whatever happens after... it is someone else's problem, yes?"

Pushing from the door, I made my way through the halls, ducking into doors whenever voices approached. The instances of nearly running into someone grew frequent as I reached the end of the ship. In a set-off room, a skylight shone from above, with five guards and ten crates in the room. *A skylight? Are you saying this entire time I could've just come from there?* I sighed.

Three of the guards sat on the crates talking, and the other two leaned against them on phones. I ducked into a dark, nearby door as extra footsteps grew near. Three more guards passed in uniforms, bodies relaxed as they continued down the hallway, two with guns at their sides. The other had a faint glow to her outline, a mole on her right cheek, and long blonde hair. *Shanessa? What's she doing here?*

When they turned the hallway, I reached for the shadows with one hand, and they bent, covering me. With the other, I pointed at the lights and they dimmed. Extending tendrils from my hiding spot, I prodded the edges of the nailed crates. The shadows hissed and I flinched from the magic shield, taking them back to my side. Though they weren't totally useless, they told me that the Alexandrite and Goldstone were in the left middle crate of the room.

My heart pounded in my chest. I smiled. The space grew sharp. Welcoming.

The three guards on the crates sat in the corner, two on the sides and one on the center-right crate. It left me with one side to work with.

I entered the room and slid by its side. I pressed my hand to the wooden surface of the crate. The shadows seeped into the cracks like oil, wrapping and latching themselves around the magic meant to keep me out. They had no weight of their own, but together we worked at the nail's rim and pried it partially open. I reached my hand in and clasped both decently sized jewels. My thumb brushed the cool and smooth surface.

Alarms blared. My heart leapt into my throat. *Damn it.* Yanking the Alexandrite and Goldstone out, I stuffed them into my pockets and bolted, missing the wide-eyed guards' expressions.

The shadows struggled to keep up, stretching thin until they caught up and thickened to set 'blockades' between me and the heavy boots and shouting voices behind or to the side.

Light flashed before and after me, cutting the shadows back from my reign. *Shanessa and your stupid Light Magic.* I formed the nearest darkness into darts and sent them back wildly. More to make her dodge than hit, as all they'd do was pierce and then disperse. The beams bounced off reflective surfaces, bright enough to sear spots into my vision. I hissed and loosed another dart blindly in her direction.

The shadows surged eagerly. Sweat broke on my forehead as I willed them outward to absorb the stray light. The flickering beams dimmed under the shadows' pull, their edges bending and warping like molten glass. My lungs burned as I cleared the open door and sprinted up the stairway to the main deck.

Guards and heroes swarmed the docks. Some flew, scanning the ground below. Two fanned out high to sweep the crates. At the top of the stairs, a wall of air slammed into me, knocking me off my feet and sending me skidding across the splintered ground between the crates.

Gasping, I rolled to my feet, scanning the surrounding faces. Rainbow hues of light blossomed from Shanessa's hand as she emerged.

At the other edge of the ship stood a woman in a long

coat, her blouse rippling in the wind, her amber eyes clear as daylight. Her caramel braided hair had strands whipped her masked face as the wind kicked debris in every direction.

"Taav-!" I cut myself off, scrambling upright. My voice changer made my voice sound low-pitched and raspy. "What are you doing?!"

Water surged from the side of the ship, rocking it back and forth, a vortex spraying cold mist into the air. A guard lunged at me, and I ducked, the shadows snapping to block his attack before piercing his shoulder like a stake. He cried out, clutching the wound with a hand as a flash of fire spiraled above him from another hero. I cursed under my breath. Part of the fire licked the damp wood, and steam rose in a hiss, creating a thick wall.

Out of the corner of my eye, Taavi smirked. With a flick of her wrist, the wind whipping her clothes died down.

Rolling to the balls of my feet, the hairs on my neck tingled. I ducked. A narrow beam barreled past and pierced through the metal poles above, missing me by mere inches. Fire roared after it, the shadows flickering and recoiling. I nearly stumbled.

Next to the water... I still have a chance.

At the top of the ship, my instructor Shanessa now stood side by side with Leor, their hair whisking heroically as her blue bonnet struggled for its life. A girl with a hawk cut, Arlene, stood between them, her hands on their shoulders. Ten guards moved in formation behind them.

I almost gagged, backing toward the water and next to a few crates. The shadows roared, rising in a mass as I pushed them outward to shield myself. They roared with excitement, stronger than the light she threw and enfolding its beams into tiny, harmless rays.

Taavi shrugged. "Now you'll learn how to handle yourself when things don't go according to plan. You're not invincible. But you need to act like you are."

I clenched my fists, the shadows pulsed at my feet. *Jump.* "I'm sorry, I should've told you!"

I leaped backward as two heroes ran at me with incredible speed and precision, reaching out their hands to grab me. I threw up a shadow wall, their hands skidding against it with sharp cracks. My breath caught, and I brushed my hand against the ship as I dropped into the water. Like a disease, black cracks spiderwebbed across the hull, the wood groaning under the strain. A ten-foot radius around the contract point crumbled instantly, splinters flying.

Breaking the waves, cold water engulfed me. I surfaced quickly, coughing as my eyes darted upward. Men and women crowded the edge, avoiding where I touched. One, Mr. Atherly, held out his hand, sending small bolts of electricity into the water. The bolts quickly reached me, a mix of tingling and sharp pricks, vibrating my muscles to spasm.

Wind roared, lifting me from the waves. Overhead, a helicopter circled, its spotlight slicing through the gloom. Another tall figure, an emblem of Ezrat's on his chest, approached, with a scruff on his chin and short, curly black hair. He wore a trench coat, and the guards and heroes immediately turned towards him, allowing him through.

"Bravo, guards and heroes!" He clapped, his voice

sounding a bit odd compared to what I heard on television. His eyes locked on mine, and he winked. "That was a test! Nothing to worry about. You did well."

What? The wind carried me back to the ship's dock, depositing me roughly beside him. *I-I...? Huh?*

"President Coast," Shanessa called and bowed, and the others soon followed her lead. "Ain't nobody told us this was a test. I swear, I thought them jewels were real important, and that person just up and snagged 'em."

"That was the point." He laughed, his posture relaxed. *Where's his German accent?* "The gems are important and still in the crate. Go look." Leor turned toward the guards, and they nodded, immediately heading down the stairs. "Now, if you'll excuse us, we have matters to discuss."

He grabbed my hand, leading me off the dock. *The hell?* I flicked my eyes where Taavi had been moments ago, but she vanished. *She left me here?! What's he doing?* Scanning the city layout, I found a very shaded place in the buildings ahead. *If only I could...* President Coast tightened his grip on me with a slight shake of his head.

"Sir, if I may!" a guard called out.

"What?" President Coast asked lightly. He stopped, pulling me with him.

"You sound a little differen' than usual, yes?"

"Forgive me." Letting go of my hand, he coughed into his mouth. "I'm sick—"

I took off. The semi-wet clothes and shoes squished

with every step. The taste of blood thickened in my mouth, the world growing darker. Under my feet, the Earth began to tremble, shaking nearby buildings. *They seriously got almost every major power out here?*

"Son of a—" President Coast shouted behind me, his voice growing closer despite how fast I pushed myself.

Light exploded in front of me, the world vibrating. But I reached the shade first, throwing the shadows behind me into a wall with spikes, their behavior almost erratic, and vanished from their sight. Gradually, I made my way back home, ensuring they didn't have someone with Shadow powers following me. As I neared the house, I pulled off my mask and gloves, undoing my hair.

What the hell was that, Taavi? You have so much explaining to do. I gritted my teeth, light flashing above me like a lightning storm. *That could've gone so badly, and you* left me. My knees, my whole body, begged to give out, causing me to stumble, yet I caught myself on the railing. I reached the doors and entered, heavily leaning on whatever wall or structure was nearest. *I don't know how I only had to hurt a few of them. Or how I got away.*

Slumping onto the couch, I tossed my mask. The room blurred, or crossed, darkness edging my vision. Blood lingered in my mouth, giving a copper scent. Taavi wandered in with a grin spreading to her eyes, no longer wearing her trench coat.

"Incredible child." She clapped. "Did you get both of them?"

I groaned, my chest tight as I reached into my pocket. A buzz arrived in the back of my head while I touched a single smooth rock and nothing else. *Crap. You have got to be kidding me.* I took it out, revealing the wet glass-like Alexandrite without a single scratch or nick on it. This one was multi-colored, changing with the shift of the light from green and blue to purplish-red, and had a weight to it. *She's going to be furious.* A mix of trembling and heat ran through me, though I couldn't quite tell whether it was my own anger or fear. "Must've dropped the—"

She snatched it from me and waved a hand dismissively, hunching over the gem to examine it. "Yes, yes, very well. Meets expectations. Go change and dry off, we'll discuss the deats of your hesitation later." She quickly peered out the window, her nose and forehead scrunching as she scanned the street. "Where's Cyril, dear?"

"Meets expectations?" I repeated hotly, then froze. *Cyril?* "W-who?" Carefully, I pushed myself into a sitting position, every muscle protesting.

"Cyril." Tucking the gem into her pocket, she continued to gaze outside. "I sent him to rescue you from your reckless attempt at grabbing both gems at once." I shook my head when her eyes widened. "Oh, there he is!"

As she went to the door, I rose to my feet. "W-wait! What-Why didn't you help me? Where did you go?"

Straightening, Taavi placed her hand on the doorknob. "I wasn't the one who decided to do everything alone. Stealing two gems in one attempt like that would've been a fool's run. But it was a decision you made, and a lesson I saw fitting, so I let you."

"I could've died," I said, the words tumbling out before I

could stop them. "Is this how it's always going to be?"

"Now, now," she tsked as someone knocked on the door. "I didn't abandon you. I still helped you through Cyril. We'll see how the rest plays out."

The door squeaked open, revealing President Coast in its frame with a jacket thrown over his head. His face and body morphed in a spiral, and his entire appearance changed. It grew thicker, revealing a thick dad-bod with honey-blond hair in a comb-over. His face became oval, his skin a whiter tan, and his eyes switched to grey. Reaching into his pocket, he took out a pair of glasses and put them on, shrugging off the trench coat and jacket over his head.

"Man, that was so annoying. I couldn't have waited long enough to get out of that thing!" Cyril exclaimed, gently touching Taavi's shoulder. "She— Aris, wasn't it?— thought I actually was the President! They all did!" He laughed in a *ho, ho, ho* way.

Who the hell is he— I swayed then stumbled, rubbing my eyes. His attention shifted to me, and his eyebrows curved upwards, enhancing a concerned shine in his eyes. "Are you alright? Did you use too much magic?"

I clenched my teeth. Part of me wanted to snap at him and ask who the hell he was. Fortunately for him, the lack of energy in my body saved him from lashing for another day, and I waved him off instead. His help was unneeded, like his concern. For all I knew, he was only with Taavi and was a stranger to me. No use in being honest. And that gem... he'd probably be disappointed I didn't snatch both if he knew as much as I thought.

Ugh, I'm too tired for this.

Using anything on the wall or banister I could reach to keep myself up, I made my way downstairs to my bedroom, ignoring whatever Taavi or Cyril said. *I'm stealing and risking my life for you, Taavi. And I have to keep doing this for Micha. For my Mother. Don't I?* A hollowness gnawed inside, taking bigger and deeper bites like a cold vacuum. All those I knew at school flashed across my mind. Shanessa, Leor, Arlene, Drystan, Mr. Atherly... Malik. What would he do if he knew what I had done? Would any of them understand?

I almost scoffed, surprising myself. *No, they wouldn't.* I looked up to where Taavi and Cyril conversed and then back down to the floor. *The heroes, people at school, they don't care. Doesn't even matter what's at stake if their lives are relatively 'peaceful'.*

My fingers curled into themselves. *... Why do I even care?* I reached the door, fighting for breath, but more distracted in my thoughts than realizing the sluggishness of my body. *The only person who can achieve what you need is you. Only your family cares about you. No one else will help.*

Shutting the door, I collapsed to the floor, feet from my bed, the dinosaur just out of reach.

****

Yawning, I rolled, an ache spreading from my back. *What-where am I?* My eyes flew open to a dark room. A senselessness wrapped my body, slowly fading as I lay on the strandy carpet. *Last night... right. I got the Alexandrite.* I found the energy to push myself up after something like ten minutes, immediately finding Chomper on the bed and dragging myself over to it. Its soft body pressed into my chest as I hugged it, leaning down to the bed.

Micha... where are you?

Reluctantly, I lay it back on the pillow, tucked under the blankets, and peeled off my musty clothes. After I showered and tossed my 'suit' into the wash, I made my way to the empty kitchen. My stomach growled as I pulled out leftover scrambled eggs and pancakes, which I practically inhaled when I sat at the table.

Yawning, Cyril walked in from the hallway, eyeing my plate. "Any leftovers?" I shook my head as he took his time getting his meal. A loud sizzle, followed by a squeal and curse like he burned himself, erupted from the kitchen. After a bit, he sat next to me. "Sorry about that! It's nice to finally meet you, Aris."

Sighing, I gave him a polite nod between bites.

"I'm guessing you don't know much about me," he continued with a chuckle, shaking his head. "Well, wait no more! I'm a third year at Mala, and an artist depending on the time of day. Well, actually, I'm more into stuff like games and puzzles, not that I'm any good—" Getting up with my dishes, I took them and unloaded them into the dishwasher. "Ma'am, last night was crazy. You were great! We make a good team. If only I had done better and somehow told you it was me! I didn't know the dock was so shaky."

As I went to leave the kitchen, Taavi intercepted me with a smile. "Aris, stay here, would you? I would like to talk."

Stifling a groan, I nodded and sat while she grabbed herself a bowl of cereal. Cyril kept talking, finished his meal, and went to the living room, switching on the TV. It buzzed in the background as Taavi came to sit down.

Inside, I felt oddly numb despite the sweet syrup taste residing in my mouth. *Is she going to explain last night and or apologize? Pft, no, she doesn't do that. She knew I was going off on my own. If she thought it was a bad idea, why didn't she stop me? Agh.* Propping an arm on the table, I rested my forehead in my palm, using the other to play with the end of my hoodie. *Or does she think I'm over it and talk about something else? Perhaps Cyril or Micha...?*

"That was reckless," Taavi began in between bites, "but with Cyril's help, it worked out."

"Last night?"

She nodded. "You have the right idea, but I expect you to tell me beforehand. That could've gone badly."

I tensed for a fight. "Are you just going to give me a lecture? I earned that gem myself."

"No, I believe draining your powers last night was enough punishment. It taught you a much-needed lesson, including the importance of stealth. You know, the one trait I picked you for." Taavi dabbed her lips with a napkin, glancing at me with clear eyes. "I actually wanted to talk about two other things."

I sighed, slouching. Intro music played in the background from the TV, and light flooded in more strongly from the windows.

"Dear, we're starting slow. We need to go bigger and do more together. No one will take you seriously until you make them."

"Last night wasn't big enough?" I asked, folding my arms and leaning back.

She waved her finger, taking another bite. "It's a start. This time, I'll go with you."

"What about Cyril?"

"He has other matters to attend to. He'll join you later when you go after the next jewel. For this, I'll go over the specifics later, but we will be targeting abandoned buildings and a few electrical grids, mostly at the edges of the city."

"Why do you want to knock down a few run-down buildings instead of literally anything else? Are you sure it's abandoned? What was the second thing?"

"Aris, good gracious, my child." She carried her empty bowl to the sink, rinsed it once, then placed it in the dishwasher. "I chose you because you learn by doing. So do it. Then we'll talk about what you overlooked." Taavi paused. The beep of the dishwasher echoed with the sound of rushing water right behind. "The second thing... I received a message from some foster parents recently." My heart leaped in my throat. The room tilted, as though everything had been waiting for that sentence to land. "They combed through the file, met with a few caseworkers. They asked to set up a date for you and your little brother. Micha, was it?"

Relief flooded me, yet it snagged on the way she said *recently*. I stood, placing my hands on the table. "When do I see him?" It took effort not to ask the others already trying to break free. *Why didn't you or they reach out sooner? How'd they find out about me?*

Returning, Taavi stopped a few feet away. "I plan on setting a date for Friday, which is in a week and a half."

"That's—Is he okay?"

Her eyes flashed, sharpening her expression. I flinched as she stepped closer. "We all have schedules we must stick to. This took effort, coordination, and care. So if this is going to work, Aris, you must prove that you can follow a plan to do this."

Music of a familiar breaking-news melody, played from the TV, growing louder. It was followed by Cyril's shout, "Hey, guys! You should come see it! Aris and I made the news!"

Pushing past me, Taavi plopped next to Cyril on the couch. I stood in the corner, watching the news do that cool flip transition and red bugs.

"This is CivicScope breaking news with what happened late last night at the docks." The lady evened out the papers on her desk, fiddling with her hands as what they said appeared on the screen. The nervousness reminded me of my sister, who also didn't know what to do with her arms when she hid something.

The man stared straight into the camera. "There was an attempt to steal not one, but two magic artifacts on the ship. While the specifics of these items are currently classified, it brings up various concerns and questions. Who are these thieves? Where did they get word of the shipment? Should we fear them? Officials suggest not, which we'll get into."

"All are great questions, I'm sure! Sandra?"

The screen faded to another lady standing in front of

the ship. "What happened last night threw us in for a loop! The President from Ezrat even came himself, claiming the whole event was a ruse! Yet we find ourselves questioning, was it really?" She gestured behind her, then began walking. "We have reason to believe someone was imitating the President, due to his voice being inconsistent with the German accent. In addition, only one gem, the Goldstone, was found and relocated. So what happened to the Alexandrite? Well, we may not have all the answers yet, but we did manage to capture footage of last night that may give us some insight."

From a helicopter's perspective, I looked so small, like another dot moving against the grid. A smear of motion against the docks. It replayed the events, with a voiceover about the 'terrorist motives' and the 'heroic' response, and tense instrumental music in the background. It cut off after I vanished in the valley, Cyril right after me.

"Who is this?" The footage switched back to Sandra, now standing on the ship. "What do they want? Until we know, we'll be referring to this person as Nyctara. Nyx for short." Ringing overtook the television, and the reporter took out her phone. "President Coast would like a word. Back to you!"

As the screen transitioned, I smiled. *Nyx. Nyctara. I like that.*

****

Under the oak tree sat Malik, Drystan, and Arlene. Another woman, beautiful, pale, and large, sat with them. As she leaned forward, she snorted, pushing up her glasses. On her back displayed a vivid tattoo of a cat, clawing from her tank top.

159

The school had been full of theories and rumors from the dock, some even mentioning the pipe bursting at our school and the fire at the government building, claiming it was connected. *Are they talking about me? No, there's no way they suspected it. Or knew about the jewels. But... it didn't hurt to not draw attention. Malik always had a way of finding me. Having two classes together just made it easier for him.*

What are you even on about? It's not like he follows you. He has his own life to be concerned about.

His group seemed so at ease, talking and playing around. Malik gestured wildly with his hands, clearly into whatever story he told them. To his left, Drystan propped himself up on his hands, occasionally adding in. Both the women sat back, but while Arlene smiled, the other woman frowned despite light dancing in her yellow eyes. She adjusted her short grey hair and snorted again.

Should I join them? Would they even want me to? I bit my fingernails. *No, I should go.*

"Looks like they're havin' a good time," a woman's voice observed from behind me.

I jumped and twisted, coming face-to-face with Shanessa, who gave me a knowing smile, and Leor, who stood casually at her side.

"Oh, yeah." I laughed breathlessly, touching my earring. "I—"

"Sorry, we didn't mean to give ya a scare. We were just tryin' to find Malik and Drystan. Thought they'd be out here by the tree," Leor said, tipping his cowboy hat. His short black hair shifted.

"Y'all lookin' to head' their way? Mind if we tag along?" Shanessa asked.

Twisting my earring, I switched my gaze between them. *I don't want to go talk to Malik's friends, but I can't just admit I'm watching them.* Slowly, I nodded and turned, walking over with Shanessa and Leor flanking me.

Malik cut off mid-sentence, eyes finding us. "Aris! Who you got there? Shanessa and—?"

He rose and met us halfway, his three friends following. I sidestepped, creating a circle as they stopped a few feet from us.

"Gracelyn, Arlene." Leor nodded to them. "Do you mind if we talk to Malik and Drystan briefly?"

They glanced at each other and shook their heads, but Malik stuck out his arm to stop them. "Is it fine if they stay?"

Shanessa folded her arms. "I guess that's alright. Malik, Drystan, we're here to offer ya both a temporary position on our team. Perhaps permanent."

"Hell yeah!" Drystan pumped his fists in the air.

Malik grinned. "Seriously?"

I stepped back. *Should I even be here?* My hand went to the elbow of my other arm. *They wanted Arlene and Gracelyn to leave, but didn't even ask me? Am I invisible?*

"Yeah, we've been keepin' an eye on ya for a while now," Leor jumped in. "You're exactly what we're lookin' for."

"What about Aris?" Malik asked. I stared at him. "I

mean, perhaps it's an idea to look at her too."

"It's..." Shanessa led off, raising her eyebrows and exchanging glances with Leor again. "Under consideration. Accepting new heroes isn't an easy or simple thing. It's about balance in a team."

I backed up more. "It's okay, I don't think this is the team for me anyway."

Leor gave a curt nod and faced them. "How 'bout it?"

"Definitely, man!" Drystan answered.

I turned as the conversation continued. *So much for that. I rubbed my arms, shifting my sleeves. They don't want me, and I'd be a fool to believe otherwise. I left and entered my school. Well, I don't need them. I have a job to do.*

Then why do you wish they asked you as well?

No, I'm probably just worried I'll be caught. Or I'm missing my family. And if that's the case, it should be gone soon when I get to meet Micha.

I will fix this. I will make things right and... I hope he remembers me.

****

A kaleidoscope of colors exploded, spilling across Taftside's cave floors. The light illuminated the jagged walls where I trained, forming holographic images from Taavi's hand. She floated next to me, her arms folded, as the scenes before us played out like a film. We've watched several clips in short succession, and this one was a woman laughing amidst a raging firestorm, with heroes surrounding her.

162

Flames licked the sky, consuming the buildings as she danced from alley to alley. Her movements were theatrical, with blasts of red-blue fire meant to impress and defend herself effortlessly. Together, the heroes quickly subdued her, using Deep Russian Amethyst to cuff her wrists and happily placing her into a heavily guarded prison. She stood no chance against all of them, despite her fighting and heat exceeding theirs. Once captured, the fires died, turning from embers to charred smoke.

I ran my hands through my hair, glancing at Taavi. *That woman is way more athletic than me.*

"Ardeo thought brute force was enough to win. She burned a quarter of the city before they cornered her, then locked her away so no one even remembers her name," Taavi said as the scene switched to a man jumping from roof to roof, tornadoes in his wake. His coat whipped around him as he shouted. "And this man, Ventus, shouted truths from the rooftops. The heroes were on him in a matter of hours."

His voice overlapped her in the background, crying, "No one chooses anymore! They erased the names of those who fought for it. Look around."

Fading again, the lights revealed a man almost invisible in the night. He limped through vacant stall booths, passing chatting heroes and security, placing a makeshift device every other stall or so. When he finished, he dipped into a nearby alley, and a high-pitched sound began. They covered their ears, looking around frantically as a type of smoke poured out from the devices.

Reappearing, the man now wore a gas mask and made his way to the Victory over Villainy statue, unaffected by the noise. Midway through, he stopped sneaking, glancing at the frantic heroes, and laughed, waving his hand so the smoke curled into their faces. Above flew another hero, spotting the man and immediately calling to others, which he didn't hear, apprehending him within moments.

"They all, besides the last, tried to take missions head-on. The last, with powers like yours, let his arrogance get to him after acting out of spite on their shortcomings to his disabilities. All of them lost." Taavi clenched her fist, and the illusion disappeared. She glanced at her watch. "But you're not going to make their mistakes. Never underestimate your opponents or overestimate yourself. They won't fight fair."

I nodded and rose to my feet, trying to prevent a smile from breaking out on my face. My hands shook. "It's been over a week. Is it time to see him?"

Waving, Taavi spun. "Go ahead. I'll show you what else I've prepared later."

****

At the park sat a woman on a bench near the playground, watching a little boy playing on the slide. His ashen hair had remained messy after only two years, and he grew about half a foot. Tears threatened my eyes briefly, but I held them back as my chest tightened. The woman beamed and rose to her feet upon seeing me, calling Micha over.

I stopped a few feet from her, recognizing her as a Shadow teacher who used to teach at Ezrat, Mrs. Parkzer. Her short black hair framed her kind face, her brown skin almost golden in the afternoon light. Micha paused at her side, his wide eyes glued to me.

"Hello, you must be Aris." She stretched out her hand, and I shook it. Her grip was firm yet warm. "We'll have enough time to talk in a bit." Squatting by Micha, Mrs. Parkzer pointed at me. "Micha, you recognize your sister, don't you? Go on, it's okay."

His hesitation melted away as he ran into my arms, burying his face into my side. I bent slightly over, wrapping my arms back around him. I choked back words, believing if I spoke, I'd start crying. The world blurred anyway.

Seconds passed, and he pulled his head back, cranking his neck to look up at me. "Why haven't you visited? Where did Mom go? Can we go home?"

My breath caught. I squeezed him then glanced at Mrs. Parkzer, who shook her head slightly, sensing my questions. "I told him, but it'll be better coming from you."

I *failed to protect and find you. But how can I admit that?* "I should've been there. I never stopped looking for you." I let go of him and knelt, taking his hands into mine. "The police thought Mom did something bad. Bad enough to take her from us." *Gosh, it's hard to keep my voice steady.* Tears brimmed in my eyes, like a dam waiting to flood over.

He stared at me with those puppy dog eyes, brows pressing together.

"I would've given anything to stay with you, with mom, to be a family. I couldn't stay with you because there weren't any foster homes in the city available to house..." I trailed off, taking a deep breath. "But I've never stopped looking for you. I swear." I squeezed his hands. "Mrs. Parkzer only recently found me and the lady looking after me, and here we are."

"Can I go home with you?" he asked again, his voice breaking as he puckered out his lips, then peered back at Mrs. Parkzer. "She's really nice, but I miss you and Mom. Where is she?" He drew out the last word in a whine.

"I'm-I'm not sure," I faltered. Then I forced a smile and swallowed. "We'll talk about that. How's school been?"

He shifted back and forth on his feet, his gaze drifting back to the slide, then straight to me. "It's so borrrrring," he groaned, tugging his arms. "Except recess. That's the best part. And Maria and Kylee played soccer with me! But not recess is all this history stuff about Shelby and Sean or uh, I dunno."

History? Is that all he's learning? "Don't you do any crafts or music?"

"Uhhh," he trailed off with a shrug and stepped toward the slide, "I draw-drew a turkey with my hand. Mrs. Parkzer put it on her fridge. But I wish Mom could see it—it has cool colors."

"Sounds fun," I laughed, releasing his hands. I wiped my eyes.

"Areeee," he drew out, "you okay?"

"Yes, don't worry about me. I'm just happy to see you."

Mrs. Parkzer patted his shoulder. "You can go back to play, Micha. I need to talk with your sister, okay?"

He stared and nodded, reluctantly running to the playground where he sat on a swing, facing us. My hands drifted toward him, as if trying to keep him there beside me.

When he made it out of earshot, Mrs. Parkzer coughed

into her hand. I met her misty eyes. "I'm sorry it took so long, Aris. I truly couldn't find any information about you or your mother. CPS nor the police were of any help. It was like hitting a constantly moving wall until I ran into Taavi, who told me about you."

Taavi found you? That's actually really nice of her. I watched my little brother climb up and slid down the slide. "It's okay, you know now. It's not like it's your fault." I inhaled and exhaled deeply. "Do you really not know what happened? Maybe anything about our mother?"

"No clue." She shook her head. "I'm his third placement, and even if I were his first, they barely tell us anything." Rubbing her eyes, Mrs. Parkzer glanced at Micha. "I do know that he really wants to live with you. He tells me he's 'waiting for you to bring him back' all the time."

"Why can't he live with me?" I asked. "I'm nineteen."

"You're still a teenager, not twenty-one," she replied gently. "Not to mention, do you have a job? Own a home or apartment? Make enough income to support the two of you?" Mrs. Parkzer sighed, folding her arms. "Even if you did, it'd take a while to get through the paperwork and be stressful juggling school, work, and a little one to look after. For now, the best we can do is arrange visits. I'm sorry."

I clenched my teeth, realizing my nails were embedded in my palms. I forced my breath to stay even, and after a moment, I managed to speak out steadily, "I understand you can't do anything about it. Thank you for your time, and for finding me."

"You're welcome to play with him. We'll stay here for a

few hours. Let me know if you have any other questions."

With a smile, I nodded and walked over to my little brother. My breath stayed short, doing nothing to ease my stiff posture. *It's not our fault or her fault that this happened. Whoever did this will pay, even if I have to suffer for it. My brother doesn't deserve this.* The outlines of the play structure stood out, but the surrounding structures were blurred. I drew back a sigh, channeling my emotions into a bottle, and tried to focus on the part I could be with my brother.

It's a temporary barrier, one that won't remain for long. Someone will answer for splitting us apart, intentionally or not. For giving my younger brother this boring, albeit peaceful, world.

Micha's voice echoed in my mind. *Where is she?*

"Be brave, my love," Mom used to say, *wrapping a bandage around my scraped knee. I was around Micha's age at the time. "You're stronger than you know, Aris. You always find time to care when others don't. Especially when others don't."*

I tightened my grip, nails cutting into my palms. I need to find my Mom. For now, this sliver of time with my brother was all I had. But I will find her for you, Micha.

Chapter 9

LEOR FEYTH

It was hard to feel like a hero when your biggest threat this week was a tomato with teeth. No, that felt more like an insult when he saw how bad actual threats could be.

A phantom pain spread through his leg. Leor straightened.

His and Shanessa's team sat around the room while he stood at the front. Arlene sat between Gracelyn and Malik with a laptop on her knees, scrolling through it. To Leor's left sat Drystan, and to his right sat Shanessa.

"This is where we're at now? Really?" Leor asked, pointing at a slide on the board.

The team nodded, but Malik leaned forward, placing his chin on his hands. "These incidents seem kind of minor, don't they? I thought there'd be more important or life-threatening tasks for us to deal with as official heroes."

"Keepin' the peace is part of the job," Shanessa said with her hands clasped neatly in front of her. "If we let anyone slide, this can turn into a full-scale mess quickly. Y'all know that as well as I do."

Her words struck a chord within Leor. *I won't fail a mission like that again.* There had to be a reason why his society had worked so far.

Leor tapped the papers with narrowed eyes. "It does feel more like babysittin'. Though Shanessa's got a point. If we keep at it, surely we'll get more 'important' tasks." The muscles in his leg tensed. "Until then, let's stick to what's assigned. It's important to ensure everyone is safe and happy."

"But someone spawning earth dunes mixed with someone else's dinosaur hologram in a dorm?" Malik raised an eyebrow. "That's what we're considering a 'threat'?"

"At least it ain't as bad as those spiky tomatoes we dealt with the other day. That was horrendous." Drystan grinned, kicking his feet out.

Shanessa shot Drystan a look, her lips pressed into a thin line. "This isn't a joke. There's a lot for us heroes to keep tabs on. If you aren't careful, it'll go right under your nose."

Gracelyn frowned. On the other hand, Arlene's expression stayed neutral, brown eyes darting between them.

"Why don't we focus on the new villain, Nyctara?" Arlene piped up. "She could be a fellow student or teacher! Even if not, there are hotspots around the city they focus on when people like her pop up. We could set up a trap and see how good she actually is!"

That shadow wanna-be? She's a temporary distraction at most. I suppose it would be better than what they've been givin' us.

All of them nodded. Shanessa shot Leor a look and relented. "I like the idea, Arlene. I'll chat with the hero management and see if they'll give us the time of day."

"Didn't she have help from a Mental power?" Malik asked. "A man replicated President Coast."

Sounds like the villain Shanessa and I dealt with as second years, Leor thought, glancing at his co-leader. *It's highly likely someone else, but we never caught him.* Her usual fixed expression gave away her thought with the end of her lip twitching. *Looks like she realized that, too.*

"Hard to say for certain," said Shanessa. "Keep your lips sealed on that information, Aegis."

Leor picked up, "Alright, if that's it, we move on. We got anotha mission to deal with of a student messin' around. Then we can train." He eyed Shanessa back. "Whaddaya say?"

****

Outside the partially burnt old city hall, crickets chirped. A faint hum ran over the sound of splashing water as glowing skeletons and fruit danced across the lawn, almost in a line dance as if it were from an old video you'd find online. The student held out her hands with wide eyes upon seeing Shanessa's and Leor's hero team, Aegis, approach.

Leor stayed at Shanessa's side. The student shrank under his gaze as he walked through the hologram, dispersing it like a splash of water. "You find this funny?" The student stammered, her hands fumbling to dispel the rest. "This is a waste of resources," Leor continued, tapping his finger. "As heroes, we're here to protect and serve, not babysit irresponsible students messing around with light magic."

Behind him, Leor heard Drystan murmur, "Kinda extra, don't ya think?"

Leor ignored the commentary. "Next time, there isn't gonna be a warning. You're gonna lose your privileges and be disciplined. You understand?"

Nodding quickly, she muttered an apology as her cheeks flushed.

As his team turned to leave, Leor caught Malik lingering near the wall of a building. He crouched beside a bench, picking up a piece of paper. After unfolding it carefully and reading, he stuffed it inside his pocket. "What'd ya find?" Leor called, letting the others pull ahead.

"A piece of trash." Malik's mouth twitched as he scratched the back of his head. "I'll throw it away later when I get the chance."

****

The smooth wood felt nice under his hand. Leor paced back and forth in front of Shanessa's desk, tracing its edge with his fingers.

"Look," he began, facing her at the edge of the desk, "the school 'pipe burst' and the city hall fire were clearly not accidents. The docks' jewel thief followed soon after. It won't take long before people connect the dots and realize Nyctara is a new villain, not a one-time deal." Leor placed his hands on the desk and leaned into it. "I think it's time we get out of babysittin' and do some real hero work, ya think?"

"You oughta quit sayin' things like that," she said. Placing her chin on her hand, Shanessa glanced at Leor. "You're the other leader around here. If you admit to doubting every little thing, they'll follow suit."

Leor's gaze met hers. "They already are. Ya know, if we start askin' questions, we might get somewhere. This... maintenance stuff isn't heroism. It's wearin' us out. Fines for magical flowers? Restrictions on enchanted toy vehicles? It's absurd. Let's go after the real problem."

"Keepin' up with maintenance is what keeps the world turning. Power isn't a toy to throw around," Shanessa countered, touching the bluish flower in her hair. She sat back in her seat. "You'd rather let these tiny issues blow up into a full-blown mess? Look, I do think our team's ready to try at a villain. However, you know that's not fully our decision."

Before he could put a stamp on the argument and agree, Malik entered, holding a crumpled paper tightly in his hand. "Sorry to interrupt. Is this important?"

Leor's frown deepened as he stepped closer. Malik laid the thin wrinkled paper on the table, spreading it flat.

"That's the Shelia fam. One of the kids is in my class. Whah'd ya find this?" Leor asked, scanning the paper. *Pretty sure she has shadow powers.*

"At the disturbance site," Malik said. "Just lying there. Think it means something?"

Leor picked it up, folded it once, and tightly gave it

back to Malik without so much as another glance. "Nah, it's only info 'bout the family. The city hall had papers like this, since the room was full of records on citizens, so this one musta slipped through when it caught fire. Ya can just toss it. Doesn't mean anything."

Replacing it in his pocket, Malik spun back to the door instead of a trashcan. "Okay, sorry for bothering you."

Shanessa met Leor's gaze, lips pressed together.

"Hold on, Malik," she called before he stepped out. Malik paused, looking over his shoulder. "There's a task we need to talk through. They're deciding who to assign it to, and we thought you'd be a good option. Can you come in early tomorrow?"

Oh, right, good. The assigned watches.

"Yeah, I'll see you."

Chapter 9.5

MALIK STYRI

He folded the paper in half, stuffing it into his pocket, and closed the front door behind him. The latch caught and rattled the frame, getting drowned out by shouting and laughter around the corner.

"Kids, dinner time!" Malik's father called.

Instantly, the giggling cut off, replaced with scuffling and the occasional, "No, you put this away," "I did it last time," "Fine, Aerin, your turn," "Hurry up or they'll start without us!"

Malik exhaled through his nose, a smile tugging at his mouth.

Rounding the corner, he took his seat around the end of the long wooden table. Its black wood was worn smooth at the edges, glossy in the white light. From the vent underneath the table, the AC turned on, and a breeze tickled his legs.

Mother sat at the head, drinking out of a wine glass,

with chicken, rice, and curry already on her plate. Father sat beside her, his plate empty. He stared at the door where the noise came from with his arms folded.

Malik touched the paper inside his pocket again. *I wonder what Leor and Shanessa want to talk to me about.*

Three bodies scrambled into the kitchen at the same time, half-colliding as they slid into their seats.

The serving began in a flurry. His little sisters and brother talked over each other, forks clinking, plates scraped. Two of them argued over who had to refill the water pitcher. His brother complained the rice looked "weird." Someone else said it looked "normal." Mother corrected posture and manners offhandedly.

"Elbows off the table. Chew with your mouth closed. Aerin."

His little sister said nothing, glancing at Father, who didn't move until Mother lifted her glass and took a slow sip, then he finally reached for the chicken. Malik waited for them to finish before getting food himself.

"Back already?" his brother, Greyson, said around a bite. "Thought heroes ate in, like, hero buildings."

"Sometimes," Malik answered easily. "I guess it depends on the day."

"Have you fought anybody yet?" the older sister jumped in, leaning forward like she wanted a story.

"Listen here. We can talk about what we do with one exception. When we're facin' any villains, it must stay secret.

Especially if they're after something. Got it?" Leor said one day during training.

"Not really," Malik lied. "A kid was messing with her powers outside the government building, but nothing other than that."

"That's lame," Emma said immediately.

"Language," Mother snapped without looking up.

"That's not language," the older sister muttered, but she lowered her voice.

Across the table, his youngest little sister, Aerin, met his eyes. She sat too straight for eight years old. Malik reached for his water and took a sip, buying himself a second.

"I could take you sometime," he added to Greyson. "If you want. Maybe you can meet my team."

His brother's eyes widened. "Really?"

Father's gaze flicked to Malik for the first time, brief and unreadable. Mother's eyes stayed on her plate. "Heroes need to focus on training. You should not have the time to show little kids around, unless you're a publicity hero," she said, soft but firm. "And you're not. Eat."

Malik nodded, shoving another spoon in his mouth while listening to the kids bicker about whose turn it was to wash the pan. He listened to Father correct the older one's tone. He watched Mother take another sip of wine.

"I found something today," he said lightly.

His father didn't look up. "If it mattered, your leaders

would handle it."

"They didn't even read it. I tried to show them."

"Then it doesn't matter nor exist," his mother replied. The table quieted. "Are you finished?"

Malik shook his head. Aerin's fork moved again as nothing had happened. She took a bite, chewed slowly, and distractedly nodded once at something his older sister said.

His mind pulled a memory forward.

Aerin's door had been cracked open, only enough for the hallway light to spill in that night. Malik had been walking past with a clean stack of towels, already halfway to the laundry room, when he heard a small, choked breath and a tiny voice kept trying to swallow back sobs.

He paused.

Inside, Aerin sat on her bed with her knees pulled tight to her chest, face turned into her pillow to muffle it. When she heard the floor creak, she snapped her head up so fast her hair stuck to her wet cheeks. Her eyes had been red, but her voice came out flat anyway. "Go away."

"Hey," Malik said softly, setting the towels down. Stepping closer, he kept his hands visible. "What's wrong?"

She'd wiped her face hard with her sleeve, furious at the evidence. "Nothing."

Malik sat on the edge of the bed anyway, careful not to touch her unless she let him. He knew she hated that. "I know something's bothering you."

"No, I don't need your help. It doesn't matter." Aerin scooted away from him. "No one cares, anyway."

"I do. It matters to me. Is it about school?"

"It's none of your business," his little sister bit back and turned. "Just... go away Malik. I'm not in the mood right now."

"Alright..." Malik rose slowly, even though every part of him wanted to stay and hold her. "Alright. I can tell something's bothering you. If you don't want to tell me, that's okay. Just know that I'm here for you, okay?" He made his way to the door.

Wiping her eyes with her sleeve, Aerin whispered after him, almost angrily, like the sentence itself was humiliating: "Don't tell Mom."

At the dinner table now, Aerin lifted her water cup with steady hands as she'd never cried in her life.

"Remember to be home Friday, Malik." Father picked up his plate and silverware, along with Mother's. "We're going out."

****

In his seat, Malik looked around the conference center. About two dozen people gathered around a table, including him. Leor and Shanessa sat on his side, and across sat a few kids from class, including Reed. The kid did nothing but stare at his fingers, casually leaning on the table.

"Welcome in, my name is Mr. Atherly," a middle-aged man said. Electricity ran in arcs across his body. He stood next to the head of the table. "I will be conducting the hero management team's meeting today, as they are all elsewhere.

Now, if you please answer when I call your name, then we can get started."

After Mr. Atherly read the list of names, he took out a binder. "Alright, I'll keep this quick. We need to have someone keep watch on students who are flagged, or have a power with a banned level. Obviously, one person can't do it alone, so we assign specifics to each individual. You don't need to go out of your way. Keep an eye on them, make sure they attend class or are doing something worthwhile. If there's nothing to report after a few months, you may switch assignments. If said assigned watch is exceptional, we'll take them off our list.

"Let's see... how about we start with... Tythea Mongo." The teacher pointed a marker at one of the students. "You will keep an eye on her. Tythea's main is Power Manipulation, and she isn't assigned to a hero team." The student nodded.

He continued down the list until half the people in the room were assigned. "Next is Aris Shelia..."

What? Malik jolted up. *Why her?* Mr. Atherly made eye contact with him. *No, no, please don't pick me. She refuses to trust anyone. If I get chosen, she'd think this entire time, everything I've done was a lie—*

"Malik Styri, you will—"

"No!" He stood immediately. Leor shook his head, making Malik recoil. "Sorry for the outburst, sir." He locked eyes with the teacher. "But I refuse to watch her. Please assign me someone else."

"Someone else you say?" Mr. Atherly scratched his head. "Ah, no worries. This type of thing happens all the time, especially if there's a conflict of interest." He pointed across from Malik. "Let's have you take his place."

The student lit up like a light bulb, his eyes flashing red-orange. His brown mullet pulled over the edge of his shoulder as he faced the teacher. "I would love to."

Him? Malik had to look away to hide his face, catching his leader Shanessa gave him a quick look and nod. *I have to tell Aris that he's—*

"Thank you for coming to such an early meeting today. That will conclude our talk. Remember our hero code, and for all those in this room, anything that's said in here will die here. No word gets out. Keep the peace as you leave. Good day."

Chapter 10

~I should've known better~

ARIS SHELIA

Rough wind battered my hair, sending it into a tangled mess behind me. I tried pulling up my suit's hoodie but to no avail. Next to me stood Taavi, focused on the distance. Clouds spiraled around the center of the city, growing tighter as each hour passed. Additional cottonball clouds rolled over, darkening the landscape to almost twilight. Lightning occasionally split across the sky, followed by the guttural growl of thunder, threatening an onslaught of rain.

Earlier today, Taavi unveiled what she'd been whipping up the past year. Well, she didn't make it; she commissioned it anonymously. Truth be told, I had no idea who made it, but it was cool. The suit appeared all black, aside from the iridescent accents of purple, green, and silver. It felt lightweight, paired with padded boots, grippy gloves, and a Bluetooth headpiece strapped inside a helmet with faint glowing lines that resembled veins.

After summarizing a few of its capabilities, Taavi shoved it to me so I could figure out the rest. It fit me great, like memory foam.

With a wave, she leapt and approached the endless lines of old solar panels. I walked after her, and the rain broke, repelling off my suit. Metal poles lay discarded between each row, giving off such a strong tang I could almost taste it. Probably set there for a future project. Taking the first one, I lifted it against an electrical grid. It wobbled, and I held it firmly, waiting. Even through my suit, I could feel the hairs on my arm and head trying to stand.

Taavi knelt and pried open one of the boxes, removing some wires with the hand covered by a white-spiked golden glove. She ripped out some rubber, then stood back.

A bolt of lightning struck, sending an impact through my gloves and boots with a deafening *boom*. A tingle worked its way through my arms, with bright light searing into my vision, dimmed only by the helmet. Sparks erupted from the solar panel, extending down the line and frying them like a burnt piece of toast. I dropped the pole, puddles splashing beneath my boots as I returned to Taavi.

"I can't use my powers in this storm," she informed me, twisting a bronze ring on her middle finger. "But I'll still help where I can."

I nodded, pulling my hood up again. It stayed for a few minutes as we made our way to a boarded-up building nestled at the edge of town. Rotting beams, broken glass, and cracks ran along the walls.

Reaching toward the shadows, I called them in and released them like a bow. The old wood and drywall split in half, folding over with a groan and crumbling, demolishing the entire building within seconds. A plume of dust mushroomed, dying quickly from the wind and rain.

With a shake of my head, I smiled and glanced at the gathering swirling clouds overhead. *This is a great idea to encourage building something new.* We targeted several more abandoned buildings, crushing them like fall leaves as the wind picked up. She kept hidden, on watch, while I destroyed, and the thunderstorm persisted with flashes. I found it odd that so few people lived at the edge of the city, frantically hiding in the confines of old, unstable places. Though it did make our job easier to not be seen.

After we reached the second-to-last building, I faced my city from its roof. Dark clouds growled above, feeding into each other. They formed a spiral, snaking down into the center of our city, growing in size until it was a thick tornado that twisted and turned. Heroes frantically flew away and around it, debris flinging everywhere. The tornado churned, ripping apart anything in its path with so little effort. The heroes flew in the opposite direction, while others set up contraptions below.

Hail struck down, switching to rain, then back to hail. Lightning strikes illuminated the city in eerie flashes. I could almost make out the screams and sirens above the pounding roar. People ran from temporary shelters to a more permanent, concrete cover, clutching children and shielding their faces. I stepped forward, eyeing the faint outline of my old house.

My lips split apart slightly. *I know they're not in our house, but what if Micha is within reach of it? Or my mother? It could kill them and I'd have no clue.*

Could I help?

By my old house, a group of heroes huddled in conversation, sheltering under the branches of a thick willow tree. None of them appeared to be acting, almost as if they had given up. Well, every so often, one would dart out to check and clear the tornado's path of animals or people, but other than that, nothing.

No, my mother and Micha will be safe. Our heroes will have to ensure that, since they're citizens... This storm is a good thing. My lips curled into a tight, forced smile. *The city must evolve. We need to figure out how to effectively handle storms like this. Implement new technology, and actually listen to its citizens. I will make them see that.*

"You've done well, dear. See them scramble or cower under cover?" Taavi's voice buzzed in my ear. "They aren't prepared for a simple tornado. What if something worse were to happen? We must help them see."

The building I stood on began to shake as the rain lessened. I pulled my attention from the tornado and leapt to another building as the one I stood buckled, its wood splintering, then cracking, and finally splitting with a snap, falling in on itself in a dusty heap of rubble, the cloud instantly battered down by rain.

"Taavi?" I pressed the button on my headpiece. "Did you do that? Or the tornado?"

"No," she answered, her voice dipping. "But stay there and listen to this." Her com turned off for a second, then statically came back to life.

"Hello! This is Sandra live from the capital, where an F4 tornado touched down! This is the first time in a century this has happened within city limits. As you can see, our heroes are handling it 'well.' There's no need for panic. Oh, we just received a flood warning. Wait, I got another- what's that in the distance?" I glanced around and saw a camera on a roof, several buildings down, focused on me. I dropped into a crouch, pulling my hood up.

The camera's lens felt like a spotlight burning through the hail. I could hear Sandra's voice crackling. "Can this be? Either that's a new villain, or Nyctara is out in the open. Is she aiding the heroes, or is she behind this destruction?" My stomach twisted.

I turned, but Taavi's voice cut in my ear. "Wait. They see you. Good, let them think it was you."

My fist clenched as I flicked my fingers, using the shadows emitted from the streetlights to attack the skeleton buildings beneath and around me, focusing on the supports or metal bindings and stripping them away. A gust of wind struck me, and the tornado shifted, seemingly standing in place.

"It seems as if she's using the storm to her advantage! Where are our heroes? Are they too held up by the tornado to intervene? Those who have mastered wind—" The headpiece cut out for a second, then the speaker's voice staticed back in with a plain, almost dull tone. Like an overlay. "Authorities warn to take shelter in secure, designated basements. Stay clear of any windows or loose items. Report any sightings of off behavior to the number below. Rest assured, the heroes have things under control."

"Taavi," I hissed. "What's the plan now? I think the camera's still on me. They suspect I'm Nyx. We need to leave."

"You've given them what they need to see," she replied. "Go, I'll be behind you."

Chills crept down my spine, like the eyes weren't just of

the camera. I leapt down as a beam of light pierced me, absorbed into my suit with a flash. I ducked behind the cover of a nearby building's debris, peeking around the corner to see Lighter, a famous superhero with an iridescent rainbow suit, land. Right behind him was his team, Emozer and Plymouth. My breath came in ragged gasps as the storm raged, pelting the heroes. I backed away slowly.

A faint cry came from my right, almost swallowed by the wind.

Sliding to a stop, I scanned the debris, frozen in place. The rubble, hundreds of feet away, shifted, and a small hand emerged from beneath the fraying wood and drywall. A boy, no older than Micha, moved some splinters, revealing his pasty face streaked with mud.

Run. Leave him, a voice that sounded like a branch off of mine whispered in my mind, *you've done enough. The heroes will take care of him.*

Taking a deep breath, I moved before I could stop myself, lifting the debris with the shadows and gently pulling the little boy out as the crunch of gravel came nearer.

He stared up at me on his knees, lips quivering. "Are you... a hero?"

"Don't worry, you'll be okay." I crouched and hugged him briefly before retreating a few steps.

Standing, he stumbled after me and fell again with a cry, catching the nearby heroes' attention. I stepped further, my eyes finding Lighter's as he sent a beacon into the sky, bouncing off his deceptively 'white' suit. The other two heroes approached. Plymouth shouted in Spanish, something about hurting the kid, and jabbed a finger at me. The other with bold eyeliner, Emozer, bolted for the little boy while the other two fanned out and advanced.

Another gust of wind almost knocked my hood off, but I caught it, turned, and bolted. Weaving through the wreckage, a small boulder flew past me, missing my head and exploding on the ground. Another struck me in the side with a crunch, crumbling upon impact as if the rock had only been smushed dirt.

The headpiece buzzed back on with the news lady, Sandra's, voice. "The tornado is letting up. There's Altruistic right now! She's circling the twister the other way. And people are already leaving their buildings to watch."

Altruistic has emotion powers. I recalled from school, sliding into a roll under a slanted wall. Another rock flew at me and struck me in the same spot at my side, exploding into jagged pieces. A radiating ache bloomed. *Including being able to affect a large group's mood. But she can only do a few hundred people at best.* The crunching of gravel behind me signaled that only one of the heroes followed. *Why is Sandra acting as if Altruistic's the reason for the tornado going away?*

A wall of asphalt shot up before me, about ten feet tall and tens of feet wide. I grinned, easily scaling it and using it to jump onto the side of a building. Throwing my head over my shoulder, I remembered that the mask changed my voice. An idea struck me, stemming from Taavi's training.

"Esta zona está preparada para explotar, creando enormes sumideros y cráteres. O me persigues y me pierdes, o salvas a tu equipo y a ese niño," I lied.

"This area is rigged to explode, creating massive sinkholes and craters. Either chase me and lose me or save your team and that little boy."

The hero threw her hands back, eyes darting around, and paused for a second. Then she *almost* smirked and retreated. Almost as if there's something she knew I didn't.

The air thickened around me, its presence so palpable you could pierce it, tightening around my ribs. I forced myself to climb upward, fingers digging into the warped siding as I scaled the building. Rain slicked the surface, and the shadows I pulled from the edges wavered with my darkening vision like they were slipping. Halfway up, a tremor zipped through my hands from the structure. I paused, breath lodged in my throat.

Wait a minute.

A faint, fleeting pressure brushed the back of my mind, like a tug at the edges of my thoughts, and those fingers were skimming through the surface of my consciousness. I froze, nails scraping the metal seam beneath my hand.

Oh, hell no.

I pulled myself over the ledge, landing low. The storm's roar faded beneath a ringing echo, like my own mind was feeding me back a delayed version of the world. My vision adjusted, shadows pooling without want, the edges of buildings warping as if someone else were adjusting my perception with a dial.

"No," I breathed, sinking lower, willing the fading darkness to form around me. It resisted enough to tell me that whatever had touched my thoughts hadn't fully withdrawn. Or that I relied on it too much.

The dying wind shifted, carrying scents of wet dust and copper, and the thought of the little boy's trembling hands returned with a fierceness that burned my chest.

I bolted, weaving through alleyways and ducking under any cover offered, striking my helmet with the palm of my hand.

Get away from me!

What if... If Micha ever got to see me as anything other than what the little boy thought...

I couldn't live with myself—Stop it! Each step's splash mixed in with the rain and wind, but I couldn't get my mind off that little child.

But I tried and tried. I really did, Mom. I sniffed, from the cold or blurriness of my eyes, I couldn't tell.

This is the only way that has brought me further to reuniting with you than asking ever has. They won't listen to me. They won't listen to anyone.

A warning pulse strained across the back of my skull. I snapped a shadow loose from the vent nearby and let it swallow me long enough to drop into the next alley, boots hitting the waterlogged pavement with a splash that echoed in the narrowing space.

I must make them. You'll both see that, won't you? No one else but you will understand. And you'll tell them, right?

The storm was easing, but my pulse kept climbing with a fear I hadn't let myself feel in years.

If they find out—if anyone finds out—who I am, this is all over. I'll be thrown away. They'd misread me so thoroughly that I could never claw my way back from the story they'll craft. The hell they care about intentions. They only care about results and safety.

"Are you a hero?"

That little boy... He got seriously injured because of me. What if he was—

No, you cannot think like that.

"I know I'm doing this for you, Micha. And mom," I whispered as the wind carried the last remnants of the tornado overhead. "Don't worry, no one has to die. I promise I won't let it get that far. Please stay safe, little one. I'll bring you both back soon and give you the life you deserve."

****

A new silver fence had been built at school, in place of the old one torn apart by the storm. Other than that, not much had been fixed. Branches still littered the field, and a thin layer of mud clung to the edges of the walkway. One window got boarded up. Otherwise, the school looked untouched. It was hard to believe that a tornado had ripped through the city days ago.

I rubbed my side, entering as best I could while suppressing a slight limp.

"She said the water came up past her windows," a girl whispered to her friend near the lockers. "I don't believe it, but she seemed so convinced."

"My dad also said the power's been out downtown," the

other replied. "It's been three days! It makes no sense. How have the heroes not fixed it yet? Do you think we're hearing rumors?"

"They probably don't know what to do. Did you see that one guy? What's his name? He just flew around in circles during the storm."

Flooding? Power's still out? The bitterness in their tones made me pause. *They're right about the heroes, though.*

"Or busy shoveling rubble. Our professors are wanting us to help them out. I plan to do it after school today, if I can."

"We're lucky it wasn't worse," a third picked up. "What if it became a fire tornado or watersprout? If Nyctara really did cause it, who's to say those aren't next on the list?"

The end of the day drew quickly, and I found myself wandering the hallway, listening to music. In about an hour, I would head out and meet Cyril at a warehouse to plan the third jewel heist.

I turned the corner toward the library, where I found Malik looking at his phone. *Is he not training today?* He glanced up as I approached, his blue eyes dancing.

"Hey— woah, you okay?" Malik asked, eyebrows furrowing. "You seem to be favoring your side."

I straightened instinctively. "Yeah, I'm good. Are you not training?"

He raised an eyebrow and drew out the word, "Right. So I suppose you always walk like a newborn horse?"

I shook my head, letting out a slow breath. "Hilarious. I

ran into something during the storm. Nothing more than a bruise." I rubbed my eyes and pushed past him.

"Hang on." My breath was loud in my ear. "Sorry, Aris, I didn't mean to, um, irritate you. You know I'm here if you need—"

"Damn it, Malik," I cut in, spinning to face him. "I'm just tired and tripped, okay? Mind your own damn business."

He hesitated, and I thought he'd press the issue, seeing that my story changed. Instead, he stepped aside, his light blond hair shifting. "Alright. Take care of yourself, then."

My mouth opened slightly. As he began to leave, I found myself calling out before I could stop it. "Malik." He turned, raising an eyebrow. "Is... your family safe from the storm?"

Malik nodded thoughtfully. "Yes, thank you. If you want to, the team and I will be under the tree tomorrow. You're always welcome to join, even if you don't want to talk."

He exited as I stared after him, my hands limp at my sides. I almost went after him. Hell, if it wasn't for my side... I might have.

The realization made me recoil. I snapped my gaze away. Would he become a 'villain' to save his younger siblings, too? Would he help me?

Why would he?

His irritating persistence to befriend me isn't surprising. It doesn't make him trustworthy or any more willing to help my cause. No, what was surprising was that despite the inner voices, the unnamed yearning inside me nearly prevailed. I almost said yes.

****

As I walked toward the courtyard, a group of younger kids ran past me. One tripped, falling to his knees, and my breath caught. He looked up, his wide eyes brimming with tears. My fingers twitched at my sides as if nudging me to offer a hand. Like he wasn't just some random kid on a field trip. He was Micha.

My little brother sat cross-legged on the floor, crayons scattered around him as he drew another 'hero'.

"Look, Aris!" he exclaimed, holding up a brightly colored stick figure with ashy hair. "This one's you. You're a mix of a Water, Mental, and Shadow knight!"

I couldn't help but smile. "I don't look like that."

He scrunched his nose. "You will when you get superpowers. And you'll save everyone, even when they don't like you."

"Even if they don't like me?" I repeated, crouching down. "What kind of hero does that?"

Micha shrugged, his expression a little too serious for a six-year-old. "The best kind, duh."

The kid fled with his friends at his side. I gripped the strap of my bag tightly, my knuckles white as I forced the memory down. Tears welled in my eyes, but I blinked them back.

An emptiness reseized its home in my chest. No, it was

something bigger than that, growing into an endless pit with no light. I could feel a hand reach out inside me, grasping for another, begging, only to be swallowed and passed by like a tree. To be mocked for even thinking of that kind of hope. Left with only air as its company. Others, people like Malik, would have their hands held and pulled out than taken care of. They would notice him. But who's supposed to take mine, lost in an abyss of dark sea?

Kids had friends who stuck by your side. They made them so easily and freely like rules and doubts had no hold.

I swallowed. The rest of the courtyard displayed obnoxiously colorful banners all around, their hero slogans faded and rain-streaked. A group of students gathered near the largest banner of heroes, still intact on the wall. "I can't believe Altruistic was there," one said. "She practically stopped the tornado by herself!"

Don't they know her powers are Emotion?

"What about that other one? Lighter and his team? He's so cool! His team must've caught Nyctara in under an hour? Or was it ten minutes and then an hour to clean up the mess?"

I turned away and left for the warehouse. The walk took half an hour. I entered through a side door, noting that the vast structure was mainly empty aside from a wall full of maps, pins, and a projector.

"Finally," Cyril breathed. He pointed at the wall of maps like a game show host. "You're late. I was starting to think you balled- bailed? on me."

I stopped mid-step, raising an eyebrow. "Bailed."

"That's what I said. Anyways, we've got it all mapped out."

The warehouse reeked of rust. A thin layer of dust clung to the floor, except for the area near the board where Cyril had been pacing, his footprints cutting a path through the grime. Against the wall floated Taavi.

"I don't recall being on a strict schedule," I answered the earlier comment, taking a stance a few feet away from the map.

Cyril waved at me with a grin. "Relax. We've got this covered. Third jewel, third time's the charm. I've scouted the place, and it's a catwalk. Security's light and the heroes won't know a thing."

"Cakewalk," Taavi corrected. "You're certain of this?"

"Certainly," Cyril said lightly, puffing out his chest. "I've been watching the place for weeks. Trust me, it's practically begging to be hit." He pointed to a part of the map marked with an unnecessarily large red circle. "They're so focused on rebuilding after the storm that they've left their precious jewel unguarded. It's almost too easy."

"Almost," I muttered under my breath, stepping closer to the wall. The map looked sloppy, with notes scrawled in rushed handwriting and pins placed with no real logic. His 'scouting' felt more like a guess. *Two stones had been stolen already. Shouldn't security be high?* "What about the heroes if we encounter some?"

"They're stretched too thin. Tornado, flood damage, power's gone, and who knows what else. They won't have the manpower to deal with us. Besides," he added, pumping his fists and pointing at himself with his thumbs, "they'll never see me coming."

I folded my arms. "And you're not underestimating them? 'Cuz underestimating heroes tends to backfire."

"Come on. Have a little faith." He laughed. "I've done this kind of thing before."

Taavi brushed her fingers over the pins. "Give him a chance. He knows more than he lets on."

"Alright. But if this goes wrong, it's on him."

Cyril clapped. "Great! Tonight we'll slip into the techy museum, and I'll use my puzzle skills to get through any defenses, forming my own for the police people to get through. If needed, I can transform back into President Coast, or we can just say we're here for the museum tour. And you'll use your shadows to cloak us and snatch the jewel. Then we'll be out of there in no time!"

"You're... planning to transform into President Coast if things go wrong?"

"Exactly. Who's going to arrest the President? It's foolproof!"

"It's something, alright." I pinched the bridge of my nose, suppressing a sigh.

Taavi drifted from the map. "Cyril's abilities are... suited for this kind of mission. I wouldn't have chosen him if I didn't believe he could handle it."

I sighed, glancing between the two of them. "Okay, just don't do anything stupid."

"Got it," he said with a mock salute.

"You'll meet at the museum entrance at midnight," Taavi nodded. "Aris, scout the area as soon as you arrive. Cyril, keep your abilities subtle. No unnecessary risks, understood?"

"Absolutely. This is going to be a piece of cake. Get it? From the cakewalk?"

While Cyril launched into more rambling explanations of his 'foolproof' backup routes to avoid cameras and distraction ideas, I caught Taavi's eye. She gave me a tiny, knowing smile. Something about this plan, or was it about her confidence in Cyril, felt off. So far, she's given me no reason to doubt her or him.

"Midnight, then," I said, stepping back from the table. "Let's just hope your instincts are as sharp as Taavi claims."

"They are," he answered confidently.

"Don't worry, dear," Taavi called out as I headed for the door. "Everything will go as planned... one way or another."

I glanced back, but she already had her attention on the map again, her fingers tracing invisible paths across its surface. Taking out my earbuds, I placed them in my ear. *One way or another, huh?*

****

Cyril caught the closing side door after the janitor headed back in. He waved at me. His dark blue clothes, sunglasses, and a bandana as a mask were barely visible in the moonlight. I slid behind him, the shadows swallowing us. I finished my patrol of the perimeter, and annoyingly, he was right. Only two security guards waited at the front entrance.

Fixing his blond comb-over, Cyril pulled some of it in front of his face as he carefully shut the door. His brows furrowed. "Did you know that most of the grease in your hair comes from your hands, not your scalp?"

"Uhm." I blinked, weighing whether or not to tell him that wasn't true. "How about we focus? Where's the jewel? Do you have the blueprints?"

"Why on earth would we need a blueprint?" He shook his head. "Can't we just use our phones' GPS?"

You have to be kidding. I dragged my hand down my face, the black gloves rough. *Okay, so the jewel will either be hidden or in a safe that's highly guarded. Likely both.*

The room we entered had a lot of pipes and garbage bins. The first door had a large screen on it, displaying a large passcode and a camera. I covered it immediately as Cyril went up and began typing on the tablet. A deep rumble overtook the room

He chuckled as the door clicked open. "The firewall was so easy to pass. I even had time to set up my own little game for the next person." I blinked at him. We entered the next hall as he put his hands inside his pants pockets. "Also, the network connected me to the next camera and alarms, which led to the surveillance room, so I managed to disable those as well."

"Surveillance room? Where is it?"

"Strangely enough, the main floor."

The corridor stretched ahead, made of polished metal tiles. Holograms shone above us, showcasing advertisements for the museum's latest exhibitions.

Cyril hummed an off-key, cheerful tune as he led the way up the stairs. "You know, I once read that if you hum a song, it confuses security systems. Throws off the sensors or something."

I tried to not roll my eyes, reaching the top of the steps where the floor expanded to a sweeping view of the holographic museum. The main floor sprawled out beneath a massive, domed ceiling made of reflective glass that refracted faint blue light. Exhibits floated with artifacts that ranged from ancient cracked pottery to futuristic gadgets.

"Look at that! A real-life hoverboard," he exclaimed, pointing at a display.

"That's a prototype from the 2020s," I said. "And it doesn't even hover properly." I gestured at a wall of photos. "Why not look at the advances in dream engineering or medicines?" He already pulled well ahead before I finished speaking. I sighed.

We moved toward the central exhibit, and the security measures became more apparent. A massive glass case rose from the tall platform with a red jewel inside. A thick, tangled web of red laser beams surrounded it, their paths crisscrossing in erratic patterns.

"It's just like in the movies. Do you think we can just jump over the lasers?"

"No?" I glanced at him, crouching behind the nearest display. "Hang on, do you think I could use my light absorption to—"

Cyril knelt beside me. "Absolutely not." His eyes flicked to the lasers. "These are motion-triggered wards, made to look like lasers, running on a rotating clock that resets every 41 seconds. Disable it or use your powers mid-cycle, and you'll trigger an alarm and traps. They thought of that already. We need to time it perfectly."

I blinked at him. "You got all of that by watching?"

"Yeah, like I said, I know what I'm doing," he replied before gesturing for me to focus. "You handle the panel, I'll time the rotation. Then I'll use the lasers to set up a trap." He pulled out a sleek pocket watch-like contraption, tapping on its surface until a small display lit up. "The system's cycling now. You've got ten seconds."

I tightened my grip on my dagger and nodded. *I can't believe I'm trusting him.*

"Three... two... one," Cyril murmured. "Go."

I dove under two lasers into a roll, avoiding another three sweeping past. Another set of lasers flickered to life, but I twisted sharply to avoid them, landing in a crouch in front of the open wire box on the wall. I sliced two of the wires with my dagger, and the lasers cut out.

Cyril walked over with a large grin, taking my position. He played with the wire box to disable alarms as I headed toward the jewel, passing two pillars into an open space. Another two leaned against the further wall. The red beryl's surface gleamed like molten fire, with a label on the pedestal holding no information on its correlation to Shelby's Crown. In fact, it wasn't even labeled as a magic object.

A thrill shot through my spine as I extended my hand. The case disintegrated at my touch, and I reached for it, but my hand passed through, and the image faded like smoke, wisping into spirals.

"What the hell?" I hissed, my voice echoing.

A voice snickered from above, "Well, 'bout time you showed up."

My head snapped upward. I backed towards Cyril as five figures emerged, and a sixth dropped from a glass-like panel hanging on the ceiling. All of them wore hero suits and masks, but I knew exactly who they all were. Her voice was unmistakable.

Great. Shanessa twisted her white and gold gloves, stepping in front of the group. I quickly lowered my polarized lenses. *If this was a trap, why them? Why not Lighter's?* Their outfits didn't match either, like they were all loners who joined together at the last minute.

"Alright, listen up. We don't want no fuss. Just give up, and we'll help ya out."

"Or," a deep voice interjected, "ya could go fight us and see where that lands ya." Leor strode to Shanessa's side. His suit shone a mix of fire-toned colors with silver-lined cracks. A stronger warmth radiated from him, brushing my face but bouncing off the rest of my suit.

"Escape plan?" Cyril whispered to me; his voice wavered yet distorted through his mask. He straightened and held up his hands. "Hey guys! I'm sure this was all just a misunderstanding, you see. We were just here to explore the museum—"

A little ways behind Leor's shoulder, Drystan shifted his weight, arms casually behind his head. "Ya think we're idiots or what?" His voice crossed as light, almost teasing. He leaned forward slightly, earning a sharp glare from Leor.

"Vortex," Leor drawled out.

Drystan, sorry, *Vortex*, eyes widened but he took a half step back. "Relax. I'm just keepin' things lively."

"If we keep actin' all lively, somebody's gonna get hurt," Shanessa said, flexing her fingers. "Stick to the plan. No messin' around."

Getting out of here might be easier than I thought. I glanced at Cyril. *Actually, with him it might be impossible. Especially when I don't want to hurt them.*

Another figure, Gracelyn, backed near the edge of the group, wore a black suit with blue and purple accents. She fidgeted, her eyes darting nervously between me and Cyril. "Are we sure this is a good idea?"

"We ain't have the time," Shanessa replied curtly, her eyes never leaving me. "If you're too scared, just step back and let the rest of us take care of Nyctara and her friend."

Gracelyn flinched but said nothing, her fingers tightening into fists. Beside her, Arlene placed a hand on her shoulder as her phantom sword flickered into existence before vanishing.

Malik also hovered near the back beside Arlene, his blond hair rippling. His piercing blue eyes, drawn to me, matched his blue, green, and white suit. Leor shot him a sidelong glance, the faint clenching of his jaw hinted at irritation. Shanessa's lips pressed into a thin line, but she nodded, lowering her hands.

I shot a glare at Cyril, silently willing him *not* to turn into anyone or make the situation worse. *We won't win this if we fight. Or if you reveal that power, so please don't escalate.* I examined the area briefly, only finding three exits. The ceiling, the one we came from, and one across the room. *Either way, I'll make a way out for you.*

Drystan and Malik should be more predictable than the other four since I've trained with them. Perhaps I can use that to my advantage. But I must be careful of Shanessa and Leor. And Gracelyn.

"Who are you guys?" I asked.

"That there is Shanessa, and I'm Leor. We lead the Aegis." He gestured with a thumb to her and took another step forward. "You're the new notorious Nyctara, ya? Thought ya worked solo."

"I do," I replied coldly, shifting into a defensive stance.

"Funny, don't look like it." Leor raised his hand, a flicker of flame sparking at his fingertips. "Last chance. Hold out your hands for cuffs or we'll make ya regret stickin' 'round."

"Funny," I echoed, "I was just about to say the same thing."

Cyril groaned beside me. "Do we really have to antagonize the man with fire powers?"

I brought the shadows close, shifting in front of him. Drystan cracked his knuckles, shifting his weight as if warming up for a sprint. His teammates' stances varied around, like they expected us to act first. *Just don't hurt them.*

"Alright, fine." Cyril stepped forward with his hands raised but stopped when I extended my arm. "Let's talk this out—"

A dazzling beam of light shot toward us. I barely had time to raise a shadow wall, the impact rattling through my arms and sending me stumbling.

"Not much for talkin', huh? Reminds me of you." Cyril dropped into a defensive crouch.

"Focus!" I hissed, gritting my teeth as Leor unleashed a wave of fire. It rampaged against the shadow wall like molten waves, the intense heat pressing against my face. The shadows wavered, almost buckling. They were diminishing rather quickly from the onslaught of lights.

A blur in my peripheral vision signaled Drystan placing himself between us and the closest emergency exit, stopping at the foot of a fully extended maintenance lift. Some of the light pierced through the wall, and Cyril covered his face, letting out a yelp.

Don't hurt them. I won't hurt them.

I twisted, curling part of the shadows into various weapons, and flung them at Arlene and Gracelyn. They avoided them easily, Gracelyn spinning away as Arlene replaced a hand on her friend's shoulder.

I need to separate them.

Meanwhile, Shanessa darted around, pulling scraps of

metal chains and wires from nearby exhibits, weaving them into a crackling, glowing type of net.

"Nyctara!" Leor shouted, lobbing multiple balls of fire at me. I jumped to dodge, but he saw and sent another one inches from my head. "What do ya say, put up a real fight, will ya?" Some of the scrap metal Shanessa discarded to the floor floated to him, snapping into place, mixing with the heat to form an exoskeleton.

There's no way I can face him, all of them head on. Cyril turned back to the box and began fidgeting with it. I shot up more walls around us, wishing he wasn't just wasting time. Gusts of wind came from above—and God who knows where?—knocking us back and forth like ping-pong balls as if the tornado itself had taken hold. I stumbled and twisted mid-fall, slashing through a hanging hologram.

A foreign, splitting headache struck me, and I gasped, letting go of a wall briefly to meet Gracelyn's yellow eyes. She was the only one whose powers I did not know fully, but I could guess her main one. It matched Altruistic's. Emotion manipulation.

She picked up a jagged piece of an already destroyed mace, hurling it at me with supernatural precision. It struck not my head, but squarely in my shoulder, unable to pierce through the fabric but managing to send a fiery jolt of pain radiating through my arm.

"Damn it." I clutched my shoulder, inhaling sharply.

"Hold still, sweetie," Arlene taunted. Letting go of Gracelyn, she summoned a phantom sword. Her grey suit with pink accents reflected its faded glow, going well with her hawk cut and mask. Her eyes darted at Cyril.

Gracelyn already had another object in her hand, chucking it at me and missing by a wide margin this time, straight into a pillar.

The concrete cracked, pieces falling off and landing at my feet. Sizzling fire and light shot and clashed against the shadows, the temperature fluctuating wildly from Malik feeding Leor's flames with wind. Cyril got knocked beside me, his sunglasses and bandana slightly askew, muttering something incoherent as he tried to go back to the laser panel.

I dodged another beam that sliced past my head while diverting a knife aimed at Cyril. I snapped, "Do something!"

"Finished!" Cyril shouted, his hand fumbling for the small device strapped to his wrist. His voice dropped an octave. "Cover me. Ten seconds and they can't follow us."

I squatted, taking a decent chunk of the rough pillar and chucked it. It collided with Shanessa's net just in time, sending sparks flying as the wires enfolded it. Cyril's fingers flew over the device's controls. Gracelyn darted forward and hurled a small metal sphere. It collided with the ground near Cyril, exploding into a blinding burst of sound and light. He let out a strangled cry and fell backward, dropping the device and clutching his head.

"Cy-" I caught myself.

Leor's flames surged, a searing wave that knocked me off my feet. My shoulder throbbed, and my vision swam. The warm air fought with my lungs, almost visible as if swirling.

Pulling myself up, I brushed my hand on the wall away

from the light, using it to summon more daggers. They aimed at Drystan and Malik, whose eyes were still glued on me, but I immediately hurled them toward the ceiling instead, severing several of the light fixtures and plunging part of the room into darkness.

"Nyx!" Drystan roared. My night vision set in, and I barely dodged as he lunged, his fist smashing into the wall behind me with enough force to crack it. At the same time, he swept his leg, knocking me off balance. In a tight turn, he punched my side, sending stars dancing in my vision. Another fist aimed at my head, but slower and I caught it, shoving it back. *Why'd you hesitate? I don't want to fight you, either. But you have no clue who I am.*

I stumbled toward Cyril, grabbing his arm and dragging him upright. He groaned.

"On your feet," I growled

"Wait, I just need—"

"No time!"

The room stretched wide around us. My heart raced. Behind laid a shattered pedestal, three exits forming a triangle across the marble floor. Above, the vaulted glass dome loomed, with a vent adjacent to it. *There. We can use the maintenance lift from earlier...* Summoning every ounce of strength, I pulled Cyril with me, propelling us as much upward as possible. At the lift cowered the janitor from earlier, lying flat against the floor. I rebounded off of it as he cried out and up to the vent cover. It rattled loose. *Leor wouldn't try to kill us if we got in. And I'm thinking that man can be useful.*

"Get back here!" Drystan shouted, leaping toward us,

but his fingers missed by inches as I dragged Cyril into the tight space above. The muscles in my body protest hotly, but the adrenaline overrode whatever fatigue settled over.

Glass shattered below, ricocheting off the walls from what I can only assume to be the glass-like panel from earlier.

Sending the shadows to cover the vent, and others toward the lift, I pushed Cyril forward. He held out his hand, and suddenly we were floating, the space expanding drastically into an old catwalk maze. In his other hand was the device, and he clicked a button, tucking it back in his pocket. *I thought he dropped that. Did I not see him pick it back up?*

"You have air powers?" I guessed roughly, rubbing my shoulder. "Actually, I have no idea what your main is."

"No," he laughed breathlessly. "Mental. Telekinesis is what I'm using right now and it's giving me a splitting headache. Though the 'puzzle' I set with the ward and other security features should keep them away from us for a minimum of ten minutes."

We burst out into the cold night air. Every inch of my body ached, pain radiating from my shoulder and ribs. Cyril ran ahead of me, and a few streets later, we paused in an alleyway. His bandana, pushed up to reveal a pale, sweat-soaked face.

"Well," he gasped weakly, taking off the sunglasses. "That could've gone better."

"You think?"

Letting out a long breath, Cyril ran his hand through his hair and shifted his weight from foot to foot. He opened his mouth to speak, then stopped, his eyes lingering on me for a moment too long then darting away. "You shielded me. It must've hurt. Are you okay?"

"Peachy." I ignored his weird behavior and rubbed my side. *We failed. I failed. What should I tell Taavi?* "Let's head back."

He stayed quiet as I turned and walked, the cold night air biting at my exposed face. The earlier energy vanished, replaced by an awkward silence that I didn't have the strength to break.

We didn't have a choice. I rubbed my shoulder. My free hand instinctively curled into a fist, my nails digging into my palm. *They hurt me without a second thought.*

People you knew hurt you when you didn't even hurt them.

I winced as we walked. *Maybe they thought I would hurt them first? Since I'm a self-proclaimed villain. They don't know it's me.*

The other voice returned. *They wouldn't care if they knew it was you or not. If they're willing to hurt you, why not protect yourself? After all, they started it.*

My pace slowed, though Cyril didn't appear to notice. He rubbed his temple repeatedly. *I... I guess. It's self-defense.*

Don't you think if they're willing to harm you, they'd also be willing to kill you?

My grip tightened, twisting the fabric beside my shoulder I held. *No. Heroes don't kill; otherwise, they'd be no better than the villains they fight. Unlike us, they have a code they abide by.*

Except... they may if it means saving many others. If it means protecting themselves and those they love. You saw it in their eyes tonight, didn't you? The people you know will do whatever it takes.

I bit my tongue and eyed Cyril. He didn't look at me. My fingers uncurled slowly, and I nodded to myself.

Bottle it. This was a one-time mistake.

I'm trying to inspire advancement. That's all this is. And if they're willing to burn me to stop me, I have every right to fight back and protect myself. It's all for their benefit, really.

Chapter 11

ARIS SHELIA

The smell of burnt coffee and cinnamon tea struck me as I ascended the stairs. At the table sat Taavi, a cup steaming in her hands. She didn't look up when I entered, focusing on the wall in front of her, lost in thought.

"You're up early," she said almost casually. "Did you have a rough night?"

I didn't answer immediately, tugging part of my sleeves up to reveal blue and black bruises blooming across my arms. More extended under my shirt, though most weren't awful. Her gaze lingered for half a second before returning to her tea.

"You didn't tell me about the Aegis," I replied tersely, curling my fingers. "Did you know about them?"

Taavi set down her cup softly. "I thought that would've been assumed. Why would it be unguarded?"

"You should've said something. We almost got captured

and would've died if it wasn't for Cyril."

Tilting her head, a faint smile tugged at her lips. "Yet, here you are. You made it out alive."

"Barely," I snapped, hitting the table. "How did you know? Do you somehow have a connection with the hero management or something? Tell me."

In a graceful motion, Taavi rose. "You've chosen a path where no one plays fair, and not everything can go as planned. I'm preparing you for the unexpected, child. This is not something that will be handed to you on a silver platter."

My mouth hung open as I searched her face. Her expression remained coldly neutral. Her eyes were unmoving.

"Don't act like this is for my benefit." I shook my head, replacing the sleeves. "I'm not your pawn in some— in some game. You're supposed to be my guardian."

"No, no, my dear. Do not be mistaken," she sighed as if correcting a kid. "I'm simply the guide and counsel to a Queen whom I love. You're free to doubt me, though. It's destined someday you'll hate me, only to realize I'm exactly who I've said I was."

Destined to hate you? I scoffed under my breath. "Yeah, right. In your little prophecy I'm more of your 'necessary evil' than a Queen, aren't I?"

Taavi's smile sharpened, almost pitying. "Labels are for the small-minded. I know how to help you."

That's for me to decide if I want to let you. I yanked my backpack up and shouldered out the door without another word.

****

"Step forward," a stern voice barked over a megaphone, crackling before going dead.

Students lined outside the school like a caterpillar, snaking and reaching the outer fence. They slowly shifted, eyeing the loud *whirring* of the new security drones hovering overhead in pairs with minor heroes, their blue lights sweeping over the field. If I so much as wince, I feared the heroes or drones would look too closely in my direction. So I kept my head down, shuffling to hide the ache in my side and shoulder, the cloth of my shirt irritating it with the smallest movements.

Yesterday, the City Council announced that the school was going to expand security measures at Ezrat. They wouldn't exactly say why, perhaps it was a precaution. I at first believed it would be student ID checks or heroes lazily glancing at faces and waving us through. But no. There were scanners, heroes on high alert, and metal detectors as if it was some high-profile event.

The girl in front of me trembled, her hands shaking like leaves in a windstorm. Her eyes darted to the heroes stationed nearby, leaning against the school's metal gates with crossed arms and half-smiles. The way their eyes scanned the crowd felt anything but friendly to me.

"Don't worry," the hero at the scanner drawled, not looking up from the screen. "This is for research. No need to worry, we're safe and under hero protection."

An unearthly bitterness rose in my throat at the words. I swallowed, stepping forward. The scanner beeped as it spun around me, but I kept my face blank.

"Move along." The hero waved, disinterested, gesturing toward the open doors.

I allowed my shoulders to drop and made my way through, passing a bulletin board full of papers and advertisements. One of them, bolded against a pink slip, caught my eye. 'This year, 43% of students transitioned into public administration or non-heroic careers. A stable choice for a brighter and fulfilling future.' *From our school? Aren't we training to be heroes?* I moved on and rounded a turn, climbing up the stairs.

"Aris," Malik called out when I reached the top, arriving at my side. "I was just looking for you. Are you joining us at lunch today?"

I readjusted my bag, the strap digging onto my bruised shoulder. I shook my head, biting back a wince. The urge to hold my side became almost overwhelming. *I need to shove it away. Ignore it.*

"Alright, in case you change your mind, we'll be a bit late," he continued, tugging at the collar of his uniform, revealing a few tattoos spiraling on his neck. "Shanessa and Leor called a meeting. We'll come meet with you afterward."

"Don't take your time waiting." I moved around him, unconsciously touching my side.

"Hang on," he said, face softening when a thought struck him, eyeing my hand, "Did you get hurt? Was it from school? People might think you moonlight as a stunt double if you keep getting injured."

The words caught me off guard. *Does he know it was me last night?* I blinked and squinted at him. *I can't say. But the more he's around me, the more it's likely he'll figure it out.* "What—do you know about stunt doubling?"

He shrugged, a glint shining in his eye. "I dunno," he deadpanned. "I mean, who doesn't want to jump between buildings while simultaneously risking a broken leg to look cool?"

"You mean parkour?" I raised an eyebrow. "Really? Do you spend all your afternoons practicing jumping fences when you can just fly?"

"Nah, just keeping it interesting. I'm more of a strategy type, like chess." I hummed as the bell rang, and he waved. "Well, see you in class."

In my first period, a few people were missing, but it dragged on as normal. Mr Atherly stood at the front, rattling off about general defensive techniques, occasionally getting into specifics like fusion defense last year's learn. The lesson was a similar (if not the same) account of what they've been teaching for years. But even as I took occasional notes, I noticed something seemed off.

"What's the best way to stop a threat?" Mr. Atherly asked, pacing the room with his hands clasped behind his back.

From the back, someone answered in a mundane tone automatically, "Neutralize it before it becomes a big deal then imprison them, ensuring the media knows we're safe."

The teacher froze, his fingers twitching. "Not quite. Preventing threats before they become one is key. But, if you face unavoidable danger, swift action and analysis of the situation while protecting citizens is required. The media isn't the biggest concern."

I tapped my pencil against the desk, my ears perking up. *At the beginning of the year, he would've agreed.* I pulled off my hood.

By the time I arrived at my second period, freshly cut grass dominated the air. Students milled about, stretching, sitting, or leaning in mid-chatter. In the center stood Shanessa in a sweater and dress pants, her blue bonnet hair clip catching the light.

"Line up, folks!"

People clustered, showing Malik on the other side, laughing with someone. He spotted me and brightly jogged over. Not long after Drystan arrived, high-fiving him and shooting finger guns at me.

"Listen up. Today's exercise is a piece of cake. We're mixin' defense and offense. Y'all get two minutes to make it without losin' your partner. Fastest times move up in class rankings." She clicked her tongue. "Work hard, as these trainings will become handy one day."

I felt Malik glance at me after I let out a quick breath. The class made our way back inside the school, through the back, and up to the massive doors encasing the training yard, which shut securely behind us once we were all inside. We filed toward the starting line where beyond loomed the obstacle course, its levels changed from the last time, illuminated by bright sunlight beaming down.

The whistle blew, sending off the pairs about every two minutes. We reached the front, and it blew again, sending

Malik sprinting down the middle.

I sighed, taking off after him and keeping close to his heels. The first section was simple enough, a series of swinging beams. Malik ducked and weaved effortlessly, coming close to being nicked in the shoulder. I got through almost as easily, giving more room to avoid the one he had a close call with. Next, bumpy platforms jutted up and down in an unpredictable manner. Without slowing, Malik jumped to the first one.

Drystan's voice cheered from across the course, "Right on, Malik!"

Malik laughed as he jumped to the next platform. "You watching, Drystan? Need an example on how to not get your—"

As I landed, a barrier shot up between us, distorting the view of Malik on the other side. *Seriously?* I dropped into a crouch, shifting to try and see around the sides. The field was a blurry wall.

"Defense phase!" Shanessa's voice rang from the overhead speaker. "Let's see how y'all adapt!"

I touched the barrier, sending a ripple through it as if it was a liquid. It's not physical, perhaps some kind of energy field from Shanessa that I can't walk through. I stepped back as much as I could without falling, scanning the wall. Off to the side, cannons unveiled themselves. They looked like those pirate ones, but instead of cannonballs, they began raining a type of foamy dodgeball with insane speed.

"Remember, folks, defense ain't just about surviving! It's about controlling the fight!"

At the top of the barrier, I spotted a faint gap. *Okay, I*

think I can make that. I ducked then took a running start, launched myself upward, twisting mid-air to clear it and avoid five projectile balls. My feet made contact with the ground on the other side, but I sprinted to catch up with Malik.

The next challenge was a series of rotating platforms suspended over a pool of murky water. Occasionally, some of the platforms would drop, hanging on for dear life by their edge, then reset slowly. Malik cleared the first platform, waving at me to stay close only for a ball to strike his arm. He swore under his breath.

We finished the section as the whistle blew, ending our time. Malik grinned as we jogged back to the sidelines, his breathing steady and somehow not ragged. I made it back before him.

Drystan jogged over, clapping Malik on the back as soon as he landed. "Told ya he'd kill it! And you too, Aris. Good job!"

I nodded, watching Malik exchange a grin with Drystan.

"Y'all did fine today," Shanessa announced, though her tone suggested otherwise. "But let's get one thing straight. The world's changin'. Heroes can't just sit back and wait to be needed. You're either ready, or you need to step aside."

I blinked at her. Everyone else nodded or brushed what she said off, continuing with hushed conversation. But her expression was serious as she dismissed us. As we headed off, I pulled up my hoodie, refraining a glance back at her.

What's with the teacher's lessons today? They seem to actually be gearing their lessons towards us.

After my third class, I made my way to the tree by instinct, passing by emptying classrooms. Right before an exit, a conversation caught my attention, the door cracked open just enough for their voices to drift out. The noise in the hallway was almost enough to mask it.

"Stop throwing rocks at the training drones," Gracelyn begged, exasperated. "You're not twelve!"

"Look, it's quicker than using my powers," Drystan shot back in his casual voice. "Ain't my fault they're built like tin cans. Should be more realistic if it's for training."

A chair squeaked, followed by Arlene chiming in, "It is less effective. You're going to get us all benched if we don't figure out how to do it properly. That includes the least amount of damage."

"Guys," Malik groaned. I imagined him throwing up his hands. "Take a breath. I don't know how Shanessa and Leor deal with you."

"Hey, at least we're trying." Drystan huffed. "By the way, 'cept for last class, I ain't seen Aris around much. What's up with her? She doing alright?"

There was a long pause. I imagined Malik shifting uncomfortably. "I think she's working through some stuff," he answered slowly, but casual enough to not be marked as cautious.

"Yeah, well, I hope it's worth it. I don't understand you, man. You ain't a hero if you're always runnin' after someone who don't wanna be saved. Or be your friend, for that matter—"

I stiffened, my fingers curling into fists at my sides.

Was that how he saw me? He's wrong, it's not... I inhaled deeply, clenching my teeth and rocking back to my heels then shook out my hands. *No, I don't want friends.* My heart ached, echoing this yearning I have to cut. *You can't trust people. No matter how kind or convincing they are, they'll end up leaving you for someone better. Leave you to do everything alone, needing help or not. Skipping the middle step is better than all those stupid false pretenses of people pretending to care.*

And on the path I'm taking, I'm not sure I want to drag anyone like Malik down with me if they did.

"Why don't you leave her alone?" Drystan continued genuinely. "I think you're bothering her."

"What do you mean?"

"It's clear she wants to not talk. Or anyone's help for that matter. Shouldn't you respect that?"

A pause. "Really? I didn't get the idea that that's what she wants," Malik said, scratching his head. "Some things fly over my head, so I might be very wrong about this, but one of my little sisters is like Aris, so I think that's just how she interacts with people. How she acts and what she wants could be two completely different ideas."

Arlene cut in, "but what if she does want that?"

"If it is, and she genuinely tells me to back off, I'll respect that. I'll stay away. I don't know for certain, but it doesn't seem like the best idea right now. I want to be there in case—"

Before I could decide whether to leave, another voice cut through with her Texan twang. "Hey, y'all!"

Leor's voice followed. "Let's kick this off."

I pressed myself closer to the wall, suppressing a wince from a bruise hitting the metal locker.

"First thing on the agenda," Shanessa said. "Nyctara is stirring up trouble, and we can't brush it off anymore."

"What do you think her reasoning is?" Malik wondered. "Is it to cause trouble? Is she angry at something? That would make her more justified, I think."

"Angry? Don't tell me you're feelin' sorry for her."

"No. Listen, Nyctara didn't appear out of nowhere. What's the reason she's doing this? If we figure that out, perhaps we can talk to her and convince her to step down."

"You serious?"

"Yeah. Shouldn't we look at the whole picture? I feel like if we don't address the root of the problem—"

"We're past that," Shanessa interrupted. "She's downright harmful, and our job's to stop her before the public gives its attention. How many more folks gotta get hurt while we 'talk with her'?"

"Aegis," Leor interjected, with a brief silence following. "'Course she's gotta reason. We all know our system ain't perfect, but the destruction villains turn to isn't a solution. If you want a better world, you gotta build it, then find a way to keep the damage in check without losing what we've accomplished."

"What do you suggest, then?" piped Arlene. Before anyone could answer, I heard her hands clap. "Wait, wait, what if we reframe the whole Nyctara thing? I mean, yeah, she's somewhat dangerous, but what if instead of hunting her down and giving her the attention she's seeking, we make her the centerpiece of a reform effort? Use her as a wake-up call to fix whatever the problem is before someone worse shows up. And it'll help bring back peace if they think the whole thing's intentional. Like a publicity stunt."

Drystan snorted. "A redemption arc? You think she's gonna flash a peace sign and roll with it if we get her to talk?"

"No! That's not what I mean," Arlene stuttered, her words tumbling over another. "I mean, we don't have to make her change. That's unlikely. We could use her to highlight another problem, instead. Like... leverage her actions after the jewels to heighten security. People already listen to heroes, right?"

"That's a risky idea," weighed Leor.

Shanessa dryly added, "I vote we guess where she's striking next and trap her there, then end it for good."

"Well, if we want Ezrat's policies to keep working," Arlene answered, "we're gonna have to fix this Nyctara thing."

"It's not a bad idea," said Malik.

Someone sighed. Leor eventually spoke again, "It's ambitious, I'll admit. But ambition gets messy fast, 'specially if our plan gets leaked or misread. Not only that, if it's approved by the hero management, it will have to be public, so we'll need more than just good intentions to pull somethin' like that off."

"Messy is where the best ideas come from!" Arlene brightly responded. I imagined her smiling.

"And while we're busy with that," Shanessa continued, "what happens to the citizens Nyctara's been hurtin'? Like from the fires and electrical grid. What'll we do when she decides she ain't gonna hide in the shadows no more and unleashes a full-blown attack?"

"Then the stronger our message's gonna be. We'll take her easily. People here need reminders of the wickedness we're holdin' off. Though, Malik brings up a fair point that we gotta figure out what she wants," Leor simply put.

Another person let out a long breath as Malik joined in, "Nyx isn't only a villain. It doesn't seem like she's flaunting her power. Last night, for instance, she didn't hurt us nor seem to want to be seen. There's definitely something bigger there. A reason we're not seeing. Until we deal with that, there will always be another like her."

A long silence overtook them. I shifted my weight, taking out my earbud and putting it away. *Why do you want to know my reasoning so bad, Malik and Arlene?* I bit my lower lip. *Is it because you don't really care unless it stops me and makes you look good?*

"Alright," Shanessa began. "We can debate all day, but the fact remains. We need to show the folks out there that Aegis got what it takes. Whether we take down Nyctara or not, we can't let her change us."

Leor agreed.

"This is the kind of messy I like," said Arlene. Who I assumed to be Gracelyn hummed gruffly in agreement due to her distinct rumbling breath.

"Fine by me." Drystan chuckled, likely with his arms

behind his head and legs crossed.

They want to know what motivates me and reframe it to 'solve' another issue? I swallowed hard, my heart pounding. *I kinda want to tell them. They might take me more seriously.*

That's crazy; the other part of me replied immediately. *After all you did, you'd think they'd believe you? That they'd let you go?* I rubbed my forehead. *No one is on your side. Ever. You know that.*

Right. Malik wouldn't believe it at first. Surprised, yes, but he'd-they'd do anything to stop me. Knowing my reason or not. He'd hate me. I shook my head, breath short. *What do I do then?*

"One more thing, y'all," Shanessa said. "President Coast took a look at our team the other day after a recommendation from the hero and villain cabinet, and I know we're just gettin' started, but you impressed him. He told me he'd get the ball rollin' so we can deal with more important matters... I believe we'll be dealin' with Nyctara more."

Pushing off the wall, I made my way out of the school. The pain in my shoulder and side had dulled, but they still bothered me like an ache that wouldn't go away. I replaced my hood as I exited the premises.

Across the street from the fence gathered a group of young men, playfully shoving each other and shouting. I stopped at the edge, spotting Reed among them.

Great. The sun shone brightly off the bench to their right, hurting my eyes. *Either try to pass him or wait for Malik at the tree.* I rubbed my arm, backing away. *Either way, I'll end up talking to someone. And lunch shouldn't be too much longer.*

Reed's gaze landed on me as I spun, and we briefly made eye contact before I pushed myself back.

I didn't make it far before I heard swift footsteps crunching on the gravel, switching to the sidewalk behind me. "Aris! Hey!" Reed's voice rang out.

I quickened my pace, hoping he'd take the hint and leave me alone. Man, was I mistaken.

"Aw, come on," he called, his voice closer. "What's with the cold shoulder?"

I stopped mid-step, readjusting my backpack. "What do you need?"

He raised his hands. "Relax, I'm just being friendly. Saw you over here brooding by yourself and thought, 'Man, she could use some company.' We used to be friends way back when, after all."

"No need. We were five. Go back to your friends." I gestured to the group watching then spun on my heel, continuing down the grass.

"Harsh." He fell into step beside me, his hands stuffed into his jean pockets. "Besides, ditching you now would make me look bad. People might think I'm slacking on my hero duties despite obviously being a catch."

I rolled my eyes. After a minute further, I stopped and faced him, mindlessly rubbing my side. "Seriously, why do you keep bothering me? Do you win some kind of prize if I don't tell you to get lost?"

He smirked, his hands behind his back. "Nah. I do get

the satisfaction of knowing I'm harder to shake than you'd like. Plus, someone's gotta make sure you don't end up in that villain prison, background *hero*."

"Careful, you might trip over your imagination."

He tilted his head back in a laugh. "Jeez, lighten up. It'd do wonders for your image."

I opened my mouth, hesitating when the light in his blue-yellow eyes died for a second. His gaze flicked to my ribs where my hand still was, his brow furrowing. The look, darkening a shade of blue, almost vanished as quickly as it appeared, replaced by his usual mocking grin.

"Uh, say, you alright there?" he asked, his tone holding a trace of something I couldn't place. "You look like you took a hit. Did you report it?"

"Leave me alone," I snapped, shielding my side from his view. I could've sworn his eyes flashed a clear blue-grey.

"Well, far be it from me to pry," he said. He slowed his pacing to trail after me. "You might wanna be careful. Kinda messes with the whole 'untouchable vibe' you've got going and you could get in some serious trouble. Or people are gonna make connections that's not there, like uh, doesn't Nyctara have shadow powers like you?"

I tightly exhaled, and tugged my hood on with clenched hands, pressing forward. *I'm not sure what started making me his point of interest, or if it paid him for mockery, but if I figure it out I will strangle it with both hands.* His steps, crunching grass a split second after mine. It invaded my mind. His presence felt more like President Coast himself was there over me, only less mature and respectful.

In the distance, a voice called out, seemingly coming from the school. Malik, Arlene, and Drystan approached the field, smiling though Malik had more of a puzzled look on his face and Drystan wore a lopsided grin with an arm around both their shoulders. *There was another during the vault attack. Gracelyn I think? I don't usually see her with them.*

"Oh, hey, it's the cavalry!" Reed said, spreading his arms wide, blocking me partially from their view. "Welcome! Did you have fun in History of Magic, Arlene?"

She waved in acknowledgement, her sleek leather jacket shifting. Her hawkcut was nicely done. The other two didn't pay attention to his comment, just looked at me.

"What's going on?" Malik asked, running a hand through his dirty blond hair.

"Nothing," I said. "His majesty merely graced me with his presence. And appears to be worried."

"Graced?" Reed chuckled quickly, putting a hand to his chest. "I prefer to call it enhancing and 'bonding.'"

Arlene exhaled in what almost sounded like a laugh. She nudged Malik with her elbow. "I'd rather call it annoying, right?"

Drystan smirked, propping up a muscular arm on her shoulder like it was a desk and leaning onto it. "Or maybe he's just workin' on his charm. Though I'd suggest picking a new hobby and or person to practice with."

"Wow, you guys don't give me enough credit. I'm doing my due diligence," Reed said, his brown mullet bouncing as he moved. "According to GMK, heroes are supposed to be welcoming, after all. You should know that."

Malik glanced at me. I shook my head and shifted my backpack higher.

"He's being himself. Not much to it."

"Which is a gift to everyone involved," Reed cut in with a wink. He stepped away, looking back at his friend group still goofing off past the fence.

"Alright then." Drystan clapped his dark hands. "Are we gonna hit that tree or just stand around here all day?"

"Tree. You coming?" Malik nodded at me as he began walking again.

I wish being alone was an option. I sighed and fell into step beside Malik, who easily fell into a light conversation with Arlene about some upcoming training. The prickle on the back of my neck from earlier died down. Drystan joked about Reed finally learning how to be friendly and something along the lines of beating him in agility training. It felt nice enough that I let myself relax a little. Like a tightening strand around my ribs loosened and tension in my neck faded.

Arlene dropped to my side. "Hey Aris, I like your hair and nose ring. It highlights your eyes," she lightly said. "We should do each other's hair sometime." Then she turned and picked back up her chat with Malik.

As if she knew I'd be speechless. And she was right. I instantly looked away, focusing on my feet. The easy warmth of the moment pressed uncomfortably against my ribs.

What would Taavi or Cyril think about this? About me

goofing off? Or that I'm allowing myself to linger too closely with heroes who make it feel easy?

We reached the tree and I ran my fingers over the rough bark, taking off my bag and setting it at its roots. I knew everything I did was for my family. For our future. But everything the Aegis did was so carefree and comfortable. They weren't walking on glass around each other. They trusted one another to be there when they needed it. This team extended their hand to everyone, even to those who won't deserve it.

A pang struck my chest. Here, under the tree offered a small refuge. Its canopy shielded from the onlooking sky, with enough shade to hide and obstruct. But it would never accomplish enough. Not like it is for them. Not with Taavi, who'd fume at me for taking a second. Or with Cyril, who couldn't blend in with these kids to save his life.

Not until those I loved were safe.

****

At my desk, I flipped through the book Taavi handed me. In the corner, alongside some check-in evaluations, sat a few old letters from Micha, before he was taken, and a notebook with a pen at the other edge.

Three more gems. I paused on a page and closed it. *Failed the last time, too. How am I supposed to do this? How does Taavi expect me to? Especially with the updated public security checkpoints and expanding restricted zones?*

Behind Micha's notes was the paper that the girl gave me, with in-depth information about the crown, jewels, and other magic objects. Yeah, the first two directions to the gems were right, no doubt to gain my trust, but the third ended up being a trap. Who's to say the rest won't be? The security would be completely revamped following our last attempt, and the information in this paper has to be outdated by now.

Did Shelby's Crown even do anything or was it a showpiece? All I remember is it being part of the statue I passed every morning. *Why did I even believe it in the first place? I know these kinds of objects exist, but a crown responsible for our peace?*

Pushing back, I let out a long breath. *If I take things into my own hands, Taavi's idea of inspiring conflict or whatever, perhaps that will work out better. After all, I do need to give my little brother and mother a better life. I need to find them and bring them back.* I paused, my grip tightening on the edge of the desk. *No, first I still need to figure out why they were taken by police. I'm no longer powerless to stand aside. Why were they?*

It can't be my Mom's engineering, nor my Dad's job as he's with Steph studying in another country. Not them, so it has to start from somewhere else.

The timing when Taavi showed up appears too convenient. She knew so much about me before I had powers. Her philosophy is reasonable, but how and why did she choose me? Could she not do it herself? I traced the lines on the ceiling. *Those bronze sunglasses she wore the first day we met must've told her something. If they're magic, did they disclose my powers before they surfaced? It would make the most sense since Taavi claimed stealth would be the main reason for success.*

As for not doing it herself... Does Taavi seem like the type to use me?

The other side came stronger. No. *She tested you for*

your growth and left assistance in case you failed. Like Cyril at the ship. She has never tried to hurt you. Only help you.

But what if she had left me to fail? Or will?

She didn't. You can tell she genuinely cares about you.

I run my hand down my face. *I guess. The real people who've hurt me are those who took my family. The heroes. And the kids at school who never batted an eye at me until Malik...* I rested my head on my desk, folding my arms around my head. *What does he want with me? I can't find any logical reason why he's so friendly. So why does he treat me like he cares and thinks I matter? People like him don't just befriend people. There's always a reason. Another person to be saved then discarded as nothing.*

No one can love someone so easily and freely. It's a damn lie. Feelings like that take time and mutual effort and bonding and... And that's not what I get or deserve.

I pressed my nails to the desk, some of the splinters digging into my fingers. *It's not only him, either. His friends, his team are kind to me. I-It must be because he is.* I relaxed my hands. *Because they feel like it's their job, yeah?* I shook my head, suppressing a groan. *Hell if I know. They're not all that innocent. They hurt Nyctara. Nyx. Me. Those 'heroes', the Aegis, harmed me when I refrained from injuring them. Without Cyril, I wouldn't have managed to escape. The whole damn thing was a trap. Yet, with the real me they're... Agh.*

At the edge of my finger lay a pen, which I tightly took and tapped against the desk. *How am I supposed to reunite my family and inspire Taavi's change, alone, against a team, no, an army of superheroes? Trying to stay unnoticed is one thing, but what did that change in the long run? It only made it for the heroes to hide what I'm trying to show our world. No, the only way to properly escalate is if people understand it. If people see who is behind it. Someone to put a name to.*

I have no chance, it's only so long until they capture me. My breath hitched. *But until then, I live in Taavi's house. She took me in, so I will help her and my family. I owe her that, after all.*

A rush of wind brushed the side of my face.

Lifting my head, a drifting piece of paper see-sawed to the desk. I eyed it and examined my room, one of my hoodies swaying on a hanger. I got up and looked under my bed and in the closet. No one.

Returning to the paper, I touch it slowly. Written in messy handwriting across the page, **Meet me outside in a week, if you really are who I think. I have something you might want, sincerely your beloved red-haired confidant.**

Chapter 12

XIOMARA REZET

Bustling with families, couples, and loners, the café brought warm lighting and atmosphere to their table. Xiomara leaned back in her chair, with her legs propped up and crossed on the table corner. Her eyes flitted to her friends, Ezra and Seth Vry mid-banter, while tracing the rim of her glass of iced tea in one hand, making that *shinge.*

A television droned in the background, drawing attention, the anchor speaking fast and clear, "Over in Ezrat, online speculation spreads after the announcement of a masked individual, Nyctara, briefly appearing during a tornado in the center of Ezrat's city. Emergency services confirm that Mala citizens and our local police responded efficiently to storm-related damages, offering aid and assistance in the aftermath. There's no confirmed evidence linking the individual to the tornado itself." The man paused, lowering his microphone. A nearby watcher turned the TV up. "Authorities further note that while the timing was alarming and dramatic, the incident resulted in no confirmed casualties and no lasting threat."

The screen shifted to footage of overturned cars, emergency lights flashing against wet pavement. "City representatives urge the citizens to remain calm, avoid the spread of misinformation, and trust in local protection units. Ezrat remains secure, and the situation is fully contained. Order has always prevailed."

Sharply exhaling, Xiomara rolled her eyes. *No mention of her attempt to steal the red beryl. They're really trying to keep it on the down low.*

Her school managed to get ahold of the footage from Ezrat, but the hero presidents decided it's best not to release it to the public. This, however, didn't prevent Xiomara from copying the file to watch on her own. *The woman surely puts up a fight. Should've sent higher heroes to deal with her though, but what can you do when the whole country is watching?*

"Dude, she's insane," Ezra said, taking a bite of a protein muffin. "You'd gotta admit they're being more or less restrictive on scientists, though. You can legally do a few more things!"

Seth snorted. "The girl's acting like another villain to feel important. She'll get caught and swept out like dust in the wind soon enough."

Chatter around them stilled as he said that. Then it sluggishly resumed. Crumbs from the muffin were wiped away from Ezra's hand as he shook his head. "I doubt it. No one can figure out who she is. It's mad! I don't know what she plans, but if Nyx achieves whatever she wants... what does she want?"

That's what I want to know. Xiomara tilted her head at Seth. "Isn't Nyctara wearing the suit you and your underground scientists made?"

He groaned. "Don't remind me." His hand dragged down his face. "Maren swore she didn't know who the buyer was. It was cool making the exo-suit tech and titanium alloys, yet it falling into Nyctara's hands stands as proof to why laws are in place."

"If I were you, I'd be supporting her," Xiomara pointed out. "If she gets caught, your operation is dunzo. You already have colleagues missing as is."

Patting his brother's shoulder, Ezra nodded. "I have to agree, man. This Nyx gave you business, and she can ruin your life with it."

Rubbing her chin, Xiomara recalled the footage again. *In the fight, Nyx blocked more than attacked. Did she not think staying offensive would give her the best result?*

"Hold up. If we take into account that Nyctara targeted electrical grids and old abandoned structures." Seth tapped his nose. "Do you suppose she'll go after food or water supplies next? If so, we can intercept her and get her to hand the suit back."

Ezra laughed. "Bro, no way she'll listen. Paid for it in full just to give it back?"

Why would she? Sliding her chair back, Xiomara stood. She waved at the brothers before exiting the café, tucking the blue streaks in her blonde hair back. *She really didn't seem like she was intentionally harming anyone. It's strange. Stories with villains in the past always left a strong mark. They used civilians as leverage. This girl... must not mean to be one.*

After a long stroll through Mala, over some deep hills and small marshes, Xiomara entered her apartment. It stood smack in the middle of town, tall and pressed in by end to end cars and other structures. She tossed her keys onto the counter with a loud jingle, then locked the door behind her. *Nyx, huh?*

She turned on the sink, letting the sound of running water fill the room. The cool liquid ran and pooled in her palm, streaking away to the drain.

Xiomara curled her hand, taking the water and forming it into a small, glassy orb. It hovered, shimmering from the window light. She smirked, flicking it to a nearby potted plant, which broke it, causing it to disperse, soaking across the soil.

I've got to figure out what's driving her. Who she is. And I have to do it without the city thinking I'm siding with her. Was she framed at all?

Digging after a figure the government wants to keep under wraps took time. Xiomara thought it would be easy since she started such a long time ago. If she had to specify, her guess was the week Seth joined Maren. But findings were slow, and now it still took her another few days to uncover a trail that wasn't complete garbage. Nyx was elusive, but even she couldn't avoid leaving breadcrumbs. Those breadcrumbs of attacks and targets pointed towards Ezrat being the villain's hometown.

The thought of going back made Xiomara want to shut all windows, lock them, and stay inside the rest of the month. Returning to Ezrat was like returning to war, and after graduating, she joined and left the military for good in her twenties, only to end up in investigative journalism at Hyzrit and traveling to Mala to see her friends. But if Nyx was there, she should be, too.

The quiet train ride went well into the night. Not many passengers rode this late, making it peaceful, almost daze-like if it were not for the constant jolting of the wagons. Or the faded confetti seats, stretched on their last thread.

"Whoever you are, Nyctara. You sound like someone who puts on a show for a breaking story. I hope you don't disappoint." She leaned back in her seat, her gaze shifting to her reflection in the window.

I hope I'm not wrong.

By the time the train squealed and pulled into Ezrat's station, the full moon took full mount in the dark sky. Xiomara stepped onto the platform, wrapping her arms around her loose long-sleeved crop top.

Same cracked pavement and faded paint, showing the town hadn't changed one bit.

"Let's see what you've got." A smile tugged at her lips. "If you're hiding here... you'd better be as clever as they say." Her eyes narrowed, a spark catching behind them. "Because I didn't come all this way to save a ghost."

Chapter 13

~But I was knowingly blind~

ARIS SHELIA

"Three more," Taavi said, bronze sunglasses pinched vertically between her fingers. "That's all we need."

I nodded, catching my breath as I paced in front of her. My hand came back wet from wiping my forehead, body aching from practice. The higher levels of Shadow took a lot out of me. To morph darkness into how I want it, stretching and thinning it to create eyes or claws or heads and limbs in some kind of working form rather than commanding it. Or the absence of space, sucking in like a vacuum and never letting go of even the user, only working for the tiniest amount of materials to disintegrate into nothing.

But when I finally get a hold of them, I won't need help. Not that Cyril sucked or anything.

The thought of informing Taavi about the mysterious note requesting a meeting had crossed my mind, but I still had a week to think it through *if* I wanted to tell her. It's not like I'm obligated to tell Taavi everything. The writer did want to meet me, not her.

Rolling my shoulders, I brushed it with my fingers, glad that the ache and bruising had finally healed. "The public and leaders are catching on. The trap made that obvious, so going after the crown is a no-go." I stifled a yawn. "What if we deflect attention to something else to keep the heroes guessing our next move?"

"That is a potential option." Taavi acknowledged. "What do you propose? Sabotage the water supply or transportation systems... Free other villains from prisons..." She trailed off as footsteps echoed closer.

Freeing villains in prison alone would be a suicide mission. Would she have an idea for how I'm supposed to do that or was it barely made up? Since my mother could be there... no most heroes guard it. I'd stand zero chance without Shelby's Crown. And I'm not even sure that's where they're holding her.

"Are you having a meeting without me?" Cyril huffed as he emerged, his body practically bounced like a ball as he descended the last few steps.

Can he hear when I think about him? I pinched the bridge of my nose. *One day. Just one day.*

Much to my amusement, Taavi shot him a look. "My friend, your grandfather and I assigned you to other tasks. Stay on them."

"Wait, wait, wait. Let me guess." He completely ignored her and furrowed his eyebrows, stopping a few feet away from me. "You're planning to kidnap the mayor! Or you want me to impersonate someone across the internet?"

What? No- wait. That's... not actually a bad idea.

I crossed my arms, leaning against the jagged stone wall. "You'll never know. I do suggest listening to Taavi."

He opened his mouth, but Taavi raised her hand. With a loud groan, Cyril turned and trudged back up the steps. Facing me, she set down the glasses. "If we're going after the mayor, you understand there can't be any mistakes."

The mayor might even know what's happening to my mother and little brother. She may be able to tell me where my mother is. Where they hold hero offenders. And if I can get Taavi to tell me or figure out a way to erase the mayor's memory of it...

I straightened. "I can do it."

"Bold yet foolish." Taavi studied me, her lips twitching between a smile and a smirk. "I trust you know well that boldness without strategy is reckless. So this is your chance to prove yourself, dear. You want this. Show me you can think ahead, adapt, and choose your outcome. Show me that you've actually learned something. Otherwise this world will fall. Remember who's at stake."

I tensed at the mention of my family. *I'll prove I have what it takes to you.* I stiffly nodded. *I'll show you believing in me wasn't a mistake.*

"There's going to be some type of dance this week the mayor will attend in the evening. Let's plan to have you take her to a set-off room in a subway near the location when she leaves. Prepare it so you can have at least a few different escape options. I bet she'll have two guards at the least." The newspaper crinkled in Taavi's hand, picked up from a nearby stand and set back down.

Even if kidnapping her might be a terrible idea...

I have to. I have to be able to get them back. And at the same time, it can act as both a deviation from the crown, a distraction to throw them off our trail, and work to incite conflict.

I will take this into my own hands, to orchestrate change and be reunited. And if that meant some people got hurt from it, oh well, that was on them.

After all, they did take away my family first.

****

Rain struck my suit like pellets of a war about to commence. I passed two subways on the way, darting through a narrow alley leading straight to the civic center. The second subway had an entrance yards away from the target's location, which thankfully allowed me to not keep testing the suit's waterproof features. And get closer with less eyes.

"Micha, Mom, I'm going to do this." I paused, almost like a response would come. "I know you would think this is insane. But they won't listen. So it's for you. For us. Just hold out a little longer, and we can be together again. I promise it won't get that far. People won't die."

I touched the stolen access badge clipped to my belt as the civic center grew closer. Its glass walls revealed quite a few people dressed in formal wear, drinking out of glassware or dancing. Occasional muffled laughter and chatter reached the dim lot, unstopped by the endless cars. I passed a dead poodle, surrounded by puddles of rainwater, flies buzzing around its head.

Wow. I don't see any blood. Perhaps it died from a disease. I winced. *Must've been recent if no one's cleaned it up.*

Next to an elevator parked the mayor's sleek black car. I exhaled, noting the tens of security detail stationed nearby, half with pistols and amethyst cuffs and the other with hero emblems. Their ranks noticeably thinned as the event wound down. By the front doors stood the mayor, talking with two other women.

After a few minutes, she waved at them and left for her car. Two guards flanked her, walking at ease and laughing. *Still far enough away for this to work.* I reached toward the shadow by the light, forming a wall and twisting it into a shape that resembled a 2D masked intruder. *Close. It's not enough. Though if I angle it, I'm sure it can look convincing. Ugh, I don't like this...* I gritted my teeth and pointed my other hand to the dead dog and connected with it. It rose unsteadily, its fur plastered to its side.

With a growl and a limp, the dog darted to the 'masked intruder', barking with a strangled gurgle. The guards' heads snapped toward it as I made both flee.

"Stay here, ma'am." one of them commanded over his shoulder, drawing his weapon as the other followed, speaking into a radio on his shoulder. Their commands of "halt" were overshadowed by each other.

Perfect. Neutralize the danger like you were taught.

I slipped to the vehicle behind the mayor and inched forward. One hand clamped over her mouth, the other around her torso to her immediate jerk and dragged us back to the shadows. Her muffled shout barely went above a whisper as she strained.

"*You don't want to do this,*" the mayor's voice seemed to seep through and nestle in my thoughts. "*Talk to me.*"

That's right. I don't want to. I need to.

I left her gagged, tied her wrists, and blindfolded her in a matter of seconds. As a precaution, I tentatively took out a deep Russian Amethyst necklace from my pocket and clasped it over her neck, avoiding the purple as much as possible. Someone like her had to have training for threats like me. A mayor wouldn't be naive or irrational about danger, even in a society like ours. I had to hurry. Plus, there was only so much time before the guards circled back.

"You'll be fine," I whispered with a deep gravely voice. "Stay quiet. I'm not here to hurt you." Sweat ran along my forehead as I dragged her toward the subway, where I took the liberty beforehand in preparing an offset room for my little guest. "Don't try to use powers you claim you don't have," I told her. "The necklace won't allow you."

My distraction of the shadow and dog lasted longer than expected, but not nearly long enough. Frustrated shouts exploded from where I sent the dead dog, paired with the sound of boots pounding against pavement.

"Where'd the mayor go? Mayor Miawei! Check the perimeter!"

I gritted my teeth, yanking her harder. I let go of the dog where I couldn't see it, reaching the stairwell, which seemed to also hate me. About three steps down, a burst of crackling erupted against my back.

"She's heading toward the subway!"

I moved in time to see a flicker of blue and white flames erupt again, licking the walls. One of the guards stepped into view at the top, outlined by the bright clouded sky behind him. Clearly older, tall, broad-shouldered, and completely unbothered. "Really?"

I cursed and released the mayor, coiling the shadows around us like ropes. She stumbled, but I didn't let her fall too far before yanking her back upright. A second guard appeared at the top of the stairs, his hand brushing the wall. A faint tremor rippled beneath my feet, resembling the aftershocks of an earthquake.

"Yeah, no you won't get far," he said. "This is sad. Why do people like you keep begging for attention? You lose no matter what, so give in and perhaps we can cut you a deal for not making a ruckus."

I didn't reply, feeling the vibrations under my feet, coursing in the ground, grow stronger. The subway wasn't an option anymore. He could easily crack the ceiling and send it on top of us.

Leave her and make a run for it?

Ugh, I can't. I promised Taavi I could do this. She might have answer— The ceiling split into cracks, dust casting down upon our heads. *And underground is no longer an option. No matter, I still have a few things under my sleeve.*

The stairwell they stood on top of was one entrance. I spun, dragging the mayor back up the stairs toward the second.

With one hand, I summoned shadow tendrils, whipping it toward the guard with fire powers. They smacked his hands, snuffing out the flames. Not effectively might I add. He backed up, pulling one hand out of reach, and shot out a heatwave back.

"Keep her in sight," the guard panted, streaks of sweat dripping from his forehead. A bead ran down his nose and hung off the tip before falling. Smoke wisped from his hands.

I returned the mayor to the parking lot. Her crying died down to the occasional muffled yelp. The sparse lighting cast long, flickering shadows, almost as if coaxing me to use them. *Okay, now or never for those Shadow Puppets.*

Throwing up a wall between the guards and us, I reached for the dead dog, refusing to look directly at it, and commanded it to lurch toward the guards. Other shadows formed around me, forming two distinct figures. A humanoid blur and a hulking bear. The bear instantly charged toward the earth guard, forcing him to falter as he created a hasty stone shield.

A third figure from the corner of the parking lot emerged, opening and slamming a hand on a control panel box. Light flooded the entire parking lot, making my creations vanish into oblivion.

I stumbled and dropped my grip on the dog instantly. My heart pounded. I lowered the mayor to the ground, keeping a hand on her shoulder.

"There's no more hiding, Nyctara," the fire-wielding guard taunted. "I told you. Those Aegis kids still have learning to do. But against professional heroes, you have no chance. The era of villains is no more."

The mayor shifted in my grasp, struggling against the ropes again. *What do I do?* I scanned the lot over and over while they strutted closer, trying to find any possible escape route. I reached for the shadows at the edge of the lot, but they replied sluggishly, retreating from the light like a tide pulling back from a shore. *Can I run? Ugh, I don't know if either of those guards have any physical minor abilities that could outweigh mine.*

"Let her go," the earth guard ordered. His hand brushed the pavement, shaking the ground underneath me. Cracks formed beside both my feet, lowering me by an inch but I kept my balance.

I clenched my fists, an ache settling deep in my chest. *Or I can absorb the light.* My head spun. *No, that wouldn't create more shadows, and they'd pounce.*

"After so many minor disturbances," the fire guard picked up with a sneer, moving to circle me. "You tried to make a name for yourself, to shatter our peace, and you failed. No one will remember you. How does that feel?"

The mayor twisted again, and I braced.

"You're outnumbered. This act of yours is finished," the earth guard added. *I get it, you called backup.* I widened my stance. "Give her back, Nyx."

There must be something. Anything. I took a deep breath, spotting the shadows underneath the cars. "Fine," I muttered. "You want her? Take her."

I shoved her up and forward, forcing the fire guard to

curse and lunge, narrowly catching her. At the same time, I ran to dive for the space underneath the cars. The earth guard was faster. He slammed his hand to the ground, the pavement rippling beneath my feet like a wave. It threw me, and I struck the ground hard, rolling to a stop against a wheel. Pain shot up my side as my body locked up.

"Not so fast," the earth guard sighed, as if I wasn't worth the effort. He expanded a stick from his jacket, which morphed into a full-on polished wooden staff, its end spiraled with an almost hypnotic black design.

My body refused to yield or move. *Are you kidding me?* A sizzling snap sliced the air after the fire guard gently set the mayor, who was now untied, down and pulled yellow cuffs from his belt. He grinned. "You know what this means."

I glared, my fingers twitching. No. *I will not fail. I will not leave Micha alone.* The pain in my side stung and held a residual ache. *I will not have done all of this for nothing.* That damn staff...

"You know, keeping you out of the news for the most part was a hassle." He twirled the electric cuffs on his finger, flashes of purple—what I assumed to be amethyst—shining as accents. "This moment is showing that our peace will last, Nyctara. I will ask again. Was it worth it?"

No matter how much I attempted to move or struggle against whatever held me down, I couldn't. The light and staff worked against me. The fire guard reached for my wrist, his grip firm as he brought the cuffs closer.

At the edge of my vision, a figure strutted to the side of the parking lot.

"Hey," a smooth, playful voice called. "Mind if I crash the party?"

Both guards froze. The figure wandered carelessly into the light, wearing a black ski mask and loose-fitting clothes. She raised her hand, and a stream of water shot forward, slamming into the fire guard's chest. He let out a startled yelp and staggered, the cuffs flying from his grip and skittering to the mayor's feet.

"What the—" the other guard started as the figure twisted her wrist.

The water coiled around the Spiral Staff, yanking it from his hands and sending it beside the cuff. The tightness on my body retreated as the earth guard scrambled for it. I rolled to my feet while the mayor took off the amethyst necklace I fastened on her neck.

"Who are you?" the fire guard demanded, staggering back up with red flames sparking in his palms.

Drawing back her shoulders, the figure shook her head. I could practically hear the teasing in her voice. "Just a concerned citizen. How about we call this a draw and let everyone go?"

The guards shared a look, then turned, placing themselves in front of the mayor who had already removed her own blindfold. She flicked her narrowed heterochromatic eyes between them, me, and the newcomer.

Sighing, the figure rubbed her neck. "Fine, have it your way." She flicked her hand, and the puddles around the lot surged upward, forming a wall of water. The fire guard's flames hissed, unable to get through. His partner cursed under his breath as his footing slipped on the wet ground, pillars of earth shooting up besides them.

"Come on, Nyx," she said, sliding to my side. The woman took my arm and began roughly guiding me away.

I tugged against her grip, looking back at the mayor. Yet the lights and objects swam. "Leave her," the figure snapped. "God, I thought you were smarter than that."

I opened my mouth but nothing came out. *I don't know if I trust her.* Weight pressed on my limbs and eyelids. *The mayor might know about my mom.* Her hand tugged again. *Do I have a choice at this point...? I have to get away.*

Reluctantly, I obeyed. Each step felt like climbing a mountain as we ran from the light.

Don't think for a moment I'll let my guard down just because you saved me.

By the time we reached the alley several blocks away, the guards' shouts were swallowed. She finally let go of my arm and faced me, slipping off her ski mask. Her blonde hair tumbled free, streaked with blue.

Her blue-yellow eyes flicked over me. "Not bad, Nyx. But if you're going to do something illegal, you might want to work on your planning and exit strategy."

I stared. "I was handling it just fine. What do you want?"

"To help, obviously." She crossed her arms with a shrug. Some of her damp blonde hair draped over her shoulder. "You looked like you needed it."

"Why bother?" I narrowed my eyes.

"Because you're interesting. I love a good story, though I thought you'd be better."

I bristled, opening my mouth. She raised her hand.

"You don't need to thank me," she said lazily. "All I want is that you make sure whatever you're after is entertaining." She turned on her heel, her steps light.

Entertaining? Does she think this is a game?

The woman only made it a few feet away when movement blurred across the rooftop above. Boots against metal faintly reached us as a figure stepped out into the moonlight.

My heart dropped.

On the edge of the building perched Shanessa, an aura of light softly encasing her body. "Where ya headed with your new friend, Nyctara?"

The woman barely flinched as she replaced her ski mask. "Friend of yours?"

I called the shadows, which inch by inch, enveloped me. Five more figures, totaling six, appeared on the rooftops around, the silhouettes outlined by streetlights.

"Seriously?" I hissed, widening my stance.

The woman eyed me, raising an eyebrow. "They seem determined," she observed. "Let's give them a show, shall we?"

Shanessa ignited a rainbow burst of light, sending the

blinding beam at us. Instantly, the woman reacted with a spiraling barrier of water to intercept it, refracting the light so both splashed harmlessly against the brick walls.

The woman then shot a stream of ice back. "I'll handle her. You keep moving."

"You ain't goin' nowhere," Leor replied, leaping to the alley with Gracelyn and Arlene. A sudden wave of heat rolled over me, fire licking his palms. He extended his hand, and a stream of fire cut through like a whip.

I dove, the scorching air pulling breath from my lungs. If not for my suit, I'd surely have third degree burns. My legs ached as I forced myself up. *We gotta counterattack him.* The woman easily held her own, but the puddles only provided so much water. *Wait, there's a canal nearby.* I darted, making my way for it with footsteps falling close behind me.

"Nyctara!" Malik shouted from above.

A pang went through my chest. *No, I can't. I gotta keep going.* Frantically, I grasped the shadows, which responded erratically. I threw a desperate glance over my shoulder, catching sight of two figures running on the building sides.

Gracelyn raised her hand. Her fingers twitched, and I felt a wave of drowsiness spread over my body.

I commanded the shadows to my side, yet they didn't. The tendrils lashed out instead, striking Drystan as he tried to drop from the building to flank me.

He stumbled, a pained shout escaping his lips as the tendrils wrapped around his arm and threw him hard against a wall.

"Vortex!" Malik cried, skidding to a halt beside him. "Are you okay?"

I froze while blood streaked down Drystan's face. *What?* This time, the shadows spun, striking Arlene, who had been closing in from the other side. The force sent her tumbling backward, her phantom sword vanishing as her head struck the pavement.

I didn't hear the crack if there was one. No words escaped my lips.

"Spectra!" Leor yelled furiously. Flames erupted from his body, roaring like a furnace as he charged forward.

My knees threatened to give out. My hands shook. *I didn't mean to hurt them that far. Never that far.*

"Keep moving!" The woman snapped as she sprinted toward me, her soaked blonde hair clinging to her face. Behind her, Shanessa wiped a bloodied nose.

I forced myself to go, racing to the canal ahead. The woman caught up next to me. I leapt into the icy water, meeting a breath-stealing chill. She formed a whirlpool around us, lifting to an angle. Flames hissed and sputtered uselessly against it.

The cold bit through the suit, numbing the ache in my legs. My chest burned. Tears threatened my eyes.

"They'll follow us," I gasped over Leor's shouting.

Smirking, the woman waved her hand, propelling us down the canal. "Not if we make it fun."

Surfing the canal rapidly, I could barely see people we

passed and couldn't help but watch. Families laughing in a store, a kid playing on a tree with others illuminated by street and city lights. Someone giving an old lady their umbrella. *Perhaps that would've been me if I had chosen differently.*

****

Inside Taavi's home, I still couldn't breathe easily. Perhaps it was from making my way home alone and running on empty after the fight. Shadows clung to the corners, almost mockingly inviting, and the faint flicker of candlelight cast shifting patterns across the floor.

Shadow tendrils. Out of control. Drystan. Arlene.

My chest heaved.

I—I couldn't—I need to apologize—I—Why?

My feet dragged and squelched as I closed the door, shaking off the excess water on the suit. The familiar cinnamon honey scent hit my nose. Tears stung my eyes.

In the center of the TV room stood Taavi, her back to me. Taking off her bronze sunglasses, she slowly turned, tucking them into her pocket. Her auburn hair was neatly pinned, and the deliberate way she drank her tea told me what I needed to know.

She knew.

Setting the teacup on a nearby stand, Taavi didn't face me. "You're late, with nothing to show for it. Where's the mayor, dear?"

I stayed near the door, setting down my helmet. "You already know it didn't go as planned."

Her hand hovered over the teacup, fingers curled as if resisting the urge to break it. She turned to me with her lips in a line, her voice soft. "Didn't go as planned? That's an understatement I daresay. What was this plan?"

"The guards had these magic objects, then the Aegis showed up, and..." I rubbed my arm, cutting myself off as she stepped closer.

"I was like you once. So were the ones before you. Yet, we were stronger. And you... you failed. A. Simple. Task."

I flinched, my eyelids and limbs sluggish. Part of me wanted to tense, to stand with my shoulders back and defend myself. Yet the other part had more control. I used too much energy, and I could feel my body giving in.

"Do you know what's at stake? This isn't just about some powerless mayor. And you—" she cut herself off, flicking her hand with an exhale. She picked up the teacup.

I took a step forward, forcing the words past the lump in my throat. My mouth tasted like lead. "I tried and almost had her. Failing or not, it worked enough to throw them off our trail, didn't it?" I asked, coughing to clear my throat. "What else did you expect me to do? Die?"

"What I expect, dear," she said slowly, "was for you to succeed. Instead, you made a mess and lost control."

The tendrils... the Aegis... the heroes hurt me first. But I still didn't mean to hurt them that much. Drystan's bloodied face, Arlene's head striking the ground.

"I didn't mean to—"

Taavi clicked her tongue. "Didn't mean to," she repeated, her voice slightly off. "That's always the excuse, isn't it? No matter, it's okay."

"Is it?"

The cup in her hand shook, then dropped, shattering and spraying liquid everywhere. A moment of silence followed, and she didn't move. I bent down to grab a shard that reached my foot, the cinnamon and honey curling into my nose.

"You practice!" Taavi stated loudly. "Yet hesitate, stumble, doubt like a newborn calf. Tell me, child, how is that going to help anyone? How is that going to bring back your precious *brother* or fix this broken world when you can't succeed on a simple mission?"

My throat tightened. I stiffened, squaring my shoulders. "*What?* You weren't there. Why am I the only one doing everything? Why didn't *you* help *me?*"

The shadows piercing Drystan, knocking Arlene...

She laughed bitterly. "You don't understand anything, nor what I'm trying to do for you. I won't let you become another wasted effort."

"For me?" I replied, my voice cracking. "Is that what this is? Why not do it yourself? You have decades of experience, right? I think you're using me because you don't want to get your own hands dirty."

Her eyes darkened. The air seemed to still, and I could only hear my breath for a moment.

"You think you're the only one with something to lose?"

she asked quietly. "You think this is just about you and your little brother? This world is rotting. The heroes, the Aegis, our society is a facade, held together by people too afraid to admit the truth. Without villains like us to inspire, to preserve, humans will die off. Structures will fall. History will be lost. Living will be pointless."

Taavi took a long breath. "I will not let this world wither and rot just because you're too weak or afraid to do what needs to be done."

"I am not weak." I stared at her, raising my head. "What are you really trying to do, Taavi?"

She returned to her original place, clasping her hands behind her. A calm smile returned. "You already know I'm fixing this world. Waking it up after watching the crack split longer, year after year, taking many with it. But I'm old and need someone willing to do what I can't. Someone who understands what it means to sacrifice for the greater good. Because I refuse to fail again!"

"And you think that someone should be me?"

"Why not? With your shadow powers, you've proven you're capable despite some... setbacks. Why not fully embrace it? I chose you, after all. You understood what had to be done. You understood this peace cannot last. Unless... you're starting to doubt me." She sighed, rubbing her temple, and picked up the broken shards of the cup. "Maybe I'm wrong. But I still believe in you."

I still believe in you. I clenched and unclenched my fists.

"Vortex!" *Malik shouted, sliding to his side.*

Her eyes found mine. "Keep that fire, little shadow. You're going to need it. This isn't over, not by a long shot. And for the mayor, I'll fix your mess."

I stepped to the stairs, pressing close to the wall. Her voice followed me.

"Don't disappoint me again."

Each word felt like a stone to the chest. Or a lead chain wrapping around me. Would Taavi kick me out and abandon me? Would she turn me in? How could I prove myself if I failed? How do I do any of this if I can't do one damn thing correctly? Do I even want to? I'd already disappointed myself. I let Micha and my Mother get taken away from me. I allowed myself to fall into a trap and failed to capture the mayor.

I used too much energy. I hurt Drystan and Arlene. I guess... they got in my way... I was tired... No, I still went too far.

Did I? Or is it just payback? You said earlier... I trailed off.

They didn't hold back when I tried taking the third jewel. At least, I think so.

You already rationalized this. If they hurt you, it means they won't hold back.

So I shouldn't either.

I ran my hand along the wall. *Or you could walk away and leave forever.* Wiping my eyes, I reached my room, eyeing the meeting note laying on my desk. *I couldn't ever do that. Micha needs me. And doing good gives silence. It's action that makes them answer.*

The image of me striking them wouldn't leave my mind. If Taavi had helped, I wouldn't have failed. They wouldn't have gotten hurt, even if they deserved it.

And after all of that, the worst part was I still had to go to school tomorrow and face them like nothing happened.

Chapter 14

ARIS SHELIA

I shoved my way through the school's entrance, the door slamming into the wall. Crowds of students formed their usual impenetrable maze, and I pulled my hood further up. If all went well, today would be okay.

Unfortunately, the universe either hated me or had a sense of 'humor'.

"Ay, look who finally stepped into the light."

My heart sank. I didn't bother turning around, keeping my shoulders low. His long strides caught up to me easily, a grin on his face as he fell into step beside me.

"Late night?" Reed hesitated, then frowned. "What's wrong?"

I increased my pace without looking at him.

"C'mon, don't be like that," he said, jogging a few steps

ahead to block my path. "We're all friends here. I wanted to check in and make sure you're okay. Did something happen?"

I exhaled. "I think you're mistaking me for someone who gives a damn about your opinion." I sidestepped, but he mimicked, holding out his arms. "Move."

"Man, you really oughta relax. You're way too high-strung these days." He met my glare and groaned. "Okay, I will. But first..." His hand shot out, brushing against my forearm before I could pull away. I winced, hard.

A wave of dread surged through me, and the hallway narrowed. The building seemed to move, and the chatter turned to accusations against my ear.

Did you see her hurt Vortex?

She can't do anything right.

My teeth clenched. I braced myself against the lockers when Reed stepped back, wiggling his finger like a mom to her toddler. His thoughtful eyes stayed glued on me. "Oops, my bad. Guess you'll feel that for the next hour."

I forced myself to breathe. *Don't react.* A cold sweat broke out on my forehead. *Actually, I think I will fight back. If he...* I flicked my hand, swirling shadows at his feet, letting them creep up his leg.

Reed laughed, almost as if forced. His friends walked up, pulling out their phones. Their faces alight. "Careful, Aris. Wouldn't want you to do something rash in front of all these people." He jabbed a finger at the cameras.

I swallowed and dropped my hand. I could feel their

eyes boring into me, waiting for me to snap. Something shifted in Reed's expression, and for a second, I thought I saw uncertainty. His hands clenched and unclenched mindlessly, as if in an effort to click a realization he wasn't ready to name.

Does he think I'd actually do it? What's he seeing?

"Damn." Reed leaned in, his voice low. "I thought you'd follow through. That would've been fun. I guess preventing another dark villain from rising is my due diligence for today." The kid stood straighter, like he'd scored a point.

A few of his friends laughed, but one in the back with a hat frowned, lowering his phone.

You all belong to a mental asylum. I shouldered Reed, causing him to stumble as I passed him. He didn't follow, but his strained laughter reached down the hallway.

As I walked, I kept my head down. *She can't do one thing right. She's out of control.* The classroom door loomed ahead. I entered and slipped into my seat, resting my head on the desk. My heart still raced, the voices insufferable.

The bell rang, and the chatter in the room quieted. As the teacher began the lesson, I stared blankly at the board.

I should've stopped him. Wiped that damn smug look off his and his friend's faces. But I didn't. Whatever he wanted to prove... He wanted to make me break... I exhaled. *Not today.*

****

I trudged to the tree and tossed my bag at the base. Rough bark scraped my back as I leaned on it, tilting my head back. No wind brushed my face, but the shade felt nice. I closed my eyes.

The second I did, Drystan's bloodied face flashed in my mind. Arlene's body hitting the ground. My stomach twisted, and my eyes flew open, blinking rapidly until the images retreated. Eventually my thudding heart slowed to its usual pace too.

A soft, rustling crunch of footsteps on grass approached. I whirled around, arms up in fists. Malik stopped a few feet away, his hands raised.

"Whoa, it's just me." Strands of blond hair hung over his forehead, almost reaching his eyes as they searched me.

"What do you want? Where's Drystan and Arlene?"

Malik shoved his hand into his pockets. "I wanted to check on you and show you something I found." He squinted. "Is something up?"

"I'm good." I leaned back against the tree. The building emotions inside me rose, as if it would spill over, fighting with every breath. I shoved it away, layering it in concrete and building thorn walls around to let nothing through. My arms folded tight around my stomach, as if it would seal it away.

I will not let it explode from its boiling pot.

"I'm not in the mood."

"Uh, yeah, no. I don't believe you are fine," he pointed out with a slight frown.

"Go away."

"Yeah, no."

I froze. "What?"

"I don't know what's going on," he replied, folding his arms. "But I can tell something's wrong. Something you need to talk about. But I'll back off if I need to, I just really need you to listen to me. It's important."

The wind and sounds of insects continued without a second thought. I fidgeted with my nose ring. "What makes you think you know something's up? And what makes you entitled to know about it?"

"Why are you doing this?"

"Why are you doing this?" I repeated.

Malik took a step closer. I should've backed away, but my legs wouldn't move. "I think you act like you want no one to care, but you secretly want that more than anything. You're my friend, acquaintance at the very least, so you matter to me. Which is also why I'm about to tell you this. Look, I know you don't want to hear, but I found something. A paper after the government fire—"

A chill ran through me, and my voice almost cracked. "I don't care."

I can't deal with this.

"Yeah, right," he pressed. "I've been trying to tell you but—"

"I said I don't care," I interrupted, my voice rising before I caught it. I swallowed. "You don't understand what I've... You don't..." I trailed off to keep the tears from spilling.

"You think I don't get it?" His voice went quiet. "I'm

trying to help you."

"I don't need it." I shot back. "You're wasting your time."

"Maybe I am," he agreed, lowering his head.

What?

The sound of approaching voices interrupted us. Drystan and Arlene appeared, exchanging a wary glance. A fresh scar ran down the side of Drystan's face, though Arlene had no visible damage. My fingers twitched. I looked away.

"Uh, is this a bad time?" Drystan asked, his cheerful tone sounding forced.

I grabbed my bag and slung it over my shoulder.

"Push me away if you want, but I'll always be waiting here if you choose." Malik called after me. I was already walking away.

"Hey! I'm going out for coffee later if you want to join!" Arlene shouted after me.

I heard Drystan say something to Malik about overstepping. Arlene shifted her weight. I didn't stop until I was out of sight, far enough that their voices faded. My chest heaved, and my eyes burned.

This may be what I deserved. Failure after failure, dragging everyone down with me until there's no one left. It was easier to be alone, wasn't it?

Malik had to be wrong. I didn't matter. Yet, I hated that part of me that wanted to believe it and let him in.

****

Hours later, in my room, a folded note rested on the bed. My name was scrawled on the outside in jagged, hurried handwriting. I froze, my heart skipping, and I opened it quickly. The message was unsigned.

"Due to the rise of the villain Nyctara, we've determined it would be safer if you would stay away from Micha. This will be until Nyctara is captured, or given up her evil ways."

The note crumpled in my grip. *But I haven't killed anyone.* I slammed the note onto the desk, and a crack responded. My fist throbbed where it hit.

I collapsed onto my bed, burying my face in my hands. *How dare they keep me from seeing him.* Tears pricked my eyes, but I blinked them away. *Mrs. Parkzer's a nice woman, I'm sure it's out of her control. I'll figure it out. I'll see him again. They can't stop me. Whoever this was will not tell me what to do.*

Chomper fell onto me from my pillow. I hugged it tightly. "Mom, Micha, I'm going to do everything I can to fix this. I promise. I miss you so much. But you'll have to be strong for me so I can right this wrong. I love you."

"Sweetie, I need to go get groceries," my mother said. "Do you mind watching Micha for me?"

I nodded, hearing him giggle from the bathtub. She hugged me, grabbed her key, and left. In the kitchen, I pulled out some jam, peanut butter, and bread.

"I'm done!" Micha shouted. "I'm all dry!"

"*Put on your clothes,*" *I replied with a smile. I heard something fall in the bathroom, paired with grumbling. "You done?*"

"*Yeah.*" *A door shut after, and he walked downstairs to the kitchen. I looked up to see his shirt inside out and backward. He skipped next to me, looking at the knife in my hands. "What are you doing?*"

"*Making lunch.*" *I set it down and squatted, touching the hem of his shirt. "You did good. Shirts are a little tricky, aren't they?*"

"*Mhm,*" *he hummed, then took a step back with a smile and bolted. Laughter erupted as he rounded the table, staring at me. "You can't catch me!*"

I stood with a smirk and followed, letting him get away with a shriek. This happened a few more times before I cornered him, capturing him with a hug.

"*No! You got meee,*" *Micha whined, trying to push my arms away.*

Messing with his hair, I kept my grip on him. "Can I fix your shirt now and finish lunch?"

He nodded and I let go. Surprisingly, he stayed and let me turn it right-side out.

I sat there for hours without moving, pressing the stuffed dinosaur against my ribs. My legs went numb. No, *no more of that.* I set the toy on the pillow, and touched the crumpled paper as if it would somehow undo the words. A bitter laugh escaped my throat. I pushed away from the desk and paced. Micha's face burned into my mind. A pit grew in my stomach.

I glanced at the mirror on the far wall, its surface dull and streaked. My reflection stared back, with half-circles under my eyes and hollow cheeks. My ash hair frayed everywhere. *Is this who I am?* Bile rose in my throat. *Someone who can't keep her little brother and mother safe?*

"I can't keep waiting," I whispered.

The small drawer in the corner drew my attention. Inside held a hastily sketched map and scrap of parchment detailing the fourth jewel and crown's location. The third jewel I'd have to wait on, and these two Taavi warned me to be patient. But patience had done nothing for Micha or me. It had only stolen more time, more distance from us. It made me hurt people and risk my life. In fact, it was like our society.

If I got all of them, perhaps I would be strong enough to forcefully take them back.

I crossed the room in three strides, yanking the drawer open. My heart pounded as I spread them across the table, smoothing the creases—the fourth jewel, hidden on a Skyship, surrounded by floating buildings. Going there without an escort or flying powers might be a death wish. A death wish I will take for my life back.

A lump formed in my throat, and I pressed my mouth into a straight line. "Micha, I know you can't hear me." I looked at the dinosaur on the bed. "But I'm doing this for you. To protect you. To reunite you with mom and get our life back."

To regain control, a voice added, *because I can.*

I shook my head. No, *this isn't about me.*

Liar. I traced the lines of the map, and the voice grew louder. *Because no one else will. Because they took everything from me, and I'm not going to let them win.*

After a few moments, I shoved the note and map into my bag. I wasn't waiting for anyone. Not for Taavi or her cryptic promises. Only part of it was to give Micha a better life. To find mom. *I have to be worth something. Things need to change.*

First, I will see what that cryptic message flying onto my desk last week was about. Then I'm not waiting to take the fourth jewel.

Chapter 15

TEGAN MULVEY

Not many workers tended the lush plants during the day. They waited until evening, when the sun lowered and air cooled — which only made her job easier.

She knew from her high-clearance job they hid it here temporarily. Why would anyone look in a store's humid greenhouse? Well, except her.

Soft leaves brushed her side as Tegan ducked, avoiding a passing family on the main trail. She bent her finger, forming a thin, invisible sheet feet away from the paths. Past it, the illusion would show any onlookers a normal greenhouse; full of red or blue or yellow colorful plants and the occasional tree, while acting as an invisible shield and completely concealing her.

They kept its whereabouts on the downlow. If anyone was watching it, they'd be undercover as a worker.

Crouching, Tegan brushed aside the cool, damp soil.

"Seriously," she muttered. "How hard is it to hide something shiny in a jungle of plants? It's like they want me to suffer."

Sweeping her hand across a patch of vibrant ferns, her illusion shifted with her. Bugs flew mindlessly around as she made her way through, avoiding all main paths that visitors were required to stay on. The humidity made Tegan's makeup melt, and her hair clung to the back of her neck in the most unflattering way. Even her trendy crop top and jeans stuck as if she went on a hike.

"This better be worth a dumb rock, or I'm going to lose it."

She glanced back toward the main path, hearing the distant voices of workers and visitors. A young couple lingered near a row of orchids, completely oblivious to her presence behind a cluster of towering palms.

Aris and Cyril had bungled their attempt for this red stone, even with *pages* of information she provided the girl. Tegan, however, never left a job half-done. That is why people needed her.

Spotting a red gleam beneath a tangle of vines, Tegan jumped forward but then froze. A second shimmer caught her eye. A *trap sensor? Clever.* Exhaling sharply, Tegan formed another light to distort it. She knelt, ignoring the dirt dusting her designer jeans, and carefully peeled back the foliage. Nestled in the soil sat the jewel, its surface refracting a dazzling array of colors.

"Hello, gorgeous," she cooed, plucking it from the ground and holding it to her eye. The weight felt right.

Straightening, Tegan rolled the red beryl between her

fingers. Her lips curled into a satisfied smile. "This was almost too easy. You'd think they'd try harder upon discovering Nyctara after it."

Her illusion of the shield followed as she exited the alcove toward the main path. Twirling the red beryl between her fingers, she passed a worker who glanced her way. Sighing, Tegan flicked her wrist, sending a puff of rainbow light in the air. It was enough to dazzle the worker, making time for Tegan to create a passerby leaving the trail, clearly moving the greenery in search. Then she vanished.

"Thanks for your cooperation," she quipped, sliding the jewel into her bag. Her smile widened as she strolled away, a bounce in her step. "Another favor owed. Honestly, I should start requiring more from them."

****

The late afternoon sun cast a golden glow over the small, weathered house at the city's edge. Tegan adjusted her sunglasses, tilting her head as she observed the place. "So this is where she's been hiding," she murmured, tapping her polished nails against her hip. "Charming, in a... run-down, rustic sort of way."

Leaning casually against the low stone fence, Tegan waited. The door soon creaked open, and Aris emerged, the edge of her mouth twitching. She wore a plain black hoodie, her ash hair falling past her shoulders.

"Well, well, if it isn't Miss Aris," Tegan said lightly. "I've been hearing all about you." She pushed off the fence and extended a hand. "I'm Tegan. Consider this your formal introduction."

Aris folded her arms. "You gave me the paper about Shelby's Crown. What do you want?"

Dropping her hand, Tegan let out an exaggerated laugh and tossed her red hair over her shoulder. "What do I want? Honey, let's not jump to conclusions so quickly." She reached into her pocket, pulled out the red beryl, and held it up. "This little thing is a piece of the crown you're after."

Aris stiffened, her green eyes locking onto the jewel. "How did you—"

"Oh, don't worry about the how." Tegan grinned. "Let's just say I have a knack for fixing messes. Though I'm not one for charity." She walked within a foot of Aris, scanning her up and down. "You can have it, but there's a tiny little catch. A favor. And trust me, when I call in that favor next week, you won't say no."

"I don't make deals," lied Aris coldly.

Tegan didn't call her out on it. "Sweetheart, you're not really in a position to bargain, are you? You want this," she said, twisting her hand that pinched the jewel back and forth teasingly, "and I want, well, who knows what I'll want later? That's the fun part."

Aris's jaw clenched, revealing a faint scar against her tan skin.

The girl's trying to see if I'm lying. Can't blame her, I kinda am. The festival is almost here though, and I need a supporting role. Who's better than a growing professional?

"Of course, if you refuse, I could always find someone else to give this to. Maybe a hero, like the Aegis? Yes, I heard about your encounters with them. Word gets around, you know." Tegan leaned back as Aris bit her lip. The girl touched her nose ring. "Your call, darling. But I think we both know you're smarter than to cross me."

Her lips pressed into a thin line, eyes hard, and her fingers twitched at her side. After a long pause, Aris extended her hand. "Deal."

"Atta girl." Tegan beamed, pressing the beryl into Aris's palm. Stepping back, she dusted her hands. "Well, I'd love to stay and chat, but I've got places to be and people to dazzle. Don't forget our little arrangement. I'll be in touch."

With a playful wink, Tegan turned on her heel and strolled down the path. "By the way, love the brooding vibe. Cliché, very mysterious, but I suggest lightening up. It's more fun when you're not so serious."

Chapter 16

~I'm sorry for the trouble I've caused you~

ARIS SHELIA

Too many damn times. I'm a freaking failure. The straps of my bag dug into my shoulder as I stuffed the last piece of the ship's and the courtyard's blueprints inside. I zipped it and slung it over my other shoulder. *I have to*—some type of emotion surfaced, lost when I shoved it back down. I slipped on my gloves and boots to my suit, rough enough it pinched my skin. *If I can't I—*

"Aris, what are you doing?"

I whipped around, my heart leaping into my throat. Cyril stood in the doorway, his glasses dangling from his hand as he chewed on the edge of the earpiece.

"Not your business," I curtly said, double-checking that I packed everything, including my daggers. Then I reran the layout in my head again and again. Create distractions throughout the city, get to the tethering station, break the control hub, make my way to the ship under the cover—

His thick frame blocked the doorway. He tilted his head, giving me a once-over. "You have enough gear to fight Altruistic and Lighter! What're you planning? Are you going to rob a bank?"

I tightened my grip on the bag. His brows pinched together as he pushed his glasses back on. "Wait." Cyril's expression shifted like pieces were connecting. "This is about the peace crown, isn't it?"

I picked up my helmet. *Knock out the guards—*

He tapped his chin. "Look, I know I'm not fighting Aegis material, but even I can tell this is dumb. Even if you already located and collected the four shiny rocks that go with it, Shelby's Crown will be heavily guarded by top-tier heroes in a secure location. Hell, pretty sure the presidents switch out themselves to take watch. Do you at least have a plan?"

I stepped to push past him, only for his hand to catch my arm. "You think rushing off half-prepared is smart?" I could practically see the gears turning in his head. "If memory serves, like with the mayor, you're not exactly on a winning streak. Are you thinking straight?"

I yanked my arm. "I don't care, and you're not my mom." It took a lot to bite back a plethora of curse words.

"Hey, no need to get aggressive. You've got options, y'know? Maybe stealing the last magic space rock isn't your best one at the moment. I'd know. Say why don't we take a break—"

"Why are you even here?"

"I could ask you the same thing," he countered instantly, then lowered his head. "Look, I'm trying to be helpful, but..." He hesitated. "I dunno. Seems like you're looking for an excuse to do something reckless. I don't want you making the same mistakes I have. Look—"

I stiffened.

"—you keep saying this is for your little brother. You can't be with him if you get caught—"

"Don't you *dare* bring him into this."

"I'm not," he responded. "But think this through. Don't do something rash when you're high on emotion."

My throat closed.

Cyril rubbed his forehead. "Y'know, I should probably let you go alone." He tilted his head up. "But I won't, since it's my problem too."

I yanked open the door and walked out. I told myself the plan would hold if I held it. That this would feel easier once I started moving. I couldn't afford another night where I lost. I couldn't afford another night where they looked at me like I was a nuisance instead of a threat.

He sighed, his voice somehow reaching me. "I'm coming with you."

I scoffed, climbing the stairs. "Do whatever you want."

****

Roars of an explosion faded; sirens wailed, their sound dim to my ears now. We've made it through the city fast, threading *distractions* of placed fires, bursting pipes, and whatever else Cyril thought up on the fly.

Above loomed the Skyship, its shadow falling over us, extending past the size of an elementary. Floating buildings connected to its body, with bridges. The same ones that I walked under on the way to high school. Lights cut through the thick clouds like jagged shards. Its engines thrummed, blending with the distant drone of automated drones. Chains hung from the ship's metal bow, as well as ladders from its sides, some pinned to the earth while others wiggled in the wind. Oars stuck out from its sides.

Cyril shuffled, his bag clinking with whatever junk he'd brought along. He wore his outfit from the tech museum, with his glasses visible behind his mask.

I stifled a yawn, rubbing the mask like that'd wake me up. Inside my helmet felt awfully warm. My body moved like it was wading through syrup. I forced myself to focus anyway, because exhaustion was not an excuse and I had already used up all my excuses.

In and out, I reminded myself, like saying it enough times would keep my pulse from stumbling. If I got inside and took down the control room, the ship would be blind for long enough to climb and cross without a flood of guards at my back.

Do not get emotional.

Nearby hovered a security drone. Its blue light swept across the area, lingering longer on the guard stationed at an outlook building. I slipped to the side wall, letting the shadows wrap around me. In my hand, I gripped the knife tighter, telling myself I'd use the hilt against the skull for a clean drop.

When the drone drifted away, I darted. The distance between me and the guard closed before he could react. My blade drove into his side, cutting off his strangled cry. It burrowed deeper. A give that should not have been there. My mind was too slow to keep up when he crumpled to the ground, a radio falling from his pocket. *He got knocked down that easily?* I squatted and turned him around. Light left his eyes while red soaked the ground beneath.

Hang on. No, wait. I nudged him as his body turned pale. *That wasn't that hard!* I touched his neck, feeling his pulse. *What have you done?* My stomach clenched. I placed my hands on the floor. *Do not kill.* The words came to me warped. *I aimed to knock him out. Not this. Not enough blood to kill him.* My breath turned short.

Did the knife get turned around in my hand? Am I stupid? I could've sworn the hilt...

The other voice sneaked in slowly. *He would've killed you first.*

No, that guard, their code. Heroes don't do that. I felt like I was grasping straws. *I killed him instead of knocking him out.*

You have to prove your worth. You're still in control. One death is worth its weight when preventing millions of others a life of misery with nothing to show.

*I just reacted— I... I glanced back up, seeing the security drone turn back. *I have to move him. I can't do this now.* Sliding my arms underneath his shoulders, I dragged his body around the corner, far enough the drone would miss. But even when I set him down, my fingers pressed against his neck again. No pulse. I kept pressing, lighter and then harder, and it felt obscene that a life could be gone while my own heart still hammered like it had won something. *He actually...* A hollow numbness settled over me as I unclipped the access card on his belt.

Inside, the control hub had rows of monitors. Wires strung like a web throughout and ran across the nonexistent ceiling. I aimlessly scanned the place, breathing heavily. Cyril stayed by the doorway, his face pale. His eyes locked to the blood smeared on my sleeve.

"Are you going to stand there?" I asked harshly, hyper-aware of the drying blood and cold sweat on my body.

I needed him to look away. Did part of me hope that, if he did, then maybe I could pretend the line still existed? That the blood no longer stiffened on my sleeve? I can't tell anymore.

From the door, a dry cold wind swept through the suit and touched my skin. I forced myself to stay watching the screens. The beats of my heart wracked my body back and forth. *Pay attention.* Each monitor had four grainy camera angles displayed.

With a grimace, he joined, pulling a small explosive device from his bag. I set the timer, its LED blinking steadily, and placed it on the wires behind the monitors.

We retreated to the hallway as the first minor explosion rattled the walls. Smoke and dust poured to the floor, and we fled. Now that it was down, the city burning with other distractions, we could vanish into the noise

Footsteps thundered outside. Cyril froze, and I shoved

him toward the exit. The exhaustion caught up all at once, turning the corridor too bright, turning every sound into something sharp that scraped the inside of my skull and doubled images.

A pair of guards rounded the corner, one with a raised gun, the other with fists. I lashed out, forming jagged blades (courtesy of the doorways) at them before either had time to react. The one with fists fell instantly. The other fired.

The shot nicked my arm with searing heat. I gritted my teeth as the fabric stitched itself back together. My arms shook. The room spun. Yet the pain faded to the background.

Another. He's not dead either, is he?

Cyril was mid-tackle with the remaining guard. He punched him in the face and snagged the gun, tossing it aside. When the guard stopped struggling, now unconscious, he rose and wiped the blood from his knuckles.

"Nyx—Aris."

I walked to the doorway, nudging the other guard's arm away with my foot. Every third breath caught in my throat. My actions were my own, seen through a third-person perspective that I watched and lived through but couldn't change.

For a moment, Cyril braced himself. I thought he might step in front of me. Stop me. Call me out. But he shook his head. "You're just going to keep going?"

"Why do you care?" My voice came out flat instead of breaking. "You're here to watch my back."

His jaw relaxed as he squinted at me. I believed I saw a

hint of relief in his eyes. *Why would-?* "You need to slow down. Why are you killing guards? Why didn't you tell Taavi you're going after the Goldstone?"

"I don't need to," my voice rose. "I'm not like you. I won't allow myself to be helpless and stand still!"

"Dude, are you sure this is still for your brother?"

"Stop bringing him up," I hissed. "You know nothing about what I'm fighting for."

"You're right," he admitted. "I don't think you know any more than I do. Again, you're not in the right mindset. You're going to lose more than you realize if you don't take a second to think. What if you get yourself killed? What if you end up killing someone close to you? Can you live with that?"

My breath hitched, but I masked it with a scoff. "You don't get to lecture me about loss. Not when you never had to fight for anything real in your life. So go ahead and leave if that's what you want."

"Don't assume you know me, either."

"Oh, please. What's the hardest thing you've done? Pick the wrong tie for a gala?"

He forced an awkward chuckle. "Please, I've made sacrifices. Like that one time I gave up my last slice of pizza." His smile died, and Cyril looked as if he was contemplating telling me something valuable. "Listen, not everyone around you is as clean as they seem. You're not the only one who's made sacrifices."

"What's that supposed to mean?" I shook my head,

exhaling like a laugh. "I think I'd know."

"Yeah, if you think so." He let out a long breath. "Just think about it, okay? I came—"

"I never asked for you to come."

Picking the first guard up under the armpits, I dragged him to the others.

He studied me for a long moment. "Fine. Don't say I didn't warn you when this all goes to hell. I'm out."

"Like I care what you think," I muttered, dropping him and moving to the door.

"Just so you know! I'm totally judging you for that knife move. Zero creativity," Cyril called out. Furthering the distance, he continued, almost too quietly for me to catch, "I know more than you think. I care. I'm not stupid. Some things aren't worth saving. Not even family."

I paused but didn't turn back.

The tethering station waved, its skeletal metal framework extending upward like a rough staircase into the sky, straight to the Skyship. I paused at the edge of the structure, scanning for security or drones. *More should be coming. Perhaps they're busy in the city or around Cyril.*

Cyril. He didn't know what he was saying. *"Are you sure this is still for your brother?"* I huffed. That *ally* had a rock for a brain.

The shifting access ladder stretched into the night sky. My shoulder protested as I reached up, gripping the cold, slick rungs. Leftover blood from the graze smeared onto the metal.

The climb was slow. Beyond and below, the city sprawled like a sea of distant lights, glittering, each one marking a life that had nothing to do with me.

No one would care if I fell.

I shook my head.

The wind picked up as I ascended, biting at my skin and tugging at my suit's hood. A whirling noise of fans behind me made my heart seize. I froze, clinging to the ladder, as a patrol drone hovered closer. Its light and camera swept across the tethering station, casting harsh beams onto it.

Move. My body refused to obey my mind, every muscle locked in place like telling me there's another way. The drone's light passed over me, pausing for a fraction of a second. I squeezed my eyes shut, willing the shadows made from its beam to bend together and keep me hidden with the night. To lower my body temperature in case it used a thermal camera or any other kind of sensor I didn't know the name of.

The light lingered. I braced, loosened my arms, and overwilled myself. I silently sprung up with a wall of black between me and its lens. I exhaled shakily, my breath visible and kept climbing faster and faster without looking back.

The last portion of the ladder shifted to a tether of thick rope, reminding me much of Shanessa's obstacle course, connecting to the giant floating Skyship. The hatch at the top was sealed, with a keypad bolted into the wall beside it. I studied it, the strange symbols on the screen rearranging themselves into something readable.

"Access code required."

I wedged my fingers under the edges of the panel and pried. The casing resisted then popped out with a crack. Inside, the wiring was bundled tight, cramped and ugly. *Okay, omnilingualism helped with interface logic like input, verification, speech, but not wires.* Every trick I'd picked up from Taavi skimmed through my mind. I traced the live line with my eyes.

The wires sparked as soon as I touched it. I jerked my hand back, ignoring the sizzling pain as the display panel switched to a warning color. Sensation crept back in sharp needles to my fingertips. I pressed two wires together. The keypad beeped angrily, flashing purple and ticking down.

A thinner line tucked behind the bundle stuck to the back. I pinched it between two fingers and crossed it with an adjacent return wire. Instant distorted screaming blasted from the keypad, then cut mid-cycle. The hatch unlocked with a soft click. "Finally." I shoved the panel back into place and pushed the hatch open.

The interior of the ship was bare, despite being built like a labyrinth. Halls twisted and grated. I moved quickly, keeping to the edges of the corridors. I stopped at a corner, peering around it. Two guards talked outside the reinforced door, both with guns over their shoulders.

"Sector five's a mess. Half the security grid is knocked out."

"Yeah, they'll have us working double shifts to fix it," the other woman replied, shifting her weight. "Wonder what happened."

I tightened my grip on the daggers. Taking them out

would be risky, but I couldn't think of another way. I'd knock them out, but their sacrifices would be necessary if needed as a last resort. And only as that.

Don't make this personal. Do not turn this into punishment because they had the audacity to talk about me like I was a joke.

"This Nyctara ain't even that good. She just runs away," the second continued, leaning her head back. "Even that new team of school kids, the Aegis, kicked her butt. Yeah, she is insanely good at escaping, though who wouldn't be with shadow powers? I bet she wouldn't last a day against Lighter or Altruistic's team."

The shadows stirred, coiling around my hands. *Those guards are just obstacles between me and what I need. I'm tired of running. Back of their heads, and or pressure points.*

"I heard that she's been enough of a nuisance to send more teams after her," the second woman added. "Hero management said Aegis gets priority to prove their worth, but really, it's a free-for-all."

I stepped from the corner. Instantly, the lights almost snuffed out as the shadows poured from the hallway walls, stretching from every surface. *Damn, I need to be careful.*

The first guard never turned around. My blade rapped against her temple. Her body crumpled. The woman with large dark eyeshadow reacted fast, swearing and raising her gun. I waved my hand, coiling the shadows from the decorative pillars around her legs. They twisted, catching around her boots and ankles, wrenching her balance out and dragging her to the ground hard, gun skittering. She struggled, cursing again in an attempt to reach her radio.

I frowned. If she had powers, she didn't use them.

"Stop squirming."

She didn't listen. I tightened the shadows, squeezing the air from her lungs as her eyes bulged in panic. When I heard her cough, I loosened its hold.

She's just doing her job. She didn't ask for this. You said knock them out.

Come on! You already killed two others. Necessary sacrifices.

I staggered, covering my helmet with my hand where my mouth should be. *I can't. Why do I feel like I just lost something?*

If you let her go, she'll call for backup as soon as she wakes up. You'll fail. You can't fail again.

My vision swayed for a second before clearing up. The guard coughed again, still pinned.

Micha will never reunite with your mother. He will never reunite with you. He won't get a life worth living. Because you were too weak to do it.

I drew a blade from my side. The guard gasped, her eyes locking onto mine. "I'm sorry." I stuck the hilt against her head before she could reply, covering her mouth. When I was certain she was unconscious, I gently let her down. Her chest rose and fell steadily. I don't know how many times I checked.

You're on your own. I have to finish this.

There's minutes until they come too.

I stepped over the bodies, forcing myself not to look at their faces. The reinforced door's sleek surface was unmarked, except for a black panel on the side.

When I placed my hand on the panel, the symbols rearranged themselves.

"Biometric verification required."

I stared at the screen, my heart dropping. *Right. I can use the guards. Agh, I should've been patient. Taken more time studying this place.* I turned back and knelt by one, heat residing behind my eyes. I hesitated before dragging her, taking her limp hand against the panel. Blinking twice, the light turned green, and the door hissed open.

In the center, hovering inside a shimmering field, was the Blue Goldstone. It looked like a midnight sky, a smooth black with trillions of stars twinkling.

I stepped inside. The jewel spun without moving, and I reached out. The field surrounding it crackled. My fingers brushed the surface of the energy field. *Nothing. Wow, these are insanely nice gloves. Who made them?* I pushed through, the field crackling and burning as I grabbed the Blue Goldstone. The heat reached past the suit, like it was exponentially increasing. My vision blurred, and the room spun as I stumbled back.

When my vision returned, I found myself beside a wall, clutching the Goldstone in my hands. I tightened my grip and stood. The room around me still had blurred outlines. I steadied myself against the wall, feeling sweat run down my body. I stepped further into the corner as the footsteps grew louder and curled the shadows around me. *No, please go away. I don't want to kill you.* Tears threatened my eyes.

Woman up. The voice mocked. I blinked them back.

"Split up," another voice ordered. Shanessa. "Aero, you head left with Leor. Eclipse, cover them lower halls. Spectra, keep an eye on the main exit. Vortex, you're with me."

If I don't escape, then they died for nothing. I slipped from the room, sticking close to the wall. The shadows muffled my movements.

Okay, I'm still unsure what Gracelyn can do. Last time she threw objects, which isn't a major power. I suspected Emotion, but I could be wrong. The Blue Goldstone warmed in my palm. *The others I do. I can plan around that. They won't have to get hurt.*

Leor stepped around a corner into view, wearing a fiery exoskeleton. Flames outstretched with him, searching with his sweeping gaze across the corridor, landing dangerously close to where I hid.

"Nyctara," he called. His breath fogged. "You can't be hidin' forever. Face us, and maybe we'll listen to ya."

Another figure, Malik, moved closer from Leor's right, then backed away.

"Ain't villains s'posed to monologue about their plans and dreams?" called Drystan's distant voice.

Please go away. My thumb brushed over the smooth surface, and I tucked it into a secure pocket. Leor's gaze snapped toward me, his mouth opening.

Immediately, I sent the shadows forward, wrapping his legs and yanking him off balance. He hit the ground hard, flames sputtering as he struggled.

Malik moved like a blur. I spun, shadows bursting outward in waves. He weaved through them with alarming precision. His knife clashed against my shadow blade, and he feinted, hitting the hilt against my side. "She's here!"

Hilt?

My shadows grew ragged as my vision swam. *Too slow,* the voice in my head taunted. I stumbled. Less and less the shadows listened to me. A slight breeze swirled around Malik as he pressed faster than I could counter.

"Stop," I pleaded, the changer making my voice low and gravely.

He didn't let up, but a slight tilt of his head told me he was beginning to realize I was terrified. "You should've thought of the consequences. Hand it over."

I formed more shadows into spears. He dodged the first wave, but I angled a second strike to his exposed side. It hit, slamming Malik into the wall. The crack of his body hitting metal reverberated through the hallway. I froze, a wave of cold running across my skin. Blood leaked from his ears and a wound running along his shoulder to his wrist, which twitched.

Get up. That was supposed to stun you. Please get up.

"Aero!" Leor's voice thundered.

Is he dead? My head felt floaty, as if I was in a dream. *None of this is real. It can't be.* The world slowed. *Did I make up that twitch? I did, didn't I? I actually killed him.*

Someone slammed into me from the side, sending me crashing to the ground. I rolled to my knees, lifting my head. Drystan returned at the end of the hall, his grin maddeningly smug. The scar on his cheek caught the light and I flinched.

"Gotcha," he said, popping his neck. His stark white hair stuck out messy, pieces plastered to his forehead or neck.

I scrambled to my feet. Blades formed in my hands. Using their shadows that sharpened with the brightening flames, I lifted a wall behind me. It shifted as I did, and I formed another by Malik to catch any of my stray attacks as a precaution. As if shielding his body would bring him back alive. Tears threatened my vision. I forced it back and swallowed.

"You're outnumbered," Shanessa's voice rang out, appearing behind Drystan. "Best to hand the Goldstone over. It's time to answer to your crimes."

One option. I bared my teeth, forcing the dark wall to twist and intermix themselves. The shadows surged as dark figures in human form. Two puppets lunged fluidly toward Shanessa and Drystan.

Shanessa's light flared in a radiant shield that incinerated one of the puppets after another. Unused shadows shrank away from the luminous, effulgent beauty.

My arms blocked my face. I hated that I knew she was holding back. Her teammates and her would be affected by the strength of this power if she went all in, despite all of us wearing polaroid lenses.

Drystan ducked under another forming puppet,

swinging it upward, shattering it into black mist. "What's this? Illusions?" he laughed. "I thought you were shadow-related. Yet you can't form proper puppets." Two more haphazardly formed behind him, nearly missing due to Shanessa's save of a light ray.

I locked onto Arlene, who appeared from the doors. A phantom sword materialized in her hand. *Lure her in. Get through there.* I threw myself around the Goldstone's stand. Her sword swung, and I ducked just in time, the blade slicing through the air above me. I lashed out with a tendril, wrapping it around her wrist and yanking her off balance. She stumbled but recovered quickly and lunged.

The blade nicked my side, stinging. I forced the shadows to constrict around her, pinning her arms to her sides. With a swing of my hand, I created more shadow puppets, which clawed at the walls and struck at anything in their path. Except for Malik. It took more effort, but I avoided his limp figure.

Her body pinned still, Arlene's head moved between me and him constantly in confusion.

Leor's flames roared as he tore free of the shadows binding him. His exoskeleton flared as he charged, sending a wave of fire streaking toward me, searing the air. I dove to the side, the heat licking my entire body, held back by the suit's fabric.

Another shadow puppet intercepted, claws raking across his armor with an ear-piercing screech. Leor countered with a swing of his fist, his strength sending the puppet dispersing into the wall.

I rolled from a blast of rainbow light. Drystan came

barreling toward me. I ducked under his strike, got elbowed and kneed in the stomach and leg, and twisted away, my breath ragged. Another shadow puppet formed beside me, a towering figure with clawed hands. It shouldered past Shanessa and Drystan, barreling Leor into the wall with a deafening crash.

My heart raced as shadows swirled around me like a living shield.

"Eclipse!" Shanessa shouted. "Check on Aero!"

Gracelyn emerged from the same doors. She slid close to the wall. I rolled to the side of the room farthest from him, dodging three strikes from three people as she knelt by Malik.

Please. If Gracelyn is checking on him then maybe—?

No. You killed him. Don't you deserve the same fate?

Drystan lunged from the side and slammed into me. Pain exploded across my ribs as I hit the wall. I forced myself upright. The shadows twisted and surged, forming another towering puppet that picked him up like a toddler and sent him sprawling.

"Leor, pull back!" Shanessa shouted. A shield flickered around her, deflecting a tendril of darkness that lashed toward her head. "Keep her away from Malik and corner her."

Arlene blurred, her phantom sword slicing through the air and her other hand extending out. I barely dodged while spinning, yanking her off balance again, the reach falling short.

Leor charged, each step leaving burnt streaks on the metal floor. I twisted their own shadows into spikes from the ground, but he batted them aside. Straining, I demanded them to be stronger, sweat breaking on my head. They pierced through the gaps in his armor, slamming him backward.

"No!" Gracelyn cried. She abandoned Malik's less-pale body and rushed toward Leor. Blood streaked his armor as he lay on the ground. Gracelyn knelt beside him, her hands glowing. Her eyes locked on me, teeth clenched. "You—"

I darted into the smoke, forcing the shadows to spread outward and mimic fleeing figures in every direction. A sharp whistle rang out.

"Don't let her get away!" Shanessa shouted, blinding light erupting around me.

A rainbow-colored blast seared past me. My vision completely darkened as I reached the hatch. I could tell I was still moving as my sight went in and out. I threw it open, the Skyship shaking. The Aegis's voices faded into the distance as I slipped through the hatch to the ladder.

When my feet finally hit the ground, I ran and found the second closest thing to cover, collapsing against the cold metal. It took all my will not to immediately allow myself to sleep. *You did it...* I touched the Blue Goldstone in my pocket. A tear streaked down my cheek. *You killed him. Malik, those guards won't die for no reason. I will make sure of it.*

Seconds later, I propelled myself back to my feet and left in the direction of Taavi's house. I wouldn't make it. But hopefully, I'd find a secluded resting spot further away.

****

The alley reeked of garbage, the acrid smell mingling with the copper tang of blood. Each step felt heavier than the last, my boots scuffing against the uneven pavement. My knees buckled, and my ribs ached as I pressed myself against the stone wall of a crumbling building. Dust clung to the floor and any exposed surface. Some puffed with each step I took, settling right back to the grime.

Ahead, a rusted door hung ajar, the faint creak of its hinges lost in the noise of the city. I slipped inside. The room was empty, save for a few overturned crates and a sagging cot in the corner. The air was thick with dust, motes swirling in the faint beams of light that pierced the grime-covered glass.

My body trembled as my legs gave out. I half-sank, half-collapsed to the floor, my back against the wall. My fingers trembled, slick with sweat and blood as I fumbled to take off my helmet. Each breath came shallow and uneven, each one catching painfully in my chest. I glanced down at my arm; the various hidden grazes had crusted over, a dark smear of dried blood trailing toward my wrist.

In my pocket, the Goldstone felt heavier than it should. I remembered the shadows. Blood. The guards didn't move. Malik went limp, pale.

I killed people. I killed him. The thought stabbed to the surface, twisting in my abdomen. *They will never see their families again because of me. He will never-* I choked.

Cyril's worried pale face. The guard before the refined door. *Did they have families too? Was it worth it?*

Leor on the floor, bleeding. Breathing? Not breathing? Malik against the wall. The sound, *the sound.*

"Are you sure this is still for your family?"

I shook my head, tears brimming in my eyes once again. *Of course it is. Don't...* The sound of Malik's body hitting the metal repeated. Blood trickled across his neck. I dug my fingers into the floor, a hollow ache growing inside me.

The last time we talked, we fought. My chest seized, and I almost choked again. I pressed the heel of my hand against my forehead. *As Nyctara, what if I killed him? I never got close enough to confirm. But it looked so real. What if- he might live? What if that wasn't actually the end?*

A sob caught in my throat, strangled. The tears came hot and endless. *He tried to tell me something, but I... I* leaned my head back against the wall, the cold seeping into my skin. *I can't do this anymore. I need to apologize and make sure he's alive. That they're okay.*

How am I supposed to face them after this? If they- if Malik knew, he'd hate me. They should hate me. I deserve it.

I'm supposed to be able to inspire progress. One way by demonstrating how rusted their ways were. But my choice has only led to people getting hurt and dying. The only people nice to me. Malik. I slid off my gloves and clenched them. That simple action hurt. It demanded too much of a body unwilling to go any further. *I shouldn't have left Taavi. I can't do this alone. She probably would've...* The distant sounds of the city faded, replaced by the pounding of my heart in my ears.

Don't think about them, part of me said as my eyelids grew heavier. *Don't think about Cyril. Don't think about Malik. Don't think about what they said.*

I gritted my teeth and squeezed my eyes shut. My stomach moved and I felt like I was about to throw up. *I need to apologize. I should turn myself in. This isn't who I am.* My head lolled against the wall, heavy eyelids drooping. Everything went dark.

****

Taavi's weathered roof blended into the overgrown brush surrounding it. I pushed the door open, the hinges groaning in protest. Near the TV sat Taavi cross-legged, already watching the door. Her amber eyes flicked to the Goldstone in my hand before locking onto mine. "Dear, you look like you've been through hell."

I let the door creak shut behind me. Cyril leaned against the entrance to the kitchen, arms crossed. His glasses glinted, hiding his gray eyes, but I could feel them.

"I got it," I said hoarsely, the words scraping against my throat. I lifted the Blue Goldstone. "What's next?"

She came over. I brought it close to my chest before letting her pluck it from my hand. "I imagine the Aegis didn't make it easy. You learn your lesson?"

Out of the corner of my eye, Cyril pushed his glasses up, but I noticed how his shoulders stiffened. *Why did that make him react?*

"Taavi." I swallowed. "I killed people."

A beat of silence. "I see." I could feel the weight of Taavi's gaze. She reached out, tucking a strand of my hair behind my ear. "It'll be alright, dear. You need to rest. The final task will wait for only so long."

She's... not mad? My shoulders dropped. "What's the

final task?"

"Patience," she said smoothly, resting a hand on my shoulder. "You've done well. That's enough for now."

Cyril straightened, catching my attention. "I'm glad you're back alive."

My head snapped to him despite my heavy eyelids. His honey-blond hair looked tousled. "No thanks to you."

"I told you not to go," Cyril replied. His lips pressed together as if he was keeping something back, body braced.

"Cyril," Taavi said, her tone light but with an edge of warning, "why don't you give her some space?"

He sighed, meeting my eyes. The fingers at his side twitched. "You don't have to listen to her."

"I think I can."

Taavi smiled. "Smart girl." She faced Cyril and spoke like he was a child. "Let her decide. Go."

He hesitated. I exhaled slowly as he turned and left.

"You've made sacrifices," Taavi said softly, "but you're stronger for it. I'm sorry for what it had to cost. I don't expect you to forgive yourself easily, but understand you're doing what no one else will. This will be worth it. Get some rest. I'll make your favorite breakfast when you wake up."

I nodded and headed toward the stairs.

"Aris," Taavi called. "Before you leave, President Coast visited. He said, 'since Nyctara obviously had some form of shadow powers, all schools were doing an in-person check on their shadow-wielding students since the file reviews turned up nothing.' We meet with him on Thursday after school, which is two days from now."

With a wave, I descended without a second glance. *I shouldn't have left Taavi in the dark. She would've stopped me from being so reckless. Or at least helped.* I wiped my eyes. *And Malik? What do I...* I need time to think. I won't go to Ezrat tomorrow. I'll tell them I'm sick. My body needed to recover, especially my shoulder and side. My mind needed the space to process. Taavi wouldn't mind, right?

Chapter 17

ARIS SHELIA

A whole day alone hadn't been enough to recover. Students and teachers packed the building, filling it with noise and clouds of perfume mixing with sweat.

I barely made it to my classroom in time. Mr. Atherly stood by the board, chatting with students. Leor was at his usual spot next to mine, flipping through a thick, leather-bound book. The sight of him made me stop. *I hurt him as much, if not more, than Malik. He's not dead.* I slipped inside, the pit in my stomach refusing to leave as I sat next to him. I kept my eyes on my desk. *Malik might not be either.*

Thankfully, Leor never glanced my way. I did see the bandages wrapped around his arms, extending beneath his shirt, but otherwise he acted unhurt. He said nothing to anyone in the entire class, leaving as soon as the bell rang.

I bit my inner cheek, making my way to agility training. When I arrived, a substitute stood in Shanessa's place. Malik and Drystan were also gone.

By my third class, I wanted to go home. A total exhaustion and ache spread throughout my body, dragging it as if I had wrestled eight matches in a row then ran a marathon.

My instructor urged me to focus on the details as I struggled to conjure a shadow knife. It flickered in my palms, unstable but enough for anyone to buy that I had moderate training. I didn't have to fake it. Frankly, I don't even know if I could do better if I wanted. My body demanded more rest than the past day provided. When she moved on to the next student, I clenched my fist and dissipated it.

Finally, lunch rolled around. I automatically headed toward the tree, music blasting in my ears and nearly stumbled when I saw a figure underneath it. Malik sat, absentmindedly picking apart a leaf in his hands.

He's alive. My breath hitched. *I didn't kill him. He's actually breathing. He's moving. I didn't kill him.*

I should leave.

Malik's eyes flicked in my direction before bowing his head back. Exhaling, I hesitantly kept walking in his direction with uneven steps. My muscles braced.

He looked up as my shadow fell over him. "Hey."

"Hey," I said beside him. Closer than I normally would, for our shoulders to brush. "I heard about your team facing Nyctara the other day. You okay?"

Setting the leaf down, he nervously sighed, "Only good things, I hope." Seeing my expression not change, he picked the leaf back up and tore it in half. "Who am I kidding? A single villain kicked our butts and put Leor in critical condition. If Gracelyn hadn't been there, he..." Malik trailed off, pressing his lips together.

I faced away from him, bile rising in my stomach. *Critical condition? He looked fine in class...* My hands felt clammy. My eyes started to blur. I...

Breathing in deeply, I pushed down the rising emotion and turned back. "He's better now. I saw him in class. What about you? Are... you alright?"

"Only a scratch," Malik said as I brought my knees to my chest. "From my shoulder to my hand. And I was knocked out. It made everyone incredibly worried. They acted as if I was on the verge of death."

"Oh... And everyone else?'

Tilting his head against the trunk, he closed his eyes briefly. "All got hurt, but not as badly." His brows furrowed. "It was unusual... Nyctara looked... terrified. Almost like she was trying to avoid injuring us. Even according to Drystan, she completely avoided me when I got knocked out. But she still... I don't know."

I swallowed. "Did anyone die?"

"Three guards."

I flinched inwardly, curling my fingers into my sleeve. He clenched a hand, bunching the fabric on his uniform. The air felt too thick.

"I know. I wish you were on our team," Malik admitted

offhandedly. "Having someone to oppose her major or minor shadow powers might've given us a chance."

No, *you don't wish.* I dropped my head against my knees. *How do I fix any of this?* Grass tore next to me. I peeked to the side, seeing him flick shredded blades of grass in the air. They caught in the wind, carrying over a few feet before falling back down.

I have to start somewhere. And even if I might never see him again after all of this, he deserved an apology at the least.

"The other day, I'm sorry for snapping at you. For always, snapping at you. There's been a lot going on and I..." I cut myself off, my heart beating loudly.

He gave a small nod and I noticed the scruff covering his chin. Our eyes met. I expected to see a coldness or disgust, but instead, his blue eyes held an understanding. Like he knew something I never said. "I'm sorry too. I shouldn't have pushed. You warned me and I didn't listen. I was ignorant and oblivious in hopes that I guessed right. That's on me." He exhaled. "I'll do better."

I broke eye contact, picking at the tear at the bottom of my hoodie. "Yeah, it's good. What was it that you were trying to show me the other day?'

Malik hesitated, rubbing his neck where the tattoos peeked out slightly. "It's something I found while on a mission. I left the piece of paper at home, so it'll be better if I show you when we have more time."

I narrowed my eyes. *A piece of paper? About the crown? Wait, no, why would he specifically want to show me? Is it about my brother?* I considered pushing it, but I let it drop.

We sat for a while in silence. The breeze rustling the leaves above us, sending bits of grass scattering. A blanket of clouds floated into the Light wing, looking almost like lightning danced inside.

"Can I ask you something?" Malik asked out of the blue.

I glanced at him, tracing the discolored half-circles under his eyes. "Yeah."

"Do you ever feel like..." he paused, rubbing his forehead. "Like being a hero, following the rules, memorizing subjects at school is getting kind of, I don't know, boring?" I nodded and he raised an eyebrow. "Really?"

"Things aren't always so black and white."

He nodded slowly. "Before Nyctara, I wondered if heroes really made a difference. I mean, the public looks up to us and we say we're important. That they need us. History says that too. But without actual issues, what's the point of us existing?"

I stared at my hands. "To maintain it, I guess."

"I don't know," Malik continued, letting out a humorless laugh. "I don't like knowing my little siblings won't have much to look forward to." He rubbed his temple. "Now Nyctara is here, we at least have someone to fight and rise against. Yet the villain is really strange. Unlike those we've observed in history class, what she's after is more convoluted.

"I mean, yeah. She did attempt to go after two stones. Could've been more. But then, she also demolished half a district, pulled a kid out of a collapsing building during the tornado, nearly kidnapped the mayor, and likely other stuff I know nothing about.

"That's what I don't get. A villain protecting and saving doesn't line up. So if it's not power or revenge, what's she actually trying to change?"

"No," I said slowly, "I don't think it's that simple."

His blue eyes searched mine then dropped to his hands. "Probably not. It'd help to know when fighting her."

I recognized his words from class: A *hero disregards themself to rescue others. Understanding your enemy is the first step to saving...* and defeating them.

"You questioned the point of heroes. If you could make it better, what would you change?"

"I think I'd start by listening to people instead of shutting them down, like back in high school with Brendan. Heroes are supposed to protect and care, not babysit citizens. And it's not just that, it feels like we're just too busy trying to make ourselves useful to notice or ignore the real problems."

I straightened. "You're right."

He shook his head. "Do you mean that?"

"Yes," I breathed, feeling an unknown pressure on my chest finally ease. "Questioning is always better than blindly following."

A ghost of a smile crossed his lips. He nudged me with his elbow. "Are you doing better? Can I do anything?"

"I'm good," I said automatically. "As good as I can be."

Humming, Malik tapped a finger on his knee. The bell rang, and he stood, brushing off his uniform. "Guess we gotta head back."

"Right." I hung back briefly, considering whether to get up after him. "Thank you, Malik."

"Anytime, Aris."

As we walked back, a strange feeling settled in my chest. He didn't know I fought them. That I almost killed him and Leor after hurting Arlene and Drystan. And he trusted me. Malik saw me as something good as I kept him at arms length.

I should tell him. If he believes in me, perhaps there's still time to turn back. If I still can. Or, he'll hate me. And I'll deserve every second of it.

****

The final bell signalled a stream of students to pour out of classrooms. I made my way to President Coast's office, tugging my hood further over my head. *Shadow power checks, huh. Has someone seen something?*

Taavi waited by the doorframe, looking up as I approached. "Glad you could make it, dear. Are you ready?"

I passed her to open the door, pausing when she placed a hand on my shoulder. Wordlessly, Taavi held out a thin purple ring.

"Why would I wear Amethyst?" Dropping my hand, I took off my hood. "I want my powers."

"It's not Amethyst, it's Sugilite," Taavi whispered, her tone so soft that I could barely hear her. "Put it on and keep that hand in your pocket while we're in there. And watch your train of thought."

I carefully took the ring. "Why? Is his main Mental?"

"Later," is all Taavi replied as she stepped into the office.

President Coast sat behind his oversized desk, stroking his beard. A wine glass rested beside a stack of papers, and a trench coat hung over the back of his chair. His brown eyes flicked between Taavi and me like we were troublesome students in a lecture he didn't want to give.

"Ms. Shelia. Ms. Higgins. Please, take a seat."

I slipped the ring on and dropped into the chair across from him. Taavi gently sat into the one next to me.

"I'll get straight to the point," Coast said, clasping his hands together and leaning forward. "Given recent events involving Nyctara, and the upcoming major festival, we're conducting evaluations of all students with shadow-related and air-related abilities. Naturally, Aris's powers are under review."

"What exactly is under review?" Taavi asked. "What is the government doing to ensure our safety?"

"We want to ensure that no student's actions harm others. Shadow powers, by nature, are often misunderstood and exploited." I touched my piercing as he continued smoothly, focusing on me, "You don't need to worry about the specifics. We already have suspects behind bars. This is a precaution, nothing more."

I nodded. Coast shifted his attention to Taavi. "Ms. Higgins, you've been instrumental in helping plenty of students adjust to their powers. I would like to formally thank you for all the work you do."

Taavi tilted her head. "Of course, President Coast."

"Ms. Shelia, as you probably know, your placement with Ms. Taavi was unconventional. The City's Council rarely approves such arrangements in a short amount of time, but given her qualifications, your age, and the circumstances, it was deemed appropriate. I trust you are getting along well?"

I stiffened, eyeing Taavi who stilled. *You played a part in fostering me, so why are you acting guilty? Is there more to it?*

"Suffice to say," he continued, adjusting the cuff of his sleeve, "your path has been guided. And I hope, now that you're older, you realize it was for the best."

"I think we're getting off track, President Coast." Taavi shifted in her seat. "You wanted to discuss the evaluations, not delve into history."

"Of course." He nodded. Ezrat's President met my gaze, studying it with a neutral expression for a solid moment. The ring on my hand vibrated. "Ms. Shelia, you've shown nothing concerning in your evaluations. Your grades and abilities are average. Continue attending your classes. You'll be informed if further action is required."

I stood. "Thank you."

He waved while Taavi and I left the office. Once out of the building, Taavi held out her hand and I dropped the ring in it.

"What was all that about?"

"Don't let anything he said get to you. Coast loves mind games, and his powers enable it." Her eyes stayed in the distance in front of her.

"Why do I feel like there's more to you becoming my foster parent than simply forgery? What was the ring about?"

"Nothing that concerns you. And the ring was to help against the President's Mental and minor powers."

I stopped walking. "It concerns me if it's about me."

She turned, her eyes seemingly flashed. "Let it go, Aris Shelia. Trust me, it's better this way."

I forced myself to bite back a response. Something in her tone stopped me. Instead, I nodded, filing the encounter away for later. A time I'd hopefully get my answers without her avoiding it altogether. That time wasn't now. I began walking again, and Taavi resumed next to me.

"Your path has been guided," President Coast said.

Taavi stayed beside me, her sandals clacking on the pavement. Distant chatter of crowds and kids came and went. After we passed a large group of people, I spotted one in the crowd with black and white hair.

I almost tripped, throwing my hands out.

My little brother skipped across the courtyard, clutching a blue backpack. His small form was dwarfed by the crowd of older students moving around him. The world slowed.

He looked up. For a fleeting second, I thought he saw

me until he turned. An older lady, Mrs. Parkzer, strode beside him, placing a hand on his shoulder and squatting to his side.

My heart screamed at me to tear through the crowd. To call out his name, grab him, and tell him everything would be okay. But my legs refused to budge. I couldn't go to him. Not after the note. Not after what I've done. My chest tightened. I choked back a sob. He shifted his bag higher on his shoulder and began to walk away with Mrs. Parkzer.

This is for him. Everything I did and was about to do was. He and Mom deserved a better life, a world where they wouldn't be overlooked, forgotten, or powerless. A world where authority couldn't hurt him like they had hurt me.

But it's not only that, is it? I flinched as Taavi took hold of my arm, nudging me forward. *It isn't just for Micha. It's for me, too. Because I deserve it. I deserve a say in my life.* I exhaled tightly.

****

School on Friday dragged painfully. My third class was nearly deserted. I stared at my notebook. I hadn't written a single word.

The sound of footsteps pulled me out of my thoughts. I glanced up, catching Arlene entering the room. She stopped near my desk. I chewed the inside of my lip.

"Hi Aris! How've things been goin'?" Arlene said lightly, sitting across from me. She shrugged off her leather jacket. "It's been a minute—okay, more than a minute—since we've talked. I wanted to check in if that's okay with you. So. Are you surviving school?"

Shrugging, I caught her warm brown eyes. "Yeah. It's been okay."

"Oh, I feel that." Arlene planted both elbows on the desk. "Like actually fine, or okay like 'everything's on fire but you're 'fine'? Either way, I'm glad you're here. Malik and Drystan can get so annoying."

I cracked a tiny smile.

"School's brutal. Nobody warned us it'd feel like juggling lightning bolts blindfolded." She wrinkled her nose. "That's definitely because my major is Power Manipulation though. But I'm glad they're starting to change the curriculum to be more action-based."

I nodded, fidgeting with my nose piercing. *Power Manipulation. What is that training like?*

"So, any interesting adventures lately? Favorite books? Weird dreams about talkin' cats?"

I shook my head. "No, not really. You?"

"Well, I'm tryin' to master the oboe. Might as well call it the "squeaky stick of doom.'" She laughed, her body turned to the side door. "Also went to an amusement park. Total rip-off. Can you believe churros cost twelve bucks?" She rolled her eyes, paused, then tapped her chin. "Oh, you still like hikin', right? I remember you mentioning that once."

I gave a short nod and she instantly straightened, eyes alight.

"Oh! We should totally go sometime. Maybe even later today! I found this spot by Taftside Peak. Super pretty around sunset. You don't even have to talk if you don't want to."

"I don't know," I started, but she gently took my hand and squeezed it.

"No pressure. Perhaps we can just chill out and watch movies with snacks instead." She let go. "Oops, sorry."

"I'm not watching a drama to sob over." I flipped through a page of my notebook. "But Taftside Peak doesn't sound bad, if you go late."

Arlene giggled, relief seeping in her voice. "I respect that." She hesitated and squinted toward the door. It opened.

I tensed as Malik entered, Drystan sauntering behind, tapping his fingers against the side of his leg. Gracelyn followed, wearing a cat necklace and a scowl while Leor marched in his cowboy attire. Shanessa was last, the light aura of hers shifting like she'd brought sunlight in with her. Her bluebonnet hair clip glinted while she waved. Arlene quickly walked over to her and helped her close the door.

Most of them settled into chairs around my desk, forming a loose circle. I closed my notebook, bringing my hood back over my head.

Drystan shook his head, exhaling almost with a laugh. "Relax. We ain't here to jump ya."

"We wanted to talk," added Malik, standing next to my desk.

"All of you?"

"Yup." Shanessa crossed her arms. Her blonde bob cut curled inward. "Listen, Malik believes in ya, thinks you're worth the shot. After last week, truth be told, we ain't got many other options left who might hold their own against Nyctara before she's sent to the pros."

I froze, furrowing my brows. *Right.* I curled and uncurled my fists.

"We've had our eye on ya," she continued. "You got moderate talent and you ain't one to back down. We could surely use someone like you 'round here."

I straightened, brushing a wisp of hair from my face. "You mean someone with shadow powers. Like Nyx's." I stared at her and Malik. "Sorry, I'm not interested. I'm not hero material and you have a full team as is."

Leor scoffed. "This ain't some hero fantasy. It's about doin' what's necessary. You seen what Nyctara's done. Folks died last week tryin' to stop her. We need to adapt or we're done. So if you don't want in, you should leave now."

"Leor," Shanessa warned. "Breathe."

I placed the notebook into my backpack and zipped it.

Gracelyn shifted uncomfortably, twisting her necklace. "What if we can't do it? Do we really think we're enough to handle this after last time?"

"Gracie, relax," interjected Drystan, sitting back and leg propped up. "We talked 'bout this. It's about puttin' in effort and fixin' mistakes."

"And makin' smarter decisions." Shanessa frowned at him pointedly. "Like not rushin' in without thinkin.'"

Drystan smirked tightly, pulling at the scar. "Hey, at

least I'm taking action."

"Aegis," Leor interrupted. "Bickerin' ain't gonna get us anywhere."

"Listen, we get it." Shanessa faced me, her blonde hair nearly touching her shoulders. "Give us one meetin' to convince you. That's all we're askin'."

Malik gently nodded. "Fine," I muttered.

He smiled warmly, shoulders loosening like he'd held his breath. The group began, and Malik discreetly leaned closer, voice lowered. "Real quick. There's something I need to mention about what we talked about the other day. Cyril. Does that name mean anything?"

I froze and kept my face still. "What about him?"

"His name popped up when I was looking into Taavi. I probably should tell you after, but..." He glanced at the arguing group and back. "I don't like what I found. Cyril and his grandfather were attached to some old council records. They are involved in some questionable stuff."

"Which is? Be specific. Why tell me?"

"Because I'm worried. It's not—"

"Malik," Leor interrupted sharply, "later."

He turned reluctantly toward Leor. Shanessa cleared her throat. "Alright, we know the peace ain't holdin'. Probably means the council needs tighter control."

"Maybe that's the problem," Leor countered. "We all saw what last week did."

Drystan tapped his foot. "Can we quit arguin' theories and focus on what to do?"

"That's what we're doin'. Nyctara got one stone from the ship during a transfer, and another days ago at the Skyship. Two others are missing, leaving one in the Crown still in our hands. Do you know what these jewels are?"

"Well, kind of."

"They're keys," picked up Shanessa in a grave tone. "If Nyctara gets all the pieces, she can assemble Shelby's Crown."

Gracelyn swallowed. Drystan's foot stopped tapping. "And if she assembles it," he said, quieter. "Rumors true, she can undo Shelby's work."

"Let's not think about it. Focus on what we can do." Shanessa glanced at Malik, like she hated even saying it. "Start by mapping Nyctara's previous hits."

"Next," Malik added, catching the thread, "we get eyes on likely targets and communicate with hero management."

"Three," said Leor, "we train Aris if she joins."

Every head tilted toward me. "Shadow does not counter shadow." I played with the hem to my hood. "It will be either a fight for control, or I take a portion and she gets the rest. Your best bet is Shanessa and Leor isolating her with shields for their own eyes. I'm sorry. My abilities won't help in this case."

Malik looked at me softly as Arlene brushed her arm with mine, brief in a way meant to be reassuring. I shrunk in my chair, hood shadowing my eyes, and let them keep talking like I wasn't the thing they were circling.

****

Rough bark dug into my back, through my hoodie. The grass blades rippled every so often.

'I'm glad you're here,' Arlene said.

My teeth clenched. *She wouldn't think that if she'd known who I was.* Frankly, I couldn't believe I had accepted her invitation to hang out later. Or that I was waiting for Arlene now that school was over to go.

Maybe it wouldn't be so bad, but she didn't deserve me to take up her time. Especially after I had hurt her and Malik's team.

The crunch of gravel brought me back to the present. Taavi appeared before me, like the day I first met her, standing with folded arms. "Still hiding under this tree?" She tilted her head, her amber eyes glinting.

"I wouldn't call it hiding."

She crouched beside me, fidgeting with the silver and red bracelet on her wrist, humming. "How are you doing, dear?"

Silence filled the space for a solid minute. "Is this really the time?"

"There's fire within you. A spark that could turn unstoppable if you let it." Her gaze drifted to the tree canopy overhead. "I see you're busy. Meet me tonight in the cave. I've got something in mind. Don't take too long." Taavi stood, brushing off her dress pants and strode away.

I blinked, staring after her, and closed my mouth. *Okay... what's that about? I wonder if it's about her history or information about what President Coast said? Maybe what happened to my mother? Eh, more likely it will be about the crown.*

The door to the school opened. Three figures spilled out in loose conversation, laughing as they crossed the lawn. Malik smiled beside Drystan, whose voice carried over to me of a loud story. His stark white hair looked messy. Arlene stood to the other side, waving at me.

"Remember the Taftside Peak hike I was talking about doing later?" Arlene asked brightly, half-jogging ahead of the others. "Well, Malik and Drystan are down to come if you're still cool with it."

I hesitated, then picked up my backpack and stood. "I guess I can come for a bit."

"Awesome." Drystan clapped once, spinning on his heel towards the mountain.

It took about thirty minutes to reach the trail, which Arlene used to tell a story about her last hike. Essentially she followed the wrong trail and ended up knee-deep in a marsh, which made Drystan laugh so hard he elbowed her.

"Okay," Malik cut in, fixing his blond hair. "Are we taking the lower trail or the summit route?"

Turning to walk backwards, Drystan called back, "I figured we weren't being cowards today."

Bouncing on her toes, Arlene pulled ahead, taking the steeper incline. I briefly covered my mouth, shaking my head.

Sunlight broke through the treetops, and snow dusted the edges of the trail, melting into slush where rock met dirt. The cave was on the other side of the mountain, so I should be able to get there at sundown.

Slowing his pace until he was beside me, Malik placed his hands inside his uniform pockets. "You sure you want to come? It's okay if you don't want to."

I bit my lip and nodded. Ahead, Arlene picked up a crooked stick and twirled it. Drystan pointed at her and said "she looked like a deranged forest wizard." to which she threatened to enchant his shoes to walk him off a cliff.

As we climbed, the air got cooler, shade giving way to dimming sunlight. I lowered my hood slowly.

"What were you thinking about under the tree?" Malik asked, nudging a pinecone with his foot.

I stepped over a thick root. "Do you think about what made you join the Aegis?"

"Sometimes. It was a pretty quick decision. Why?"

"You seemed sure of it."

He gave me a sidelong look. "I still question things, but I've made peace with it."

A snowball flew over my head, and another at Malik, who barely ducked in time. Arlene yelped as Drystan threw one at her, which missed and exploded against a tree. I almost smiled as Malik chuckled, making a few of his own.

After a few exchanges of snow, Arlene shouted from the ridge. "This is the best view in the entire city! Hurry up!"

We climbed the last stretch, the trail ended and the world fell out from under us. The valley stretched wide and golden in the late light, enriching the colors. Wind tugged Arlene's short raven hair as she pointed out the winding roads and clusters of sun-capped rooftops spilt like glitter between fields of deep brown or green. Clouds shifted below us, shadowing the sparkling lake far past the city and Ezrat's spacious walls, wedged between more rows of mountains.

Critters scampered around up here, shifting rocks and leaves with the refreshing moist wind. A large bug scrambled across my shoe.

"I always forget how big the world feels up here," she said.

Drystan dropped into the dry snow. "We should fake our deaths and chill out here."

"Do you even know how to light a fire?" Malik replied. "It is chilly."

Drystan opened, then closed his mouth.

Arlene brushed my arm with her fingers. "Aris, if you could live anywhere with no rules, what would you do?"

I shrugged, touching my nose piercing. *Find my family or disappear.* "I guess a rural place to spend time with family."

"Yo, real talk," Drystan interrupted, rolling onto his stomach. "I met this guy by Mala who's got a power like Nyctara's crew. Ya know, the other one when she went after the gem in the tech museum. Well, his name's Cyril. Hilarious. Says the most clueless things."

I stilled, then ran a hand through my ash hair.

Malik raised an eyebrow. "Anything useful?"

"Not even a little," Drystan replied, grinning. "But hey, he did spill info on underground scientist movements between Mala and Ezrat that our crew ain't keeping tabs on."

"How does he know about that?" Arlene frowned, sitting next to me.

"He wouldn't say."

"Sounds like he talks too much," I muttered.

Cyril could turn a conversation into something harmless, something harmless into something dangerous, and something dangerous into becoming hidden, with teeth underneath. I liked that about him. And that might be the problem. If he talks to people so freely; I don't know who he's helping. Or why. *I'll ask Taavi about him tonight at the cave.*

"Good to know," Malik patted Drystan's shoulder, snapping my attention back. "Say, on the way back, do you want to race?"

Drystan straightened. "Oh you're so on."

Nudging my shoulder, Arlene gave me a look. I sighed, the edges of my mouth twitching.

Chapter 18

CYRIL SHEPHERD

Leaning against the doorframe, Cyril idly turned a metal puzzle piece between his fingers. Inside the room sat his grandfather in a recliner, staring out the window into a garden. He wasn't sure if the man had actually noticed him coming in, but moments when his grandfather rested almost at peace were rare.

Sadly, his grandfather wanted to see him.

"Did you know," Cyril started and pushed himself off the frame, "that if you stare into the sun long enough, your brain will auto-adjust and filter out its brightness?"

His grandfather sighed heavily, rubbing his temple.

"It's like when you close one eye," Cyril continued helpfully, "and your brain fills in the missing details."

Turning from the window, his grandfather's dark eyes settled on him with a long, unreadable look. After a moment of silence, he spoke in a gruff, weathered voice, "I'll keep that in mind. Have you been keeping up with Taavi, boy? Did she send anything?"

Placing the puzzle piece into his pocket, Cyril chewed on his bottom lip. "Yeah. I'm just relieved we found someone else to replace me."

"So she likes the girl."

Nodding, Cyril gave a thumbs up. "More than me."

"That's good." His grandfather nodded. "We did the right thing. I was worried about letting you help her. Say, didn't ya hear she got caught?"

"What?" Cyril exclaimed, in part confusion.

With a chuckle, his grandfather kicked up the leather chair's footrest with his feet and reclined. "That's what they're saying. Three suspects in custody. They're sure one's her. I take it as false since Taavi's yet to call."

That's what I thought, but I couldn't tell if my mind was playing tricks on me again.

Walking to the small table where a half-finished puzzle sat, Cyril picked up a jagged piece. They were spread out in a mess, and he began sorting them. *She's still free. No thanks to me. What a terrible ally and friend I am.* Halfway through, Cyril paused. "Did we do the right thing?" he asked quietly. "She's a person we ruined the life of."

His grandfather hummed noncommittal. "Yes, but in turn, we made her into a storm. Storms don't care what they destroy, but they may instigate change."

Cyril turned a puzzle piece over in his palm. It was worn at the edges, bent from too many attempts to fit where it didn't belong. "Storms can be redirected if you shape the environment around them."

"Which is why she's better than you. After all, you suggested it when your powers weren't enough."

He flinched, shutting his mouth. That's not how Cyril remembered it, though maybe he recalled it wrong.

By the time Cyril eventually left, the sun dipped far behind the horizon. He slipped his glasses on as he made his way back to Mala. The path wound past a river, and he stopped on the bridge, leaning over the railing and staring at the stream below. It was calm, flowing smoothly.

The trickle of water soothed him enough to close his eyes. Which only brought up the memories. Explosions. Aris's frantic face, scrambling toward him. They barely made it out.

Aris shouted at him with full strain in her voice, "I'm not like you. I won't allow myself to be helpless and stand still!"

Cyril flinched. The skyship dock, with blood on her sleeve and an emptiness in her eyes that said more than she'd ever admit. This is all his fault.

I'm not sure if I want this to be happening anymore. He tightened his grip on the railing, then let go, leaving the water rippling below. *I'll try to reason with Taavi about it. We cannot be doing this to her. Yet Taavi may not listen.*

At Mala, Cyril found himself wandering in the library. He picked a table in the far corner and spread out the notes and books he gathered. The librarian suggested he look at a decades-old, worn document of a Council memorandum, so that's what he found. Lots of nonsense fluff had been added to the wording, but below in the bottom right, Cyril found his grandfather's scrawled name.

He rubbed his nose, taking off his glasses. The door to the library creaked open, and Cyril set the paper back, relaxing to see it was just another student. His mind hurt as if scrambled.

If I organize these papers, they'll start making more sense. He nodded to himself, exhaling. *Yeah, that feels right. There has to be a reason why I don't exactly recall suggesting a replacement. I'll figure it out.*

Chapter 19

~I should've done more, but...~

ARIS SHELIA

After training, I met Taavi by the cave mirror. Papers and maps scattered the wooden desk and stone floor, with two in particular held in her hand.

"Well done, dear." Taavi set down the two photos, and pointed at the first. "The final jewel with the crown will be located underneath the frozen sea, inside a temple. For one month only, there's a brief three-week window when the sea won't be frozen." She clicked her tongue. "I'll look into getting you supplies for breathing and temperature."

I recalled the woman who saved me when I failed to kidnap the mayor. "Wouldn't it be easier to bring someone with Water powers?"

"Depends if you can trust them. Even if you get inside, you won't have to fret about fire heroes or the Aegis. You will have to worry about better, professional heroes and Council guards. Unless..." Taavi walked her fingers through the air, the silver and red bracelet on her wrist sliding down. "You can sneak past with your stealth. Then you only have to worry about escaping."

I ran a hand through my hair. "You sure it'll be there?'

Nodding, Taavi tucked the maps into a shelf. I squatted and gathered the rest of them, handing it to her.

"I presume there will be various traps and wards. You'll need more than your shadow and Cyril's mental abilities to counteract it, so don't be surprised when I hand you jewelry to wear."

The mirror caught my reflection as I passed it again, materializing my little brother to my feet. My heart jumped as I moved beside Taavi again, escaping its range. *Once I have the crown, I will get you and Mom back. I have to.*

They'll forgive me if I succeed, right? They'll have to understand.

The cave phone on the wall buzzed loudly. I picked it up, suppressing a sigh. Taavi shook her head at me, turning back towards the desk.

"Hello?"

"Aris! Darling, it's Tegan. I need to cash in my favor now. Can you come to the amphitheater?"

I frowned. "Now, now? I'm kind of in the middle of something."

"Ohhh, please," she pressed. "You owe me. It's for the festival. I promise it'll be worth your time."

"I'll think about it." I hung up. *It can't be that bad.*

Taavi raised an eyebrow as I snatched my hoodie from the steps, then sprinted up the stairs without a glance back.

****

The amphitheater at Lumea's square bustled when I arrived. Workers dominated the area, setting up decorations and lights with music blaring in the background of some type of pop. The stage at the center was massive, its backdrop painted in bright golds and reds, the words '150th Anniversary-Victory Over Villainy' emblazoned across the top. About five heroes cleaned Shelby and Sean's statue.

In the middle directed Tegan, with people constantly coming and going at her side. She spotted me immediately and waved, a bright smile on her face that could blind anyone with Polaroids.

"Hey!" she called as I made my way over. "Thank you for coming!"

I took out my earbuds, stuffing them into my pockets. "What do you need?"

"I need help with a... performance. See, I want to put on a show for the festival," she clarified, extending both hands out to the stage. "Something large, dramatic, and memorable. Something that says: *me.*"

"Okay? What do you want me to do?"

Leaning in, her voice dropped as she winked. "I know you have shadow powers like Nyctara—" I heard the wink in her voice, avoiding directly stating it. "—so I want you to stage an attack. Something that looks real enough to scare but not hurt. It'll be paired with my magic so we can portray me as the hero who saves the day."

I drew back, stopping myself from giving a short laugh. "You're kidding." *You literally could've said anything else that would've been better than that.*

"Think about it," she said, nudging my wrist. "You'll practice and flex what you can do without being a terrible person, and I'll get the recognition I deserve. Win-win, really."

"You want me to 'pretend' to be a villain so you can look good and be famous?"

Tegan shrugged. "Say it like that, it sounds bad. But yes. You won't have to do much. I can use my illusion powers to make it worse than it actually is."

"What if I say no?'

"You owe me, remember? That little favor I did for you last month wasn't for free."

"You forget this festival is our city's biggest occasion. There will be a crazy amount of heroes and police that will catch me before I start."

Laughing, she covered her mouth. "Caught? You? Please. Don't you want to show someone what you're capable of? That you're not someone to be underestimated and shoved aside?"

"This sounds like a terrible idea," I pointed out, folding my arms. "And what if another wannabe villain actually shows up? What then?"

"Yeah, yeah. Look, heroes love their narratives, don't they?" She tucked a red strand of her hair back from her eye, and flashed a dazzling smile which I swear could cause ten car crashes. "It'll be perfect for our 150th anniversary! Villain shows up, wreaks a bit of havoc, and the city's beloved rising star, *me*, swoops in to save the day. Nobody gets hurt. And really, there's nothing better than to remind the people of why we host this festival anyway."

Blinking, her voice softened as I didn't move. "I get it, it's scary. But I've got you. My illusions will make sure no one gets too close to us. I"ll even make it look like you've escaped in a dramatic puff of shadows and the audience will be too busy applauding me to even bother chasing you." Her eyes sparkled. "Come on, don't tell me you're afraid of a little spotlight. You're better than that."

I clenched my teeth. *This would be a great opportunity for Nyx. But the risk of getting caught...* I looked her up and down as I tapped my arm with a finger. *I do owe her. That gem was no easy cost, either.* "Fine."

Tegan beamed, clapping her hands together. "I knew I could count on you! This will be amazing."

By the time I left, my mind spun. I walked back while fidgeting with my nose ring, focusing on its rougher, prickly edges. *I have too much going on right now. I'll just have to make it quick.*

****

More banners stretched across the streets, with one fluttering over my head as the sun dipped below the horizon. I stood beneath the shade at the edge, wearing my suit and scanning the crowd. Heroes and police walked everywhere and vendors lined the sidewalks, selling hero-themed merchandise to magical trinkets and fried food.

In the center was the amphitheater, draped in red and black streamers. The massive stage's backdrop depicted a sprawling mural of the city's greatest heroes. Among them: Lighter, Emozer, Plymouth, and Altruistic.

At the foot of the stage gathered four of the five college hero Presidents. Emblems placed right over each heart. *You never see all five together.*

Near the stage, Lighter spoke to Emozer and one other hero I've never seen before. Snippets about their '3-week freezing stay next month' reached me. Plymouth stood at the base of the amphitheater steps, and Altruistic hovered above the crowd, talking into her earpiece. Hundreds more heroes, including the Aegis, talked nearby the pros. Gracelyn leaned against a railing, her gaze flicking between the stage and the surrounding area, while Drystan bounced on his feet. Shanessa wasn't with them.

Perched near the center of the stage was Tegan, wearing a small bronze tiara. Her braided red hair shifted over her shoulder as she waved to the mass of people, revealing a black ebony necklace. Her freckled face lit up in a smile.

This better be worth it. I crept towards her, reaching the platform she stood on. Tegan's eyes met mine and she gave a small nod, spinning on the heel of her foot to face away. Her right hand clenched, and the light shimmered across the floor.

Taking in a deep breath, I pulled the shadows from the edges, intertwining them the best I could with her light. With a flick of both our fingers, they erupted and took the stage, flooding over the audience, smoke and darkness filling the entire festival. Gasps and shouts erupted from the audience, when a beam of light shone from Tegan, cutting through the shadow.

"Nyx! I know you're here," she called, her fingers brushing the ebony necklace. The shadows recoiled at the gesture. "Very brave of you with all these heroes."

Sighing, I raised my hand. Sweat beaded on my neck as two shadow puppets emerged, one a creature with spikes for limbs, the other a blob. Both seemingly went after Tegan, stalling when a large gust of wind shook the curtains. It rippled them and the illusions, which Tegan began to attack, her black necklace peeking out under collar. The closest slices of darkness to her lurched away or snapped from my control then back like a caught leash.

Heroes and officers assisted citizens in vacating the premises, while others attempted to fight with Tegan. She copied her illusions to my shadows, spreading them far apart across the festival, spaced just so from her position that it appeared she was fighting alone.

Altruistic and Lighter darted into sight, flying side by side in the air, eyes glowing a soft blue-green with a grey aura wrapped around their bodies, growing stronger and stronger so the darkness itself stepped back for the light to touch those below. The crowd immediately calmed, evacuating in a guided and orderly fashion.

This sensation rolled through the audience like someone dragged a hand over a row of candles and snuffed the panic clean out.

Stage lamps caught Lighter splitting the glow into thin spokes that skimmed over heads, banners, and occasional phone screens held up to record the "attack." Altruistic hovered half a body-length from him the entire time. When Lighter drifted a fraction ahead, the aura stuttered at Altruistic's edge, the nearest people blinking like they'd woken up mid-dream—then it snapped back the second Altruistic corrected, glancing at Emozer who paced on the ground beneath them.

All three are doing a power fusion. I stepped forward and out of my cover, letting shadows explode outwards around my suit. My lips twitched upward. Combined, figures appeared with falling debris. Taking the lights from above, I dimmed them significantly with my other hand. Then, targeting the electrical panel behind Tegan, it exploded, sparks flying.

This is what Taavi was saying about conflict. I exhaled, shoulders back, feeling like I could do this for miles. *Tegan's right. This is kind of fun.*

More screams came from the audience, and the ground thudded. I jumped, dodging an axe chucked at me. I narrowed my eyes. *That doesn't seem to be fully illusions. Are things actually falling? Do her illusions somehow give weight?*

Tegan kept at it, charging and slicing through puppets and figures like nothing. I sent a stray tendril to the necklace she wore. It frayed instantly. *Huh.* I couldn't help but glance towards the hopefully empty audience, where dust significantly kicked up. *No, she's insanely good at this. It's probably a part of the act. Maybe she's a pro hero?*

"You've killed people," Tegan began, her voice right next to me. I spun, but saw nothing. Black filled my vision. "And will kill more unless someone stops you. I will be the hero our world needs to restore peace."

I brought up my arms to shield my face, a wall of shadow mimicking in front of me. Explosions overtook the area again, throwing me back.

Amid the remains of people evacuating, a figure abruptly halted and faced me. My throat tightened, my tongue twitched to answer a question nobody asked. For a split second I almost forgot what I was doing. I bit down hard enough to taste copper. *Is that mind reading or another type of Mental? Where's Cyril when you need him?*

A whisper from Tegan slithered to my ear, "Aris, leave now through the fountain. I will handle the rest."

For half a beat, I stayed rooted, because the words didn't match the chaos around us. Handle the rest. Like she hadn't just turned a festival into a mouthful of smoke and screaming. Like the stage wasn't shaking under my boots. Like the air didn't taste like burnt wiring and panic.

Another figure separated from me with a cloud of smoke. An exact copy of my outfit, moving fluidly center stage.

I backed toward the stairs. After a second, I turned and sprinted, cloaking myself from view.

When I reached several buildings away, sure of no one following me, I paused in front of a TV. The news lady's mascara ran down her cheeks as Tegan wrapped up the battle, with fake Nyx fleeing and multiple heroes pursuing it. Dust settled, with actual structures shattered on the ground. Police swarmed the area, hurriedly uncovering the debris off of several bodies. Many civilians sat off to the side, blood and bruises painting their clothes.

I gulped, backing away. No, *no, no. Again? We gave them enough time to evacuate... I...*

"A devastating attack hit us tonight at the 150th Victory over Villainy festival. Tens are dead, hundreds injured." The news lady wiped her eyes. "The consequences would've been worse if it were not for Cosmic Storm, a local last-year student, who managed to defeat Nyctara alone. However, we're not in the clear yet, as our top superheroes are still pursuing and in search of this villain and any accomplices."

The camera panned to Tegan, waving and bowing at the crowd then disappearing in a puff of smoke like a cringey magician.

I clenched my teeth, my stomach lurching. *That woman is going to pay. She lied to me!* Adjusting my gloves, I strode away from the TV.

The headset buzzed. I clicked the answer button. "What?"

"Aris?" Tegan answered cheerfully. "We did it. And let me say, I love having Nyx as a friend!"

"We?" I laughed, slipping into a rundown building. The cracked concrete reached toward each wall as if to collapse them. "You made me a murderer. While you got fame, Nyctara is becoming the most wanted criminal our country's ever had."

"Well, hey—"

I snapped. "No, listen. You said no one would die or get hurt. That it was all for show. But you've killed people and I'm stuck taking the blame for it."

The other end stayed silent for a moment before Tegan responded. "I get it. Not everything went perfectly. However, we should really look on the bright side. Not everyone died, which, FYI, was NOT because of me, let me make that clear. Nyx did that. And you did use your shadows, did you not?" She didn't stop to let me respond. "And now... I'm famous for beating a rising villain!" She squealed to the point I could almost envision her lifting up one foot.

"Your illusions gave that impression," I growled. "You and I both know that never happened. People died. The festival you worked so hard to build got obliterated."

"Oh chill out." Her voice wavered. "It's for the greater good and all that. And listen, I have more control over my illusions than you think. Something else had to have happened in order for both the festival and surrounding structures to have collapsed. So whoever killed them, those deaths will not go down in vain."

I touched the headset. "What do you mean?"

"I'm saying, we either had another party there or you don't have as much control as you thought. Besides, this shakes people up. Get them talking. A little instability wakes society to a problem, don't you think?"

I shouldn't have agreed to this. I ripped off my helmet, ending the call. My ash hair spilled out onto my shoulders. *I shouldn't have let it get this far. Any of it.* I stepped through a broken window, making my way back to Taavi's house. *I shouldn't be doing this. I put myself at risk and hurt hundreds of people. All this for that stupid gem Taavi wants. Agh, I should've told her about this.*

Hot sun reflected off a building's windows. Immediately, I could feel my strength dimming, even as I stuck to the shade. I passed my school, the park, and a diner. People focused on the television, the news lady still covering the damage of "Nyctara" and the rescue of "Cosmic Storm."

A fountain's water flowed smoothly, an endless stream to the base where I could make out my reflection. For a second, I saw my mother instead, morphing into my brother, then back to me.

Mom. What happened to you? Tears filled my eyes but I wiped them away. *Why can't I find you? I can't even keep your last wishes of staying with Micha and ensuring he's safe. What would you say when you find out what I've done? Would you forgive me? Would Micha? Is there any way I can fix any of this?*

I squeezed the edge of the fountain, helmet resting at my side between my arms. "Taavi said that what I'm doing would make life better for you both," I whispered, glancing around to check if anyone was around. "That I'd fix this messed up world for Micha. That maybe I could save you from whatever they found you guilty of. And now I'm in too deep, I'm worried it's the only way to save our family. To save me from what I might become."

I sucked in a deep breath, slipping back to head to Taavi's house. *Shelby's crown is the only way to finish what I've started. To give me the power I lack so I can free my mom and give my family the interesting life they deserve. And if I fail, everything I've done was worthless. So in a way, it's to save my future as well.*

****

Taavi awaited me at the dinner table, with steamed vegetables and chicken on the counter. Her lips pressed in a puckered out line, a cup of water in her hands. When I sat, her eyebrows pointed up and she set the cup down.

I placed the helmet on the table and took a piece of chicken and vegetables. When I began eating, she breathed in deeply then out through her mouth. Her finger tapped the cup rhythmically, almost as if deciding what to say.

The muscle in her hands flexed and relaxed. Almost ten minutes passed before she tilted her head towards me, eyeing the food I put into my mouth.

"Just say it," I said between bites. "I know what you're thinking."

With a hum, Taavi stood with her dishes, walking to the sink. "Do you? Is that why you did it?"

I set the fork down. "I owed her a favor."

"Oh, child." Taavi shook her head, walking back over. "You are being someone's puppet. I bet she wore an ebony necklace."

"I'm not her puppet."

How did she know?

"You know why I picked you. Time and time again, you've seen what those before you have failed to do. Why... Why risk the same huge mistake?"

"I owed her, okay? Do you think I wanted to hurt- to

kill people?" My voice broke. I lowered my head to the plate.

"Yet, you still refused to tell me. Why can't you trust that I have the best intentions for you? Your stealth and power are the reason you'll succeed in your mission to save our world. Without it, you're just another failure."

"Failure? Wha—You don't really care about me, do you?"

Taavi rubbed her eyes. Sniffing, she pulled back her shoulders, meeting my gaze. "Do you really think anyone changes the world without false pretenses? You wanted power. That's what I gave you."

I stood, picking up the helmet. "No, I wanted to save and protect my family." I brushed past her, looking over my shoulder in the doorway. "You don't know me. And I know even less about you."

"I see you're angry." I froze. "That you need to prove who you are and you're tired of hiding it. You can't outrun this." Her voice grew softer, almost gentle. "You decide what kind of villain you're going to be. One who tears the world to ash, or the kind to build something new from the ruins."

Turning my head over my shoulder, I squinted at her.

"You made another mistake, dear. Learn from it or it'll cost you everything." Taavi tapped the table. "There's a reason I told you when we first met not to attack the festival. I fear the lashback hasn't come into full effect yet."

Taking in a deep breath, I turned back. "Whatever. I'm getting that crown with or without you."

Chapter 20

ARIS SHELIA

"Promise me you'll look after Micha," Mom asked.

I shifted the strap of my backpack. Questions floated back and circled in my head. *Who called CPS on us? What is Mom framed for? Should I try asking the police again? Pft, no, that's pathetic. I'm running out of options.*

Hot sun bore on me until I entered the school, beyond the metal detectors and multiple security guards. Inside, AC ran frantically, louder than the strangely absent chatter. Students filled the halls, though most watched their phones or spoke in low voices. Few bothered to look anywhere else besides their friends.

Though I briefly searched, I couldn't find Malik or any of his friends. *Are they avoiding me?*

Pft. You couldn't get rid of Malik when you wanted to. He must be busy in the Aegis.

The clock ticked, catching my attention. The first bell was set to ring in five minutes. *I'll see if they're in class today, I guess.*

I climbed up the stairs to my first class, where a familiar face waited outside the door. Arms folded, leaning against the lockers with his curly brown hair brushing his forehead, was Reed.

Upon seeing me, he stood straight and grinned.

I took off my hood and an earbud, slowing to about a foot in front of him.

"What do you want?" I asked, deadpan. "Are you going to prevent me from getting to class?"

His smile dipped. The kid rubbed his chin. "Look, I'm not here to fight. Actually, that's what I wanted to talk about."

"Not in the mood." I sidestepped but he shot out an arm to block me. "Dude. You need to get a life."

"You aren't making this any easier," Reed managed, his voice sounding strangled.

"Is someone holding you hostage or something?" I faltered toward the end. Within his tone held something I've not heard from Reed. A type of conflict that held rough in his voice, eyes shining like he regretted being here.

"What—no." He lowered his arm. "It's not that. The school—no, do you ever feel like you're not the main player in your own story? That no one cares? It's like everything I do I'm being laughed at or replaced. I say that 'cause my friends... I've realized that I haven't felt like that since being assigned—*someone* to watch..."

That no one cares... Friends... Words I didn't want found itself a burrow in my heart. Its thudding skipped a beat. Others from his mouth, "assigned someone to watch," spoiled it over it. A lemon sour tang to milk freshly poured, curdling it enough I could ignore the first feeling.

I replied flatly, "This isn't my problem."

"I know–"

"We can talk another time." I passed him. He lightly grabbed my shoulder. "Reed. I will—"

"Please, hear me out. The school— I wanted to..."

The halls were beginning to empty. Another familiar face ascended the stairs with his dress pants and cowboy-esc boots. Leor's eyes squinted when he ended at the doorway to our class. Then he slowly backed up, nodding to the hand. "Aris?"

"All good." I brushed Reed's hand off and entered, Leor a step behind me.

That's weird. Feels like Reed really thought we were friends before. As if I'd actually listen to him.

What did he mean about his friends and no one caring? I took my seat as the teacher handed out papers, stuffing my bag under my chair.

Why do I care? The thought came sharp. Its absurdity almost made me smile. Inside, I could feel words hooking under my ribs as my chest resided with the thought, giving with the potential of what his words could mean and still aching what was unsaid between us.

Besides me, Leor adjusted his hair, quickly glancing at me. The warmth of his power heated my side. "Malik was searchin' for ya this mornin'. He said he'll be by the tree during lunch since he won't be in class," he whispered and faced away to take the paper. "Also, no sweat on joinin' us. Just thought ya be a great fit."

****

Outside, the tree waved in the wind. A branch dropped to the floor, right in front of Malik's feet. He leaned against the trunk, arms at his sides. His piercing blue eyes, once staring above, now tracked me as I walked closer. A piece of his dirty blond hair curled over his forehead.

"Hey, how's it going?"

"Not bad," I answered, taking an earbud out of my ear. "Leor said you've been looking for me."

Nodding, Malik rubbed his eyes. "I have. Have you been doing okay? I've noticed you're more comfortable around us, yet somehow you're more distant than usual." Something was for sure on his mind.

"Yeah." I forced a smile. "Just tired and busy with school."

"Right..." He glanced away and scratched the back of his head. "Well, I read or uh, heard something interesting recently. Thought I should get your take on it."

"What is it?"

"Some students were talking about the house you live

in. That's the place near the edge of the city, right? They said it belonged to an old woman named Taavi. I'm assuming you live together."

I felt the blood drain from my face. "What about her?"

"Was she the woman you talked to under a tree like this a few times?"

"Why do you care?"

"Just wondering... Things happen and I wanted to make sure you're not in trouble or the sort. Speaking of, if you ever need somewhere to go, you are always welcome to come to my place. My parents wouldn't mind helping out."

Words evaded me. For a moment, I stood there, mouth slightly open. "Uhm, I don't need that," I answered, forcing myself to look away. "But... thanks?"

"Anytime." He walked past me, brushing my arm with his. "Offer always stands. I'll see you, yeah?"

I hummed in response and stared after him as he walked away. *Why did he mention Taavi? How did he notice? I* ran a hand through my hair. *Whatever. Honestly, after next week, I'll quit showing up to school. Then I won't have to deal with people pretending to like me.* I glanced away from him to the ground. *That's all it is.*

****

I leaned against the rough stone wall, arms crossed. Cyril stood across from me, flipping a dagger in his hand. His black jacket hugged close to his thick frame. On the fifth or so flip, he dropped it, almost slicing his hand open in the process.

343

I snorted as Cyril muttered and squatted to pick it back up, fumbling with the handle.

"I'm assuming he is coming with me?" I asked, facing Taavi, who was perched on her air chair.

Cyril tucked the dagger into a sheath on his thigh, then winked. "Good to see you too."

"Yes dear." Taavi nodded, tucking a strand of hair behind her ear.

I pinched the bridge of my nose. "Fine."

"You don't have to trust or like him," Taavi pointed out. "Though I strongly suggest otherwise, dear, since you have to work with him. Cyril has experience navigating wards and traps. He's essential for this mission."

Cyril gave an exaggerated bow.

"And what about you? Are you coming?"

She leaned back. "I haven't decided yet. After another week of you and Cyril training together, if I'm confident you can handle it, I may stay behind. But if not..."

"Okay."

Taavi stood, the silver and red bracelet on her wrist catching the flickering light as she gestured for us to gather closer. "Yes, good. Now, let's discuss the specifics."

She waved a hand, and the mirror on the wall shimmered before displaying a projection of the frozen sea. The surface was a vast expanse of jagged, shimmering ice, with cracks spidering across it like veins. Beneath the ice were faint, blurry outlines of a building.

"The crown's last jewel is in a temple beneath this sea, guarded for the three weeks it's not frozen," Taavi began. "It's been buried there since Shelby Feyth, protected by pro heroes, at least one hero President, and wards powered by every type of magic." Taavi waved her hand again. The mirror shifted, displaying images of various artifacts and tools. "Each ward will require a specific counter to deactivate. These objects will neutralize the magic protecting the temple."

The artifacts rotated slowly; the only two not part of our suit was a shard of ice and a vial.

"Both of you will carry at least two of these vials," Taavi continued. "Aris already has her suit, so we'll focus on getting Cyril his."

"What about the wards themselves?" I asked.

"They're embedded in the walls of the temple," she said. "Each one must be deactivated before you can proceed. Once you're past them, you'll retrieve the crown at the center of the temple. But removing it may trigger a failsafe."

Cyril raised an eyebrow. "You mean like in those treasure hunts, where the roof collapses and water rises if you take the treasure."

"In this case, I highly suspect a flashflood. Could be any number of things," Taavi said flatly. "Seeing its design, the temple appears prepared to collapse thirty minutes after the crown with the black opal is removed. You'll need to get out quickly."

The image on the mirror disappeared. I twisted my

earring, staring at my reflection.

"Sounds fun," Cyril muttered, stretching his arms. "Glad I'm not the only one doing it anymore... Wouldn't it be a lot easier if we had someone with Water powers? Especially against heroes who definitely will?"

Nodding, Taavi touched her feet on the ground and began walking towards the training tunnel. "Yes, like I told Aris. But we'll have to make due. Now come."

Cyril gasped, pushing his glasses further up his nose. "No, don't tell me... Already?" He skipped ahead, walking in line with Taavi. "Only select last years and top heroes learn it!"

I shook my head, a few steps behind them. "What are you talking about, Cyril?"

Taavi tapped the wall, opening the door to the tunnel and stepped inside. She beckoned us to follow, smiling. "For the next week, you will be training together and with me. I will teach you how to combine your powers with others. I've only shown you the surface, Aris."

****

Little kids laughed on the playground, with adults observing from afar. I sat on a hill overseeing the park, tearing apart blades of grass in my hands. Mrs. Parkzer's house, presumably with Micha inside, rested on the other side, the kitchen light on.

"Hey, can we get ice cream?" Micha asked, skipping *besides me, our hands swinging.*

My mother laughed, taking his little fingers into her

palm. *"You already had a cone an hour ago."*

"Yeah!" He giggled. "And I want more! Pleaseeeee mom!"

I wiped my eyes, smiling. "Probably shouldn't have told him Water wielders like you can make ice."

Her eyes gleamed. "That does complicate things. Perhaps we should get food instead?"

"No, I already ate!" Micha declared.

Frowning, my mom raised an eyebrow. "Really? I think you're lying to me."

Covering his nose, he giggled. "No! Am not!"

"When you lie, your nose doesn't twitch. Your left eyebrow does."

I inhaled slowly and leaned back with my hood falling down. My stomach growled. *If only I could go back and make it last forever. Now I'm about to change everything in a few days... Is it possible to go back?*

"You ate today, right?" a voice said behind me. I didn't move as Malik sat beside me, with one leg stuck out and his arm draped over the other.

I shook my head.

"I haven't either. I was thinking about going to get something from a restaurant."

"Okay... why are you here?"

He sighed, tilting his head towards the sky. "I needed a

walk from training. They made me sit through a three-hour ethics presentation yesterday. Definitely a waste of time. I already know not to vaporize someone for cutting in line or for calling me a name."

I exhaled sharply before I could catch myself, sneaking a glance at him. "You sure?"

Running a hand over his face, he groaned. "Oh my gosh. Please spare me."

"Alright. How's your family been?" I smirked.

"Well, all three of my little siblings think I'm some kinda genius because I'm in the Aegis. They're wrong," he answered. "Do you ever talk to your brother about school stuff?"

My heart dropped. I lowered my head. "Micha's eight now. We haven't talked much the last two years, but I'm pretty sure he thinks I'm a shadow ninja hero or something."

"Why haven't you talked much?" Malik asked softly. "Aren't you two close? Is it something to do with that foster situation Drystan mentioned? Shouldn't they be scheduling monthly or weekly hang out sessions?"

"It's... complicated. I can't do much about it." I clenched my hand. "But I'm trying."

"Hey." He placed a hand on my shoulder. "Let's get your mind off of it. Here." Standing up, he held it out. "Come with me."

I hesitated. "Where do you want to go?"

"It can either be a surprise, or there's three options for

you to choose from. One's a restaurant."

I took it and stood. "How about we walk?"

Shrugging, Malik scratched the back of his head. "Sounds good. There's a place in the forest I could show you. Suppose we can walk around there?"

I nodded as we began walking toward the woods. After we exited the city, crossed over some hills, a large mix of oak, pine, and aspen trees began to surround us. Most of the journey was in silence until we reached a semi-clearing.

In the middle, Malik faced me, widening his stance. I squinted at him, dropping my hands out of my pockets and to my sides. "Wanna spar?"

I drew my head back. "What?"

"You heard me." He took a few steps back, beckoning me to do the same. "Whaddya say?"

Rolling out my wrist, I wiped my mouth with my forearm, hiding a smile. A small voice in the back of my head warned me against it. Warning me against showing him what I could do, by the off chance he'd recognize my style as Nyctara. But the louder voice wanted to test it. The shadows at his feet twitched. *She uses more tendrils and spikes if anything, so I'll avoid that. I'll be cautious.* I flicked my fingers and they exploded in a puff of ink around him, erasing my line of sight.

The air around me dropped drastically. Goosebumps rose on my arms. A bubble made its way out of my shadow smoke cloud, carrying Malik inside. My shadows themselves bent around, almost as if struggling around pressure. He broke out and took to the sky, gliding straight over me.

Wind picked up, taking rocks and branches with it. They aimed straight at me, which I blocked or knocked aside.

His attacks reminded me of Taavi's power. Of her trainings or her fighting besides me. Or more recently, our practice to combine our powers. I knocked another rock out of the way, summoning a staff.

Malik dropped behind me, sweeping his leg to kick mine out. I jumped over, spinning with my own leg out. It connected to his chest, knocking him away. A branch struck me in the side at the same time, sending me stumbling towards him.

Grabbing my elbow, Malik twisted. The momentum pulled me flat on my back beneath him. Placing a foot on my chest, Malik leaned over. "Gotcha. Give up?"

Bending my legs, I raised my eyebrows and tilted my head. "Nope."

In a smooth motion, I flipped myself to my feet, sending Malik stumbling back. Taking his wrist, I spun around his back and kicked his knees from under him. Coughing, he tried to wiggle out but I held a tight grip. After a moment, he froze. *That old trick?* I did not loosen my grip.

A rough wind swept over, sending my hair above my head. Suddenly, we both took the sky in a bolt. I yelped, clutching to his arm. He slowed down tens of feet above the trees.

"Now do you give up?"

I hummed, biting my bottom lip. I let go, combining Light Absorption and stealth with the shadows to hide myself from his sight as I fell beneath the first set of branches.

"Aris! The hell?" he shouted, sweeping both his hands to the area I fell.

What am I doing?

Closer to the ground than I'd like to admit, the air solidified under my feet. My heart raced as he barely caught me. I let out a breathless laugh, feeling my grip on the shadows loosen. *Perfect.* I jumped up off it, then to the next, reaching his side and catching his arm. He gasped as I revealed myself again and instantly lowered us back to the grass. I could see his hands shaking at his sides.

"Did-did we just do what I think we did?" Malik asked, rubbing his forehead. His sharp blue eyes met mine as he exhaled slowly. "That was reckless. What if I didn't catch you in time? You could've gotten really hurt..."

I'm so freaking lucky Taavi made me practice with her. And Cyril. I flopped to the ground. "I know what I'm doing. Combining our powers is not that hard. It's fine." *And that hero teams get a head start at learning fusion.*

Shaking his head, he sat on the rock by my head. "Seriously... You fight like someone who doesn't care if she gets hurt." Silence wrapped the space between us in a hug. Then he continued in thought, "Not to mention, I've been practicing basic combination moves with the Aegis the past two weeks. It's never been that easy with someone."

I shrugged, sitting back up. A leaf, tangled in my hair, fell in front of my face. I worked it out as I spoke, "we could practice it more if you want. I know it's usually reserved for last years, but it could be fun." I said it as if these little 'practices' didn't make us act like first years.

"Yeah, okay. Only if we're more careful." He nodded. "What would you want to try?"

"How about something close to what we just did?" I suggested. "You create an updraft, and I can use it to aid me in parkouring up and across hollow trees."

"I'll have to form the shields right where you step to preserve my energy."

Standing, I went to the closest tree and pulled myself up to the first branch. He gave me a thumbs up, so I leapt into the air, stepping onto nothing and onto the next branch. We continued doing this until I reached the top, where the branches thinned enough to barely support my weight.

"Want to try going to another tree? You'll have to do five air-shields in a row," I called down.

When I saw the thumbs up, I leapt. I made it three steps before the fourth air shield summoned too far out. My foot completely missed it.

My stomach lurched as I plummeted. Wind rushed by my ears, almost loud enough for me to miss Malik cursing. *He's not going to be able to catch me.* My heart raced. *Why did I think this was a good idea? I shouldn't trust him. Shouldn't trust anyone.* The fall slowed only slightly before I struck the ground, sending me rolling a few feet to the side.

Leaves crunched, growing louder as Malik knelt at my side. A dull ache spread across my body. "Aris, are you okay?" he panted, sweat brimming on his forehead. "I'm so sorry, I misjudged. Are you hurt?"

I squinted at him. "I'm fine." I stretched out my arms. Leaves skittered on top of me, swept up from a breeze. "Maybe bruised, but that's to be expected." He didn't move, eyes focused distantly on me. *Why is he...?*

"Sometimes you remind me of my sister," he eventually admitted.

"Don't you have two?"

"Yes, well, they do. One acts very similarly to you, and the other has asthma. She falls a lot during recess, trying to catch her breath. Yet, she kept pushing herself, refusing to stop or even take a break unless her body forced her to. Then she lies and tells me she's fine." I furrowed my eyebrows, waiting for him to continue while he straightened his sleeves. "I joined Aegis to protect people like them. But sometimes I feel like a volunteer doing menial tasks, disciplining, or like a fraud. As if I'm one mistake away from turning into the people we're supposed to be fighting."

"That's stupid," I said. "You have the best intentions out of anyone. You're not one mistake away from anything."

"How would you know?"

I rolled over and broke a twig in half. "Because I've made a hundred. It's not that easy. It's a path you decide to take, not a single decision or mistake. Those instances don't define you, but what you do about it does." I pushed myself up. "You're a good person, Malik. You make it hard to hate people. Even if you overstep."

Chuckling, he scratched the back of his head. "Thank you. You know, you're not as bad either."

I flinched, lowering my head. *As much as you know. If you've known what I've done, you wouldn't even be looking at me.* His smile stared at me anyway. *I don't deserve people, friends like you. If it's real.*

Malik stepped forward, extending his hand. This time, I don't take it and stand on my own. *This was reckless. If Taavi knew, she'd lecture or kill me.* The shade around us twitched, like it was itching for me to use it. *What am I doing? I should be practicing for the temple, not whatever this is.*

Then why were you watching the house Micha's supposed to be at?

I wanted to make sure he was okay.

Now you're with Malik, with scratches and bruises from goofing off.

I opened my mouth, realizing I was clenching it too hard. A shadow tendril expanded from my right in a whip, slicing across two large nearby trees. Both groaned and began falling towards me and Malik. Air brushed past me in a wall, but neither tree stopped. *You got to be kidding me.*

Holding out my hand, I bent the shadows to mimic it. Even together, they didn't hold. "Let's try making a fusion shield around us," I strained, looking over my shoulder.

Malik shook his head. "No. I'm not going to do it right. I-I..."

"Dude, now's not the time." I moved the shadows to a dome-like structure as both trees snapped, smashing right into it and forming multiple cracks.

Sticking out his hand, a shimmer spread across the shadow. Almost like a bubble, creating a hazy see-through area. Both trees rolled to the sides, puffing dust out in clouds. I dropped my hands, coughing and breathing heavily. Malik sat, looking as if the world was spinning. *We... did it. Now to make it so Taavi never finds out.*

Chapter 21

EZRA VRY

Ezra tilted back in the metal chair, rocking it onto two legs while he absently toyed with a soccer ball resting beneath his foot. His dark curls hung damp from the humidity inside the basement. Throwing his head back, Ezra exclaimed, "Dude, we can't keep sitting here doing nothing. I'm losing my mind!" He let the chair thud back onto all four legs and pushed himself upright.

Across the table, his friend Xiomara sat with one leg propped up on the chair beside her. Her blue-yellow eyes flicked up from the notebook she'd been doodling in. "For all the years I've known you, you're always losing your mind," she pointed out. "What's the urgency this time?"

Ezra gestured in circles with his hand. "The crown! You don't think it's insane Nyctara's going after it? If those jewel thefts are what people are saying—pieces that belong to it—that thing's like... world-ending levels of power. Shouldn't we do something about it? Like go after her?"

Xiomara raised an eyebrow. "How exactly do you know this?"

He glanced over at his brother who stood at a workbench, soldering wires onto a black piece of armor. The faint glow of the soldering iron lit up Seth's focused face, his brown eyes narrowed. Occasionally, he'd switch between that and this weird gadget ball.

"Well," Ezra began, scratching the back of his neck, "I heard it from a... reliable source."

Seth snorted, not bothering to look up. "Reliable, huh? You mean you overheard someone at school gossiping about her. Aren't you about to graduate? You should know better."

Ezra shot him a look. "Okay, yeah, I didn't want to say anything until I was sure. But it checks out! People are talking. They know she's been stealing jewels that belong to it. Besides, I hear an older woman's involved. Can't get the name, but she's got a reputation for being shady as hell."

The soldering iron hit the workbench as Seth set it down. "You're basing this on rumors."

Xiomara rested her chin on her hand. "Yeah, let me get this straight. Are you suggesting you want to follow a supervillain whom you never met, who doesn't trust anyone, into a temple under the frozen sea to interfere with something that could disrupt our world. That's guarded by pro heroes. Did I miss anything?"

"Sayin' it like that, it sounds bad," Ezra shrugged. He scratched his head. "Wait, it's under the frozen sea?"

"It is bad," his brother interjected. He turned to face

them. "Nyctara, Nyx, whatever you want to call her, is not someone you chase down. She ain't looking for help." He glanced at Xiomara. "You, as a reporter, should be incredibly selective about the information you share with people."

"She wouldn't have even made it this far if it weren't for Xiomara," Ezra pointed out. "She owes us. Plus you helped make her suit, Seth. If that information leaks, you could be in deep trouble."

Xiomara closed her notebook. "I saved her from getting caught only because it was entertaining, not because I'm her babysitter. She didn't ask for help, and I don't expect her to thank or repay me. And Ezra, I'm not interested in being dragged into something because you're restless."

"That's my point. You helped her, and she didn't turn on you. The crown, though..." He let the thought trail off, shaking his head. It felt as if a weight rested on his shoulders, growing heavier with the deflating hope they'd agree. "If we're there, we can slow it down. Maybe keep her from doing something stupid. Or at least... I don't know, be on her good side and not die?"

Seth shook his head, leaning back against the workbench. "You're assuming she'd even let us help her like this is a rescue mission. From what I've seen, she's not the type to take advice or allies kindly. She killed people."

"If we show up uninvited, she'll assume we're there to stop her and kill us too," Xiomara added.

"We don't follow her trail and hope for the best. We find a way to make her trust us without showing up empty-handed. You said it's under the frozen sea. What do you say, Xiomara? She'll need a pro like you to fight against other Water and top tier heroes."

Seth sighed, pinching the bridge of his nose, already sensing his younger brother's decision. "This is stupid, dude."

A faint smile tugged at Xiomara's lips after she shifted her head side to side. "It is. Ez was already going to do this with or without us. Going alone will get himself killed. And if she gets that crown and loses control, we're all screwed." She paused, her gaze growing distant. "It'd be a hell of a story to tell."

"You're both insane." Seth looked between them.

"By chance." Xiomara set down the pen. "But you're coming with us, aren't you?"

"You did bring up a good point about the suit." Seth dropped his gaze to the armor on the table. "Also, if I don't go, you two won't let me hear the end of it. So I kind of have to."

Ezra grinned, clapping Seth on the back. "That's the spirit, bro!"

Standing, Xiomara stretched her arms and back lazily. "Alright then. Now, how do we even get to the temple beneath a frozen sea?"

Ezra's grin widened. "Leave that to me. I've got a plan."

"That's what I'm afraid of," Seth muttered, grabbing his jacket.

Chapter 21.5

MALIK STYRI

Water trickled from his faucet—a constant drop of sound, resounding in his head. *Do something. Anything.* He braced his hands on the sides of the porcelain sink, staring back at his clouded reflection with messy wet hair. Droplets of water collected on the tattoos surrounding his neck.

There are many more missing people from the demolished buildings across the city. And I didn't see Aris come to school the past week. Is she okay? His grip tightened as he tried to tell himself to stay out of it. *Should I check? Wouldn't she just brush me off again like every other damn time? Like every other damn person.*

Except for recently, whenever Malik tried talking to her, she kept their conversations short. There was always a faraway look in her eyes and he never knew when he overstepped. But he'd be lying if he said it wasn't adding up.

Couldn't there be any other explanation?

Aris had Shadow like Nyx. No, shadow powers aren't definitive. But the way she's always shielded off from everyone. Or was that just her?

During school, she arrived with injuries after an attack and tried to hide it. And the other day, when she flawlessly combined her power with his as if she had practiced it beforehand... That part he also tried to ignore, yet the way she timed and angled her powers was very close to Nyctara's. *She didn't use the same moves. I could be reading too much into it. The other possibility is being a missing person or sick or...*

Days ago, he spotted her with an older woman under the tree. Taavi, he recalled. Didn't Aris tell him that's her foster parent? A name that was on the paper he found at the burnt government building. That name was the furthest he allowed himself to read before he felt like he was intruding on Aris's life. But he did look Taavi Higgins up after talking around.

A daughter of archivists, friends with Cyril Shepherd and his grandfather, Ashby Feyth. Clean record, but has only joined one hero team that had been disbanded since 2132.

Wait. The paper... it had Aris's current address.

Pushing away from the sink, he threw on a shirt, checked the paper, and left his room. In the background echoed the television, mixed with his three younger siblings voices as they played.

Through two halls, Malik made it to the front door before shouting behind him without expecting an answer. "Pops, I'm heading out. I'll be back soon!"

Outside, the late afternoon wind pressed against his back. Malik shoved his hands into his uniform pockets as he strode across the sidewalk. A street vendor across the street lowered metal walls, his cart of skewers still half full. The smell made his stomach growl.

It took nearly an hour on foot to reach the neighborhood at the edge of the city. The sky melted to soft blues and oranges. That small house sat tucked behind a crooked fence and two scraggly trees with dark windows. Overgrown ivy clung to the porch rails with no car in the cracked driveway. He walked the perimeter, pretending to scroll on his phone.

"What if I'm wrong?" he wondered aloud, rubbing the back of his neck. "What if I ruin our friendship by accusing her?" He exhaled sharply and kicked a loose rock off the sidewalk.

She had to be hiding something. But if she was Nyx... it didn't fully make sense to him. Why would she be causing mass panic and hurting people? Why would she nearly kill him and his friends? What happened?

A branch breaking snapped his attention. Aris emerged from the side of a building, holding something behind her back. The hood she wore was down, revealing the edge of her jaw. Despite being ways away, the suit she wore with iridescent greens and purples looked eerily similar to Nyctara's. Malik couldn't be sure from this distance.

When she saw him, she froze.

"Give me a second," she stammered, running past the fence and slipping inside the house.

Blinking, Malik replayed the interaction in his mind like a photograph. Slowly, he pulled out his communicator, thumb hovering over the Aegis channel. But he didn't press it.

His fingers trembled. If his siblings were in danger, he'd want someone to act. But Aris... if she was Nyx, she would never hurt them. He knew that because she had her own little brother. And Aris would tear the world down for him.

He closed his eyes and lowered the communicator. "I don't know if you're her, but if you are, I need to know why."

The communicator buzzed. "Yo, Malik, my man." Drystan's voice sent a relief through him. "Nyctara struck again. We have eyes on her next to the school. You coming?"

"Cover for me Dry," Malik answered and paused. *Eyes on her next to the school? Wait... but Aris is here. She can't be in two places at once. That's not one of her powers. Am I wrong about her? But she's still missing school, and looked panicked. Is someone framing her?*

"I have to check something first. It's important."

"Do you need any help?"

"No, this is something I need to do alone."

"Okay, I'll do my best, man. Stay safe."

Chapter 22

~If I turn back now, who would I be?~

ARIS SHELIA

He saw me in the freaking suit. I shoved it under my bed, switching into a shirt and sweats. I placed my piercings back in. *There's a chance he didn't put it together. I didn't have the helmet on, and I was pretty far away. I hope so.*

Fixing my hair, I double-checked I didn't leave anything on and rushed back upstairs. My footsteps thudded as I passed Cyril and Taavi and burst out the door, stumbling out onto the front porch. The air burned in my lungs.

Malik stood in the same spot, arms folded. "Sorry for showing up unannounced. You've been away from school, so I wanted to see if you're alive."

I walked to him, reaching for my hood but realizing I didn't put on my hoodie. "It's good, I was getting changed." I gestured to the house and brushed my arms. When I looked back, I caught him squinting at me. "What?"

"I've never seen you not wear a hoodie."

"So? Don't get used to it."

Another moment passed before he sighed. "You doing okay?"

"Why wouldn't I be?" I twisted my nose piercing.

"I'm making sure. You haven't been at school." His eyes searched mine for a second. A leaf fluttered, landing near his foot. Another spun once before dying still a few feet away. His brow pressed together, and a piece of his dirty blond hair fell in front of them. "Can I ask you something?"

"You did." I tilted my head. "But sure."

Malik gave a half-chuckle. His fingers drew from his cheeks to his chin. "Not that. Remember what you said two years ago in class?"

"I've said quite a few things since then."

"You once asked our teacher if locking villains up actually helped anything or one change," he prompted. "I've been thinking about that lately. Do you really think people grow more when they're hurting or when they're safe?"

I blinked. "Sorry? What kind of question is that?"

He sat down on the edge of Taavi's split porch steps, motioning for me to do the same. "Ever since that day, it's never left my mind. And then Nyx comes, sporadically destroying for no clear purpose yet indirectly reinforcing how you and most people say war creates sole progress. I'm unsure why you think those two things are connected, but I've been wondering if peace does too. Perhaps it just takes longer to notice."

"What kind of philosophical fortune cookie are you quoting from?"

"Partially, it's from class. You know, that place you haven't been..." He glanced away. "Sorry, I've been worried."

I shook my head. "Yeah, alright, that's fair. I guess, depending on who you ask, progress *can* slowly come from peace. Though it's nowhere as significant as during conflict."

Malik rested his head on his elbows, staring up at the sky. "You talking about war?"

"Yeah." I sat next to him. The splintered stairs creaked, shifting under my weight. "If you think about it, lots of inventions came due to a need or motive, even if by accident, such as Penicillin and antibiotics for soldiers. Take away the reason, there's less desire and push to discover more. Conflict is important."

He hummed, tapping his chin. "You see, I used to think that peace was a welcomed in-between... like the break before something important actually happens."

"Used to?"

"Think about it. The stuff that really lasts, like art, literature, science, medicine... only thrives when we're not trying to survive. Especially after a war to heal."

"You sound like a propaganda poster." I rolled my narrowed eyes.

He smiled. "I just think... Fear isn't the only thing that drives people to change. What about curiosity? Or love? Or wanting to make someone proud?"

The air stilled for a second. My throat tightened as I looked down at my hands. They felt empty. My little brother's face flashed in my mind.

"Anyway," he added quickly, "you probably think that's naive or stupid..."

"Not naive. Just... not always how the world works." My fingers curled. "I mean, people need motivation, and peace doesn't usually bring that. What I have seen is what it lets people fear and ignore. Or what it allows them to do."

Like a government who separates your family under its guise, then refusing to give me answers about it for years.

"Have you ever heard of the Great Reforestation?" Malik asked suddenly, his eyes on me. "It happened long after the wars, during one of the most peaceful eras in history. People from all over the world collaborated to restore forests that had been destroyed by conflict and industry."

"Really? People don't usually join forces even for an important problem like that."

"Yeah. It was about making something better simply because they could and needed to for the future. Think about art and music, too. Most of it comes from people trying to express beauty or process emotion." His blue eyes lit up. "Has fighting ever given you anything you wanted long term?"

I stared into the distance. *I guess that's true.* Malik, reminded me of my mom a little.

Her voice slipped in my head. *"Don't let the world decide*

what kind of good you are. We're not perfect, but hold onto yourself."

The last time I saw her, at her arrest, she told me not to worry. She taught us it doesn't matter if anyone else sees or remembers what we did. What mattered is still choosing to do the right thing despite it.

"We'll get this figured out. All I need you to do is be strong and look after your little brother."

I tried, but they wouldn't let me. Tears brimmed my eyes as I closed them. *Micha begged me to take him back... And even if Mrs. Parkzer's a nice lady, I just want to hold my little brother again. To eat dinner with you, Mom.* The muscles in my neck felt tense and pressed together like my back. *To even have Dad and Steph return before they are allowed.*

Only Taavi had been the one who'd given me the option, who'd gotten me close enough to save you and make our lives better. Who forgave me for making mistakes instead of punishing them. She acknowledged that you were gone instead of ignoring my desperate attempts to reach you.

I recalled my second meeting with Taavi easily. *"Progress comes through struggle. History has proved this, time and again. So what's left for someone like you in a world where innovation has been stifled away?"*

In our fourth meeting, I had asked her, *"If everyone breaks the rules, wouldn't that just cause mass destruction?"*

"Not everyone needs to, child. Only one. You want a better life for those you love, don't you? A life with purpose and choice. Something you can control. Do you think the Council will give that to you? Or will they decide what's best for Micha like

they did for your mother?"

I tried to get them back peacefully. Multiple times. To talk to the police, anyone in charge that could help. But they wouldn't give me answers. Only more questions. When I tried reaching out to my older sister or my father for help, there was no response. As if the line simply didn't extend far enough. I don't know if they were busy or simply never got it. I don't know if anything I said would've allowed their early return.

The only one who had tried was Taavi, who now waited inside for me with Cyril to pack up and see us off.

So has fighting ever given me what I wanted long-term? Not yet. But it will. Better than standing still.

Opening my eyes, I half-snapped, "Fighting forces people to move." My voice almost broke. "Even if they hate it, or if it hurts. Peace, fake or not, gives us permission to stay fearful, broken, and passive to what's really going on."

Raising his hands, he waited for me to catch my breath. "Okay. Okay. That's fair." He hesitantly reached out a hand, as if to touch my arm, but dropped it after a second. "But... Aris, who gave you the job of fixing this?"

I didn't answer, sliding farther away. *Is he...?*

"I've known you for years. You act like if you stop, everything falls apart. Who told you that?"

Pollen hit my nose as wind blew it from a tree, sending it circling exactly to where we sat. I stayed still, ignoring the itch.

"You don't have to carry anything alone. You know that,

right? You can talk to me."

Still, I said nothing. He sighed.

"I don't need to know everything," he added, softer now. "I can try to help fix whatever it is. Or at least, help you not do anything drastic."

I found myself gazing at him longer than I should've. Inside felt like Newton's cradle swinging too fast. I stood, jerking away. "No, thank you. It's nothing and I-I have to go back inside. Taavi's expecting me. You should probably go home before I get in trouble."

I spun around and stepped inside. Cyril and I had a task to do. Unlike the Crown and my family, Malik could wait.

****

Shards of frost stung through the suit. I tugged my helmet tighter over my head, feeling the suit heating struggling to keep up with the bitter cold. Ahead, the frozen lake stretched out in a jagged expanse, its surface glittering like shattered glass under the pale light of the sun.

"Should've brought someone with fire powers," Cyril mumbled under his breath, fogging up the inside of his mask. His thick frame looked awkward in the sleek suit, and he kept fiddling with the gauntlets like he expected them to fall apart.

"Oh my gosh," I said with no bite in my voice. The snow crunched under my boots. "You've been complaining since we left. If you're too cold, go back."

He snorted, a puff of condensation escaping his mask. "Like Taavi would let me live that down." Then he punched in

370

my general direction. "Plus, I know you want me."

I used my sleeve to wipe off my helmet. Each step sunk deep into the gradually wetter snow. With Cyril lagging behind, the journey most likely extended another hour or two. The ice didn't end as much as rot into slush, sucking at our boots, when we reached the edge. The lake at last cracked and opened like a jagged seam. Its still black ominous mouth didn't sparkle like the snow, but brought in the light as if it belonged.

I faced Cyril, who panted over his knees, his hands braced on them. I could imagine his red sweaty face behind the mask. I opened my mouth to say something but stopped. In the distance past him, three figures approached us, rising and falling into view over the distant pure white hills and gaining rather quickly.

"Company," I muttered, removing a dagger and lifting my arm.

He slowly turned, raising his hands. I could already pick out the people's appearance. One woman with blonde hair peeking out of her sleek coat walked ahead of two men, about the same height. One of the men struggled through the snow, like he hated the weather, and the other practically pranced through it as if it were second nature.

"Pleasure to find you, Nyctara!" the woman called, lowering her coat's hood and revealing blue streaks in her blonde hair. An axe strapped to her back peeked above her head, shifting with her body.

I pulled my shoulders back. *From the mayor?*

The man who moved happily through the snow, hopping in quick, foxlike pounces, lifted a gloved hand in greeting. "It's hard to find you, man. Looks like you could use some help."

Cyril rubbed his forehead, eyeing me. "Aw, do you know these guys? I was kinda excited to get warmed up before plunging into the lake of hypo-hypothermia." He clicked his tongue, slouching as if pouting.

I ignored him and responded curtly as they slowed. "No thanks. We're doing fine on our own. What do you want?"

The woman's eyes scanned me before she chimed in brightly, "to help." Snow collected on the parts of hair which escaped her coat. "You needed it last time, so I'm expecting more or less now, too."

"That would be great!" Cyril blurted. He immediately switched his tone after eyeing me. "Except, we don't even know your names or powers so... best go by ourselves. Even if it might be something super useful like Water powers..."

"Funny you say that." The woman chuckled, her arms folded. "Name's Xiomara. I have Water powers."

"I'm Ezra!" the man jumped in and jabbed a finger at himself. His muscles sharpened enough I could see it through his clothes. "My power's earth and nature. Though I also have three minors as well..."

"Ezra," the third man coughed.

Rolling his eyes, Ezra gave us a pointed look. "And that's my bro."

The third man raised his hand barely, like he was thinking about sticking it out for a handshake but dropped it.

"I'm Seth. No powers, though I do engineering and science." A rough, sharp burst of wind struck us when he said the last word. I stumbled. The hood to Seth's coat flew down, revealing wavy brown hair. He sighed, a puff like smoke flying from his mouth, while he tugged it back on.

"Sounds like we could use the help." Cyril nudged me with his elbow.

How can we trust them? Yeah, Xiomara saved me that one time and never asked for a favor in return. So what's making them want to help us? It's too easy. Maybe the heroes planted them or something...

Biting my bottom lip, I inclined my head to the woman. "Xiomara, is it? How'd you know we were here? And why do you want to help?"

"You make it too easy to find you." She ran her gloved fingers over her hair, shaking it and letting it catch on the handle of the axe. "We knew you were after the jewels, which could only lead to the crown, and well, that's a story if I ever saw one."

"We kept tabs on you since you made the news, wearing the suit Seth made," Ezra added. Seth groaned.

I blinked. "Wait, he made this?"

"Well, yeah! Someone had to."

"Had help," Seth grunted, moving towards the edge and nudging the slushy water with his toe. "Do you want our help or not?"

Breathing in, I jumped when Cyril placed a hand on my

shoulder. His eyes told me what I already knew. Having help from someone with Water powers could mean life or death on a mission like this. But that still didn't change the fact of what they're after.

A light in his eyes told me he knew what I was thinking, and let go. "Alright, tell you people what. We don't tell anyone Seth here made Nyx's suit, or that you helped us and got her out of kidnapping the mayor. In turn, Nyctara and I keep the crown and no one gets hurt." Cyril cracked his knuckles.

I stared at him as all three shrugged and agreed. Xiomara held out her hand confidently to me. "Like I said when we first met. Let's keep it entertaining. A good story is always worth the time. So promise me an interview."

"You walk in front and don't get near the crown, then we have a deal." I shook her hand, and pointed with my head to the water. "Take us to the entrance."

Flicking her fingers, like she was removing a bug, water exploded up as a geyser and wrapped around us, similar to the ball end of a sorcerer's staff. The rest of us secured our breathing apparatus as she lowered the group into the water, veering straight for the shadow of an extravagant temple, distorted from the wavy watery light. It felt like flying and floating at the same time. Where my weight was like it would be on the moon.

Xiomara steered at the front. Seth and Ezra hovered shoulder-to-shoulder behind her, Cyril and I flanking, tight enough our elbows almost brushed in the current.

Tens of feet from its walls, its form now extending far above us, she slowed as a teal honeycomb pattern emerged in a dome, encasing the structure. *Water ward. Out here?* Removing the one-handed axe, Xiomara struck it, a *wobble-wobble* sound emitted like a type of bass drum sloshing with water, and she alternated with her foot until there was a hole large enough to let us through.

The bubble squeezed inside, lowering us to the floor. My feet found solid ground of loose dirt and rocks at the temple's side, clouding each time my feet made contact. The building's white walls, textured stone or slate, expanded fifty feet high like castle towers, and only one entrance, with a paved front, could be discerned in the dim water. Dozens of arches spread over the sides like windows, where above, on top of each spiral tower shone a spike, pointing to the icebergs floating above. Stairs elegantly climbed to the entrance where we now awaited, not cracked whatsoever.

"Cy-Puzzler, is this the only entrance?" I asked.

He tapped his chin, spinning in a circle. "No, there are two. Unless we make one, then there will be more."

"Have you been here before?" Seth inquired Cyril, typing and swiping a screen on his glove. "There is no public information on this castle. To the public, this doesn't exist."

Shrugging, he winked and ignored the question. "The second entrance could be more of an escape route for guards. But either way gets us in, so it doesn't matter to me."

If there's an attack on the Temple, they'd likely assume we'd find another way in. I'd wager it'd be near impossible to break the walls though. "Let's go through the front." I decided. "I think it's time to diverge from the shadows and show them what we're made of."

It'll be guarded but hopefully unexpected.

Xiomara swatted her hand, moving the bubble to the front. The brothers adjusted masks around their faces. Hitting the front door, she lifted both hands.

Here it is.

"They'll know you're coming, Aris." Taavi told me. "Be ready. I'll keep the jewels here in case you fall."

This is the day I'll get the crown. Then who knows what I'll do first? I grinned.

Sending a barrage of black mass at the door, dancing around Xiomara's ice spikes and Ezra's underwater plants of seaweed or other, the thick doors, built not to bend nor break, budged open instead.

Xiomara popped the bubble encasing us. Rushing water swarmed in, pressure popping my ears, creating spirals of bubbles flying to the surface. Rays of sunlight wiggled past them, reaching us and through the temple's thick windowish walls.

We swam inside, the walls giving way to a spacious ballroom-sized entrance filled with water. Two spiral sets of stairs in the back led up to an overhang. Stationed between us and the steps, eight guards, clad in green armor and playing card games, all scrambled from their lounging positions. Scants of light revealed their wavy forms.

I knocked the nearest one out with a combo of my dagger's hilt and a shadow tendril, careful to avoid his oxygen mask. Ezra and Xiomara managed to utilize the security's muddled clamber, taking out six in unison, working with an oddly-grooved sphere Seth threw and stunned whoever it touched. (It jumped smoothly, and touched each of the guards' feet, like a marine animal headbutting its glass tank.) And Cyril trapped the last one in the right corner, her eyes crazed as she rocked her head back and forth in her hands. Bubbles exploded from her mouth in rapid succession, climbing over each other in a battle to the surface.

Up the stairs and its railings sprawled vines with spikes and seaweed, leading to a green and brown cracked glowing wall. Ezra swam to the left-hand staircase, reaching out his hand that touched the next ward. The plants lengthened, curling to him. Rocks lifted and spun around him as a shield. I watched Xiomara's own axe lifted and gravitated towards him, restrained by her sheath. She made her way towards him.

The ward broke and collapsed like dust, shaking the building once. At the top, ten more guards lined in formation, half without breathing masks. *Five water/ice.* Light seared down from the overhang, right past my eyes as if traveling through air and bounced off the right staircase, inches from my leg. I went to shoot up a wall, but the shadows felt heavy and resisted.

Xiomara and Ezra crossed arms, forming a whirlpool of rocks and plants. Cyril touched Seth's shoulder, feet from the other two. They huddled, forming throwing knives to fling at the guards.

The five water guards above spread apart, two with bubbles forming at their hands, and three with ice. Five others stayed behind them. The one who shot light took another's hand and vanished, while one of the last three guards swam to the water's sides, placing a hand on an arm.

Seventh has power manipulation. I blinked, managing to get the room to be a normal-yet-greenish light instead of close to none. A swish of water sounded close to my head. I spun, sending out a hand and absorbing a bolt of light. In the middle of the room the light user and the man reappeared, both with a rainbow aura around them that reflected off parts of the water and walls. This wall of air split the water down the middle, leaving a layer of space isolated straight at me.

Taking the chance, I formed six shadow puppets. Two animals, two hybrids of animal humans, and two with the sole purpose of taking their hits. Something hummed in the back of my mind while I had the sixth one slice the water the air guard reached to touch.

A ball flew over my shoulder, expanding at their feet and encasing them in a deep Russian Amethyst box. Cyril appeared at my side, laughing, his voice distorted coming to my earpiece. "That should block them until they pass through it. Say, Nyctara, what about we try that Paranoia Bleed while the air is still up?"

Reaching out my hand, I took his and expanded the shadows like a blanket around us. I aimed them at the two guards and let it surge, hearing its whispers like a nightmare.

Together we turned, and I disintegrated my shadow puppets. Xiomara and Ezra had two Water guards nearly submerged in the floor at the stairs, half-guarding themselves and Seth from ice projectiles. He handed them both a box, a wall of ice erupting above his head and melting upon bubbles hitting it.

Plants spun around a whirlpool, with rocks shooting from the ground and surrounding the rest of the water guards.

They regrouped together, with the light user and air user circling back and helping the water guards out from Ezra and Xiomara's trap.

Water circled our group, weighing my body down. Pressure slowed my body, like it was locking up. *Damn it, do something Xiomara.* She hugged herself, body curling in as if she was the most targeted and affected by it.

The last two walked up. The guard touched the sphere, and a shockwave rippled through me. Through my suit. My muscles spasmed.

Ice formed around the sphere, encasing us inside next to the stair landing. My muscles tensed so much, and ache spread across my neck. Despite the water, the pressure constantly on my body, I punched the ice. Shadows warped around me, expanding and avoiding my group, splitting the ice.

I shot out an arm, using a shadow tentacle to wrap around the guard and squeeze him. The pressure released. My breath came back easily. Spears of light hit me in the chest then, making the world go completely white. Again, I heard the splash, yet this time someone touched my arm. Energy sapped from my body. *What the hell? Why do I feel so weak?* I moved to use my shadows and they refused. They stopped responding to me.

Stupid power manipulators. They grabbed my arm as Cyril appeared at my side with Seth, his eyes glowing white. He wedged himself between us. The man instantly froze and backed up, shaking his head, eyes wide. His skin went pale and he dropped to the floor.

"They got me," I managed through the mic. Jagged ice

walls expanded between us and Xiomara, who kept attacking with Ezra. "My guess is an hour or more without my powers."

More air separated the ice from the water, and bubbles floated at an alarming rate towards us. Cyril threw out his hands as if he could stop them. Below us formed a vortex, pulling the three of us inside. Shards of ice and debris fell into it, shattering or breaking upon impact against our bodies. Almost like it's tearing flesh.

"Get me close to them," Cyril grunted, shielding his face from the ice shards. "I got an idea."

Seth shoved his glove in Cyril's face. "Got it. Hold on to me." He pushed out his other hand to me, holding a thin, hollow looking sword. I kicked, fighting the spin to take hold of the weapon. It moved through the water with zero resistance.

Together, they pushed off me. Seth activated a button on the glove and spoke into his mic. An outline hand of water reached out, assisting the glove and dragging both of them out of the vortex, straight to the group of guards.

I used the sword to stop the ice from mostly hitting me, spotting a spot in the wall where I could stick it. On the fourth spin, I jabbed it. My body yanked to the side, then floated out. The sword easily dropped from the wall, which I cleared easily.

On the other side, Xiomara laid on the ground with Ezra still fighting over her. Her legs and arms twitched, as if wanting to push her up but refusing to.

I glanced back at Cyril, who managed to touch two of the guards' heads simultaneously. A ripple shot through, and their eyes rolled to the backs of their heads as they crumbled.

Seth held two more swords, swinging them at three guards. Cyril forced his way to four more. Each dropped after his hand left their head. *What's he doing?*

Back to Xiomara, I dropped at Ezra's side as the light and ice died down. "Is she okay?" I asked, kneeling at her side.

"Yeah, dude." Ezra stared at Cyril, head forward. "One of the guards had paralysis as a minor ability."

That's fantastic. Three more guards remained, their movements sluggish compared to the beginning. Cyril and Seth played off each other. Gadgets exploded, waved, lit up, or spun around the guards while Cyril got himself closer. After a brutal stretch, he touched their heads and all three dropped to the floor like ragdolls.

The water stilled. All I could hear was my own hard breathing. Both men made their way back to us. When Cyril landed, I checked him over. Minor tears in his suit in the process of reknitting itself. Other than that, nothing.

"What happened to her?" Cyril asked, out of breath. He got the same explanation I did and made a joke that they turned her into a turtle on land, which no one but Ezra acknowledged. (He patted him on the back.)

Adjusting his gloves, Seth knelt at Xiomara's side and ran a hand along her side. "You're right. Paralysis seems to be what it is."

"The doors up there lead to more stairs," observed Cyril. He pointed past the overhang supports, toward the far wall beyond the stairs where doorways waited. "Pretty sure the water level ends after this. That's what the blueprints said, anyway."

Seth picked her up in a cradle carry. "Alright."

Passing the guards, Ezra used the plants to tie them up. Four doors lined the wall, and we went with the farthest left. Each step up felt easier, until we broke the surface. There, another glowing ward with silver cracks shined.

Cyril took out a pressure gauge from his pocket, and a thermometer from Seth's waistbag. He pressed both against the ward and breathed on it until a dull split spread from its middle.

On the third crack, Ezra body-slammed the ward and it fell into dust. We braced and opened the first door, where more stairs and a second door waited. We closed the other and decided to rest there until Xiomara could move and my powers revived.

"Nice move back there, Puzzler." Ezra punched Cyril's shoulder. "Wanna tell me how you did it?"

"Feel like guessing?" Cyril tapped his forehead.

Leaning against a wall, I lowered myself to the floor next to Xiomara. *Love mind games, don't you?* I ran through the list in my head of the categories of powers.

"I'm thinking you used either a minor, emotion, mental, or power manipulation."

"Correct," he answered, then yawned. "Well, let me know when you have a more specific guess. I'mma take a nap because these ladies are taking forever." Cyril drew out the last word while stretching his arms.

"Talk some more and I'll make that a reality for you," I

called, bending my knees and resting my head against them.

I heard a huff as I closed my eyes. The next floor or room awaits. Is it more guards? Or will it be pro heroes? If it is, that means the next area will have the crown. I wonder what hero President awaits there? Surely both know we're coming. But why are they allowing us to come to them?

Soreness crept into my limbs. Would it be the rooms themselves? Or about the wards? Are they cocky enough to think we don't have a chance? I shook my head. Guess we're about to find out.

Chapter 23

ARIS SHELIA

Energy crawled back to my bones about the time Xiomara shifted. She sat up quickly, removing her mask and letting her wet hair fall down her back.

I looked away while she stretched. Warmth spread under my skin. An hour had passed before the gaping emptiness that had taken my powers retreated.

Flicking my fingers at the shadows in the corner beside Cyril. They twitched, twirling into a spiral over his head. He met my eyes, then tilted his head to look at them with a raised eyebrow. Letting out a long breath, I released them and stood, turning to help Xiomara to her feet. *This is the best we'll get. We need to keep going.*

"Finally!" Ezra got to his feet with his brother. "Alright, what's the plan?"

Seth went to Xiomara's side, softly asking if she was okay. She nodded, shrugging him off. Her hair mostly dried as she pulled it back into her mask.

"Well, it makes the most sense if the crown wasn't at the top of the building…" Cyril said softly. "So let's stay on this floor."

Taavi said there'll be professional heroes here as well. They must be on the way to guarding the crown. As much as I want to avoid them, they'll lead us there. Well, I could use my powers to cloak all of us and we can still sneak past…

"They'll be expecting us," added Xiomara. "Mainly you, Nyctara. So Lighter will be there. And I assume his team."

Seth nodded, picking up where she left off. "Meaning they've set up traps against shadow powers." He faced me. "You need to stay by us and restrain your use of them. Do you have any others besides Shadow?"

I squinted. *I don't like that idea.*

What else do you suppose you do then? They are obviously trying to help you get the crown. It'll be quicker this way.

Relying on others has always ended badly. We accepted their help only for the water powers. Who's to say they won't get hurt because of me? I can't stay by their side. This is my fight. But the Crown is so close.

Oh, is that what this is… Blinking, I tightly answered, "okay, yes, two. Physical and omnilingualism."

A vein on his forehead bulged as Seth focused on the ground for a second. He pointed at Cyril. "And you. Your powers."

"That's no fun. I wanted you to guess." He sighed, then relented, "Puzzle creation, mental, and replication of people's features. Kinda like shapeshifting."

"You were the one who impersonated President Coast," Ezra realized. "That's crazy awesome."

Seth pinched the bridge of his nose.

"I've been told." Cyril smiled, running a hand over his head. I saw his eyes flick to me as I visibly tensed. "I bet she had it under control without me. I only wanted some credit and action."

That smile used to be so irritating... Yet I don't hate it so much anymore.

"It's all good. I know what that's like."

"Guys," Seth interrupted. "We're expecting Lighter, Emozer, Plymouth, and Altruistic. All of which will fight swiftly, with precision, to end it. Nyctara, you have to stay with either Puzzler and I, or Xiomara and Ezra, in case they use a counter defense on you. Especially watch out for Lighter. Xiomara, keep an eye on Altruistic."

"You're sure she isn't Emotion?" Xiomara eyed him.

He shook his head. "Her eyes don't change colors."

Holding up a hand, I waited for them to all watch me. "I don't think I should stick with you. If you distract them, I will slip past and into the next area. That way you won't be at risk protecting me from Lighter and their defenses."

Pressing his lips together, Cyril shifted his weight back and forth. "That works. At the same time, we should listen to

Seth. They prepared for your Shadow powers Nyx. You can't get hurt if you want to succeed on your mission."

I folded my arms. He took my silence as an agreement and went to the door and opened it.

Seven full sets of steel armor lined the left wall, with varying weapons of axes, maces, swords, spears, and bows. On the right side held shelves of old, rotted books and split wood. Light shone down on the dusty room, casting little shadows among it. At the other end rested another door.

My footsteps echoed. We crossed the room without trouble after Xiomara and Ezra checked it over.

The next door slid open, revealing an extremely empty, well-lit room. It formed a semi-circle: one side curved, the other straight and flat. On the other end opened a tunnel, like an entrance to a slide, only going up.

Cyril stayed beside me as the trio entered first. We closed the door, and a dull pattern of squares appeared on the floor, staying white. An emptiness settled over me, exactly like the power manipulation earlier, as if the bright light seared into my soul and squeezed me out like a rag.

Both Ezra and Seth shared a square, which didn't react to their feet. Neither did Xiomara's.

"Hey, Puzzler," I whispered. "Can't you use your telekinesis and fly us to that tunnel?"

"Theoretically, yeah. If I hadn't used so much high-level power on those guards earlier," he responded, tentatively tapping a toe on another square. Nothing. "Though I don't see the big deal with them. They're not doing much."

I hovered my foot over one, and a thrumming pound entered my head. I lowered it back to where I stood, biting my lower lip. *Why doesn't it like me?* About twenty squares separated from here to the tunnel. Each one extended a foot. I *think I can jump that.*

"Ohhh," Cyril said aloud, watching me. "It's a light room against Nyctara. Almost like how fries and ice cream don't go together."

"You need help?" Seth called over his shoulder, making Ezra look back. "Does it hurt?"

Backing until my shoulders hit the wall, I widened my stance. *Three steps before the first square.*

Ezra held out his hand. "Yo, are you trying to clear it? I've done jumps like that doing sports, and it's not easy unless you know what you're doing."

On my toes, I ran and leapt, clearing the air. Below felt like a hand of light closing around my ribs. The thrumming in my skull spiked hot. Wind gently brushed through my suit as one foot landed square in the entrance tunnel. The other skimmed a square, rolling my ankle. Pain cracked both in my head and up my leg so hard I bit my tongue. For a sick second I pitched backward. I threw my hands forward and caught myself on the rim, hauling my entire weight inside. The pounding left once I fully entered. Another grey ward met me just beyond its entrance.

I flicked at the crack, using shadows to crawl through and separate it. Dust crumbled in its place as the others joined. Sliding forward, I scaled up the tunnel's walls, ignoring each dull spike up my leg. Only Cyril struggled behind us, using his telekinesis and the brothers to help himself out.

Out the other end, a hallway extended with another pulsing wall. This time, a mix of red, orange, and purple. Cyril brushed it with his fingers, making it ripple.

Multiple colors. Previous wards had related a color to its power needed. Like the last, a grey ward signaling shadow to bypass. This one appeared different. *Perhaps it's multiple. Fire and... what does purple mean? Mental?* The same thought seemed to cross Seth's mind.

"Looks to be fire and power manipulation." His arms crossed, and he tapped a finger on his elbow. "My guess is that the only way through is combining three or more powers."

Silence overtook the space, and for a heartbeat, I swore I heard voices on the other side, around the corner. Like the pro heroes were already waiting for us to step into their trap.

Xiomara inclined her head. "Adds up to what I've researched. Ezra and I can combine our powers well." She faced me. "Are either of you trained on fusions?"

Cyril gave a thumbs up. "We are fantastic at it! I mean, Nyx is. Even did it with—" he cut himself off, adjusting his mask. "You know."

"Who's better?" asked Ezra. "Cause your boy and Xiomara's got it handled."

"I-um, am not that great," he admitted.

You literally practiced with me. Rolling my eyes, I stepped forward. *Water and Earth/Nature with Shadow. This'll be interesting. Has a trio combo ever been tried before?*

Taking a metal ball from Seth, Ezra rolled it between his fingers. "Don't feel overwhelmed. I'm pretty great at this."

The ball flung from his fingers as if he threw it, straight at the gate. Water droplets formed from the air, spinning around and inside the sphere. Extending my hand, I focused, pulling the shadows toward them. They wrapped through the water until it blackened.

Together, it smashed into the wall, and the ball split into pieces, clattering to the floor. Ezra pinched his fingers, and the metal shards lifted. Water wrapped around it again, this time forming into a sword.

Morphing the shadows together, I created a plant-like puppet, taking the weapon between its leaves and slicing the wall. It puffed in a cloud of smoke. I released it.

We continued, rounding the corner to yet another yellow, shimmery field. Beyond it led a path of no flooring, only pillars. In the middle held a platform, where Lighter, Emozer, Plymouth, and Altruistic sat at a table. All faced us in unison. Beyond them, tucked away in the corner, was a metal gate.

Lighter rose first, his light aura shifting with his rainbow iridescent suit. "Ah, Nyctara. The wannabe infamous villain. About time we met face to face."

Cyril and Seth went to the side, fidgeting with his gadgets. Xiomara and Ezra moved two pillars in front of me.

"There's more than two of you," Altruistic muttered. Her suit ranged a variety of colors, but she wore no mask or helmet. Only dark eye shadow and earrings adorning her ears. "Shame. Only thought one of us would have to fight."

"This is a temporary arrangement," Xiomara said lightly. "One that's become oh so very intriguing, *Gwen*."

Altruistic shot up from her seat only to have her arm caught by Emozer. "How do you know me?"

Lighter waved her off. "We're getting off topic. Your identity is public to everyone, Altruistic. Nyctara," he continued, stepping on the first pillar, "why do you want the crown?"

Isn't it obvious? I stifled a breathless laugh. Why ask such a dumb question? My teeth clenched. You should already know. You were the ones who took away my family.

Between us, the field faded and we moved. The heroes shifted by their table while we approached, staring at us with unamused expressions.

Plymouth gave a side smile. "¿Por qué siempre se pelean? It never ends up working well for them."

'Why do they always fight?'

Halfway there, I slid to a stop. *Wait.* Back when Taavi first found me, she told me the stories of villains before me. Those who tried to reach the public's eye and crawl to fame. To disrupt the peace, yet were always quickly subdued.

"Part of why you may succeed where they failed," she said, "lies in your powers and strategy. You'll never win facing them head on."

"You okay?" Cyril stumbled to my side.

I shook my head, seeing the trio paused two pillars ahead with wide stances. "I got an idea. Get Xiomara to throw a mist bomb and cover me."

"Gotcha," he replied.

A minute later I saw my chance. Mist expanded into the air, completely clouding the entire area in wet fog. Well, up to the tables where the pro heroes waited.

Cloaking myself, I leapt to the side pillars that edged the wall. Before I could make it, this *slither* ran up my spine, and suddenly chills expanded across my body. Each step, my body trembled like crazy and my heartbeat raced, then dropped. *Agh, Emozer!* All the pillars swayed and tilted. The last one between me and the wall broke in three, one third floating into the air and over where the densest part of the mist was. The other two thirds fell through another beam which simply vanished as if it were an illusion.

Red streams of light cut through the mist, extending to where I hid. Sudden as the chills came, they left, replaced with an overwhelming surge of warmth that made my chest want to puff out and drop my shoulders back. To hold my head high because I *knew what I was doing.* Insisting I step out of the mist. Despite it, I froze. The feeling raised a sense of discomfort and unease. Too familiar to Reed's when he used his powers on me back at school.

A figure dropped on my pillar in front of me, dusting his suit. His smile glimmered that of a sunburst. "Really thought you could sneak away in the mist, huh?"

Three shadow puppets formed at my sides. I sent daggers and balls of spikes at him, which he easily avoided or blocked with a light shield.

"I was hoping you'd be one for more conversation. It

makes this a lot more fun."

Metal scraped in the background, followed by water splashing and thuds of bodies hitting the ground. It took all the effort I had to not take my eyes off Lighter. His gaze darted behind me, and his smile faltered for a second. I used the chance to crash him, smothering his figure with walls, shadow puppets, and spikes.

Leaving a single space in the smother, I used an arm to absorb as much light as possible and touched the ground with the other. Decay spread across like water, taking both of us down with it.

I jumped, managing to bounce off the debris to other pillars. The original vanished from view.

In the middle, the mist vanished, revealing Plymouth backing up from Cyril and Seth attacking her. Altruistic and Emozer hounded Xiomara and Ezra, getting close enough that Emozer managed to brush her shoulder.

Water split from Xiomara's, spinning around them like a water tornado. It took Ezra to another column. Altruistic threw her head over her shoulder, spotted me, and grabbed Emozer's arm.

Weight hit me in the chest like a falling boulder. This voice resounded in my head. *You can't do this. That's why you needed help. You can't do anything alone. You're incapable.* Deep grinding of concrete blocks shifted over all exits. *If anyone gets hurt, it's because you weren't strong enough to finish what you started.* My entire body tensed so hard until I felt a vein bulge in my neck.

Another figure emerged beside the two, crunching

gadget wires splayed under their feet, scattered on the floor. Some still smoked. *Lighter. I thought- agh stupid teleportation.* His lips rounded, like he blew at Xiomara and Ezra, which sent them crashing against a wall. She struggled to get back to her feet while Ezra didn't move from his position on the ground.

This is all your fault. Give up.

Clutching his side, Cyril reached me, gasping. *Do it. Let's do it.* Each piece of shade twitched, then moved as one, like another blanket over the professional heroes. Shadow puppets rose from the ground, got obliterated, and formed some more. Swirls of gold threaded through them, despite my teammate dropping to his knees.

I zeroed in on Altruistic. The voices in my head worsened and my body seemed to recoil away until the black thickened around her. It stopped, yet she still fought inside it. I could see her feet shift back and forth. Emozer darted at me, his feet crunching the debris. Groaning, Cyril shook his head. *Think.* I recalled the shadows to me after Altruistic fainted. Her body almost rolled off the edge. *Every weakness you've reviewed. Think.* They collected at my feet. *Every power has an opposite.*

A scent of gas entered my nose. Six metal boxes sprung before me, coming from Cyril's hand. "Go now!"

Shadows expanded into a large wall. I turned and fled, scaling the pillars. I passed the table, ending up at a metal gate. With a tap of my fingers, it was wasted into dust. I wiped my mask to clear my head and went through.

****

I rubbed my mask. It helped steady my rapid heartbeat.

I can't believe I made it past them. I hope the others got it covered. Like a stadium, seats circled the middle, where the crown lay on a pillow placed on the carpet. All of the surrounding seats were empty but one.

The man raised his head, his face fully covered by a spherical mirror. A convex view of the room and my reflection shone back to me of my black iridescent suit, helmet, and hood. I couldn't see my face. An ebony necklace peeked out on his neck. On his wrists decorated multiple bracelets and rings, many with gemstones except amethyst. His white suit appeared floaty, like an innocent cloud.

"Welcome Nyctara," he greeted with a light, feathery voice. "Have you come seeking power or fortune?"

I strode forward directly to the crown, with no inclination to answer. Shadows swirled at my side. My finger with the ring Taavi gave me buzzed constantly, its strength increasing.

"I see that guess isn't completely accurate. Cute little ring, by the way." A few feet away from the crown, he finally stood. "You're here to avenge something, aren't you? Tell me what happened."

"My little brother and mother were taken from me." My mouth moved before I could prevent it. I shoved my hand to my face but kept speaking. "No one would tell me why or what happened. No matter how much I looked. In a world where everyone pretends it's peaceful, why is mine not?"

"I see," the man smoothly cut between me and the crown. "How does destroying a city and heisting a crown help with that?"

I coughed, my voice catching in my throat yet forced to continue, "It gave me control. The only way people will listen to me is if I make them. The only way this life will change is if I force its hand. Taavi said our world needs villains." Tears brimmed my eyes. My hands rested empty without Micha's. "Yes, I hated how my life was. How boring our society is with its constant rules. But I'd give anything back to be with my family again. Yet no peaceful measure got me there. This is all I have left to get them back."

Someone's large shadow draped over me from behind. I could tell it was Cyril by the rounder outline.

"You," the man called, "are you Nyctara's ally?"

"I am. Name's Puzzler."

"And did you have anything to do with Nyctara becoming a villain? How do you know her?"

"... yes, I've watched her for some time."

"To what extent?"

"To do with her becoming a villain? Most of it."

Like an illusion, a video crossed my mind of Taavi writing on a piece of paper. Next to it lay a flashdrive. I walked closer, seeing my face plastered on it. Video-Taavi held up the paper with a wide smirk. "Finally, a person worth my attention." In the image, Cyril moved to the side and it cut off, switching to Taavi, Cyril, and a man talking to the police.

"Nyx, snap out of it!" Cyril demanded.

I jerked back, and spun on my heel to directly face him. I thought I knew what it was trying to tell me. No, I knew. And I couldn't keep the fierce anger or hurt bleeding out of my voice. "Taavi got my mother arrested? And you watched? You *let her?*"

"Yeah, well kind of-" he stammered. "Look, I'm not supposed to tell you-"

Pathetic. I whirled back to the man I decided to call Revelator. "You. Ask him what he means."

"Nyx, I'm not supposed to tell you. At least not here. You aren't ready..." Cyril tried, his voice growing closer.

"I'm guessing that this Taavi also wanted you to get the crown for them," Revelator prompted, dancing away as a shadow tendril lashed at him. "You're allies aren't who they think, huh? Must make you mad they're always lying to you."

"Shut it!" Jagged figures emerged from the shadows and launched themselves at the man. The majority of the light in the room snuffed out, leaving enough to still cast shade but make it hard for anyone else to see. Anyone but me. "Explain, Cyr-Puzzler. Why would Taavi do that to me? And you *knew?*"

Holding up his hands, then doubling back to cradle his side, he answered with a high-pitched voice. "Not here. I'm not trying to hurt you. I'm on your side."

"I'll make sure you get the vengeance you need," Revelator said softly, and grunted, destroying two more shadows. He hummed under his breath, fully facing me. "If you turn yourself in and help detain all your allies."

"I said, *shut it.*" My voice sounded strangled.

I threw my elbow with my body at him. A mix of tendrils, sharp edges, and spikes, puppets, and walls of thick black crashed in on him. Disintegrating black spread from my foot, edging to Revelator. He wrapped his arms around his torso, dropping to a kneeling position, then doubling over. Blood dripped from his lips and ran down his ears. Purple bruises lined his jawline and neck. Blood puddled beneath him. My legs were stuck. My head spun.

Those guards I killed and hurt. The Aegis, my own friends, nearly died. Malik.

Two hands wrapped around my head, one in front and the other behind.

"Sorry, I have too. I can't let you know." Came the only words from Puzzler as the world dove into nothing.

Chapter 24

ARLENE WEAVER

The constant tick of the roller coaster increased as her cart reached the top. It slowed, then shot like a bullet train in zero gravity. She could hardly hold onto her handrail as the momentum tugged her side to side, nearly colliding with Drystan.

He screamed, a large grin plastered on his face that tugged at the long scar. Strands of his white hair flew back until the coaster reached its final turn. Arlene was breathless.

They stumbled off when she felt a vibration in her right pocket. Taking out her phone, Arlene saw five missed calls from Leor and two from Shanessa. *Frick.* Her *friend* showed the same on his phone. She dialed Shanessa back, who informed them of Nyx's current attempt on the crown. Apparently, it was looking like she would get it.

Tsk. Arlene followed Drystan to their car, weaving around civilians and kids alike. *To think we could've made this*

Nyctara thing a cover up instead of letting her hit social media and the news. How did she make it so far?

Her phone rang again. It was Leor. She answered, entering the car. The boss immediately switched to grainy and glitch footage of Nyctara and four others fighting the pro heroes. They were holding their own. The video jumped or cut, making Arlene guess what happened in between. *Oh, I wonder if one of Nyctara's friends has electric powers.* "Hear me out," she said aloud. "If she's going for the perimeter pillar run, why don't we collapse the second one...? Oh... right. Let's not kill her. And they can't hear us. Fine, fine, next idea." Arlene looked up to Drystan chewing on sunflower seeds. "Man, can you please stop chewing during a crisis?"

A shout made Arlene focus back on the tiny screen. Emozer touched Plymouth's back, most likely drawing power. *That would...* Tears dripped down her cheeks when she watched two of the villains slam against a wall. And winced when it was followed by Altruistic falling unconscious. Lighter signaled to his team.

Cutting away, Leor centered the screen on himself. "Can Drystan hear me?" Receiving confirmation, he continued, "Nyctara is giving one hell of a fight. Thankfully this still gets us information about any other powers or magic objects she may have, including her fighting style. The second one, I think refers to himself as Puzzler, wasn't a surprise. The other three were, however. Never heard or seen of them before."

"Why is she after that crown again, boss?" Drystan asked, turning. "They're keys?"

"It's a relic from the ol' Victory Over Villainy festival. Symbolized the ending of that era. Fact, is said to have helped end it," Shanessa's voice answered. Arlene couldn't see her on the screen as the car jerked onto another main road. "Lookin like her team learned fusion combos. I'm guessin' they must be last year or professionals then."

Leor picked up, "And if word gets out, I betcha more wannabe villains will escape or rise to the occasion of taking the crown. We must keep this on the down low. President Coast has every professional hero monitoring civilians as we speak."

"Isn't the crown insanely powerful when assembled?" Arlene wondered, nearly dropping her phone when Drystan veered again. "I heard it's been the fall of many villain heists. Honestly, the pros only need to flood the room to win."

"They need the right powers," Drystan added.

Minimizing the call, she opened social media and looked at the tag. The topic "Nyctara" was trending, yet no videos showed up about her except older ones from days to weeks ago.

Both the leaders paused. "We'll go with that." Shanessa said. "Malik and Gracelyn are half an hour out. Make sure you make it by then or we'll miss them." She hung up.

Chapter 25

~Maybe this was who I was meant to become~

ARIS SHELIA

Cold carpet poked my suit. An emptiness clogged my brain. *I'm not at home. Wait, where am I?* Opening my eyes, I spotted a man with a spherical mirror as a mask unconscious between me and a pillow. Beyond, Cyril sat in the first set of stadium seats, one hand clutching his side and the other holding a crown. *We won?* The top of his mask pulled back to reveal his eyes, squinting at the metal. One black gem rested in its center, a black opal, with fractals of rainbow colors ricocheting off its center. *Did I almost die?*

Isn't there a failsafe on Shelby's Crown or something?

Xiomara and Ezra sat a few seats down, with Seth laying unconscious at their feet. A large slice extended down Xiomara's legs and arms, dried blood trimming the edges. Ezra's suit, from shoulder to waist, looked shredded.

What happened? Why does my head hurt like an invasive

*surgeon operated on it? We fought four pro heroes, then...
nothing. How'd I get into this room?*

Sliding my hands to my chest, I pushed myself up. All
three snapped their heads up to me when I moved. I bit back a
curse when my body protested harshly, tightening in all the
wrong places and crying from strain. Static sharpened behind
my eyes.

Fully on my feet, I stumbled over to Cyril, catching
myself on one of the armrests. "That's it? That's the crown?" I
held a hand. "Can I see it?"

He thoughtfully looked at me before placing its cold
metal in my hands. "You were out for a while. Xiomara said
she'd get us out when you got back up and running. We hope
Seth will be too, but he's taking a turn for the worse it seems."

"We'll have to take him to a special doctor. I can't wait
any longer," Ezra exclaimed, throwing his hands down. The tone
in his voice underlaid a kind of seething I've never heard from
him before. "Let's go!"

****

Cyril and I entered the city after a three day journey,
our suits and the crown shoved into bags, weaving through the
alleyways and sticking to wherever I could get shade. My black
and white ashen hair stuck to my sore neck. At my side, Cyril
limped like an old man, cradling his side. Hunger gnawed at my
stomach. *We need to eat.*

We separated from the trio midway back. Xiomara
promised we'd 'keep in touch' and told me to remember what
they've done for us as they rushed away.

By midday, we reached Taavi's house, sliding in through the back door. After I threw my suit inside my room, Cyril and I met upstairs with the crown, where he called Taavi. She said she was on her way home, and to start dinner. We decided on making chicken sandwiches. Well, I made them. Cyril rested beside the table, tending to whatever happened to his side. I could tell it bothered him enough that I insisted he didn't move.

The door squeaked open minutes after the timer beeped. I heard something hit the door, then the couch. A scent of cinnamon honey struck my nose as Taavi entered, sliding into the seat at the end of the table.

I walked over and set the silver crown in front of her. Her face immediately lit up as she carefully lifted it, spinning it around between both hands and inspecting the black opal. "This is it," Taavi confirmed with a voice more excited than I've ever heard from her. "At long last, we will save this world from itself. I will make those who let us suffer pay. It won't all be for nothing, Ashby. No it won't."

I set the chicken in between them with seasoning, hotpads, bread, and mayonnaise.

"Child." Taavi licked her lips. "Would you be a dear and go to Taftside Peak to retrieve two of the gems I hid there? One is under the desk, and the other in your training room dummy. It's about time we assembled your crown."

I plopped down in the chair to her left. My whole body filled with a buzz, as if I couldn't wait. But my eyes felt heavy, overtaking the buzz with a droning headache. The throb in my ankle returned. "Can I rest first?" I rubbed my eyes, taking the stuff for my sandwich and putting it together.

Her jawline clenched, but she gave a soft smile and nodded. "You've done well, little shadow. You deserve rest. Let's do it tomorrow. Would you both like to tell me how it went before you're off to bed?"

Yawning, Cyril finished his bite before speaking. "Three others joined us. Said their names were…" he went off. Taavi stayed expressionless throughout. We finished our food by the time he ended the story at the crown. There, he tilted his head back and forth as if weighing what to say, simultaneously chewing on his inner lip. "A man was there with a mirrored mask." I noticed Taavi's grip tightening on the edge of the table. "Whatever he asked, both Aris and I felt inclined to answer. But she knocked him out prior to figuring out our identities. Then I used my memory absorption on him. He should have zero recollection of us using your name, Taavi. Or any other privy information."

I furrowed my eyebrows, shaking my head. *Did I hear that right?* "How did I get knocked out, Cyril? You said he did it."

Cyril recoiled back a split second, small enough only someone looking closely would see. "Yeah, you knocked each other out at the same time."

Humming in acknowledgement, I stood up and took care of my dishes. *I don't know if I believe that. I mean, Cyril has stumbled over his words a lot and talked nonsense, so maybe that's what it is. But… I don't know. He did have my back in the fight, so it'd be hard to think he's lying to me.*

Then again, others have lied to me plenty.

I used the stairs' railing on the way to my room. There,

I showered, and lay in bed with Micha's stuffed dinosaur in my arms until sleep claimed me.

****

Crickets chirped outside. Darkness enveloped my bedroom as I sat up. Sliding out of my bed, I crawled in front of my mirror. My suit piled up beside it. Yawning, I ran my fingers through my hair, taming its wild strays.

You got the crown.

I *did.* I smiled and straightened.

Want to have one last night of fun?

I eyed the Nyctara suit. *Kinda.* Then sighed, pushing it farther against the wall. No, *I asked to rest. Taavi would want me to rest. It's a big day tomorrow.*

You've done everything she's asked. What's one little night going to do? She doesn't control your life.

That's right... I rolled over and picked up my helmet. *I do deserve some fun before assembling the crown. See the city once more before I set it right and find my mother and little brother.* With my foot, I flung the suit to my hand and changed quickly.

I made it out of the house in a blink, scaling rooftops underneath the half-moons watery light, breaking streetlights and skylights with each pass. The wind brushed through what little the suit allowed, cooling my skin. A sharp musk battered my nose when I turned, climbing a larger building. At its top, I overlooked the sleeping city with sparkling lights. Only few cars or people dotted its land, but otherwise, it remained still.

I traced my finger on the roof, the path I touched rotted away, leaving me with the word "NYX". Flipping off the building, I landed and drew the words both on the next few buildings and ground: Peace lets you ignore.

Up another set of buildings, I allow the shadow puppets to rise and roam, keeping them out of any late-night heroes' way. A dead mouse's body twitched with them, and skidded past me to a three-story overnight daycare. Shrugging, I extended my hands, taking some of the shadow puppets and forming nearly invisible giant black hands at the capital.

Someone grunted nearby, followed by the sound of fighting. I instantly vaporized the hands and looked down, where a hero sliced three of my shadow puppets in half. He looked up and instantly spotted me. My blood ran cold. *Aero. I mean, Malik.*

Bending his knees, Malik took flight right at me. I shot out a wall to intercept him and scrambled back to the center. He flew around it, landing at the edge gently. Forming daggers at my hands, I threw them and he dodged effortlessly, making his way closer.

"Wait!" Malik tried. I transformed them into a spear, twisting and jabbing it at him. "I only want to talk." Holding the spear, he pulled himself up and slammed his feet into it. It poofed upon hitting the ground. "Nyctara, listen to me."

I backed away, panting.

In a singular motion, Malik pulled off his mask. In his other hand clutched a piece of paper, which he held out to me like an offering. "I'm not here to fight you."

On it, I made out two words. My name, Aris Shelia.

"What's that girl got to do with me?" I grunted, forming a sword. "Looks like one of a million papers from when I lit a government building on fire. What do I care?"

"It is. And I think you do more than you're willing to admit." Malik exhaled.

I scoffed, aiming the sword at his neck. Three shadow puppets slowly rose in formation around him. "Yeah, right."

When they leapt, he lifted his arms to shield himself while shouting, "I know it's you, Aris!"

I dropped the shadow puppets, the sword vanishing at my side. I fought to breathe while strangling out a, "What?"

"I know you're Nyctara, Aris Shelia. I haven't told anyone I figured it out, because I want to believe you'll come back." He pushed out the paper until his arm fully extended. "I didn't know how to tell you. Honestly, I didn't fully put it together myself until last week. I thought it would break what little you had left. But the people you live with aren't who you think they are."

Managing a half-laugh, I used the back of my arm to wipe my eyes. "What makes you think I'm her?"

"Read it."

I reluctantly took the paper, flattened it out, and read.

<u>FAMILY STABILITY PROFILE — CLASSIFIED / ISA</u>

Subject: *Shelia family, 781-ML-29-U.* **Tier:** *Lower-middle class, five total people-- four adults, one child. Three live in-city. Two located in the country Almicen Nepif. Child in foster care. Recent adult lives with Taavi Higgins. Mother sent to work,* *unfit to raise children. See next page. Person of interest.*

Risk Factor? *Six speeding and seven minor traffic violations.* **Powers?** *2 SHADOW-C 2-4M, WATER-D 3M, check next page.*

Felonies? *Three, none active.* **Compliance Index:** *63.9/100.* **On watch?** *Yes.* **Notes:** *youngest experiences night terrors. Three indicate above-norm curiosity; detailed record of deviance or dissent page five.*

Hero-Program Eligibility: *YES. Flagged: perceptive bias.*

"How-how did you find this again?" I asked, flipping it.

Family powers: *Isaac Shelia (Father)- Shadow (Isaac's Mom- Shadow, Dad- none)); Rayla Shelia (Mother)- Water (Rayla's Mom- Physical/Mental, Dad- Water)), Steph Shelia (Eldest)- no powers, Aris Shelia (Middle)- shadow, Micha (youngest)- too young, 8, unknown.*

He answered softly, "Like I said, after the government building went on fire a month ago, I found it on the ground as Aero. I thought it was trash, but when I saw your name on it I kept it. I didn't get to reading all of it until..." he trailed off when my hands clenched.

On watch: *Rayla Shelia (Mother) arrested due to multiple police reports and footage from Ashby Feyth and Cyril Shepherd. She was accused and found guilty of: stealing and using magical objects, uncertified hero using powers in public as display and to 'rescue citizens', endangering children and government officials, and forgery.*

Locations: *Youngest child sent to the last household with availability. The Hanover's--they work nights. Eldest child sent to* *live with Taavi Higgins, a recently re-certified caregiver. Father and older sister out of the country for a research assignment. Attempted to contact with no answer.*

Water blurred my eyes. The back of my throat burned as the words stopped there. My fingers trembled, making the paper unreadable before fluttering to the ground. The shadows themselves shrank back.

"If I'm really Aris, why would you bring this up to me so late?" I choked. "How can I trust that you didn't make this up? Am I supposed to believe my allies, my foster mother used me from a piece of useless paper?"

"I know I should've told you sooner. Yet after years of knowing you, I couldn't believe you would... be Nyctara." A single tear ran down his cheek, mirroring mine. "You can still come back and turn yourself in. You're not alone. We can fix this together."

"Yes I am," I snapped before I could stop myself. I clamped a hand over my mouth. Well, where my mouth would be if not covered by the helmet. "I've tried over and over. I-No, no, this doesn't change anything." My heart lurched when I spoke, fighting with my body. *Talk to him. Let him help you.* My knees trembled, threatening to give out. "You know nothing about me. So stop pretending."

Shaking his head, Malik locked eyes with me. "You keep telling yourself that. I'm not them." He gestured sharply at the paper. "I-"

He got cut off by a young scream slicing through the air, "help!"

The voice rang inside me. *Micha??* I spun on my heel

and darted to the edge of the building.

The overnight three story daycare from earlier gaped with holes, cracked foundation, and missing windows. On the bottom floor, barely visible past the dust, was Micha and two other kids. Above, the entire concrete floor dipped, riddled with wires. Cracks spread around it as it hung lower and lower.

"Get out of there!" I screamed.

I moved before I could think, leaping off the roof. The floor above him creaked and snapped as it gave away. With a scream, my little brother shoved the other two away before getting buried underneath a mountain of rubble.

"Micha!" I cried, tears running freely now. I made it inside what's left of the structure, with Aero hot on my heels.

Aero's voice cracked, "Aris!"

"Get them out!" I barked. "Get the other kids out. A hospital or somewhere safe. Go!"

He picked up the two other kids and dipped out faster than I had time to remove the debris off of my little brother. My mask clouded, blocking my vision with the dirt and grime. I fumbled it off. *Damn mask. Please be alive.*

I reached where his body vanished and threw off sheets of drywall or broken metal. Every piece I yanked free slid into another. Dust packed my throat. My fingers found wires, nails, heat—anything but him. I couldn't tell if the wet on my hands was blood or my own skin splitting until I managed to uncover most of it. It didn't crush him. I dragged him partially out, his foot caught on a beam, forcing me to set him down. Micha's breaths were shallow, yet his eyes stayed open as he watched me.

"Aris? Is that you?"

I stopped and knelt at his side, taking his hand. I ran my fingers over his bloodied knuckles, then his dusty hair. He squeezed my fingers. "Yes, it's me. Don't worry, I'll get you out of here and to a hospital. You'll be okay, Micha."

He blinked hard, eyeing my suit. "No. No, that's—" He squinted. "What are you wearing?"

"Nothing." I let go and removed the last heavy piece of metal, ignoring that it cut through my sleeve.

My little brother coughed hard, letting his arms go limp. "That looks like... Nyctara's suit. Wait, don't tell me?"

The beam thudded as I dropped it, then turned back to him, dropping to my knees. "Don't worry about it." I caressed his bruised cheek before sliding my shaking arms underneath his knees and back. "You're seeing things, Micha. Just focus on breathing."

"You're the bad guy," Micha managed, his voice breaking. "I don't understand. Do I even know you?" He coughed again, shaking roughly.

Groaning beams filled the silence as I stared at him. My heart stopped. The pit returned and claimed it, like a black hole. "Please," I tried. *What should I say? What should I do?* "It's-it's not what you think." His breath hitched. "Hey-hey. No, no, don't do that. I'll explain after I get you to a hospital. Do not fall asleep." His eyes drifted closed. "No, no, no!" I shook him. "Keep your eyes open. Stay with me. Micha, please."

Leaning forward, I tilted his chin, checked his airway, and wiped the dirt off his face. Nothing.

"Micha?"

A spotlight knifed down on us as my brother stilled.

"Micha? Hey now." I slid my arms under his limp body, drawing him close into a cradle. I shook him again. "Micha!" I screamed and checked his pulse, feeling it fade into silence. Limp and lifeless. Not a breath, not a sound came from him. I tried to remember how to breathe. "No, don't die on me! Please, don't die. Damn it!"

A constant chopping sound grew louder, forcing me to turn. Everything slowed. In the air, a helicopter lowered with a camera sticking out, focused on me. Tears streaked down my face. I choked back a sob, bunching my little brother's shirt into my hand.

What was I doing? Why was I so reckless?

"You're going to lose more than you realize if you don't take a second to think." Cyril told me at the Skyship. "What if you get yourself killed? What if you end up killing someone close to you? Can you live with that?"

The faded fabric of Micha's torn shirt fell back to his side as I let it go. Part of me wanted to pick him up and run to a hospital, like they could still do something. Like no matter what the hell happened to me, if I could bring him there, do anything to bring him back, I'd risk it. It didn't matter if they caught me or not. What mattered was him. And now...

I choked back another sob and gently set him back to the ground. My fists clenched so hard, the nails would be making my palms bleed if it wasn't for the suit.

The helicopter above lowered.

Cyril and Taavi set me up. They lied to me, locked up my mother, and now my little brother is dead. My brother is dead. Why should I keep going? I sniffed, whipping my nose with the back of my sleeve. *All of this was a lie to get me to do what they wanted. Maybe I'll turn myself in. Micha...*

What would your family think of you now? Are you really going to let it all go to waste?

Agh! Leave me alone! I leapt to my feet and clicked a button on my comms. Micha's limp body bore into my head. I stole a glance at it, which made my heart feel like an arrow pierced through. *My brother is dead because of them. Me. What would my mother say if she saw me now? I'm such a damn failure.*

All for this damn Crown.

"-local daycare center, Nyx without her mask had been spotted at the feet of a dead little boy. The boy looks no older than ten years old, with multiple visible wounds over his body. This just came in, the villain behind all this destruction is Aris Shelia herself. Foster kid of Taavi Higgins, where she currently resides at the-"

The pain in my chest hurt. It all hurts.

Cutting my comms off, I ran a hand through my hair and bit back another sob. *If I stop now, his death will have meant* nothing. I briefly bent over to hold his pale hand. *I can't leave him....* I carefully set it down and eyed the helicopter. *Damn it, no. I won't let this be it. I will follow this through on my own terms. I'll avenge you and Mom. I'll make them pay.* I took off, the drywall snapping underfoot and the helicopter doing it's best to stay on me. *Where the hell did Malik go? Where is Taavi and Cyril?*

On cue, my comms buzzed. "Aris, meet Cyril and I at Taftside Peak. Hurry."

"Taavi, what the hell did you do?" I hotly responded. The call ended on her side.

I pushed faster until I reached the edge of the city, slipping into any shadow on the way to lose my tails. *It said Cyril and his grandfather signed off on my mom. They claimed she did numerous illegal things.* I skimmed around the mountainside. *Taavi was only mentioned to be my foster parent. Yet I refused to believe she didn't know a single damn thing about it. They used me. Used my family to get me to do what? Get a crown? My muscles felt sore from how much I tensed them. They are going to answer for what they've done to me. No one touches my family.*

I weaved through trees and over logs, reaching the entrance to the cave and stormed down. Heated, angry voices reached me long before I made it down the first path.

"Why?" Cyril exclaimed. "Why do I have to cover up for you and my father for a memory I have no recollection of making? Aris is my friend and I hate-"

"Enough! Out of all people and as my first villain, I thought you'd be grateful since you failed your job so miserably. Don't blame me. You know I didn't register until after her mom was arrested. I had zero idea about your grandfather's idea to bring someone else into the picture. Lucky for us we found someone mad enough at the world to work with. Hand them over!"

"He used your sunglasses to find someone with Shadow, like you asked," Cyril shot back. "Yeah, you didn't know "we" were planning on giving you a processor, but you neglected to tell Aris my grandfather framed her mother just so you could coerce her into a closer space and use her."

"I am not using her!" It was the first time I heard Taavi yell. "This world deserves to crumble for locking up all those I loved. I watched as it became still without being able to do anything about it. These heroes fear breaking a fake peace they made up. And to fix it, I needed to find someone to do the work for me. You know I'm old. Do not mistake Aris as my revenge. She's still my foster-daughter!"

I burst to the bottom steps, finding the crown locked in Taavi's hands. Three of the crystals rested securely in their places. Across from her, Cyril had his back against a wall, clutching the remaining two pieces.

"Taavi?"

Chapter 26

ARIS SHELIA

"Good, you're here." Taavi tossed the crown to me. I caught it. "Convince Cyril to hand over the other two gems. He's not being very cooperative."

Sliding to the other end of the exit, Cyril hugged them close to his chest. "Aris, please you have to listen. I never wanted any of this."

He darted out of the cave.

I let him go, silently facing Taavi who sharply waved her hand. "Don't let him get away! After him! He has the two gems to your crown."

"I don't take orders from you," I snapped. "I'm getting those gems on my own accord and assembling this damn crown for myself. And by the way, I don't appreciate a traitor. Especially one posing as a 'mother' to me after removing my own." At that, I exited the cave, sprinting at him.

He made it halfway down the mountain before I caught up to him. His body morphed into an exact replica of me as I reached him. Apparently he knew that would happen, because a handheld metal patterned box skipped between us and exploded at my feet, encasing me in a solid box of deep Russian Amethyst. Cold washed over me instantly, holding my power.

What jewels make up the crown? Holographic words floating before me asked. I placed said crown on my head. "Black opal, tanzanite, red beryl, alexandrite, and goldstone."

Wailing with a flash of white, the box fell apart. Cyril only made it tens of more feet during that time, reaching a bridge. He transformed back into himself, and I sent out a black tendril, wrapping it around his body. Many more added, twirling him upside down to reveal a black ebony necklace on his neck.

"You knew! You traitor." I slithered a tendril around his neck. "Why would you get me to trust and care about you only to stab me in the back?" I walked onto the bridge, hair a mess.

"I-" he started, sounding strangled. I covered his mouth and shook him. Both of the gems fell to the ground, one clanking on a rock. Everything in me wanted to squeeze. To break him and watch him suffer. At this point, I don't even know if I'm trying to stop him or hurt him. That terrified me. A muffled voice spoke around the darkness I encased him in, "Aris. Please."

Prying both gems from his thick clammy hands, I let him go gently. I slowly took off the crown and placed the last two jewels inside.

A massive ripple echoed through the city. A mix of

sound and light, tearing through structures and silence itself, resembling a bomb that went off. Glass exploded, cars flipped, alarms went off. Lights flicked on and off. Heroes rose into the air. The bridge we stood on itself vibrated and groaned, wires snapping in half. My heart raced as I dove off it with Cyril onto the bank, the whole thing collapsing into the canal below, the crown still clutched in my hands.

I dragged myself to my feet and placed it on. My vision went white, then faded to a time I played with Micha and his dinosaur.

"You promise?" he asked with a puffed out lip.

I rose to my feet, meeting his wide, pleading eyes and kissed his forehead. I hope so. I really do.

"We'll have to see," I said.

The vision switched.

"Open your eyes!" Mom said.

In front opened up a wide theatre, with gifts wrapped on the side and a video call, waiting to be answered.

"What's all this?" I asked.

She walked to my side. "Well, I know how much you like the older action movies. So your Dad, Steph, and I rented out a theatre to watch some together. As for the gifts, well, you have to open them and see."

"W-what?" My eyes blurred. I blinked it away and swallowed. "You really didn't have to. But how is Dad and Steph going to join?"

"Aha! I knew you'd ask. After persuading the librarians, they're borrowing a computer for this." Walking over, Mom connected the video call to them. Steph immediately answered. The frames lagged, but it was really them on the other side.

A crackly voice broke through. *"Hey little sis. Miss me?"*

Another, my Dad's voice, followed. *"Is that really you, kid? You're so grown up! Has it really been a year already?"*

Snapping me forward, the vision brought me back to my mother being dragged away, Micha clinging to my side as if he let go, they'd take him too. And that's exactly what they did.

Taavi found me. She took me in and fed into that anger. She trained me, giving me missions until the paper of the crown was handed to us. I could've stopped. Said no at any time. Yet, I loved being given a choice. I hated those government officials, since they took my Mom and refused to tell me anything. So slowly, it shifted. I went to school, trained, got bothered by Reed and oddly acknowledged by Malik, Drystan, Arlene. While moonlighting as a villain, taking jewels and fighting them as another person.

I snorted. *They invited me to join their team in facing Nyctara also.* Cyril. Tegan. Mrs. Parkzer. The trio who saved me and joined us in battle. All of it was a lie.

No one actually wanted me. They all wanted to use me or protect themselves. And to think this all started because Cyril wasn't enough to fulfill what his grandfather and Taavi hoped to achieve.

No. It had to be me. Not a single damn person can be trusted in this world except my mom and little brother. And now one was dead because I recklessly destroyed the building he stood in.

So many people have betrayed you for their own personal gain. That part of me came back, stronger. *All you wanted was your family back. Look at where that got you.* I lifted my hands to fling off the crown, but stopped as it continued, *Hang on. Instead of giving up, it is now your time to show them what it means to mess with you. Show them you aren't someone people can walk over and use. You are Aris Shelia. You are Nyctara.*

I am not a puppet. Micha did not deserve to die.

"Shelia! Aris," a voice called. I blinked rapidly, and my vision adjusted. Smoke curled around the canal. Through the haze, I spotted Aero making his way to me. *Cute.* "Take it off."

"And why would I do that?" I asked, wiping my blurred eyes.

Light flashed through his eyes. His lips wavered, and there I saw two deep Russian Amethyst daggers in both hands. *He could've and still can kill me. Why hasn't he taken the crown yet? Isn't it more important than whatever fake friendship he's shown me? Why doesn't he try to destroy the crown?*

"You aren't acting in your right mind."

"Everyone says that." I floated above the ground, my head two feet over his.

"And here we are." He threw a dagger to my feet. "Whatever you're going through, you don't have to destroy the world for it. We can work it out."

A broken sound caught in my throat. More than anything, I wanted to collapse and disappear. To let all of this go. For it to never have happened. For my mom and little brother to be back with me and forgive me for everything I've done. For someone to hold me while I fell apart, despite all of it.

That's not something I deserved anymore. It's not going to happen.

"Our city is beyond saving." *I know you don't actually care about me, Aero-Malik. Well jokes on you. You people are not the only ones with secrets.* Another wave erupted from the crown. One I could feel deep in my sternum, like needles to my very core. *Nothing I do will bring him back.*

Specks of heroes flying in Lumea's distant city faced me. Screams swirled into the night while colorful vengeful fires collected and spread over neighborhoods. Buildings tore in half, occasionally caught by a hero. Over a hundred of them flew toward me. In the front of the hoard, I could make out members of the Aegis. *It'll take them some time before reaching this place.*

I'll let the city fall. They never wanted to change. I'll show them how.

Below, Taavi ducked out from behind a rock. Cyril appeared next to her. "Child, we've achieved our mission. You've done fantastic in bringing the city to its knees. Let it rebuild while we plan our next attack."

My laugh turned into a scoff. "I'm not doing this for you. I did it for him. For my mom." Three waves from the crown split the air. Its force was strong enough to fling me higher in the sky and back down again. Blood dripped from my nose and lips, tasting like copper. "I'm not your pawn, anymore Taavi. You knew the crown would kill me. And I know what you both did to my family," I spat the last sentence, its words leaving a vile taste in my mouth.

"Yes I knew. You're a symbol," she said simply and came closer. Her caramel braid frayed. "Proof conflict is inevitable for change. That doesn't mean I think of you any less. I love you, like the daughter they took from me."

"That's bullshit!" Aero pushed off the ground and floated in front of me. "She's taking conflict into the extreme of war. Conflict means misunderstandings, arguments in pair with other humane emotions like love. It doesn't mean we have to kill and destroy all we know."

Clutching my hand, I formed a shadow dagger in my hand. *Use the crown and mix it with your own power,* a voice sweetly said. I called on it's power, and each gem glowed so bright, I could see it from my head. Fire swirled around the shadow, mixing with a silver, purple, blue, and gold glow. I aimed my hand at Taavi. "You never loved me," I said coldly with tears streaking my cheeks. "No one ever did." The dagger flew straight at her.

Chapter 27

STEPHANIE SHELIA

Flopping onto a bench, Steph dipped her hand into the fountain, watching the water ripple circles around her fingers. Her dad sat next to her in his wheelchair, hunched over his phone and doom-scrolling with a tired frown. She had just taken him out to a quiet dinner. Now they waited outside the restaurant while a breaking news headline claimed the television.

Beep beep. "*We bring you to a worldwide emergency. Lumea, the city which houses Ezrat, is under attack by Nyctara, otherwise known as Aris Shelia.*"

Steph froze. Her dad's phone slipped from his hand and landed face-down in his lap.

"*With the help of Taavi Higgins, Cyril Shepherd, and others, she has now claimed the crown and jewels that aided Shelby Feyth and Sean Weaver to bestow peace upon our land. Is this the end?*"

The news lady cut off, the screen switching to a video of Steph's little sister. A silver crown rested on her black and white hair, floating with her. Green light bled from her eyes.

"I know what you both did to my family," Aris said on the screen with a voice so raw and hopeless, Steph had never heard it before. Not even when their grandparents died. It sounded so stripped and hollow.

What are you doing? Where's Mom? Or Micha? Abruptly standing, Steph nearly knocked the bench back as she made way for her father to wheel to their house. On the way, nearby televisions and radios updated them. Steph decided she would be the one flying back and her father would get the next flight out after sorting this mess here.

"This is insane," her dad muttered under his breath.

Steph double stepped. "Tell me about it. We've only been gone for four years. Now I wish we hadn't gone at all."

Footage played of citizens being shielded by heroes, majority panicking and a scat few protesting against Nyx. Yet their protests ran short as they often had to scramble away from wreckage and flying debris.

"We interviewed Lighter, one of the professional heroes whose team faced our nation's greatest threat in over one hundred and fifty years."

"We should've been more aware," he admitted hoarsely. Discoloration and wounds painted the skin Stepth could see. His emblem was gone. "People like me got used to having fun and showing off. It never occurred to us that a villain could break through all of our protocols we had in place and actually get this far." He swallowed and pulled his shoulders back, head lifted high and eyes clear. "But we will not back down. The five magic schools are already implementing changes to their curriculum, encouraging new ideas to form so this does not happen again. Nyctara will not win against Ezrat, and in whole, Lumea."

Steph packed her things with insane efficiency, blew her dad a kiss, and was out in two licks of a cow's tail. The drive to the airport felt molasses slow.

Inside the terminal, a bearded man in a long black trench coat flanked by two others caught her attention. "Excuse me, miss. Are you related to Aris Sheila or know who is? We're looking for her sister and father."

"Who are you?" Steph picked up her suitcase in case she had to use it as a shield.

The man who spoke bowed. "I apologize for the urgency. My name is President Coast, head of Ezrat." He resumed his stance. "Now do you mind answering my question?"

Aris Shelia. Not Nyctara or Nyx. Nodding, she gently placed the suitcase back. "I am her sister," Steph said carefully. "My father has business to finish up, but he will follow soon. I am traveling to go speak with her."

"Perfect. That saves time." Waving to a guard, President Coast inclined his head. One of the security men picked up her package and the other presented an official badge. "Come with us. It'll be faster in my plane because of the pilot's minor power. We'll pick up your mother on the way."

Pick up my mother? Rolling her shoulders, Steph quickly followed him. *They're scrambling. I'll take it as a good thing that my sister hasn't been killed yet.*

One of the guards leaned over, whispering to Ezrat's President, "Daylight is burning the longer we're away from Nyctara. Should we send in professional heroes? They're waiting on your command."

"Ms. Shelia," President Coast immediately corrected, hushed but harsh. "It's Ms. Shelia until I say otherwise. Have backup within view, and keep it to the Aegis for now. You know what happens if we forcefully take the crown."

They boarded the plane. Steph sank into her seat, staring at the patterned floor while the engines roared to life. *Please, don't be too far gone sis. I don't know what the hell happened, but I'm coming.*

Chapter 28

~Or by chance, endings are only what you choose to see~

ARIS SHELIA

The dagger flew straight at Taavi, a slice of rainbow in the air. Aero blurred between us, faster than I tracked. The multi-colored dagger sank into his shoulder, burning through flesh and fabric in a hiss of light. He didn't flinch as it faded, replaced by blood. I recoiled at the sight as he turned, revealing a glowing arrow embedded on his other side, as if aimed straight at me.

"Aris," Malik gasped. "Please... stop."

I nearly fell, losing a few feet of air. "What are you doing?" I rasped as he lifted a hand to the dagger, fingertips brushing the edge.

Two more waves erupted from the crown. Five heroes dropped in front of Aero, separating us in a wall of bodies.

Aegis.

Shanessa drew in a deep breath, holding a light-infused chain. Smoke emitted off of Leor's exoskeleton at the seams, his eyes almost red, reflecting his own fire. Gracelyn stayed furthest back, touching Malik's shoulder.

Arlene and Drystan came at me together and attacked with everything they had. I blocked most of their strikes on reflex. A bar of shadow as Drystan circled behind, and a thud of my shadow sword-against-sword with Arlene.

Shanessa and Leor advanced after, using the distractions of their team to strike me with the chain across my shoulder down to my hip. It seared past my suit, engraving in my flesh.

The smell of burning assaulted my nose. My vision swam as two fists connected with my ribs. Trying to breathe in, I realized I couldn't. Thudding overtook my heart. The crown exploded outwards again on its own accord, splitting across the field and mountain, knocking them all back with tremendous force.

Spectra and Vortex almost knocked over Aero, who managed to catch both of them and set them down as if they weighed nothing. His hand went back to cradling his shoulder, blood seeping through his fingers.

His boots rustled the grass as he walked towards me, hands at his sides. "You are right," he said calmly through clenched teeth. "Our city, the people betrayed you. Taavi lied. Cyril used you. But I'm not letting them be the reason you lose yourself and die." He touched the bleeding wound at his shoulder, removing some charred residue. "You had every reason to give up." Another shockwave ripped from the crown, this time into the sky. He winced. "I've watched you fight and try to be happy. I've seen you try to move on and protect people when no one did the same to you. You are not someone who deserves to die for other people's mistakes."

My breath hitched. Spots filtered through my vision, black at the edges. "Stop acting like you care. I'm not worth saving nor a project for you to 'save.'"

His voice cracked. "I'm not acting. If you're going to burn everything down, I'll stay between you and the edge. I know you, and it's okay."

My fingers twitched. Shadow coiled instinctively, hungry and waiting. He lowered his head, stepping close enough that the rest of them became a blur behind him, and whispered so only I could hear.

"You've carried everything alone for too long. I wish I could've done more. But I genuinely am your friend, Aris."

My head thrummed with the crown, as if urging me to attack him. Yet the memories...

One of the first times we interacted, it was around the time my mother got arrested. He had stopped me in the hall, and I told him, "I don't need friends."

"Yeah, well." Malik shrugged. "Too bad. You've got one anyway."

"You don't know me."

"Maybe not," he admitted. "But I'd like to."

There were also the times he sat outside underneath the tree with me, saying hi when passing in the hallways or going on the hike. Arlene and Drystan were there for that one.

Or when we did a power fusion together by accident.

That doesn't mean he won't betray you like everyone else. I flinched. *It doesn't mean he will, either.* I lifted my head as the thrumming grew stronger. Another set of waves emitted from the crown, forming split clouds in the skies. *I lived my whole life thinking no one would ever stay loyal to me. Care about me or my life except my family. That I could trust no one.* I shook my head.

I think one thing holding me back was myself from trusting that someone, one day, might. People aren't perfect, they'll make mistakes. But it doesn't mean I should live my life around expecting it all the time.

Taavi and Cyril show you otherwise.

My arms moved to lift off the crown, but it flashed. Burning strung through each vein, slowing my muscles and tendons. Colors of the main powers strayed from me. A line of fire and water intermixing to create smoke. A flash of air creating a tornado guided by earth straight to the city. Light and shadow forming bombs and blinding spells. Random emotions flooded people's expressions, like tears running down faces or furrowed eyebrows and clenched muscles. Some held their head, cradling it.

You've been shown time and time again. You've tried to forget, but you never could. What makes him any different?

Trees fell in clumps. Rocks from the mountain slid down, and buildings bore multiple holes. Like the daycare.

"Get the crown off her!" Spectra yelled, taking Vortex's hand and jumping. At my level, she let go of him and he caught my leg, dangling from it. On the other side, Arlene ran on air, like another was guiding her steps, summoning her phantom sword. "Aris, you are my friend. I know you're still in there. I'm sorry I didn't see you were hurting, but wrecking a city isn't the solution."

I glanced down at Drystan. He swung his legs back and forth. "Man, honestly I was unsure about you at first." I raised my hand, fighting a sigh. "But I knew Malik and thought if he was chill befriending you, you'd be cool. He was right, you are. I don't always understand you, but you are not a villain." Kicking him, I shook my leg and flung him into Malik.

A gust of wind surrounded me, and the three were blown away, replaced with Taavi. She created a barrier around us, and the pressure built significantly. I felt it in my eardrums. I felt the crown shift side to side, but it stayed on. The temperature in the bubble dropped and rose, yet Taavi seemed unaffected and my suit did well regulating myself.

"Aris Sheila!" a distant voice called. I spotted two people flanked by President Coast and his security detail. One I haven't seen in years, and the other...

"Mom?!"

I pierced the air bubble. It exploded, battering my ears. Instantly, other heroes were on Taavi, herding her away.

They're here to stop you. Don't go.

"Come here." She opened her arms and I bolted towards them, feet skitting the ground. I collapsed into her, wrapping my arms around her back. She rested her head on mine and I let it go. I tried to choke it back, to fight the sobs, but they ripped out. "You don't have to explain. President Coast told me." Her heart thudded against my ear, its presence comforting.

Someone rustled the grass to my left, and wrapped her arms around me too. Steph squeezed me, speaking in low murmurs.

Somewhere, a voice reached me. I couldn't make out how far it was. "She's right there! On the ground. Now's your chance to grab her!"

I deserve whatever becomes of me.

"Hold up, y'all. Not without the President's orders you don't," Shanessa answered, walking in front of the hero with Leor.

My Mom squeezed tighter. *They're only here to stop you.* The voice in my head repeated. *You don't deserve to see them, or talk to them. Remember what you did?*

Seeing them immediately reminded me of Micha and I tried to pull back, but her grip strengthened. I leaned back in. "Mom, Steph," I stuttered. "I killed him. I killed Micha. He's dead. A-and I couldn't find you. I kept trying and I was useless and I failed you and..." I braced myself.

Instead of crying, or accusing me, demanding I explain myself, both shushed me in unison. Steph clutched my suit harder and my mother smoothed my hair. Like if I said I did the worst things imaginable, they would still hold me. I didn't have to say anything else.

"Ma'am," Aero greeted from behind me. "It's nice to meet you. I'm Malik. Aris's friend."

I felt my mom smile. "Nice to meet you too."

"And my name's Arlene, and this is Drystan," Spectra added. "We are also Aris's friends, though Malik's closer."

You hurt all of those who pretended to care about you. What do you deserve?

"I'm sorry," I mumbled into my mom's chest. I turned my head, bleary-eyed. "I'm so sorry for hurting you."

Slowly, Malik dropped in front of me and joined my mother and sister, wrapping his arms around me. "It's okay. Aris, it's okay. I know why you did it. You'll still have to go through the system, but we'll make sure to fix everything while we do."

Don't believe them. A headache coursed to my skin. A thrumming and hum emitted from the crown. I abruptly shoved them off, getting to my feet as if touching them any longer would draw blood. Or scorch them. Searing heat met my hands as I tried to take it off. Instead, it held on, clinging like an insect.

I took flight again. White overtook my vision, displaying two different views. A world decayed, full of blood turning flooding rivers black. Lava claimed mountains, and torn structures dominated the area. Heroes lost in the wreckage, attempting to save citizens.

The other remained peaceful with serene structures and even newer technology then what we know now. People laughed and played. I thought I even saw Seth working on a new invention in broad daylight.

These images switched to the three story daycare Micha died at. One, he laughed in front of me, holding his toy dinosaur. That one I knew I had saved him. The other repeated my memory, covered in dust, my little brother took his last dying breath.

Fading, one side was replaced with a faded grey of my father, mother, and sister. The other presented all five of us, with Malik, Arlene, and Drystan too, our laughter like bells. Like the world waited right there, waiting for me to step in it.

I chose this path. Energy coursed through my veins. It surged, growing faster. Roaring assaulted my ears. *I put this crown together, piece by piece. I wanted to make my world a better place. I think I did, if only a little. For the most part, I'm the one destroying it, instead.* This feeling sank into my chest of deep despair, mixed with... I wanted to yawn and close my eyes. The world fractured like glass, shards folding inwardly.

I still couldn't see. But I reached toward the crown. Pain stabbed and sliced through my body when I touched its points. Like a burn so hot, it turned cold and numb. *I need to calm down. I have to take it off. I need to breathe. I need to—* I *need to—*

I can't. Tears continuously streamed down my face.

Another voice, one I haven't heard in weeks, huffed in a mocking laugh. Other voices below retaliated against it, but it grew closer. Then, a familiar hand brushed my arm, exactly like that day on the obstacle course when Reed passed me, and a dull wave of neutral blandness washed over me. All the anger and anguish momentarily paused before the wave retreated, as if fighting with the crown itself. A suffocating grief swamped its print, but it was working enough.

"Remember how easy it was for people to mess with your head, Aris? Every time I'd shove past you on the course or corner

you in the hallway, you went stiff and silent. All I really did was watch you."

Are you here to gloat? Why did you come, Reed? I thought, shaking my head. Another fierce ripple extended from the crown, diving deep into my chest. Why can't you go away? Almost as if in response, it kept going.

"Yeah, I guess I pushed too hard. Whatever. This isn't the same as before. Use that emotion instead of letting the crown control it. Hit back. And don't think I've gone soft. I'm just not going to let you wipe yourself out like an idiot and make our school look bad..." A pause. *"If anyone's going to beat you, it sure as hell won't be a crown. I had a job to do."*

Another course of numbness spread over. I yanked and the crown gave a little, then flung off, hearing what I assumed to be it shattering on the ground. People must've leapt for it before the waves ceased in an eerie silence. Two seconds later, I plummeted. My body felt weightless. Air ripped from my lungs.

Someone-no two people caught me, landing and setting me gently on the ground.

"Hey, hey, stay with me," Malik demanded. I felt a hand brush mine.

Another voice added, "This ain't funny. Gracelyn, come here." Someone-something grumbled

Sounds jumbled together. Flaming hot agony radiated over my entire body. Or was it cold?

I breathed in, then out.

Chapter 29

ARIS SHELIA

Numbness dominated any feeling I could have. I thought Taavi was right the day we met. Our world did need a wake-up call. And no one else was willing to do it.

I never thought it would have to be me.

Micha's laugh rang faintly, too bright to belong in this dark. My throat tried to close around his name, but my body didn't listen. It hadn't been listening for a while.

My family was all I needed. They knew that. She knew that. Guess her, Cyril, and his grandfather played their cards right, huh?

I guess leverage works when you know what someone can't live without. Out of its peaceful, yet dull life and into a new era. They did everything right. They almost won. But they never took into account the possibility of someone like Malik. Someone, with seemingly no reason, tried to befriend a villain like me.

Why did he?

That question had never been answered. I couldn't understand. He shouldn't have cared when I gave him plenty of reasons not to. I would constantly ignore and snap at him. But each day, without fail, he reminded me. Was his fault caring for others too much?

It helped that we had two classes together. But that gave him more reason to bring his other friends in too.

Drystan stayed closer friends with Malik. Yet he would never shun or look at me like other students did. He would talk to me like a person. Like a brother content with barely knowing his introverted sister, but still there in case she needed him.

And Arlene... That woman tried to be my friend, no matter whether I liked what she did or acted like I cared. I wouldn't have gone hiking that day if she hadn't somehow convinced me she liked me, at least a little.

All of this. To think if I hadn't said yes, maybe my little brother would still be alive.

Or if I had, would I ever have become close to Malik, Drystan, and Arlene?

You know, maybe Taavi was onto something, but she didn't have all the pieces. If only I had begun to realize that sooner, I could've stopped myself. I could've helped her. Maybe even forgive her and Cyril for what they'd done. Like my family, like Malik, did for me.

Chapter 30

MALIK STYRI

Fresh dirt and grass lined the soil. His knees were soaked from the musty rain, hands dirty from planting trees and flowers at the President's request. Whether this was a place to rebuild or remember, he wasn't sure.

Arlene and Drystan sat silently beside him, occasionally glancing into the distance or at their feet.

Heroes and citizens still bore marks of the crown, with wounds healing. Its remains got scattered across the globe this time. Obliterated into slivers and tiny pieces. Around, the ruined structures had new brick and concrete replacing the old drywall and wood. Slimmer metal outlined it, and new stained glass, colors vibrant like a fairy-tale or fantasy landscape intertwining as one, filled windows where there used to be a simple dull wall.

Aris's mother immediately got released following her daughter's attack. Hyzrit agreed to expunge her record, trading her remote prison work with Taavi and Cyril.

Amethyst chains racked their bodies, dragging like how Malik felt inside. They didn't fight, though Taavi seemed on the teeter between annoyed and pleased.

Reed was also there at the time, and joined the hero team Ranlea on scene. They offered him the position after he made the call to the helicopter, exposing Aris to the world as Nyctara. Yet, Malik also saw him arrive in the end, reaching for her with his power in an attempt to dull the crown's power. He wanted to end it without more blood. A man that had exposed her and tried to save her in the same breath.

Whether that made Reed a coward, a hero, or something far more human, Malik didn't know.

At least she threw the damn crown off.

"She succeeded," Malik uttered in a half-laugh. "Breaking us apart forced our city to put itself back together. All it took was—" Tears escaped his eyes. He covered them with the palms of his hands. He hadn't slept well since that night.

A hand found his back, rubbing across his shoulder blades. "I know." Arlene whispered. "We'll be here every step of the way. Just tell us what you need."

"Tell me what to do," he immediately said, hating how desperate it sounded. "Who can I—"

"Not right now," Drystan answered. "Sit. Breathe. We've got it. You don't need to do anything."

With a deep breath, Malik sniffled and tilted his head back to look at the sky. A large oak's branches extended over his head, like cracks splitting the blue and white background.

He'll make sure this world is ready for what's next.

Chapter 30.5

TAAVI HIGGINS

Inside the cell, a solid metal door swung shut with a click. Taavi lifted her head, amber eyes catching the faint light as the figure lingered beyond the first set of amethyst bars. Her fingers tightened at the hem of her blouse, then stilled.

"I told you we should've been upfront from the very beginning," she said.

"Oh yes, you've grown bitter in your later years," the old man huffed. "Too much time spent archiving with those parents of yours, I gander."

"We both know intent means nothing in this life. Heroes don't care about reasoning. They discredited all of our work, dismantling decades of research because it made people uncomfortable. If you want something done, you can't wait around for someone else to do it. You must do it, or guide one who can." She took a breath. In a softer, near broken voice she allowed herself to speak. "I love the girl like my own, Ashby."

Cyril's grandfather clicked his tongue, eyes studying her for a moment. "And that was your downfall." Lifting his hand, he touched an amethyst bar. "Don't fret, I can still get you out of here. Third time's a charm."

Taavi's eyes drifted, growing distant beyond the walls. To a world done holding its breath. To the last two and a half years spent with a child eager for someone to prove her wrong.

"Why would I leave?" she asked softly, almost offended. "I do not know her outcome."

The question hung between them. Ezrat had learned what it was never meant to face. It had reacted and fractured like the crown. The hero school and city would never return to the quiet lie it once called peace. There's still so much more that could be done.

Taavi looked back at the old man, her expression settled, resolved. "If given the chance," she said, "I would do it again."

Opinion- Nyctara: the shadow over our peace

By Xiomara Rezet   March 23, 21xx

The name Aris Shelia is now known to many as Nyctara (Nyx) — the villain who wreaked havoc across Ezrat and threatened the country this past month. Heroes and news coverage captured her seizing the ancient crown once used by Shelby Feyth, wielded it, and shattered it in a matter of days.

To most, she was another villain after power or fortune, which had been handled. That is not the case. No, Shelia is a student like you and me, who cared deeply about her family, and took an ideology to an extreme when she wasn't heard.

I've been able to talk and battle at her side. Something very controversial, I'm sure. But curiosity pushed me to understand the person behind the mask. What made them so motivated? Villains usually go after a bank or person, making their motivation clear and monologuing about it to be understood. But this individual varied attacks and had allies. She was seemingly random with her goals, yet strategic enough to allow the government to cover up her disruptions.

It wasn't until much later did I discover more to her motives. Many of her attacks seemed to be after stones, relics once embedded in Shelby and Sean Weaver's crown. How did she get the information about these objects? That part remains unknown.

Signs pointed to desire for power, so I thought that was all of it. I was wrong. A more desperate drive guided each decision she made.

In interviews with classmates, former rivals and allies, and her family, their answers differed. But one point remained consistent. Her mother was unjustly arrested, followed by no communication or explanation from officials, and the separation from her close younger brother, Micha Shelia. He is now dead.

The Presidents and Council declined to comment at this time.

According to government documents, following the arrest, Aris was relocated to the house of Taavi Higgins. An angry old woman, found out to be a radical hidden villain, set in the belief that peace makes our world stagnant. And how do you fix that? War.

This is where I believe Shelia took a turn for the worse. With her family taken, reports of her being a 'lone wolf,' a preference of being isolated, her questions ignored, and a mentor luring her to take action, it makes sense. If you stepped into her shoes, even briefly, and asked yourself: Would you have made different choices?

I think the focus shouldn't be on Nyctara as much as it should be on the problem she fronted. Think of her actions as a warning.

What could have been done before all this happened? Why is it that we need someone like her in order to pay attention to our own problems? These are all things we should be asking.

Editor's Note: I want to make clear that Nyctara's actions, by no means, were excusable. But evil doesn't appear overnight. It festers, then explodes. That's why Aris Shelia's actions were understandable, not excusable.

<u>Acknowledgments</u>

Thank you so much for reading! As a young author, completing a second work is astonishing to me. I would really appreciate it if you could leave a review for me on Goodreads or Amazon! Or even email me feedback. I would love to hear from you! Gmail: lorienrosebriscoe@gmail.com

I'm very thankful to be at the end of this. It was a great time writing though! The ideas in this book have interested me for a while, and it felt so nice and real to finally get it on paper. I'm trying to live up to my name.

Once again, Anilee Briscoe, thank you for drawing my book cover. You're a great older sister. (She takes commissions!)

This book has been professionally edited.

I had some insanely wonderful betas this time around. While not as many as my debut, I feel like they were equally—if not more—helpful. They always challenge my worldbuilding, characters, and dialogue and make excellent points to get the writing better. It's great to see into their minds for a first draft and after a hefty edit!

Hint: Strange, another odd set of bolded letters on page 382. Wonder what's up with that?

Note: If you want to take a look at my debut: Magic's Escape: Wingless, or any of my upcoming novels, that would be amazing!

<u>About the Author</u>

Lórien—yes, named after Lord of the Rings—wrote Between the Lines to Villainy from 16-19 years old. She's been a storyteller since kindergarten, and finished her debut, Magic's Escape: Wingless, between 14-15.

In the United States, she multitasks between sports (Basketball, Softball, Soccer, Wrestling, Fencing), art, percussion, filming and editing videos or live streams, doing random fun things (skydiving, ziplining, survival skills, motorcycling) or scribbling story ideas in the margins of her notes. Lórien's studying toward her B.A. in Film and Media Arts with five minors and one certificate at the University of Utah.

Fans of underdog heroes, fractured families, and philosophical "what ifs," will feel right at home in her morally tangled universes focused on family and trust—typically with no romance.

Stay tuned, because Lórien is revising the second in the Magic's Escape duology "Magic's Escape: Shadow of the Ikris," and writing more stand-alone survival inspired novels.